MY
BARE NAKED
HEART

DAVID AVERY

WALT WHITMAN PRESS
NEW YORK

My Bare Naked Heart is a work of fiction. Names, characters, places, and incidents are used fictitiously. Any resemblance to actual events, locales, or persons, living or dead, is entirely coincidental.

WALT WHITMAN PRESS, NEW YORK

Copyright © 2016 David Avery
All rights reserved.
ISBN-10: 0-9977645-0-3
ISBN-13: 978-0-9977645-0-5

CONTENTS

1	Fairies	1
2	Dusty	6
3	The Magnificent Seven	11
4	Dream Land	19
5	Helicopters	24
6	Wonder Bread	35
7	Axis Shifting	48
8	Measuring Up	65
9	Snow Balls	80
10	The Truth	93
11	My Heart In My Hands	100
12	Thanksgiving	112
13	Explorers	128
14	Stalled	152
15	Angels	174
16	Out With a Bang	187
17	Shadow Dancing	202
18	The End of Innocence	236
19	Inquisition	268
20	Darkness and Light	279
21	Judgment	290
22	Commencement	297

"One homosexual can pollute an entire government office."

- United States Senate Appropriations Committee Report on *Employment of Homosexuals and Other Sex Perverts in Government.* 1950.

1 FAIRIES

*Inverness College
Inverness, Vermont
September 1957*

I HAD THE heart-pounding feeling I had made a disastrous mistake. My parents had just dropped me off at Inverness College for the start of my freshman year. But, I didn't want to stay. I wanted to get back in the car with them and go home. I had felt a rumbling of panic as we passed through the iron gates of the rural campus and drove along the single lane of the winding, elm-lined road. I had stared out the window at the verdant landscape and the stone bridge that carried us over a brook that burbled as it emptied into a swan-filled lake. We stopped in front of Canterbury Hall, the ivy-covered dormitory where I would be living during my freshman year. The campus could not have been more beautiful. I could not have been unhappier.

I brooded over how I should have said yes to NYU instead of this preppy, all-male college in the mountains of rural Vermont. I had grown up in Connecticut surrounded by green lawns, shady trees, and people who looked like me. The thought of living amidst the gritty tumult and parade of unfamiliar faces in Manhattan had scared me. As I looked around me, the thought of living in the middle of nowhere with all of these young men – and no women – scared me even more.

I stood in the window of the second floor lounge and peered down through paned glass at the curb below. My father opened the passenger door of the car for my mother. It was her '56 Ford Country Squire station wagon, a lumbering behemoth with simulated woodgrain side paneling. The way-back was now empty. The books, clothes, and new bedding that had shared the ride with me were arranged in my dorm room with a neatness that would never be duplicated after my mother left. She hesitated for a moment as my father held the door for her and said something to him I obviously could not hear. Anxious thoughts ricocheted through my head. How could they leave me here? Would they look up and search for my face? Would they grace me with one last wave good-bye?

Only minutes before, I had wanted them to hurry up and leave with the hordes of other parents who had had the decency to drop off their sons and leave without fanfare. I had been eager to rip off the bandage of their departure so I could get on with the new life that awaited – and terrified – me. At this moment, however, I wanted nothing more than to get back in the car with them and return to West Hartford, the place from where I had wanted to escape for as long as I could remember.

My mother checked her hair in a hand mirror she pulled from her purse. My father flicked his cigarette butt into the gutter. He looked up at the sky as if he were a pilot about to climb aboard a plane and fly it away. He lit another cigarette and slid behind the wheel. They did not look up for one last wave or a final glimpse of their only son. Instead, they sped off without turning back, and I was left with the memory of our stilted farewell.

"Good luck, son," my father had said as he had shaken my hand.

My mother had pressed an imaginary crease on the lapel of my blue blazer and straightened my tie. "Your father and I are very proud of you."

MY BARE NAKED HEART

"Yes, Mother." I had responded with an ersatz formality I had summoned from deep inside, because I thought the situation and my parents were calling for it. The forced stoicism seemed so ridiculous. The sad part of it is, I desperately wanted to be hugged and held by both of them, even if just briefly. I am a different sort of parent than mine were and would have hugged me tight if I had been them. But, in 1957, parents were afraid their sons would turn into fairies if they showed them too much affection.

The truth was, my biggest fear was I just might be a fairy. That thought terrified me to the core of my being, far more than the fear the Russians would drop an atom bomb and start a global nuclear war, which was everyone else's big fear back then. Yes, I genuinely liked girls. I had even creamed in my pants as I fooled around with Allison, my girlfriend, on Saturday night. It had been in the back seat of the Ford that had just whisked away my parents and my former life. Surely, that meant I wasn't a fairy, a fruit cake, a fag or whatever people called guys who shared some of the same feelings I sometimes had, right?

I had hungered for Allison with extreme frustration. She had a diabolical way of stringing me along, but never giving me exactly what I wanted or needed when I wanted or needed it. For someone who was bored by baseball, she sure marked the boundaries of her sexual limits with set bases, and it was clear to me she was protecting home for as long as she could. On Saturday night, however, however, she had allowed me to take matters further than she had all summer. She had let me lift up her dress and slide my hand down through the top of her underwear. She had not resisted as I lingered on third. I was certain I was about to slide into home.

But, no.

"Maybe at Thanksgiving," she had said when the slow grind of my hips signaled I wanted more. Those three words were the most hope I had ever been offered of losing my virginity. My cock throbbed inside my khakis like a hound on a tether. I kissed her and continued to probe warm, mysterious places I had touched, but never seen. The more I kissed her and slid my fingers over her wetness, the more aroused I became. Soon, I felt

3

that well-familiar feeling and knew I was passing the point of no return. A churning, rushing, dervish rose up within me, and I shot a warm, wet load into my underwear. I stifled a moan, embarrassed at what was happening, afraid she would think it revolting. My breathing deepened, but otherwise I came in silence.

I pulled up in front of her house. There were no lights on inside. We kissed again, and she professed how close she felt to me. I felt the same way, I said, and tried to ignore the goopy mess in my pants. I held her hand as we walked up the pathway to her door in the darkness and made plans to see each other at Thanksgiving.

When we reached the front porch, the lights at the front of the house snapped on and blazed us with blinding brightness.

The front door swung open. Allison's father stood in the doorway, his arms crossed. He beamed a smile that slid from adoring to dyspeptic as his gaze drifted from Allison to me. He was always polite to me, but not-so-deep down, I knew he despised me. In his mind, I was not the responsible boy next door with the bright future. I was just some guy who wanted to fuck his daughter. He started to ask how our evening was when he stopped mid-sentence. He had caught sight of the wet stain that was now the size of a slice of baloney spread across the crotch of my rumpled khakis. My stomach lurched. I placed my hand over the front of my pants. But, it was too late.

His eyes narrowed to slits and bore into mine. "Good night, John. Good luck at Dartmouth." He yanked Allison inside and slammed the door shut.

"Actually, it's Inverness," I muttered to myself as I slunk back to my car, wondering how I could ever face him again.

I wanted Allison and hungered for more than she was giving me. But, my other undeniable truth was I also liked guys. As much as I ached to distraction for girls, I was afraid I had the "deviant homosexual tendencies" you would read about in psychology text books or newspaper articles about police raids of bars and other establishments that catered to the homosexual. That confused and terrified me. If I was your normal, clean cut, boy next door, why did I sometimes have abnormal, perverted desires drumming inside me with a deafening roar? I had never acted on them and had prayed I never would. But, as I scanned the faces of these other young men in search of anyone who might share my secret, could I trust myself?

2 DUSTY

I WASN'T SURE what to do. The halls and common areas were awash with square-jawed, sporty boys wearing tweed jackets, navy blazers, and striped ties. My ears rang with the din of their voices as they acclimated to our new environment and to each other. Clusters of new friends had formed even though none of us had been here more than an hour or two. I hadn't met anyone yet and was hyperconscious of being alone. In West Hartford, I had a wide circle of friends I had known my entire life. I had never lived anywhere else, and the comfortable familiarity that enveloped me there had become stifling. That was the major reason I had been eager to leave. I also had an intuition a bigger life was meant for me, one not possible in central Connecticut. Now that I was getting what I wished for, however, I couldn't help but wonder if what I had back home wasn't so bad after all.

I returned to my floor and stopped by the bathroom to take a leak. Its walls were covered with hospital green tiles you don't see much anymore except in old institutional buildings. There was a row of sinks against one wall, a row of urinals against another, and a row of stalls against the other. An opening off in the corner led to the shower room with which I would later become well-familiar and still think about to this day.

MY BARE NAKED HEART

You couldn't fully see into the showers unless you stuck your head inside. I would later see there was a small alcove with towel hooks and a wooden bench. Around the corner was a rectangular room with eight shower heads. It was a gang shower, of course, with no curtains. There never were back then. I had the fleeting image of what the room would look like when all of the shower heads were in use and cascading water over the nude bodies of the young men I had seen in the hallways but not yet met. "Stop it," I told myself and forcibly dispatched the image from my mind.

I heard the sound of spraying water, and it struck me in passing as an odd time to be taking a shower. But, the thought left my head as I stepped up to the urinal and pulled out my cock. I hadn't used the bathroom since leaving home with my parents several hours earlier. I closed my eyes and savored the relief as my strong, steady stream splashed against the porcelain. The tang of fresh urine tickled my nose. After a few moments, I looked down to appreciate the relaxed, elongated look of my cock as the urine hummed through it. I rubbed my thumb across the thick vein that ran the length of the topside before splitting off in tributaries at the base. Like every eighteen year old male, my cock was an endless source of fascination I had spent untold hours exploring.

Finally, I finished. I shook it dry and was careful to splatter the remaining drops of piss in the urinal instead of on the front of my pants. I sighed audibly and was relieved to be relieved. At the same time I flushed, I could hear the shower turn off. I wondered who would be emerging and whether I might see him naked. "Stop it," I told myself again. "Stop it!"

While I washed my hands, I heard a friendly, "Hello."

I turned around to see who had said it. The word "hello" was on my lips, but it lingered there for a beat or two as I took in the sight before me. I caught myself and said, "Hello" again, forcefully this time, in case I had swallowed the word the first time and not been properly heard.

"Hey, there," he said. "I'm Dusty McCaffrey."

My mouth had not dropped open, but it may as well have. Dusty was an almost overwhelming sight to behold. He was nude, toweling himself off at the entrance of the shower alcove with an absence of abashment. About twenty years later, a motion picture called *The Blue Lagoon* would be released starring an actor named Christopher Atkins who bore an uncanny resemblance to Dusty. Dusty was six feet one inch tall with a lean, cut, v-shaped torso. He had ringlets of curly hair that were multiple shades of blond naturally bleached by summers in the sun. His hair wasn't long by today's standards. But, it was for 1957 and not what you would often see in New England. His eyes were a deep cerulean blue that swallowed me up and made it difficult to speak. It was not just his looks, however, that made him so compelling. There was something more. He had an aura about him that transcends looks. His smile? The warmth in his eyes? The confidence with which he carried himself even though he was nude and I was fully dressed in a blazer and tie? Whatever it was, the whole package was something you almost never encounter in just one person.

"Hi, Dusty," I said. "I'm John Branson. Nice to meet you."

"You're from West Hartford, Connecticut."

My face twisted in surprise at how he knew without me telling him.

"I'm the resident advisor – the 'RA' – for Canterbury Hall," he said. "I'm a senior. I recognized your face from the freshman directory and remembered your name. I'm here to keep people in line, but I'm also around if you ever need someone to talk to."

"Great," I said. Great was right. Dusty was one of the most handsome young men I had ever seen. It was a breathtaking sight to have him standing naked before me. His body was mostly smooth except for a dark brown treasure trail that bisected his abs and lead south in the direction I most wanted to take my eyes, but didn't yet dare. When you are what I am, you are careful to look at what your body aches for you to look at without being noticed. You develop excellent peripheral vision. You go undercover and collect stolen glances. But, even all that never fully satisfies the hunger of which those who are like me know.

"Where are you from?" I asked. He started to towel those curly blond locks. I had my moment and seized it as he dried his hair.

Good Lord!

His cock was long, thick, and floppy. It was just as beautiful as he was, if not more so. It bounced from side-to-side as he toweled his head. He was clip-dicked with a wide brown band around the middle of it, which suggested he wasn't hard, but he wasn't completely soft. His cock had a smooth, shiny helmet perfectly proportioned with the rest of it. If I had to guess, I would have said he was a thick five inches long at that moment and would have been at least seven to eight inches fully hard. The memory of that first sighting of his beautiful, naked body and truly glorious cock is seared into my memory. I have never forgotten it after all of these years, and it will be with me until I take my last breath.

"Where am I from? Orange County, California," he said. "And my family actually grows oranges. We have an orange grove my grandfather started." It's hard to believe it now, but back then, Orange County was mostly agricultural. It was mile after mile of nothing but orange groves. "I'm sun-kissed," he said.

I grinned. It was impossible not to. "That explains your nice tan."

He beamed that smile of his, the one that pulls you in and doesn't let you out. "Hey, thanks," he said, patting the well-defined line separating the golden hue of his flat, tanned belly with the stark whiteness of his thighs. Because he had drawn attention to the line of demarcation, I granted myself the right to take an open look at what my mind ached for my eyes to devour. I was mesmerized by the thick, jiggling pendulum between his legs and stared at it openly for as long as I dared.

"My family has a bungalow for weekends and vacations in this little town called Laguna Beach. Have you heard of it?"

I shook my head, no. My mouth was dry. I licked my lips, not with desire, but because I was afraid I might not be able to speak otherwise.

"Not many people back east have. I get down there every chance I can. It's small. Peaceful. Quiet. At night, when you lay in bed, you can hear the crash of the waves. It's my favorite place on Earth."

My eyes met his. His smile was warm, not leering. He moved in close enough to shake hands.

"It's real nice to meet you," I said.

"Same to you."

I stole another glance at his glorious cock. The door to the bathroom opened. He took that cue to wrap his towel around his waist. He also reminded me to show up for orientation in the second floor lounge later in the afternoon.

"You remind me of somebody," he said as he turned to leave. "I'm just not sure who."

"I get that a lot," I said, which was the truth. I was not a matinee idol, but I knew my dark-haired good looks, shy smile, and the brown eyes that opened into my soul if you looked at them in the right light had their appeal to people who wanted what I offered. I often reminded people of someone else, they just could not remember who.

He nodded, smiling at the same time. And then he was gone.

That was the first, but certainly not the last time I saw Dusty naked. As I type these words, I can picture his bare body in all of its magnificence just as it was that afternoon. I later asked him if he had been aware of the effect he had had on me that day. He laughed and said there was a *Mona Lisa* air of mystery behind my smile in my freshman directory photograph that had caught his attention. He had been curious to meet me because of it and wanted to make a positive first impression, which of course he had. I didn't know it yet, but I had just met one of the most extraordinary people, both inside and out, I would ever meet in my whole life. Years later, when I was watching that sexy, but ridiculous movie, *The Blue Lagoon*, I would break down weeping in the middle of it and have to leave the theater at the memory of Dusty. But, that was years later. Back at this first meeting, I was thinking only for the short term that this impossibly handsome older brother type of guy was someone I wanted to get to know much better.

3 THE MAGNIFICENT SEVEN

THE REST OF that first afternoon passed by in a blur. I would meet my roommate. I would have the orientation session in the second floor lounge where I would be introduced to the young men with whom I would live for the school year. I would meet more guys than whose names I could remember. I would come to know six of those guys better than I had ever known anyone. Some of them would be brothers to me for the rest of our lives. Some of them would drift away sooner than I expected. One of them I would come to despise and never speak to again. On that first day, however, I could not know any of that. I had a vague idea I had begun the odyssey of my adult life. But, my immediate desire was nothing grand. I just wanted to make a home for myself in this unfamiliar world and make it through the first day.

My roommate had not yet arrived when I returned to my room after having been dazed by Dusty. I did not have it in me yet to walk the halls of the dorm and introduce myself to my new floor mates. That's amusing for me to recall, because somewhere along the way to adulthood, the more gregarious side of me would emerge. When I later would be dropped into new situations, my first instinct would be to analyze my surroundings and connect with those in my midst. Much of my career was spent overseas, and I have had to interact with people at high levels and in unfamiliar cultures far more than most. I have an openness to new people that has served me well in professional and social situations. I hadn't developed that quality then, however. My natural inclination was to close the door and not have to face anyone, which is exactly what I did.

I lay down on the bed, folded my arm under my head, and stared at the ceiling. I exhaled and loosened my tie. I was exhausted from trying to project that I was relaxed when I wasn't. It was a relief to have a moment to myself with the door closed.

I looked over at the bare mattress on the bed next to me and wondered if the Rorschach-like spots were cum stains and if they were, who had delivered them and under what circumstances. Most of the stains had to have been from wet dreams and jerking off. I knew without being told girls were off limits upstairs in the dorm and getting caught with one in your room was grounds for suspension. But, I sure hoped there was a chance I would have opportunities to dip my toe in that kind of trouble without getting busted.

Back at home, I had my own room with a lock on the door that allowed as much privacy as I wanted. Sleep nude? No problem. Jerk off after school? No problem. At night? No problem. In the morning? You get the idea. One of my principal worries about having a roommate was whether I would have enough privacy to satisfy my insatiable appetite for masturbation. I closed my eyes and wondered whether I should take advantage of the privacy to rub one out before my roommate arrived. The images of Dusty and his big, floppy dick were just minutes old and had the clarity of temporal proximity. My cock began to stir.

My right hand headed down a well-traveled route. I squeezed the crotch of my khakis. I traced the outline of my cock through my pants and could feel it awaken. I lingered on the head and caressed it. I reached down with my right hand and gave my balls a squeeze. I stroked my shaft from the outside of my pants and took satisfaction in the size of my semi-hardness. The fingers of my left hand toyed with the zipper. It would take only a quick minute or two, and I would have the relief I needed.

The sound of fumbling keys on the other side of the door caused me to sit up with a start. My cock hardened further with the adrenalin surge that arrived with the shock of the interruption. I glanced at the tent in my khakis. Damn! My eyes darted around the room in search of something to cover it. The doorknob turned back and forth. I stood up and grabbed a book to hide the bulge that jutted out from me. I cursed to myself and tossed the book onto my desk. As the doorknob continued to twist, I removed my blazer and folded it over my arm while I approached the door to open it. In a moment, my new roommate and his parents were standing before me.

"Daniel Wright, right?" I laughed, and he did, too even though it was a play on words that had long been overplayed for him even at this young age. "I'm John Branson," I said, holding out my right hand, careful to keep the folded sport coat folded over my left and positioned in front of me.

"Great to meet you," he said with a bright smile. My new roommate. His eyes were warm, a light brown flecked with gold. His hair was auburn, which he wore in a crew cut. His nose was freckled from years of boating on the Chesapeake Bay, not far from his home in Potomac, Maryland. He was about five feet ten inches tall, a little shorter than I am, and he had a broad-shouldered wrestler's build.

As we shook hands, my cock betrayed me again and surged even harder. It was now a turgid pole, as hard as it ever gets. I was afraid a drop or two of pre-cum might have leaked out of it. What the fuck was wrong with me? I willed my hard-on to go away. I didn't want to be standing here with my heart pounding in my chest and a boner throbbing in my pants. It was not lost on me that the reason for my current priapic state was the unexpected kick of almost getting caught with my pants down and my cock out. I had never been so close to getting caught before, not even by my parents, sister, or our housekeeper. It was a crazy sense of exhilaration that left me terrified and thrilled at the same time.

Daniel's parents were too busy looking around the room and making the kind of small talk parents make to notice their son's new roommate just happened to be holding a folded blue blazer in front of him. Daniel looked sideways at the blazer before turning to examine the four corners of the room that would be our home for the next year.

Miraculously, my boner subsided after several minutes. I put my blazer back on and tightened my tie. The pre-cum that had escaped from my uncooperative cock had not been enough to leak through. I was relieved to think the whole incident had passed without notice.

I helped Daniel and his father carry Daniel's belongings up from their car while his mother placed his folded clothes into drawers. She was distraught by the sight of his mattress. She fretted out loud that it was stained by so many "accidents" and announced her intention to talk to the housing department about getting a new one. Even Daniel's father wasn't going to touch that comment and pretended to be distracted by the voices of other arriving students out in the hallway. I could tell Daniel wanted his parents to leave, just as I had with mine not too long ago, and get on with his new life.

Shortly thereafter, they granted Daniel's silent wishes and left. His father had shaken his hand in the same stilted way mine had, albeit with the added bonus of a hard slap on the back. His mother hugged him and kissed him on the cheek. She wiped a tear from the corner of her eye, and I imagine she would have said, "I love you" if I hadn't been there. Daniel's father made one of those awkward comments about being "careful of too many hijinks" fathers make in front of their sons' friends, thinking it made them seem hip to the ways of the younger generation, when it only underscored they weren't. And then they were gone.

Daniel and I had a long moment of uncomfortable silence as the reality sunk in that we would be living together in the confines of this small room with the stranger facing each of us. But, it didn't last. Soon, the conversation flowed easily, and it turned out we both had a lot in common. We each loved baseball, basketball, skiing, squash, boating, camping, politics, and Elvis. We both loved the Yankees and hated the Brooklyn Dodgers. We each thought James Dean was the coolest and Brigitte Bardot the most beautiful. And so on. By the time we

MY BARE NAKED HEART

headed down to the lounge for the first orientation session, Daniel and I had bonded.

Sure, there were differences. Daniel wrestled, which I detested. I ran, which he disliked. I wanted to major in international relations and work as a diplomat for the State Department. He wanted to major in biology and be a cardiologist after going to medical school. There were other dissimilarities that would later become apparent. But, for now, all was good. Extremely good. Daniel was smart, funny, and handsome. I sensed by the easy way we fell in together he felt the same way about me. There was a strong chemistry between us, and we each knew it. Whatever else came my way at Inverness, at least I had drawn a lucky number in the roommate lottery.

In the lounge, Dusty moderated some "getting to know you" type of exercises. In most situations, my mind and body rebel against such forced endeavors. But, Dusty had caught my eye, and anything he said was something I wanted to hear. I made a conscious decision to cast aside my natural prejudices and see where this took me. I was glad I did. Dusty did a compelling job of setting strangers on the path to becoming lifelong friends. He made us each realize, without forcing us to admit our collective fears of uncertainty and loneliness out loud, this was a unique opportunity in our lives to connect with other young men to form enduring friendships.

When I think back to those early impressions of Dusty, I shake my head in amazement. He was just twenty-one then and displayed greater presence and professionalism than you would expect to see in a man double his age. You would think someone so good-looking and perfect would be oblivious to the challenges faced by mere mortals who had not been as blessed by the gods as he. But, that was not the case at all. I could tell by the way he conducted himself that first afternoon he had an uncommon ability to connect with others in a sincere and meaningful way.

That same afternoon, I would meet five other young men who would play big parts in my college experience and in the rest of my life. There was Anthony, a handsome, hunky, and hilarious Italian guy from New York who would be branded with the nickname "Meat" the next morning in the showers for the

15

reason you might suspect. There was Eddie, who had an elfin grin and a spirited sense of fun. We renamed him "Shorty" when he claimed to be five feet six inches tall but proved to be five feet three after we held him down one night and measured him against his will. There was Howell, the most generous, loyal guy you would ever want to have as a friend. His cock was so small we nicknamed him "Howl," as in "Howl with laughter because your cock is so small." There was Ted from Schenectady who we nicknamed "Sasquatch," because he was so hairy. And there was Freddy from Shaker Heights, Ohio who we sometimes called "Rita," after Rita Hayworth, because of his movie-star prettiness.

You'll hear more about all of them, probably in more detail than you would ever want to. In addition to Daniel and me, we formed what I described as "The Magnificent Seven." During an important period of my life, these young men played a pivotal role as I transitioned into manhood. I didn't realize immediately who would be who and what I would have. But, I soon would and so would they. Before the first week was out, we would each recognize the kindred spirit amongst us and bond together with an uncommon tightness.

That evening, as we dressed for dinner, I had assumed Daniel and I would be going together to the dining hall. I knew him the best and had not yet figured out who I had met today would become my friends. As we prepared to leave our room, Daniel said he was meeting up with a guy named Mike, a high school classmate from Potomac who lived in another dorm. He spoke as if he had mentioned it before, which he hadn't. There was an awkward pause. Of course, he said, I was welcome to join them. But, the invitation was an afterthought, and we both knew it.

I understood how it would be preferable to meet up with a familiar, hometown acquaintance after a draining day like the one we just had. I read people well, and I knew he wanted to meet up with Mike without me. I know it sounds needy of me, but my feelings were bruised at the presumed brush off, particularly since I still felt unsettled in my new surroundings and because we had seemed to connect so well.

MY BARE NAKED HEART

At the same time, Anthony called out from down the hall to ask if Daniel and I wanted to join the group of them heading off to dinner. Daniel begged off, saying he was meeting up with his friend from home. I hesitated a moment and realized I could turn right or turn left. I have a weakness of becoming too attached to people too quickly. But, I also have a strong sense of self. Even then, I tried not to chase after people unless they were chasing me right back. That's not to say I didn't long for certain people to be in my life in bigger ways than they were. I looked at Daniel, who I hoped would become a new close friend, and told him to have a good time. I headed down the hall in the direction of the guys who had waved at us to join them while Daniel headed off in a different direction.

My relationship with Daniel would be a complicated one, though I must confess I was the one responsible for most of the complications. For the time being, however, I was forging pathways with new people and could not be happier my worst fears of being alone and miserable had not been realized.

Later that evening, I would return to our room to find Daniel already in bed, the lights off, his breathing sound and steady. I made an effort to stay quiet, and Daniel did not stir. After I crawled into bed amongst the clean sheets spread taut, I listened for confirmation Daniel was asleep. When I was assured he was, I pulled my cock out from my boxers and proceeded to jerk off into the paper towel I had snagged from the bathroom. It was a quick release, and I moaned quietly as a gentle squirt of sperm exited my cock.

I would not learn until Daniel and I grew closer he had only feigned sleep. His eyes were open as he faced the wall. He had heard every rustle of my sheets as he listened to me masturbate and the low moan that escaped my lips as I ejaculated. He would later admit that after I drifted off to sleep, he would jerk off for a second time, the first being shortly before I had stumbled back into the room. I would also learn he had known exactly what I was doing with my blue blazer when he had arrived with his parents. He coined the nickname "Woody" for me, a name that has stuck with me to this day in some circles, though only the members of The Magnificent Seven would know its genesis. I was exhausted and spent in every sense. My day had ended up being terrific. As I drifted off to sleep, I could not help but think of how much I was looking forward to freshman year.

4 DREAM LAND

IN THE MORNING, I lingered in the nether world between sleep and consciousness, drifting back and forth between the two. I shifted in the bed from my stomach to my side and back again, not asleep, but not awake. My cock had roused itself before the rest of me. It throbbed against the elastic of my boxers, and I pressed my boner against the mattress with the weight of my body. It surged to full hardness, straining to escape. I felt a flushness pass from my throbbing cock to my balls and down through my taint to the pucker of my virgin hole. I ground my boner into the bed, drifting off into a dream in which I was grinding it into . . . someone. Who was it? I couldn't tell at first. The faces and bodies were flashing by too quickly. Then the ball on the roulette wheel landed on just one: Allison, my girlfriend from back home.

It was Thanksgiving break. *We were in a room bathed in white light streaming through Venetian blinds and streaking across a gigantic bed. We were naked. She said she had waited months for me and was nervous. I said I wasn't, but I was. As much as I ached to lose my virginity, the thought of what might be on the other side frightened me. I said I had missed her, that she was so beautiful to me. I leaned in and buried my face in her neck and breathed in her scent. I lifted my head up again to take* in the glory of her body. I couldn't believe how lucky I was, how great life was. Her breasts were firm and fleshy. Her body had the smooth softness only a woman's does. And the bottom of the triangle of black public hair pointed in the direction I most wanted to slide my cock.

"Tell me you love me," she said.

"You know I do."

"No, I need to hear it."

"I love you," I said, though even in my dream it felt wrong to say the words that felt so sacred to me unless I knew for certain they were true. Did I love her? I didn't know. But, I knew I needed to say so or else I would be denied entry to the warm, wet tunnel of love that beckoned me.

I looked down at my cock. I was surprised to see it was not the cock I knew so well. Somehow, it had surged in size from the seven and one-half inches I knew inside-and-out to a monster that had to be ten inches. And so thick! How was this possible? I gave it a squeeze. It felt so hard, thick, and heavy. It throbbed with a burgeoning torrent of sperm clamoring to be released. Pre-cum flowed from my dick hole in anticipation and glazed the head of my cock with shiny wetness.

"I want you inside me," she said.

I rubbed my huge, shiny wet glans against the moist lips of her vagina that lead the way into a world I had spent countless hours dreaming of, but had never experienced. Until now.

"Wait," she said. "It's too big. It will never fit."

Those words were magical for me to hear. My cock surged even harder and fuller to a degree that surprised me it was even possible. I whispered for her to take a deep breath and relax, I would be gentle. She looked up at me with a trusting look in her eyes. I grabbed the python between my legs and pressed the head against the outside of her wetness, begging to be let in. I paused to savor the sensation that felt new and warmly familiar at the same time. It was as if I had found the key to the heaven I had been searching for my whole life.

I leaned in and kissed her mouth. My tongue intertwined with hers as my cock loitered at the opening of her vagina, ready to plunge to the depths of the place I most wanted to go. It was too much. I couldn't wait any longer. My desire was too strong. In one smooth motion, I slid in deep, to the bottom. It was soft, wet, and hot all at the same time. I pulled back up, my hard, juicy cock almost all the way out, with only the head sheathed by the initial inches of her vagina. It was the most incredible feeling I had ever felt.

I lingered for a moment and then plunged back in as deep as those ten inches would go. And then again. And then . . . I felt a sense of panicked terror I was going to cum far too early, way before I was ready. I wanted this to last forever, not three slow strokes. But, it was too late. I felt the familiar rumbling from the depths of my loins. I could not stop it. My cock throbbed and pumped the potent mixture of semen and sperm up from inside me, through my pulsating ten inch shaft. I deposited the warm, messy load deep inside her. She moaned in delight, and I held her close. My arms wrapped around her as she lay beneath me, as if I would never let her go.

I wanted to luxuriate in the post-orgasmic glow, but something wasn't right. I felt a wetness and heard voices that were out of place. My eyes opened. It took a moment for my brain to register where I was. No, I was not in some ethereal white bedroom losing my virginity to Allison. I was not in my bedroom back at home in West Hartford. I was in my dorm room in Vermont. My cock was not a throbbing ten inch monster. It had all been a dream. How could that be? It had seemed so real, so intense. I exhaled. When I did have sex someday, is that what it would feel like? Would it be that incredible?

In the hallway, I could hear Dusty's voice full of good cheer and enthusiasm even at this early hour. I reached down and felt the outside of my boxers and my sheets. Damn! They were wet with warm semen rapidly turning cold. I hadn't had a wet dream since junior high. Why did I have to have one on the very first morning of college? With my new roommate in the room? I sighed. The pleasures of the dream had already retreated into the recesses of my brain.

At least the dream was about Allison, which was of considerable consolation. I sometimes had vivid, powerful dreams about guys. As the excitement of those dreams ebbed, each time a nagging fear crept back into my consciousness like poisonous mist rising from a bog. I have mentioned before one of my fears at that time of my life was I might be a fairy. If I had just had a wet dream about Allison and explosive, satisfying sex with a girl, it meant I wasn't a fairy, right?

Dusty pounded on the door. "Wake up boys! We have a big day ahead of us!"

Daniel swung his feet around and planted them on the floor. He wiped the sleep from his eyes. "What's with him?"

"I know," I said. "I'm not ready to get out of bed." That was true in more than one sense. I was trapped. I couldn't let Daniel see I had had a wet dream. I had to wait for him to leave or at least turn his back so I could slip out of bed without him seeing. And I needed to piss like a race horse. My worst fears of diminished of privacy were coming true, and it was only the first full day.

Daniel stood up and shuffled over to the closet. My eyes followed him as he crossed the room. He had a well-toned body with a meaty ass I looked forward to seeing uncovered. When he turned to reach for his shaving kit, my eyes widened in disbelief. I looked again and saw the unmistakable bulge of morning wood, a sizeable ridge that stretched to the top of his boxers and strained against the cotton fabric. He rubbed his eyes again and yawned. I tried not to stare, but it was impossible not to. I thought of those X-ray vision glasses I had once ordered from an ad in the back of a comic book. If only they had worked as advertised, I could use them now to see what lurked beneath that hefty bulge. As he pulled his T-shirt over his head, however, a miracle happened: his big dick flopped through the fly of his boxers.

It bounced lazily a few times. And then he simply tucked it back inside. I had pretended not to notice, though if I had fooled him – which I later learned I hadn't – I certainly wasn't fooling myself. The image seared into my brain, and I can recall it with clarity even all of these years later. His cock was big, a solid seven inches, just a little shorter than mine. But, his was wider and flared out in the middle. It was narrower at the base and the head, and it widened in the middle like the sexiest of soda bottles. Well-proportioned. Hefty. Long.

I was practically cowering in my bed, afraid he might see my semi and the wet spot from my dream. He was cut from different cloth, however. He had a strong sense of self and didn't care too much about what other people thought. In his world, so what if your boner flopped out of your boxers and your roommate saw it? Just slip it back in and never give it another thought. I took note of how casual he had been about it and his lack of embarrassment. One of the many lessons in self-confidence I would learn from him was not to worry so much what others think, even if it was something private like this.

"You coming with me to the showers, sleepy head?"

"You bet," I said. "Let's go." I sat up and slipped off my boxers. I wrapped my towel around my waist and grabbed my shaving kit. Had he noticed the wetness on my boxers or on my sheets? I wasn't going to care. At least not too much.

One of the reasons I look back at my college years with such fondness is I had been hungry for the brotherhood of male companionship. It was not just the cockfest I would be exposed to on a daily basis in the showers and the dorms. Or the random acts of nudity that arise when rowdy young men live together in the oasis of an all-male college, particularly in those times. For sure, that was part of the fun. But, the camaraderie of bonding with young men and the close friendships we made at this formative time in our lives is something I cherish even more.

Daniel and I headed out the door and down the hall together. The sounds of raucous laughter escaping from the bathroom made me wonder who I would be seeing naked in the showers and whether Dusty might be one of them. *Stop it*, I told myself. *Stop it!* I would later come to terms with those thoughts and where on the spectrum my sexuality fell. But, until I did, I would continue to be terrified by what excited me. I still didn't know what was ahead of me. For now, I was happy to be walking down the hall to the showers with my new buddy and a little more confidence in my step.

5 HELICOPTERS

THE BATHROOM WAS busy that first morning. All of the sinks were occupied with guys shaving and brushing their teeth. You could hear the sounds of rowdy voices and water spraying in the shower. I nodded and exchanged hellos with some of the guys I had met yesterday. Daniel headed to a stall to take a dump, and I made my way to the urinal to take a long piss. After that, I headed into the shower for the very first time.

I hung my towel on a hook in the small alcove at the entrance. Now that I was naked, I poked my head around the corner. There were four naked guys in there already.

"Hey, fellas," I said as I sidled up to one of the open nozzles.

There was a round of friendly greetings from my shower mates while I turned on the water and adjusted the temperature. As it happens, these were some of the guys with whom I would come to be closest in college and formed a portion of what I described previously as The Magnificent Seven. In the flesh with their bare asses and bouncing cocks on display was, Anthony, Howell, Eddie, and Ted. Or, as we would later sometimes call them, Meat, Howl, Shorty, and Sasquatch.

I was determined to be on my best behavior and not check out the cocks of my new pals. I had sensed intrinsically my whole life without ever being told I would be relegated to pariah status if people knew of the secret desires that swirled inside my head. I did not want to risk that, especially not on my first full day here when wary first impressions were still being formed. I kept my head up, my peripheral vision on the dimmest setting. With a few minor adjustments to the hot and cold faucets, I was soon immersed in a generous cascade of gloriously warm water.

"Where's your roommate?" Anthony asked. "He's AWOL again." I hadn't mentioned it to Daniel, but the guys had been put-out he had not joined us for dinner in the dining hall on our very first night together. There was a perception he had ditched us in favor of his friend from home, the one who lived in another dorm. It had not gone over well.

"He's using the toilet," I said, jutting my chin in the direction of the main part of the bathroom. "He'll be right in."

"He seems pretty full of himself," Anthony said. The words hung in the air, and I would later think how rich that comment was coming from him. They were the same words I would hear people say about him from time-to-time, and with some justification.

"He's cool," I said. "He just wanted to see a friend from Potomac who lives in another dorm." I had felt a sting I hadn't wanted to feel last night when Daniel chose to have dinner with Mike instead of me. But, I had understood why he might have preferred the familiarity of someone from back home. I had moved past it and now felt silly it had even bothered me.

"I dunno," Anthony said. "I picked up kind of an attitude about him."

"C'mon," Howell said, his hair soapy with shampoo. "Seems like a good guy to me, too."

Eddie agreed.

Anthony shrugged and lifted his arms up to rinse off his chest and armpits. He was physically imposing, and he knew it. He was six feet three inches tall with broad shoulders and dark-haired Italian good looks. He had a half moon of hair across his well-defined and impressive pecs, but otherwise was hairless on his chest and back. In later years, when he entered his twenties, his hair would grow across his chest and ass. But, he was only eighteen then and still mostly smooth. When he turned around to rinse the shampoo out of his hair, I could not help but catch a glimpse of his cock out of the corner of my eye. What I thought I saw shocked me. Could it be? Reflexively, my head snapped back for another quick look. It was not much longer than an instant, but I saw what I needed to see. It was, by far, the largest cock I had ever seen.

"Hey, Anthony," Howell said, "Branson just checked out your cock."

My faced turned crimson at the shame of being caught. I turned to Howell and snapped, "Fuck you, I didn't check out anybody's cock. Why the fuck would you say that?" Terror rose up within me, and my heart threatened to pound its way out of my chest. How could I be so careless? After unwavering vigilance from my earliest awareness of the secret desires within me that I somehow always knew to keep to myself, how could I slip up now, on my first full day of college when people were forming first impressions that would govern our next four years? Fuck!

Anthony's gaze met mine. His eyes were menacing. The room fell silent except for the sound of spraying water, and if anyone could hear it, the pounding beat of my heart. No one spoke. Until Anthony did, that is. "So, you were checking out my cock, were you?"

My mouth went dry. "No."

"No? Then why did Howell say you did?"

"It's bullshit. I didn't."

Anthony continued to stare back at me, his eyes leveled with mine. "Is this what you wanted to look at?" he asked. Even with our eyes locked, I could sense from the periphery he had grabbed his cock in one hand and was slapping it against the other. Each time it hit with a loud smack, baiting me to look at it and prove him right. But, I did not look down or say anything. I wanted this all to stop. I wanted to turn back the clock and to have this all never to have happened in the first place.

"Is this what you wanted to look at?" he asked again, enunciating each word as if they were separated by periods.

My eyes stayed steady with his. I was not going to give in and admit anything. I couldn't.

After a long beat, a huge, shit-eating grin spread across his face. "Look all you want, I have nothing to hide."

Howell's face broke out in a broad, good-natured smile. "C'mon, we all checked it out. We're just ribbing you. How could you ignore that huge anaconda between his legs? It's a fucking monster!"

"It's no big deal," Anthony said to me with a smirk of false modesty. "I'm used to it."

"I definitely wouldn't call that 'no big deal,'" Eddie said, nodding his head in the direction of Anthony's cock.

Anthony slapped me on the back, a mischievous smile emblazoned across his face. "Sorry, bud, I was just messing with you. Check out my big dick as much as you want, seriously. All of these other fruits did. I don't mind at all."

My eyes were still leveled with his, and my sense of personal well-being was telling me he meant it. "I actually kind of like it," he added, his right eyebrow raised in a conspiratorial arch.

I took a giant and fateful leap and allowed myself to look as well.

Holy shit!

I took in the magnificent sight before me for a longer look than that initial furtive glance. Eddie was right. They all were. Anthony's cock was gigantic. It was long, thick, and symmetrically shaped, like a heavy, wrinkly cucumber hanging between his legs with a shiny glans poking through the lips of his thick foreskin. Back then, not everyone my age was circumcised routinely like guys who were born after World War II. It was often a hallmark of socio-economic status. Upper middle class whites, like me, usually were. Lower class whites usually weren't. Ethnic types usually weren't either unless it was for religious purposes or there had been a medical issue.

Anthony was Italian, and he was a first generation American. So, of course, he wasn't cut. His flaccid cock was about seven inches long with a well-proportioned head protruding from the opening of his foreskin, as if it were so big it needed its own supply of oxygen. He had a long piss slit and a large, smooth, shiny glans. His cock was wide and undulated from side-to-side when he moved. Later on, when I would see it hard for the first time, his length and thickness would cause me to gasp audibly in disbelief. Fully engorged and on the precipice of ejaculation, it was a legitimate ten inches long and seven inches thick. To this date, in all of my many years on Earth, Anthony's cock was the largest I have ever seen in person. I certainly never expect to see another one so big in the flesh during this lifetime.

"Damn," I said. "That thing is fucking huge!" I didn't know what else to say. There were no other words. I allowed myself to look for a long, leisurely series of moments. But, not so long as to raise any further suspicions about me. It was one thing to look at a friend's gigantic cock with admiration and respect. It was another to look at it with desire, which I certainly felt, but was determined to hide in the deepest recesses of my being.

Daniel walked in to the shower. "Hey, guys," he said. "If you're having a big dick contest, count me in!"

"Sorry, bud," Howell said, taking an open glance at Daniel's ample goods. "You don't stand a chance. Anthony's got everyone beat."

Daniel was smiling gamely until he looked over at Anthony's cock. His mouth opened in surprise, his lips forming a perfect "O," his eyes widening in disbelief. Daniel stood under the open nozzle and turned on the faucet as he allowed himself to take as long and leisurely a look at Anthony's cock as he wished. Daniel didn't care what anyone would say about him taking his time to gander at Anthony's cock, unlike me, who was worried I might be looking too long. Naked, in all his beautiful glory, Daniel's body was taut and athletic. His skin had a golden hue. His stomach was tight and smooth with the outline of a six pack. His cock was beautiful and impressive in its own right, as I had described before. But, he was no match for Anthony.

"That's a big Italian sausage you got there," Daniel said. He pronounced "Italian" as "eye-talian." While it did not quite rise to the level of a slur, it had an edge to it that was not lost on Anthony.

Anthony smirked. "No points for originality, Wonder Bread. I've been called that before." His eyes looked down at Daniel's cock with disdain. "And, I've seen bigger."

I never fully understood why it is some guys look for conflict with someone they see as a perceived rival without ever giving the other person a chance. Usually, these guys have more in common than they don't, and you'd think their similarities would bring them together instead of making them rivals. You see it when fights break out in a bar for no reason other than someone rubs someone the wrong way. Or gang warfare erupting over a lingering glance in the wrong direction. Or two alpha males in a college dorm angling for who will be top dog – or who has the biggest cock. I liked both Daniel and Anthony and didn't want there to be any petty bullshit.

"I think everyone's got me beat," Howell said good-naturedly. "I'm hung like an acorn." That was one of the things I would come to love about Howell. Not his tiny cock, but his desire for people to be happy and to get along. He sensed the rising tension between Daniel and Anthony and deftly stepped in to defuse it at his own expense. I was embarrassed I had snapped at him, especially when he had been right about me and especially as I grew to realize how devoid of pretense he was.

"How do you two guys look, side-by-side?" Eddie asked of Howell and Anthony.

"The better question is, how do you and Anthony look side-by-side?" Ted asked, looking at Eddie. "He must be a foot taller than you."

"I'm six foot three," Anthony said to Eddie. "I'm guessing you're five foot three, tops."

I would come to learn that Eddie was pretty easy going, but he was very sensitive about his height and any inference he was short. "Nah, I'm five foot six."

"Bullshit. Come over here," Anthony said, pulling Eddie over to him and squeezing his arm around his shoulder so he couldn't squirm away. The warm water was splashing wildly everywhere, and we all were laughing. Eddie resisted, but Anthony was too strong. I found it supremely erotic to watch tall, hulking Anthony pull Eddie next to him against his will. Both of them were good-looking and sexy in each of their own ways. Eddie was short, but he had a tight, toned body and a meaty, apple-cheeked butt. He was handsome, with brown hair and a lively smile. He had a happy, bouncing cock with a tight set of large, hairy balls. We would later become particularly close, and I liked his sense of spirit and fun from the very beginning.

"I'm saying five foot three," Anthony said. "But, your cock is big. At least you have that going for you, shorty."

Eddie broke away, but not before Anthony slapped his ass hard enough to leave a red mark.

Howell stepped over to Anthony and stood next to him, facing us. The physical differences of their anatomy were stark. Anthony was just a few inches taller, but his cock was a long, thick, wrinkled appendage that swayed heavily between his thighs. Howell's cock was just a crown that rested snugly on top of a loose set of low hanging balls. We all laughed, and I swear it was in good spirit and in keeping with the camaraderie building between all of us in the forced intimacy of this warm, wet, shower. Yes, the laughter was precipitated by Howell's tiny cock. But, I assure you we already had bonded as friends. He was laughing with us, and there was no malice intended by anyone.

Daniel called attention to Ted's incredible hairiness. He was the only one of us to have a swath of fur across his entire chest, back, and ass. "You're a fucking Sasquatch," Daniel said, which prompted another round of laughter. Thereafter, none of us were able to think of Ted by any other name than "Sasquatch." He truly was one of the hairiest guys I would ever see in my life. His head was covered by curly black hair that, with great irony, would fall out by the time he was in his early thirties. His chest, back, ass, and legs were covered by long black hair as well, and he had a thick, black bush cushioning a thick cock of average length. I would later learn he also had the ability to cum in gushing, copious amounts. I would watch with wonder as it matted his hairy chest and abs with sticky whiteness he would need to scrub off in the shower rather than just wipe, like I did with mine.

By now, I was all showered and shaved. There was no real reason for me to remain in the shower other than I was enjoying everyone's company and what seemed to be an extraordinary closeness and rowdiness that was starting to feel titillating. I had showered with buddies before in locker rooms after sports. But, we never laughed and openly spoke of each other's cock and bodies like we were now.

Daniel turned his attention to me. "I have to admit, my roomie looks pretty gifted in the dick department. He almost gives me a run for my money."

I blushed as I realized it was my turn to have my cock on display and under group scrutiny. My cock is circumcised, and when hard is about seven and one-half inches long. It's as thick as the cardboard tube in a roll of paper towels, which I can slide about half-way down with some effort, but no further. I've come to learn it is bigger than most I have encountered in my life without being extraordinarily large. I am more of a show-er than a grower, giving Daniel the misconception his cock was bigger than mine. He and I would come to know each other's cock well enough to correct his misperception. But, at this moment, he thought he had me beat.

"I don't know, Danny Boy," Anthony said. "It's close. I think Branson might be bigger."

By now, my cock was at ease, elongated and loose from the warm water, the steam, and the bawdiness. I was caught up in the raucousness of the moment and have a strong sense of fun when I am not busy being serious. And the truth is, I am a bit of an exhibitionist. Now that the spotlight was on me, I wanted to give a show that would be remembered. I started off slow, swiveling my hips from side-to-side with a slight twist. In a moment, I had my cock spinning like a helicopter rotor, a secret skill perfectly suited for a reception like this rather than the solo performances I had given in my bedroom mirror back home. I had not underestimated my audience: they roared and howled in delight.

"Look at you," Eddie said. "The boy next door with the dirty parlor tricks!"

I smiled mischievously and laughed, my cock still spinning amidst the spray of the water. "It's the boy next door you should be worried about."

"I'm not worried, and I can do that, too" Anthony said. He began gyrating his hips and soon his big dick was swinging around in a circle that truly was a sight to behold. Daniel joined in as well and broke out in the giddiest of laughter. Eddie could do it as well with what I would later learn was a solid six inch hard cock that looked disproportionately huge on his five foot three inch frame. Howell, of course could not, but it was fun to see him try. Sasquatch's cock was thick, but not long enough. It was fun to see him try as well.

Looking back through time, I am profoundly grateful we were able to share the greatest gift of bonding with all of this naked silliness. The world can be a grey, dreary place if you let it be, especially as you fully enter adulthood and are burdened by the responsibilities that come with it. There is something so humanly special about the freedom of young men at play in the prime of life, especially when that play is without inhibition. I am long past those years and experiences. But, I will argue with anyone that there are few things more glorious, beautiful, and pure than a shower full of naked young man laughing and cheering as their cocks spin like helicopters while warm water sprayed down upon them.

I was not so naïve as to be ignorant of the silent undercurrents passing beneath us as we established in unspoken ways certain dynamics there would be amongst us. Daniel and Anthony would always be rivals in ways that sometimes would cause tension to hang in the air for all of us. Howell would be the fun-loving good guy with no agenda who got along with everyone. Sasquatch would be the hairy, low-key guy in the mix of things who went along with what everyone else did and would join trouble, but never cause it. Eddie would be the short, adorable mascot who was always up for fun, with the added bonus of being the most generous, unselfish friend in the very darkest of times. I would pass among different roles ranging from diplomat, observer, voice-of-reason, consigliere, and the guy who sought opportunities to push his own boundaries when he wasn't watching other people push theirs.

By now, I was showered and clean. I knew my new friends better, and I had showed everyone a trick of my own. It all felt very good. Perhaps too good. I had started to feel a low-rumbling in my groin. Despite the standards for uncommon openness we had all just established, a boner in the shower would be going too far. I decided now would make a good time for an exit.

In the alcove, I ran into Dusty. He had a towel around his waist and was ready to uncover himself and enter the shower just as the others were preparing to wrap things up and leave. We had not had a chance to speak outside of our initial introduction in the bathroom yesterday and a few words during the "getting to know you" exercises he had moderated. He said a friendly "hey there" and asked what was going on in the showers and, with a chuckle, whether it would be safe to go in. I laughed and said it was. I had thought about Dusty a lot since I had met him yesterday, and I am sure my face displayed my open happiness at seeing him. I felt a tingle at being naked in front of him for the first time. As we spoke, I couldn't help but notice he had stolen a quick peek at my cock that, in its early stages of tumescence, was making a good first impression. I smiled and said I'd catch him later.

After I wrapped my towel around myself and grabbed my shaving kit, I turned around to take another look at Dusty. He had turned around to take another look at me as well. Our eyes met and we each looked away with a tinge of shyness. Then, without hesitation, we looked back at each other. Dusty and I were in the beginning stages of some kind of a connection of which neither of us yet knew where it would take us. But, it was safe to say we both knew it, even if it was unspoken. We each smiled shyly without saying anything this time. Then he stepped into the shower, allowing me to steal a fleeting glance of his full, white, meaty ass before he disappeared around the corner.

I grabbed a paper towel from the dispenser by the sink and rushed back to my room before Daniel returned. Thinking of all of the cock play and wet, naked bodies I had just seen was causing my own cock to harden. When I reached my room, I closed the door and rubbed out a quick one into the paper towel. My balls ached afterwards and my load was on the smaller side given I had just awoken from a wet dream less than an hour before. In the moment after I came, I closed my eyes and savored not just the fleeting moments of my quick orgasm, but the memories of what I had experienced since my parents had dropped me off not even twenty-four hours before. My head was still swirling from everything I had encountered since my arrival. It was so much to take in, and it is a lot to remember all of these years later. Wherever I was going, however, I liked the path I was on.

6 WONDER BREAD

A FEW WEEKS had passed, and I had settled into the routines of my new life as a college freshman with more ease than I had expected. I was exploring a number of areas of study and was particularly enthralled by a course called "Emerging Governments," which I hoped would lead to a major in international relations and a career in the State Department, a long-time dream of mine. The course was taught by Professor Johnston, who would become a mentor to me, and you'll hear more about him later. The Magnificent Seven grew closer. We had fallen into a routine of goofing off and hanging out in each other's rooms and the second floor lounge when we weren't in class. We played pick-up games of softball in the quad. We had meals together in the dining hall. We would talk smack about girls and sex. On weekends, which usually started on Thursdays and sometimes on Wednesdays, we would drink beer and any kind of alcohol we could get our hands on.

Daniel and I had gone grown particularly close over the past few weeks, a development I had hoped for to the core of my being. He was also in my Emerging Governments class. He had received a C+ on our first essay assignment, which had been a jarring wake-up call for him. I had received an A, which impressed him, and he asked for my advice on how to get his grade up.

We would sit side-by-side at the long wooden tables in the hallowed library, our knees so close they sometimes touched. I reviewed drafts of his essays and provided suggestions on how he might improve them. We spoke in low whispers so as not to violate the sanctity of the library's silence. My eyes followed his as they scanned the pages and his brain registered the red marks I had made. I listened to the sound of his breathing. I examined the soft, fine hairs on his neck. I inhaled his scent, which smelled faintly like the clean freshness of Tide laundry detergent, but distinctly human at the same time. When he looked up and his smart eyes met mine, I swooned at the mental and physical closeness I had with him at that moment. I never wanted it to end.

We would repeat these encounters twice a week over the first few months of school. On his second paper, he received a B. On his third, a B+, and he would hover between a B+ and an A- for the rest of the semester.

I received a mixture of As and A+s in that class, which I say not to brag, but to say it impressed Daniel and made the playing field between us more level. It was sometimes hard to be close friends with someone who lived as charmed an existence as he did. While I was accomplished in my own right, almost everything I could do, Daniel could do better. I was handsome, but Daniel was more handsome. I was a good athlete, but Daniel was a better one. I was popular amongst our friends, but Daniel was more popular and people gravitated to him in ways they did not with me. That he sought my opinions on the papers for this class helped to balance things out.

This Friday had been a good one. Daniel had received his first A- in Emerging Governments, and I had received my first A+. We had celebrated by playing squash at the athletic center. Daniel had beat me handily, of course, in three out of the four matches we played. But, I had squeaked by in the final match and won by two points. He laughed that he was losing his edge, and we both were in high spirits. Daniel was also excited about a date he had for the evening with a girl he knew from Potomac who went to Mount Holyoke. She was up for the weekend with another girl for a double date with Daniel and his friend Mike. Daniel had messed around with this girl over the summer, and he was fairly certain he was going all the way with her tonight.

After squash, we lingered in the showers talking after we had rinsed the sweat from our bodies. As always, I savored the bonding that strengthened our closeness as we dallied naked in the warm spray of the water long after we had any practical need for being there. I knew he felt the same unspoken sense of enjoyment. Otherwise, he would have turned off the faucet and headed to dry off already.

"This girl, Carol, she has an incredible body," Daniel said.

"Yeah?" I said, thinking few bodies could be more incredible than Daniel's. As I mentioned before, Daniel had a beautiful body. He was five feet ten, just a little shorter than me. His shoulders were broad, and his torso v-shaped from working out for his high school wrestling team. His skin had a vibrant, unblemished glow to it. His areolas were dark brown, and each was a little larger than the size of a quarter. His belly was flat and had the trace of a six pack. If your eyes continued traveling south, and mine did, you would see he didn't have a treasure trail, just smooth skin until you hit a band of tightly curled pubic hair sprouting a few inches above and on either side of his cock. Yes, I was in heaven.

"Did I ever tell you? Her tits are like grapefruits, and she let me play with them last summer at a party at the country club. I could have sucked on her nipples all night. Mmmm, so delicious." Yeah, he had told me before. More than once. But, I still liked hearing him talking about it.

He turned around and rinsed his face under the water, which gave me an unobstructed view of his beautiful ass. Daniel's ass was high, if you know what I mean. It defied gravity. It was smooth and hairless. It was tightly muscled, and if you were to squeeze it, it would be firm instead of fleshy. I wanted to grab it in the worst way, to feel its firmness and to rub my index finger along the length of his crack and gently press it in and touch the pucker of his hole.

He turned around again, and we continued talking as the water cascaded upon us. We each took casual glances at each other's cock without it being a big deal or anything other than normal curiosity. That's not to suggest we weren't sizing each other up. We were in every possible way. To say I was thrilled at our shared level of comfort would be a wild understatement.

While we lingered, Dusty joined us. "Just came from a run," he said. In an instant, he too was enjoying the warmth of the water with us. I stole a peek at his long, bouncing cock when his eyes were closed. I noticed Daniel did, too.

I remember thinking how great it was I was able to stand there in the showers and enjoy such laid-back nudity and conversation with two of the most beautiful young men I had ever seen. The dynamic between the three of us was different each in its own way. Daniel and I were roommates and good buddies. I had an infatuation with him I had no reason to think was reciprocated. Dusty and I had not spent as much time together as Daniel and I obviously had, and I did not know him as well. He was older than us, and as the resident advisor, was an authority figure of sorts that meant our playing field was not level. But, there had been an unspoken something between us that felt more than platonic.

Dusty and Daniel were cordial to each other, but they did not share what I had with each of them. Since Dusty had joined us, Daniel was not as chatty. Even though I was in my own naked heaven, I could tell that with Dusty in the mix, the intimacy of the moment had passed for Daniel. He turned off the faucet and headed to the alcove and his towel. His cock was long, loose, and relaxed from our extended stay in the warm shower. It swung heavily from side to side as he walked, the wide brown scar of his circumcision stretched as well. Mine was in a parallel elongated state. Our widths were about the same. But, if you were to look closely, and I was, mine was just a little longer than his.

I would have been happy to continue loitering in the shower with Dusty until the aquifer ran dry. But, I took Daniel's impending departure as my cue to leave. I never fully understood the dynamic that draws people to others who might not want them as much when there is someone just as desirable dropping almost every hint they are available. I was as guilty as anyone of the failings of such behavior. Even with my lack of experience in such matters, I sensed Daniel viewed me as just a friend, albeit a close one. With Dusty, however, I sensed he might view me in a different, more intimate way if we could ever move beyond the stolen, but unflinching glances and spend time getting to know each other better. You would think I would have stayed behind with Dusty. Instead, I was drawn to Daniel and the hopeful uncertainty of what friendship with him meant and whether there was the possibility of more. We left, and I didn't look back. If I had, I would have seen that even though Daniel's ass was better, mine was the one Dusty followed.

Daniel and I finished toweling off in our dorm room. He talked more about Carol and his expectations for the evening. I listened. By the time he slipped his feet into his underwear and pulled them up, his cock was in a state of a semi-hardness that required him to bend it between his legs when it came time to tuck it in. I watched openly. I couldn't help myself.

"You're staying in by yourself tonight?" Daniel asked, not understanding why anyone would want to do that. "You sure you don't want to go out drinking with the guys?"

Despite the hunger for male camaraderie I had been satisfying with my new pals, I sometimes needed time to be alone in my own thoughts. This was one of those nights. Howl and Shorty were rounding up guys to go into town to get drunk and play pool at one of the townie bars. Normally, that would sound fun to me. But, tonight, after a long week, I just wanted to stay in. Daniel eyed me with a mix of bemusement and bewilderment. Soon, however, he finished dressing and was ready to leave. Before he did, he pulled a foil-wrapped condom out of his dresser and held it up to me. He winked and put the condom into his wallet with a huge, shit-eating grin spread across his face.

Looking back through the lens of what happened later that night, Daniel must have thought I had been up to something when I said I wanted to stay behind. But, I really just wanted to read.

After he left, I settled into Somerset Maugham's *The Razor's Edge*, which I had read three times before. It was a popular book in those days, particularly among young men like me who were looking out at the broader world beyond them and wondered how they were going to find their place in it. It's about a guy named Larry Darrell who returned from World War I traumatized by his combat experiences, in particular the death of his close friend, a fellow soldier named Patsy. There were only fleeting references to Patsy, but Larry had come unglued by the tragedy of Patsy's death and set out on a global journey in search of meaning and adventure.

Conventional literature back then almost never had overt homosexual themes, and readers with persuasions like mine were left to read between the lines for what they hoped they might see, but never did. I couldn't help but wonder as I read and re-read *The Razor's Edge* whether Larry's love for Patsy had been more than fraternal and whether the loss of that love was what had motivated Larry to set out on a search that would never end. Was Maugham telegraphing a secret message to knowing readers like me who were searching for meaning hidden in plain sight? I couldn't know for certain, but I couldn't help but hope he was. The book had resonated with me from the first time I read it. Soon, I was engulfed in it again until I drifted off several hours later.

○3

A pounding on the door roused me from my slumber. I had fallen asleep in my clothes with the book on my chest. I looked at the luminescent dial of my alarm clock. It was almost midnight.

"Branson! Open up! Hurry!" It was Anthony. He pounded on the door again.

I stumbled to the door and flung it open. "What's going on?" I asked, my eyes adjusting to the brightness of the light in the hall. Anthony was there with Howl and Sasquatch.

"It's Wonder Bread," Anthony said. Ever since Daniel had made the comment about Anthony's I-talian sausage, Anthony had stopped referring to Daniel as "Danny Boy" and only referred to him as "Wonder Bread." I hadn't understood the reference at first. Then, Anthony explained Daniel was the whitest person he had ever known. I was confused. Didn't everyone eat Wonder Bread? Even with Anthony's explanation, it took me a while to get it and even longer to understand the description could have applied to me as well.

"We have to hurry," Howl said. His tongue was thick with drink, and he was bleary-eyed. I looked at the others. It was the same with each of them.

I was alarmed. "Is he hurt?"

Anthony smirked and shook his head, no. He had a bag of Wonder Bread in one hand and a pair of binoculars in the other. I was curious why, but figured some type of prank at Daniel's expense was impending.

In a flash, we were on our way outside of the dorm and had circled around to the back of it with everyone imploring me to be silent. We stopped outside the window of the first floor housemaster's lounge. The window was heavy and large and opened up a foot or so at the bottom. Anthony peered inside and motioned for me to do the same.

What I saw drew me in and captured my full attention. Daniel and Carol were fooling around on the couch on the far side of the room. Carol was on her back in a state of partial undress. Daniel was on top of her. His pants were still on, but his shirt was off and his blue blazer was spread over the seat of a chair. They were kissing with squirming passion, and Daniel was slowly grinding his pelvis through his pants into Carol's midsection. They weren't quite there yet, but Daniel's prediction they would be going all the way tonight looked about to come true.

Sasquatch handed me a flask of whiskey. I took a long swig while Anthony flashed me one of his trademark shit-eating grins.

Howell brought the binoculars up to his eyes and trained them on the sight before us. He gasped. Daniel had shifted his weight, allowing us a clear line on Carol's breasts, which Daniel had rightly compared to grapefruits. He cupped them in his hands before leaning in to suck her nipples. All the while, he continued to grind against her through the cloth of his pants and the fabric of her dress.

After sucking on her nipples and groping her breasts, it was time to take things further. He stood up, unzipped his pants, and pulled them down. His underwear had tented upwards, showcasing the firm, solid bulge of his erect cock. Carol grabbed it, running her hand up and down its length and giving it an assessing squeeze. She pulled down the top of his underwear and his boner sprung out of it. Unlike my earlier, fleeting glimpse of the rod that had flopped out of his boxers the first morning in the dorm, this afforded me a long, unimpeded view. Daniel's cock was a solid seven inches, as I had mentioned earlier, and jutted up in the air at a forty-five degree angle. His balls were full and heavy in the flush of arousal.

Anthony took a turn with the binoculars. "Way to go, Wonder Bread," he said under his breath.

While Anthony had the lenses up to his eyes, I couldn't help but grab a glimpse of the huge bulge in his pants. My own cock was hard as well, and I had to imagine Howell's and Sasquatch's were, too.

"Give me a look," Sasquatch said, taking them from him. We all watched as Daniel reached for his wallet and pulled out the foil-wrapped rubber he had flashed me earlier. With his fully engorged cock pointing upward at attention, he tore off the foil wrapper and unrolled the condom down the length of his shaft.

"Holy shit," Howell said. "Wonder Bread has a big cock."

"He sure does," I said.

Daniel positioned himself over Carol and bent his boner down towards her. Sasquatch let out a low whistle. "He's going for it!"

"Let me see," I said. Howell handed the binoculars to me. What I saw was so electrifying, I peered through them without blinking so as not to miss a single instant of the extraordinary show going on before us. Daniel pressed the top of his cock against the opening of Carol's vagina and moistened the tip with her wetness. Without giving her a chance to adjust, he plunged inside her, all the way to the bottom. She flinched in pain and pressed her hand against the lower part of his abdomen to slow him.

Through the lens of the binoculars, I had a view that brought me even closer than if my face were flush against their bodies. Daniel's full, heavy balls were pressed against the opening of her vagina. No one trimmed pubic hair back then, and both Daniel's balls and Carol's bush were untrimmed and long-haired in a way that would be fetish-worthy in today's pornography, but were conventional for the times. Daniel pulled up so only the head of his dick was covered. Between the cheeks of his firm, rounded ass, I caught a quick glimpse of his hole, the first time I had seen anyone's other than my own. Then he plunged back in and then out, again and again.

"Tsk, tsk, Wonder Bread," Anthony said under his breath as he grabbed the binoculars back from me. "You're going too fast, your technique is terrible."

No one else said anything. We were too entranced.

"Look at him, he's like a jackrabbit the way he's pumping up and down so fast," Anthony said, louder this time.

"Shhh!" Howell implored.

"That poor girl's going to be sore," Anthony said, even louder this time. "This is a complete disgrace." He took another swig of whiskey and reached down into the bag of Wonder Bread. I thought he was reaching for a piece to snack on, but he had something else in mind. He pulled out a slice and tossed it like a Frisbee through the open bottom of the window. It landed on the floor of the lounge without Daniel or Carol noticing.

"What the hell are you doing?" I asked. It was one thing to watch them surreptitiously. It was another to interrupt them. I knew Anthony and Daniel both very well by now. While I would bet good money Anthony would find humor and pride if he had been the one being spied upon, Daniel was more tightly wound and likely to view the situation with affront. I valued my friendship with Daniel very much, and I had a terrible feeling this drunken, lecherous fun was going in a dangerous direction.

Anthony reached for another piece of bread. I tried to stop him, but he shoved my arm away. Howl and Sasquatch each joined Anthony by reaching into the bag to pull out slices of the bread. In unison, they spun them through the air of the open window pelting Daniel and Carol in rapid fire. The first one hit

Daniel's ass in mid pump. One after another, the others struck various parts of their bodies.

Carol shrieked.

Daniel bellowed, "What the fuck!"

The guys reloaded and continued the barrage of flying bread.

Daniel withdrew his cock from Carol and stood up. Even in the low light, I could tell his face was twisted with anger. But, I wasn't interested in his face. As he strutted towards us, I was transfixed by the image of his hefty cock, still sheathed in a Trojan with the reservoir tip, still fully engorged and jutting straight up at a forty-five degree angle. It flipped left and right and left and right as he rushed over to the window. In the background, Carol was crying and trying to cover herself up with her dress. Daniel was screaming he was going to beat the shit out of all of us. The other guys laughed raucously and fled. I was still horrified and mesmerized by all I had just seen, and my face was the last one Daniel saw before he slammed the window down and whipped the curtains shut.

I caught up with the guys when we reached the front side of the dorm. They were bent over with laughter. "Did you see his face?" Sasquatch said.

"His face?" Howell asked. "What about his cock? I'd give anything to have a cock that big. Did you see it sway back and forth like a metronome as he stomped across the room towards us?"

I shook my head. They were fueled by alcohol and were not as vested as I was with my feelings of friendship and otherwise for Daniel. If it had seemed funny before, it certainly didn't now, and I was dreading the fallout that was sure to come. "This is not good."

Anthony took another swig and slapped me on the back. "Oh, lighten up, Branson. Don't be such a pussy."

I had had enough and not just because it's never fun to be the only sober one in a group of people who are toasted. "I'll catch you guys later," I said and trudged upstairs.

Before I reached my room, I stopped at the bathroom to grab a paper towel from the dispenser by the sinks. The events that had just unfolded had left me both uneasy at the presumed fall-out from Daniel and exhilarated at having witnessed him fuck Carol at such incredibly close range. I was still a virgin then and had never seen a stag film. I had seen nude photos in magazines, but nothing as close and graphic a depiction of a wet vagina getting fucked by a big cock as I had just seen through the binoculars.

My cock was throbbing in my pants even before I reached my room. Once inside, I ripped my clothes off and threw myself on my bed without turning off the lights. I was as horny and turned on as I had ever been in my whole life at having seen the live sex show I had just seen. I started stroking my cock furiously, imagining in my mind the image of Daniel's apple-cheeked ass pumping up and down on Carol, his thick cock sliding in and out of her wet vagina, his unexpectedly large and hairy balls slapping against her taint.

In the delirium of my rapture, I had not heard the sounds of Daniel's steps in the hall or his hand on the door. It flung open, and he stormed into the room. I was startled in the worst possible way. His face was incandescent with rage, and he slammed the door behind him. I put my hand over my boner, but there was no hiding what I had been doing. I was completely naked, lying there on my back with my hand gripped around my cock in mid-stroke as he had burst into the room.

"You're such an asshole," Daniel said. He shook his head with disgust as he looked down on my prone, naked body and my erect cock.

"I'm sorry," I said. "Really, I am."

"You're fucking, pathetic, you know that? You're a fucking degenerate sicko." He paced back and forth as he spoke. "You think I didn't know what I interrupted when you had your sport coat in front of you when my parents and I arrived on the first day of school? You think I don't hear you beating off night after night after night? I thought we could be friends. I even let you win today at squash. But, I was wasting my time. You're an asshole. I'm done. I'm going to the housing department in the morning and getting a new roommate."

"Please, don't do that," I said, sitting up, my boner in open view, a full drop of pre-cum leaking out of the slit of my dick hole. "I really am sorry." I started to stand up so I could reach for some clothes to cover myself up. But, Daniel planted the face of his palm squarely in the center of my chest and pushed me, roughly, backwards onto my bed. He ripped his jacket off, then his shirt, and then his pants. I tried to stand up again. But, he pushed me back, forcefully, as he had done before.

"Is this what you want?" He dropped his underwear. I was surprised to see his cock was hard. I was further surprised to see that in the rush to pull his pants up and chase after Carol as she fled from the room in tears, he was still wearing the condom he had been wearing while he was fucking her.

"No," I said. "Stop it."

He unrolled the Trojan and threw it to the floor. He began jerking his cock with rough, furious strokes as he stood over me. I was frozen. I wanted to sit up again. But, I was powerless as I watched this manifestation of anger unfold in slow motion. It didn't last long, however. In less than thirty seconds, a large plume of cum shot out of his cock. It arced through the air and landed on my chest. A half dozen more pulses followed, falling with warm, wet splats that stretched from my stomach all the way up to my collarbone.

When he was done, he looked at me with disgust. He flicked his wrist, and the thick blob of cum that had pooled on his right hand flew through the air and landed on my face. He turned out the light and crawled into bed without saying another word.

At first, I was stupefied at what had happened and just lay there. Once I pulled myself together, I reached for the paper towel I had planned to use to wipe up my own cum. Instead, I used it to wipe up Daniel's, which had splattered across my torso and my face. You might think having the object of my secret affection jerk off on me would have been hot. But, it wasn't. Not at all. I had never seen him this angry, not even close. Daniel had jerked off on me in fury and with contempt. I was shaken. I felt denigrated in a way I never could have imagined. He had wanted to defile me, and he had succeeded. Moreover, I was shamed my

prurient conduct had caused a potentially fatal rift in our great friendship.
 The truth was, I had a serious crush on Daniel, and now he surely despised me. How could we ever play squash again? How could we ever lounge around our room, bullshitting in our underwear and drinking beer? How could we ever sit, knee-to-knee in the sublime silence of the library and the music of our own whispers? The thought of him walking over to the housing office in the morning and moving out was devastating to me. I had known all of this would go down badly, and it had. My boner subsided, and I did not jerk off. I felt an overwhelming wave of sadness. I wanted to say something, but didn't know what to say and was afraid of making matters even worse. Instead, I closed my eyes and lay silent in the darkness while my heart continued to pound and a storm of misgivings raged inside my head.

7 AXIS SHIFTING

I WISH I could say everything was fine in the morning, that Daniel had not woken up angry, and that everything was back to normal. But, nothing was fine, nothing was normal. Everything was worse. I knew it as soon as I saw Daniel was gone when I woke up. He had slipped away before I was awake, something he had never done before. My heart sank as I pictured the efforts he had undertaken to tiptoe around the room so I would not wake - and so he would not have to talk to me. I imagined the scorn with which he must have looked at my sleeping body. I wondered if he had noticed the dry, crusted remnants of his cum across my chest and relived his anger. It took little imagination to realize there would be no easy banter with him today, no warm shower just the two of us with our camaraderie of friendly nudity. There would be no breakfast together in the dining hall, no day together in the library, and no softball in the quad with him and the other guys from the floor. To say I was crushed would be just the first word of many that could describe the depths of my despair.

I grabbed breakfast by myself in the dining hall and not just because the other guys were still sleeping off their hangovers. I needed to be alone to process what had happened last night. I lingered over a second cup of coffee and then a third as I read yesterday's *New York Times*, which had just arrived, as it always did up here in rural Vermont, one day late. But, my eyes started dancing over the words, and I returned to the dorm to grab my books and head to the library.

I ran into Anthony in the bathroom after I returned to the dorm to brush my teeth. I wasn't in the mood for small talk and said I'd catch up with him later. In the haze of his hangover, he mumbled an acknowledgment. He did not ask about Daniel and last night. He shuffled over to the urinal and pulled out his thick, wrinkled cucumber of a cock to take a long piss. As I washed my hands at the sink, I was not so distracted by my troubles to miss an opportunity to steal a long, leisurely glance at his magnificent cock. I found myself holding my breath as I watched and listened to the strong stream of piss that gushed from his dick hole and splashed against the porcelain. His large cock was a small blessing of sorts: until the moment he shook off the remaining drops of piss and folded that long, fat, wrinkled trouser snake back in his underwear, I forgot where I was and the supreme sadness I felt.

I saw Daniel in the library during the afternoon, which was not a surprise. He had arrived with his friend Mike, also not a surprise. They set themselves up in a cozy alcove of leather-backed chairs just across from the long tables where Daniel and I usually sat when we studied together. I looked over at them with a wary smile and nodded my head in friendly acknowledgement. If I had any lingering expectations things were fine, however, they evaporated in an instant. Mike glared at me, no doubt blaming me because his date had stormed off with Daniel's and returned to Mount Holyoke instead of staying for a weekend fuckfest. Daniel looked right through me, which felt even worse.

My fragile equanimity cracked as I turned to my Emerging Governments text book. My heart was pounding with the realization my worst fears were coming true. How could Daniel just completely avoid me? How could he look right through me? I tried to force myself to concentrate on the pages of text before me. But, my thoughts reverberated in my skull at deafening levels, and it was impossible not to think of anything else.

My mind replayed on a continuous loop how he had walked in on me and caught me masturbating in the bright light of our room. He had to have known it had been precipitated by me watching him fuck that girl. Did he think - or know? - I must be some kind of fairy who was hot for his cock? I thought of how he had jerked off on me in anger. I didn't even need to close my eyes to relive it in slow motion. The violent thrusts of his hand on his dry cock. The pulses of semen that arced through the air and landed with warm, wet splats across my torso. The final dismissive flick of cum that had spiraled through the air and streaked across my face. The disgust in his eyes as he stood over me. His hefty cock still throbbing after unloading a reservoir of sperm across my body. How I had been paralyzed with helplessness. I couldn't take it anymore. Even though I had a mountain of studying to do in preparation for upcoming mid-terms, I packed my bag and left the library without looking back.

For the rest of the afternoon, I moped around my room. The minutes ticked by with agonizing slowness. I hoped against hope he would return, but he didn't. That night, I went out with the other members of The Magnificent Seven for pizza and pitchers of beer. Afterwards, we ended up at a townie bar to play pool and toss back whiskey shots. Anthony and the other guys were reliving the events of last night with raucous laughter, the story getting bigger and more exaggerated with each retelling. I was still upset by it all and did not think it was funny. To make myself feel better and forget, I drank too much in order to feel worse in a different way. After I stumbled back to the dorm, I passed out on top of my bed. Daniel was not there. He never came back that night.

As I lay in bed the next morning nursing the angry pounding in my skull, I started to accept he might not ever come back. Even in young adulthood, there was a steady consistency to Daniel. When he said he would do something, he usually did it. It was becoming clearer to me his pronouncement he was moving out would not be an exception. Until my arrival at Inverness, I had kept my unexplored desires, the ones that both electrified and scared me, under control. I had cracked open the door to those desires in the wonder of what might be on the other side, and I had found only pain. I resolved to slam that door shut before whatever was on the other side caused me any more trouble. The pain was proof, I rationalized, that those desires were morally wrong and against natural order. I sensed that the heavens were speaking to me, and I decided to listen to what I thought was hearing. In the meantime, I knew I needed to reconcile the probable loss of my best and dearest friend who meant everything to me.

☙

I ran faster than usual when I went for a run on the track in the afternoon. It was healing to imagine the blood coursing through my body, to breathe with my lungs heaving at full capacity, to chase away the unhappiness within me.

After I passed the two mile mark, I noticed Dusty was running on the track as well. We were running the same pace on opposite ends of it, and I hoped it stayed that way. I liked Dusty, of course, even though I did not know him well. Yes, he was uncommonly good-looking and, yes, he had a beautiful naked body I would behold every time I had the privilege of seeing it in the shower. But, it was impossible to forget he was older than me, and there was a remoteness about him. He would smile and ask us with genuine sincerity how we were. If he perceived someone was off, he would check in on them. But, he did not eat with us or hang out in our rooms. He did not join our bawdiness. He could be irritating in his futile efforts to keep the noise levels down on the floor and his ineffective attempts to curb our rampant abuse of alcohol.

From the glimpses I caught from the corner of my eye, I could sense he was increasing his pace to catch up with me. I sped up to avoid him, which was cold, particularly when he had only been nice to me. But, I was serious about wanting to be alone.

Dusty, however, was serious about catching up with me.

By mile four, he had succeeded. "Hey, Speedy," he said, that ever-friendly smile spread across his face. Dusty never would have sped up to avoid me or anyone else. I was embarrassed at my unfriendliness and hoped he had not known what I was doing. We made small talk through my fifth mile, which was as far as I had planned to run. Dusty could have passed me at any time, but he didn't.

As I have written above, I did not know Dusty well at the time. The shyer part of me was starting to wonder whether I would use up all of my conversation with him too soon. Through a career that took me around the world and called upon me to engage with people from many cultures, I learned how to be an effective and engaging conversationalist. Back then, however, I was an awkward eighteen year old who tended to be swallowed up by insecurity in encounters like this one. I worried for nothing, however, because Dusty and I had a lot to talk about. We fell into a natural rapport, as if we had known each other for years. Dusty was like that. People would meet him for a short time and feel they had known him forever. As I mentioned in my recollections of the "getting to know you" exercises he conducted during freshman orientation, he had an uncanny ability to pull you into his world in a way that made you never want to leave. I don't know what it was about him or me that day, but the haze of friendly remoteness I had felt about him dissipated.

By the time Dusty and I finished up at the track, it occurred to me I had not thought about Daniel for the last mile and a half. It felt liberating, and I was supremely grateful to Dusty for his unknowing assistance in pulling myself together at least for a little while. I was not so self-absorbed, however, to realize that however far Dusty had intended to run, his run ended when mine did. He had to have known something was off about me, that I was pre-occupied and in need of cheering up. Whatever his reason was for running with me, however, I was glad he did.

We walked back to the dorm in sweaty togetherness along the pathways of the well-manicured campus and its ivy-covered buildings. The trees were brushed with the golden, amber, and scarlet hues of mid-fall. Somewhere on campus, the groundskeepers were burning fallen leaves, a practice long since banned for reasons of environmental unfriendliness, but one I remember with nostalgia as an aromatic harbinger of changing seasons. There was a chill in the air, but neither of us felt it. I couldn't help but notice there was a smile on my face I couldn't wipe off.

When we returned to the dorm, we each headed off to our rooms to grab our soap and towels.

"See you in the showers," I said with friendly enthusiasm.

I made it to the bathroom first and soon was enjoying the sensations of a hot, steamy shower. Daniel was not completely out of my mind, but he had moved to the back of it. At this moment, Dusty was moving to the front of it. While I waited for him to join me, I fluffed up my cock out of habit. I wanted to make sure every part of me made a positive impression, even though I had no specific intentions or expectations, only general ones. I was just glad to be extending my time with him.

I lathered up my body. I rinsed off the soap. I washed my hair. Where was he? I had been enjoying him and didn't want the magic of the moment we had been sharing to disappear. Had it been too much for me to say "See you in the showers" with friendly enthusiasm? Had he picked up a vibe from me that made him uncomfortable, like what had happened between me and Daniel? If he had, there would be few things worse than being naked and alone in a shower with a probable fairy unless you might be one yourself.

Before I could go too far down that road, I heard the door to the bathroom swing open. In a moment, Dusty had hung his towel on a hook in the alcove and had stepped into the shower in all of his naked glory.

"Good, you're still here," he said. I couldn't help but notice he had stolen a quick glance at my cock. He blushed when he saw that I had caught him.

"I'm glad you made it," I said. "The truth is, I've had a rough weekend, and I was enjoying your company." Now it was my turn to blush. Had I really said that?

If I was worried about Dusty's response, I didn't need to be. "I could tell you needed a friend," he said without hesitating. He was intuitive that way. "What's going on?"

How could I explain what had happened with Daniel? How we had watched him through binoculars as he fucked Carol on the couch in the housemaster's lounge? How I had been so turned on at watching his big cock slide into Carol's vagina at close range, his balls slapping against her taint, that I had raced back to my room to jerk off? That Daniel had caught me and jerked off on me in anger? How my feelings for Daniel transcended ordinary friendship? "It's nothing," I said.

He shrugged, unconvinced. "If you ever want to talk, I hope you know you can trust me."

I didn't want to talk about it anymore and didn't say anything.

Dusty soaped up his hair, and the conversation lulled. He leaned back and closed his eyes as he rinsed his head. With his eyes shut, I took in the full glory of his naked body. Every curve and angle of his face had exquisite symmetry. His cheeks were high and firm. His jaw was square and strong. His lips were soft and full and a tantalizing opening to the unknown beauty that lay within him. His neck was long, the muscles in it taut. Even his Adam's apple was an object of beauty I desired to kiss if only I ever could. His eyes were still closed as he rinsed the shampoo from his hair. I would later see his handsome face twisted in the pain of a tormented soul. But, at this moment, he was at peace with the uncomplicated expectation of shared time with someone he wanted to know better, which I was thrilled to know was me.

His shoulders were square and solid. They looked broader than they were because of the narrowness of his waist. His pecs were solid and wide. His nipples were soft brown. The water cascaded down his torso in rivulets that swirled past his navel and converged over the tight, curled ribbon of brown pubic hair that framed his long, floppy dick. That dick would be a singular beauty in its own right, even if it were not attached to such a beautiful human being. My eyes continued down, past the scar of his circumcision that was stretched by the warmth of the water and the steam of the shower. They continued past the water streaming down from the curled rim of his corona to the tile below. I admired the rounded bulges of his thigh muscles, honed from the miles he ran on the track and the country roads of

Vermont and Orange County. To say I was dazzled by his beauty would be an understatement of the highest degree.

I looked up and started at the realization his eyes were open. He had been watching me the whole time. My heart seized, and I recalled the terror of when I had been caught checking out Anthony's monstrous wrinkled cock. But, Dusty just looked back at me with the same openness and warm attentiveness he always did, as if it were perfectly normal for my eyes to inhale the divine nakedness of his body. I averted my eyes and gulped. "Sorry," I said.

"Sorry for what?"

"For – for looking."

"Nothing to be sorry about. It's not as if I haven't checked you out when I thought you weren't looking."

Our eyes met again, and I held them there. He continued to wash his arms as he had been before. The difference this time was he allowed his eyes to lower from my gaze and descend down my body with unbridled openness. My eyes stayed on his as I watched them absorb every inch of me. They took in my shoulders. They lingered on my chest. He zeroed in on my navel and followed the treasure trail that led down to my groin. My bush was thicker than his, a tangled copse of black hair that hugged my penis. I had tugged on it earlier so it would make a formidable impression. It had shrunk some. But, now that he gazed at it with open admiration, it started to awaken. It fully hardened in only seconds, faster than I can get out of a chair these days. It was beyond my control, and there was no way to hide it. But, if I was supposed to feel embarrassed about it, I wasn't.

Dusty's demeanor turned serious. He stared at my now-hardened cock, mesmerized. His eyes moved back up my body with a slow, measured steadiness that felt like a warm embrace at a moment when I felt supreme vulnerability. I knew standing openly in the showers with a boner was a reckless act that could destroy my past, present, and future. My eyes had followed his the whole time, and now they were even with mine again. They were heavy with what I now recognize was desire, though I was still unschooled in recognizing those cues. I wanted him to say something, to say anything.

The corners of his mouth curled upwards into the most admiring smile. "You have a truly beautiful body," he said. "And your cock, it's – it's beautiful, too."

I looked down at the seven and a half inches of wonder jutting straight out in front of me. "Cocks, they do funny things, you know?"

Slower than mine, but with steady alacrity, his cock hardened, too. I watched, transfixed, as it filled, widened, and lengthened without any manual assistance. In not much longer than it had taken mine, his cock was fully erect. Unlike mine, Dusty's curved toward the sky, like the most beautiful cock-colored banana you had ever seen. I was conscious my breathing had slowed. Whatever was happening right now, we each knew an uncommon human connection was occurring, even if neither of us fully understood that connection and what it meant.

"So, there. We're even," he said with a smile that dispelled any nervousness or shame I might have felt. "Actually, almost even," he said. "I think you're a little longer."

I appraised his magnificent cock. "Perhaps," I said, "But, I think yours is a little thicker."

We stood there in the showers staring at each other with silly, drunken grins on our faces. Neither of us touched our cocks, but each of them pulsed with unmistaken passion. When I think back through time, I remember how my cock was so hard it hurt, one of the most powerful erections of my whole life. I also remember feeling how a primal desire had been awakened from the core of my being, a desire that frightened me with the confluence of intensity and authenticity. This was me. This was what I wanted. I could not deny it any longer. It was one thing to fantasize about cocks when I jerked off. Or to have a secret crush on Daniel that existed only in my interior thoughts. It was another to be standing here in full naked arousal with a guy as fantastical as Dusty and wanting more as we bathed together in the comfort of warm falling water.

The sound of the main door to the bathroom door opening and then slamming shut brought an abrupt end to the moment.

The desire on Dusty's face evaporated. He shook his head as if he were trying to shake away unwanted thoughts. He looked again at my hard-on, but I could see by the way he clenched his jaw he recognized the impossibility of the situation. We exchanged glances, his eyes wistful. "This was fun," he said. "But, I better get going." He turned to leave, presenting me with a view of his athletic, milk white ass and the wisps of hair that lined his crack like brown velvet. I wanted nothing more at that moment than to press my face against the cool whiteness of his ass cheeks and quietly savor them. *Don't go*, I thought. *Please, don't go. We never have to leave.*

"See you later," I said. But, he was already on his way out, and he did not turn around.

⋆

I returned to my room and got dressed. Daniel still wasn't there, but I wasn't thinking about him. I paced back and forth in my room like an unneutered tiger tantalized by the scent of a nearby female in estrus. I could not stay still. My body tingled with the charge of the shared shower with Dusty and the sexual tension that was fraught with madness. I was tormented by the fresh memories of our tandem hard-ons that had pulsed with unexplored longing as the warm water cleansed our bodies, but not our desires. Had all of that really happened? Had I really seen Dusty's spectacular hard cock curving upward towards the heavens? Had he really admired mine and hungered for it in the way I hungered for his? Had his penetrating eyes probed the depths of my secret desires as if he knew me in a way I did not even know myself?

I lay down on my bed. My hand found its way to the hard-on that throbbed through the fabric of my pants. I stopped. I stared at the ceiling and realized this would not be enough. I knew in my heart what I wanted was not in this room, but down the hall. I stood up and started to pace again. As I did, I caught a glimpse of my face in the mirror on the back of the door. It reflected the hunger inside me. I stared back and thought of how I could feed that hunger if I had courage. Did I have it? Could I take what I wanted? Would he give it? I did not know for certain. I only knew I had to try.

My mind was awhirl as I marched with determined purpose down to Dusty's room. My shoulders were tight and my heart pounding.

His door was ajar. I pushed it open the rest of the way.

"Knock, knock," I said. I tried to be cool, even though I felt anything but.

"Hey, there," he said, looking up at me, his expression pensive.

I stood there, waiting for an invitation to enter, one that was not forthcoming. "Can I come in for a minute?"

"Sure, of course," he said, his face softening.

I had never been inside Dusty's room before, and I looked around. His room was bigger than ours, and he had it to himself. He had the standard issue twin bed, but a better desk, a tattered leather couch, a beat up coffee table, and two cushioned chairs. He was reclined in a chair, one of his long, lanky legs crossed over the other. He was wearing an ivory-colored Scottish fisherman's sweater and faded jeans that were so worn the openings at his ankles were frayed. His feet were bare. His blond, curly hair was still wet, a reminder of what had transpired in the showers. There was a book in his lap and red wine sitting in a water glass on the floor next to his chair.

"Have a seat," he said, gesturing to the couch.

In the background, a record played on the hi-fi. But, there was a silence of spoken words between us. He wouldn't look at me even though I couldn't stop looking at him. "Is that Chet Baker you're listening to?" I asked finally.

He nodded. "*My Funny Valentine.*"

"Thought so," I said.

More silence. What had happened? He was serious, distant. He had regrets about the charged intimacy in the shower, I was sure of it. Did he think I was a fairy who was trying to come onto him? Was I a fairy? Was he a fairy? I hadn't known what I was expecting when I left my room and marched down here. But, I didn't expect cold silence and fog. I should not have come.

MY BARE NAKED HEART

"I should go," I said, starting to stand.

He softened. "No, stay." He paused a beat. "Please."

"You sure?" I wanted to stay and leave at the same time.

"Would you like a glass of wine?"

I nodded.

He set his book on the floor and reached for another glass. "Sorry, I don't have any wine glasses, just these water glasses I lifted from the dining hall." He flashed me a smirk, knowing I would be amused.

"*You* swiped glasses from the dining hall? I like that. I have some dirt on you after all, Mr. Perfect."

He laughed for the first time since I had come in. "That's not the only dirt you have on me."

"Don't worry," I said. "Your secret's safe with me."

The melodious voice of Chet Baker played in the background, but another awkward silence descended upon the room.

"What are you reading?" I asked, fumbling to regain an equilibrium between us.

He picked up the book from the floor and read the cover. "*The Razor's Edge, by Somerset Maugham.*"

"Hey, that's my favorite book," I said, surprised even though the book was popular in that era and was making the rounds in the dorm with the few of us who read books for pleasure.

He looked at me with skepticism. "Your favorite?"

"I've read it three times. There's something about Larry Darrell that speaks to me, and I try to find meaning in every word he says. He's searching for answers to questions about himself and about life. I guess I have questions, too, and want to travel the world like he does."

"I'm impressed," he said. "This is only my first. But, I'll admit I saw it in your room and thought if you were reading it, I would give it a try." He handed me a glass of wine, and our hands touched for an instant. He sat back down.

More silence.

"The thing is," he finally said, "is that I wasn't really reading it when you came in. I was trying to. But, I couldn't concentrate and was just staring at the same page." He paused. "I can't stop thinking about what happened in the shower."

I felt a weight leave my shoulders. "Me, too," I said.

"I'm sorry about what happened," he said. "I shouldn't have."

"It was my fault," I said. "I popped the first boner."

He winced. He started to say something and then stopped. Then he said it: "That boner was pretty incredible."

"So was yours."

More silence.

The book slipped out of his hand, and we both lurched forward to grab it with a fateful consequence: our heads - and mouths - were now just inches apart. Either of us could have pulled away. But, neither of us did. We teetered on the precipice of the rabbit hole through which we were about to tumble into a fantasy world that both frightened and excited me. I remember the thumping of my heart. I remember the heavy sound of my breathing, the air rising in my chest and flowing out through my nostrils. I remember the sound of Dusty's short, labored breath and the rustle of his clothes. He licked the dryness off his lips. I gulped, and we leaned into each other.

Our lips met. His were luxurious: smooth, full, wet, soft, and strong. Our tongues searched for each other's and intertwined. They probed with intense desire to taste, touch, and explore. His stubble scratched against mine, an unexpected pleasure that felt as if two sheets of the finest sandpaper were rubbing against the other. My eyes clamped shut. I savored the incomparable thrill of kissing him, a thrill that enveloped me and jolted me to the core of my being.

Even with the expansive range of my unexplored desires, the thought of men kissing was not something that had ever entered my mind. Kissing was something I did with girls. I had never seen men kiss, never seen a picture of men kissing, never seen it on TV or in the movies, never read about it in a book or in a newspaper or in a magazine. Jerking off with or getting your cock sucked by another guy were things you heard stories about and would sometimes be the subject of sniggering accounts of suspected fairies you might have known. But, kissing was something I had never seen or ever even thought of. Now that I was doing it, however, I never wanted to stop.

I ended up underneath Dusty as he lay on top of me on his leather couch. My cock was rock hard, bulging at the top of my pants. I could feel the pulse of his hard-on twitching almost in tandem with mine as he ground it into me. Our arms wrapped around each other, and nothing felt more beautiful and natural than to have him hold me tight. His mouth tasted of salt, sweat, and red wine. He smelled of Old Spice and a raw, sexy, manliness that was a natural scent all his own. I don't even need to close my eyes to recall it today with such clarity. Having our bodies grind together with increasing urgency, dancing in the most exotic play world was like being in a heaven of which I had never dared to dream.

Dusty lifted his head, and I opened my eyes for the first time. That first kiss, and the intensity of the manhandling that immediately followed were so electrifying, I can say in all honesty that anyone on the planet would be lucky to experience half of what I experienced even once in their life. Dusty and I had been swept up into each other and melded in a way I never wanted to come uncoupled. It was as if I had just opened a door to a magical world I wanted to swallow me up and never let me leave.

I exhaled with a heavy sigh. I opened my eyes again and left the heaven that had beckoned me. I knew without asking that Dusty and I had tarried in the same ethereal world. He took a deep breath. He smiled the broadest, truly happiest smile you would ever want to see on another living being. He leaned in and kissed my lips again. He bore his blue eyes into mine. Our minds swirled together as if they were linked by an electrical connection that passed through the air. My eyes bore back into his. Years later, when I traveled to Santorini and Corfu and would see the bluest waters of the Aegean, I would think of Dusty's eyes and the bliss of this moment.

"Is it wrong of me to confess I wanted to do that with you from the very first moment I saw you back on the first day of school?" he whispered. "Maybe even since I saw your picture in the freshman directory and wondered what was behind that shy smile and those mysterious brown eyes?"

I stared back into his eyes, which sparkled with euphoria. I wish I could say I felt the same way. But, something was happening. The spell had broken, and I felt terror percolating inside me. I gulped and tried to sit up. What had I done? God, no. I had kissed a guy? Dusty's eyes searched mine, aware of my shifting demeanor and emerging turmoil. I licked my lips and tasted him on them. I felt sick. I bristled at his touch and turned my head, my face contorted with confusion and regret.

"Shhh," he said, holding me tight. "It's okay. It's okay."

I closed my eyes again and tried to pull myself together. But, it did not feel okay. Not at all. The room had started to spin. I stared into his knowing, caring eyes looking for assurances I needed to find in myself, not someone else. The pleasure and joy I had just seen in his had transformed into a probing, wariness. "You're okay," he said, his tone measured. "Trust me."

It was one thing to dream of jerking off with a guy in an adolescent way. But, it was something entirely different to kiss one. And not just kiss, but kiss with as much passion and raw desire as we had. As I had said, it had never occurred to me ever that men would kiss and embrace in the way we just had. Yet, I had done it. Even my body had betrayed me, my cock hardening and leaking pre-cum. Is that what fairies did? Did this mean I was a homosexual, destined to become one of those lisping pansies who were the private nightmare of everyone like me who secretly desired more from our male friends but struggled to process why? It did not feel right anymore. It felt very wrong. I felt the room closing in on me. I squirmed and broke free from him.

"I have to go," I said, standing up.

He stood up, too. "Don't leave like this."

I shook my head. "No, I'm okay," I said, even though it was obvious I wasn't. I turned to the door and pulled it open. I did not look back, but I knew Dusty was at my heels. In the hallway, the light was brighter and the air somehow was easier to breathe. Dusty grabbed my forearm and locked his fingers around it. "John, wait."

At that moment, Daniel exited the staircase and entered the hallway on his way to our room. My eyes met his. He froze at the sight of Dusty and me. His eyes darted to mine, to Dusty's tight grasp on my forearm, to Dusty's eyes, and then back to mine. Dusty dropped my arm as if he been splashed by scalding water. His eyes met Daniel's again and then he looked away. Daniel stared at us for the longest of moments, no doubt wondering what the hell was going on, but not saying anything. Then, he turned in the direction of our room and did not look back.

I had been knocked sideways by how the bliss of Dusty's embrace and the heaven of kissing him transformed into terror at the realization of what that embrace meant and who I might be. I felt as if a monster had awoken inside me, a lavender Mr. Hyde who would rise up thereafter when I least wished him to and wreak havoc on my life. Deviant, perverted, sick, illegal – those were the words that crowded my mind. I shake my head with sadness at how different times were back then. They allowed the sweet beauty we had just experienced to feel sordid. It scared me to the core of my being to think of what all of this might mean. Dusty reached for my arm again, but I recoiled from his touch and turned away.

I fled down the hall with a brisk step, and I did not look back. I felt as if I couldn't get away fast enough. I didn't mean to be so cruel. I just couldn't help myself. If I had looked back, I quite imagine I would have seen someone who wanted to run after me, but didn't dare. I wasn't thinking of Dusty's feelings, however. I was only thinking of myself.

Daniel had dropped his bag of books on the floor of our room. He looked at me without saying anything, and it was clear things were still not right between us. He stripped to his boxers, climbed into bed, and turned out the light on his side of the room. I tried to pretend everything was normal, even though nothing was normal. There was a loud, deafening roar inside my head. *I had kissed Dusty! We had ground our boners into each other!* I stripped down to my boxers as well, climbed into bed, and turned out my light.

Daniel whispered a quiet, "Good night" that was said so low maybe I would hear it or maybe I wouldn't. I could respond – or not, all without consequence. At that moment, I didn't care very much about Daniel and whether things might be okay with us.

What I cared about was I had just had an evening of boner-gawking and the most passionate, powerful, fumbling encounter I had ever experienced. Everything I had ever known about myself had turned on end. I had not only kissed Dusty, I had been pawed and manhandled by him – and I had loved it. Yes, I had kissed a guy. *I had kissed a guy!* As rattled and frightened as I was, I also had to admit it had electrified me in a way no kiss had ever done before. That terrified me even more.

Looking back through time, if I could take back that kiss, I would, without hesitation. But, not for the reasons you might think. The axis of my world shifted after that kiss in ways I could not have anticipated. As much as I thought that kiss was just about me, it wasn't. I did not yet know it, but because of that kiss, the lives of a half dozen people and those who loved them would be upended in ways I would not yet realize until they had been upended. But, that would come later. For the time being, there was no taking back I had kissed a guy. And an extraordinary one at that.

8 MEASURING UP

THE NEXT MORNING, I woke first, before Daniel did. A light, steady snore rumbled from his throat, but I didn't mind. I was just glad he was back, even if I did not know for how long. Whatever happiness I felt to have him home again was overshadowed by the roiling cauldron of emotions that consumed me as I grappled with the confusion of what had happened between Dusty and me. It had been more than just a kiss, of course. Our bodies had surged to overdrive and not just our cocks had come to life. An enveloping electricity had tingled through our bodies to the ends of every extremity. A light had turned on in my soul, and I knew with all certainty Dusty had looked into that light. Our minds had melded for the duration as each of us divulged without speaking the shared secrets of our innate desires. It terrified me to think of it.

    I pulled a trick from Daniel's playback and left the room early to shower. I wasn't avoiding Daniel, however. I was avoiding Dusty. I just couldn't face him. Facing him meant facing myself, and I didn't have the wherewithal to do that. At least, not yet. Everyone on the floor was still asleep, and I had the shower to myself. My head felt a heavy haze, as if I had had too much to drink the night before even though I hadn't. I soaped up my body and washed my cock more than was necessary. It started to awaken. I stood under the shower and let the water wash the haze from my head. The healing effect brought me some relief, and soon I needed relief of a different kind.

I flipped through my usual fantasies. Brigitte Bardot. The Marilyn Monroe nudes. Daniel's morning wood that had flipped out the fly of his boxers. The binocular view of Carol's pussy getting plowed by Daniel's big cock, his hefty balls slapping against her taint. I tried to visualize anything other than Dusty and his golden beauty, his milk white ass, and the banana-shaped cock that rose up to the sky. I wanted to forget him and what had happened in here last night. But, it kept coming back into focus. I gave in.

My heart raced faster as my right hand picked up the tempo. A blinding flurry of images passed before me in rapid fire. *Dusty's cock. The tight brown curls of his pubes. The ribbed flatness of his abs. The flawless nipples I had wanted to suck but had not dared. The warmth in his eyes. The fullness of his lips. The raw power of how he had wrapped his arms around me and ground himself into me as I had laid on my back on the cold leather of his couch.* I felt that inevitable, overpowering, rushing feeling, and an insistent surge radiating throughout my body. My eyes shot open. I gasped. My knees buckled, and I leaned back for support against the slippery wetness of the tiled wall. Spurts of cum arced through the air, landing on the wet tile of the shower floor where they were swept up by the flow of the water. As I caught my breath, I watched as the ribbons swirled in circles to the drain where they congealed in blobs on the narrow grates.

I closed my eyes again and rested my forearm against the tile. I held my head under the water as I savored the ebb of waning ecstasy and tried to catch my breath. *Damn*, I thought. *What the hell am I going to do?*

When I returned from the showers, Daniel was awake and said, "Good morning" a little louder than he had whispered, "Good night," but not much. It wasn't particularly friendly or unfriendly, but at least it was something. "Morning," I said in much the same tone. I turned my back to him while I dropped the towel and pulled on my underwear.

I said, "Later" when I left the room, and Daniel said it back. But, the obvious chill with which each of us said it didn't mean we were back on speaking terms.

For the rest of that day and for next several days, I spent little time in the dorm. When I wasn't in class, I buried myself in my text books in the library. When I wasn't in the library, I went to the gym and lifted weights or went for a run. But, I gave a wide berth to the track, where all of this trouble started. I ran instead on the streets of the village and around the outskirts of the campus so Dusty and I would not cross paths. It was not just him I couldn't face. It was my own fears. I had hoped running would let me escape my inner turmoil. But, the reality was, it trapped me in my own thoughts. The only relief was to run at the peak of my physical limits, when it was all I could do to breathe and keep my legs moving through the protests of exhaustion and the frenetic pounding of my beating heart. Even with my strong desire to run from those thoughts, I could sustain such exertion for only so long until I was on the verge of collapse.

The campus was too small for me to avoid Dusty completely, however. We passed each other at a distance at least once or twice a day. I could tell by the way his eyes would search for mine that he needed to speak with me. If I had been thinking of anyone but myself, I could have given him an opening. But, I didn't. I made sure I was either with the other guys or was dashing off to somewhere else when I would come in range of him. I wasn't just avoiding Dusty, of course. I was avoiding a harder conversation with myself about who I was and what I truly wanted.

Daniel appeared to be back, but not like he was before. We barely spoke to each other. The easy, friendly camaraderie we had was gone. He was polite in a strained way and spoke with as few words as he could. It was a passive aggressive way to punish me for my perceived role in what the guys had come to call "*Wonder Breadus Interruptus*." Daniel seemed content enough to fuel his grudge for the indefinite future.

If the circumstances had been different, I would have made a concerted effort to fix the situation with Daniel. But, my encounter with Dusty had left me on edge, and Daniel's behavior seemed monumentally petty in light of my other problems. Yes, we had caught him in one of the most private of moments in which you would ever want to be caught. And, yes, Carol had fled into the night in her father's Cadillac, the red lights on its finned tails blazing bright in the darkness. But, so what? If Daniel wasn't so busy cataloguing an imaginary mountain of perceived assaults on his dignity, he might even laugh with all of these guys – his friends – who would have responded in kind by laughing with him instead of at him. Daniel just wasn't wired that way, however. He would rather mull in his anger and nurse his tattered ego. I was too caught up in my own interior drama to face Daniel head-on. I left him to study on his own as he sat in smug, punishing silence at his desk. I needed a break. From everything.

"Later," I said, leaving our room without saying where I was going, as I would have before.

"Later," he said in cool, measured response.

The truth was, I was exhausted from the past week. It takes a lot of energy to be as angry as I was at Daniel for being as angry with me. It took even more energy to manage the sadness I felt from the gulf in our friendship. It also takes a lot of energy to be afraid, much less terrified. Even in my ignorant denial, I knew I was terrified at what had happened with Dusty and what it might mean for me. I was exhausted from being exhausted and was glad to be out of my dorm room and the tension that hung in the air.

There was raucous laughter coming from the room that Sasquatch and Shorty shared just a few doors down from my own. I walked into the room and was greeted with warm enthusiasm, which I appreciated at that moment more than any of the guys could ever know.

"Branson! C'mon in," Howell said, handing me a whiskey shot as I walked in the door. I knocked it back and gasped with audible pleasure as the liquor burned down my throat and into my gut. The room smelled of fart, sweat, alcohol, and stale cigarettes. I didn't care. I was just glad to be here and away from the tension with Daniel.

"How's Wonder Bread doing?" Anthony asked. "Still sulking about *Wonder Breadus Interruptus?*"

The guys burst into loud, boozy laughter. They still had not tired of laughing about or dissecting the events of that night into the minutest of details.

"It hasn't been too much of a party in our room," I said.

"Those tits were pretty awesome," Sasquatch said, squeezing them through the air in his imagination. "I'd be sulking, too, if I had watched her stuff them back into her bra and drive off into the night."

"That's because you're a pussy who's never gotten any snatch before," Anthony said, throwing a pillow at Sasquatch. He lifted his leg and farted, the sound reverberating off of the wooden chair.

"What do you know? I've had tons of pussy," Sasquatch said, throwing the pillow back at him.

"I still can't get over how his cock swayed back and forth like a metronome," Howell said right before downing another shot.

"That's because your cock is smaller than a squirrel's," Anthony said. He threw a pillow at Howell, who always laughed in good-natured agreement to every reference to the size of his cock.

I didn't want to talk about Daniel, Carol, and that night. I had come here to get away from all that. "How can you guys stand it in here?" I opened the window to let in some fresh air.

At that moment, Shorty returned to the room. He was muddy and wet from rugby practice. "Geezus, it reeks in here!" he said, laughing in mock horror. He was quite a sight in his rugby shorts and shirt. Mud and wetness streaked across his clothes and the exposed skin on his compact, muscled frame. His face was ruddy from exertion, and his close-cropped hair was awry.

"You should talk, Rugby Boy," Anthony said. "You're just adding to the stench."

Shorty stripped down to bare nakedness. "And that's why I'm going to take a shower." He grabbed a towel and snapped it at Anthony before wrapping it around his waist.

"Give the drain a rest and don't beat off in there," Anthony said. "One of you degenerates unleased a load in there this morning. It was still sticking to the drain when I took a shower his morning. Fucking disgusting. I almost stepped in it."

I blushed with shame – and arousal – at the knowledge the cum Anthony had seen was mine. I was relieved, however, when the conversation shifted in a different direction and no one seemed interested in starting a witch hunt to find out the source of the semen. It occurs to me only now, however, that it might not have been mine, and the reason there was no interest in hunting down the culprit is that it could have been any of us in the room at one time or another. Sasquatch passed the bottle of whiskey around the room. As I had said before, he was the friendly, hairy guy who was always in the middle of trouble, but never caused it. By now, the guys had become loaded enough to dispense with the shot glass and guzzle straight from the bottle. No one was stumbling drunk yet. But, the fire of the whiskey in our guts had lowered inhibitions, mine included.

Shorty returned to the room after showering, a towel around his waist and nothing else.

"How tall are you again, Shorty?" It was Freddy Hamilton who asked that. I have mentioned Freddy once so far, I believe, and only then to say that he was handsome and from Shaker Heights, Ohio. The handsome part was an understatement. We would sometimes call him Rita, because of his movie star prettiness, as beautiful as Rita Hayworth, Shorty once said. Freddy's eyes were a violet blue. His skin had the smooth, unblemished purity of ivory, and his hair was a honey brown laced with golden streaks of blond. He was square-jawed with a mouth that struggled to contain straight white teeth so large they looked like they belonged onscreen. If I have only mentioned him once, it was because I view him as a fallen member of The Magnificent Seven. Yes, he was incredibly handsome, and yes he was friends with us in the way that we all were. And, yes, he played a big part in all of our lives back then. But, for reasons I will get into later, I would never speak to him for the rest of his life or mine, even if he begged on his knees for forgiveness.

MY BARE NAKED HEART

"I'm five foot six," Shorty said with a noticeable edge. Shorty was like short guys everywhere: he hated being called out on his height. He had perfect posture, as if he could capture every available millimeter by stretching his spine to its limits. His penny loafers had a bit of a heel. Not so much that you might notice unless you looked close, but it was there. He also lied about his height.

I look back with irritation at the recollection it was Freddy who initiated the inquiry into the truth about how tall Shorty was or wasn't. You'll understand more about my irritation later. At least for now, it all started in fun. Everyone laughed at Shorty's insistence that he was five feet six. But, no one laughed louder than Anthony, whose laughter was fueled in part by the whiskey that burned in all of our bellies.

"What? Are you fucking kidding me?" Anthony said, spit spraying from his mouth. "There's no fucking way you're five-six. I'm six-three. You gotta be at least a foot shorter than me."

Shorty crossed his arms. "I'm five-six. You don't know what the fuck you're talking about."

Anthony threw his head back and laughed. "Can you believe this guy? He can't pull this shit on us." Anthony stood up and roughly shoved the chair back against the desk and approached Shorty, where he stood next to him, side-by-side. "I'm about a foot taller than him, right?"

Shorty uncrossed his arms and squirmed a bit. He smiled in his wise-cracking way, but he was not laughing with us, impish smile notwithstanding. "You're not going to listen to this big galoot from Brooklyn, are you? I bet he's never even seen a ruler before."

I like to remember Shorty from this night. He was defensive, funny, and self-assured, even if the self-assuredness was fueled by false bravado. Yes, he was short. But, all of us loved him and were charmed by his sense of humor and his sense of fun. He had a twinkle in his eye and in his smile, and he had an easy laugh. I also like to remember him from that night, because it is a reminder of how strong and fit he had been, even if he was short. His shoulders were broad, his chest well-developed, and his biceps thick and rounded from playing sports and lifting weights. He was good-humored, smart, and had a scrappiness that served him well in rugby, soccer, squash, and just about everything in life he pursued.

"'Big galoot!'" Anthony bellowed. He scanned the room in mock outrage, his eyes red from the liquor. "Can you believe what this short fuck just called me?"

Shorty curled a bicep for us. I don't know what he intended next, but Anthony raised his arms and lunged towards Shorty. Shorty clenched his fists and raised them to his chest. With his trademark smirk and cockiness, he baited Anthony. "I'll say it again: I called you a big galoot from Brooklyn."

If you didn't know they were great friends, you would be worried about what might be happening next. If Shorty was worried, he didn't show it. Anthony pinned Shorty's arms above his head and used his left leg to pin both of Shorty's legs against the wall. Shorty was strong for his size and struggled valiantly, but he was no match for Anthony. After just a few moments of scuffling, Anthony leaned down into Shorty's face and said, "You short little fuck, we are going to cut the bullshit and find out how tall you really are. Five-six my ass."

"C'mon, Anthony. 'Uncle.' I'll say it," Shorty said.

Anthony leaned in close to Shorty's face. "I don't want to hear you say, 'Uncle.' I want to hear you say, 'I, Edward Laurence Olsen, am five feet three inches tall. I am also a liar. I have falsely represented to the entire world that I am five feet six inches tall.'"

Shorty shook his head. "Nope, not saying it."

"Okay," Anthony said, his face just inches from Shorty, who still squirmed, his smile defiant as Anthony had him pinned against the wall. "We're going to prove you wrong." Anthony pointed at Freddy and told him to grab a ruler, and he told me to help him hold Shorty down.

I was caught up in the fun, and as much as I liked and respected Shorty, his claim of being five feet six was ridiculous. Even with my judgment dulled by alcohol, this focus on Shorty was in good fun, and I was willing to help put that canard to rest, particularly with the rowdy encouragement of the room. I helped Anthony hold Shorty against the wall, though I did not have my face in Shorty's like Anthony's was. While Anthony clearly was forcing Shorty to participate in something in which he did not to want to participate, I couldn't help but notice Shorty's eyes and Anthony's were locked. Their defiant smiles were testosterone-powered, not mean-spirited. I also couldn't help but notice that in the scuffle, Shorty's towel had fallen off, and he was now completely nude.

Anthony and Shorty were unlikely friends, and I wondered about them sometimes. Shorty was from New Canaan and his father was a partner in a Wall Street law firm that Shorty's grandfather had founded. His mother came from old money and fit the stereotype. I was there on Parents' Weekend when Shorty introduced Anthony with pride to his parents. If Anthony had missed the thin-lipped smile of disapproval from Shorty's mother as she absorbed his ethnicity and her perceptions of his social status, I had not. I knew from Shorty's downward glance of disappointment he had not either. Anthony was a first generation American who had been born in Brooklyn. His father was a marble cutter from Italy and had come to America with the skills of a master craftsman. He had made a business of cutting marble for the grand apartments and buildings of New York, like the kind where people like Shorty's family might live. He was skilled enough that he was able to move his family out of Brooklyn and into the solidly middle class prosperity of Floral Park. Anthony was also the first person in his family to go to college. That might have bothered some people in my social circles back home, but not me or any of The Magnificent Seven. It made me respect him even more.

By this point, Shorty's struggle against the grip Anthony and I had on him was just pretense. There was no escape from being pinned against the wall, and he had resigned himself to having his height being measured in front of everyone once and for all.

"Stand up straight," Freddy said as he knelt before him with the bottom of the ruler placed even with the mark where Shorty's heel met the floor. Because Freddy was eye level with Shorty's naked groin, he was the first to see what the rest of us had not noticed yet. "It seems Shorty wants me to measure something else."

We all looked at Shorty's cock, which had swelled to semi-hardness. Shorty had a full set of balls that usually rode high and tight instead of loose and dangling. In repose, his cock followed the contours of his balls and projected out farther from his body than someone whose balls were loose and whose cock pointed loosely, straight down between the legs, like mine. He had a curly bush of dense pubes that connected with a thin, dark treasure trail that rose up to his flat belly. In a state of progressive arousal, his cock was thickening and lengthening before us.

Anthony howled in drunken delight. "I think there is something almost Shakespearean in how the lady doth protest too much, and now your cock betrays you. You're a fucking pervert who's getting a charge out of all of this, aren't you?"

Shorty pretended to struggle. But, he was no match for the grip we had on him. He burst out laughing, joining the rest of us. Of the many qualities I loved about Shorty, the ones that stood out most were his sense of humor, his bright smile, and how easy it was to get him to laugh. In this case, there was nothing he could do as we measured his height against his will. In the sense that he joined everyone's laughter instead of revolting against it, he was the diametric opposite of Daniel. It was the precise antidote I needed at that moment from all of the other stress that had been consuming me.

Freddy had finished measuring, and the top of the ruler was pressed next to the top of Shorty's head. "Edward Laurence Olsen, you are officially five feet three inches tall."

Shorty's cock was now fully hard. It was approximately six inches long and looked disproportionately huge on his short, compact body. It curved sharply upwards, and in full engorgement, his glans rested against his belly button.

Anthony leaned into Shorty's face. "Five foot three. Now we know the truth."

Then Anthony did the most extraordinary thing. He took the index and middle fingers of his right hand and placed them on the topside of Shorty's cock. He pressed it down far and then released Shorty's cock so it bounced back up, snapping against his belly. He did it a second and then a third time as the rest of us roared in drunken laughter. No one in the room could have gotten away with such a brazen expression of curiosity except for Anthony. To have touched someone else's cock like that with innocent fascination, making Shorty's boner bounce up and slap his stomach in front of everyone, would have been utterly unthinkable for anyone but Anthony.

"This is fucked up," Shorty said. "Are you done yet?"

Anthony shrugged. "I've never seen a cock that stood straight up like this. It's flat against your stomach. Mine sticks straight out when I have a stiffy."

"That's because your cock is so fucking huge," Howell said. "It's too heavy to stand up like that."

"Shorty has a big cock on a small man's body," Freddy said. "I think we need to measure this, too. What do you say guys?"

The bawdy laughter escalated to a higher decibel level, and there were a series of shouted yesses.

"I can't do it," Freddy said, the ruler in his hand, his eyes on Shorty's hard-on.

"Do it!" Howell shouted.

"Nah, I'm not touching that thing," he said looking at it with disgust. Then he handed the ruler to me.

I took the ruler and stood there listening to the chants of the guys to go for it. As curious as I was about Shorty's cock and wished I had the courage to press down on it so I could experience for myself how it would snap back against his belly, that would require courage I did not have. Even with my judgment clouded by whiskey, it felt like a step too far. My eyes locked with Shorty's, and he looked back at me with a look of resignation. I could tell the fun had gone far enough. I tousled his hair and set the ruler down on the desk.

"Go cover yourself up, you little fruit," Anthony said, slapping Shorty's bare ass hard enough to leave a red mark as he stepped away. Freddy leaned in and did the same on the other cheek, a gesture I would remember afterwards.

I have cherished the memories of the special relationships I developed in those formative years while I transitioned from young adulthood into manhood. I also have cherished the complicated tangle of friendships amongst The Magnificent Seven that went beyond just me. As I mentioned above, Anthony and Shorty had an unlikely closeness that challenged my narrow perspectives on class and ethnicity, to say nothing of their differences in physical size and appearance. Anthony and Shorty transcended all of those differences in ways that might not ever have happened had they not been thrown together on the third floor of Canterbury Hall where New Canaan and Brooklyn could meet. I think, too, of the thin-lipped disapproval of Shorty's mother who lived in a prison of her own prejudices and had dismissed Anthony with a polite smile and a coldness in her eyes. The irony is Anthony would become a leading seller of junk bonds on Wall Street and earn a fortune that would make him far richer than Shorty's family. Shorty would become a lawyer and join the Wall Street law firm with his grandfather's name emblazoned on the imposing letterhead. The friendship between Anthony and Shorty that had seemed so unlikely would continue in New York where they both worked on Wall Street.

When I think back on how young, vibrant, and alive Shorty was that night, my eyes burn with tears at the memory. He had been in such high spirits when he had first returned to his room, his muscled frame streaked with mud and sweat, and his face flush with victory on the rugby field. He was handsome, strong, and always up for fun. He had an easy laugh he had shared with us even when held down and having his height measured against his will. He was a tremendous spirit and the most loyal friend you would ever want to have.

I wish I could always think of Shorty in the beautiful prime of his existence. He would become an early victim of what was called GRID in the early '80s and later called AIDS. God, how it hurts to write this! When he became too sick and needed a place to die in the summer of 1985, his parents refused to let him return to their home in New Canaan. Without hesitation, however, Anthony and his wife, along with their four daughters, moved Shorty into their summer home on the ocean in East Hampton. They could not have been more generous with their love or more heroic in their efforts to make Shorty's final months less horrific than they otherwise would have been.

The last time I saw Shorty alive was when I drove from my home in Amagansett to East Hampton that awful summer when

MY BARE NAKED HEART

So many friends of mine had started to become sick. It was a sunny day, and Anthony's wife served us iced tea and cucumber sandwiches on the back porch overlooking a wavy Atlantic. Anthony's daughters fawned over Shorty and made sure the sun wasn't shining directly on his fragile skin. The conversation was light and reminiscent, but there was no ignoring the sadness and sense of finality in the air.

After an hour, he was too exhausted from our visit to continue. I walked over to him and leaned forward. I kissed him on his forehead and said, "I love you." He said it back and squeezed my hand. His body was just a jumble of bones sheathed in withered skin, and I had a vivid recollection at that moment of how he was this night in Canterbury Hall, streaked with mud and his smiling, handsome, happy face flush with vigor. That afternoon in East Hampton, his eyes had a faraway gaze as if they already were trained on life in the next world, and I knew I would never see him again. I stepped aside as Anthony lifted him into his powerful arms and carried him inside. As I watched Anthony lay him down in the bed with such tenderness, I turned my head to the ocean and bit my lip hard so I wouldn't burst into tears in front of Anthony's wife and daughters. Driving back to Amagansett, however, I cried so hard I had to turn off to the side of the road and pull myself together before I could continue the rest of the way home.

Thinking of the sad times makes the memories of the happy ones so important. I look back on what happened that night in Shorty and Sasquatch's room as one of the very happy ones. Yes, the behavior may have been coarse. But, we were friends, and it was just roughhousing with a higher degree of intimacy and challenged boundaries that brought us closer together and strengthened the bonds between us. No malice was intended. It was also a welcome distraction from the tensions I had felt with Daniel and Dusty. The sight of Shorty, pinned against the wall with a boner that looked disproportionately large on his small frame had caused my cock to twitch. As he stuffed his boner into his underwear and pulled on some pants, I decided I needed to go back to my room to jerk off.

As I left Shorty and Sasquatch's room, I crossed paths with Dusty, who was returning from the library. Our eyes met, and I looked away. I turned back and saw he had gazed up at the ceiling in quiet despair. It occurred to me for the very first time, I am ashamed to say, that all of this had to have been difficult for him as well and my inner equanimity was not the only one in upheaval.

"Hey, Dusty," I said, not knowing what else to say.

He turned his face to me, surprised I had spoken to him. "Hey," he said back. I knew there was more that needed to be said, but "hey" was all I could muster at that moment.

I sensed in the way he looked at me that my fumbling, inarticulate gesture was understood for what it was. His face softened. "Have a good night," he said.

I wanted to say the words back to him. But, I just nodded and turned back to my room with my heart pounding in my chest.

Daniel was in bed reading. The room was mostly dark, illuminated only by the small lamp on his nightstand. He looked up at me for just longer than an instant and turned back to his book without saying anything. I had been hoping he would be asleep so I could jerk off. I needed relief in every sort of way. My heart was pounding in nervous agitation at having just spoken my first words to Dusty since we had kissed. The tension of living with a roommate who had been the best friend I had always wanted to have last week, but was a silent enemy this week was eroding my sense of happiness and well-being. And my cock was throbbing at the thought of what had happened with Shorty just moments ago and my role in it.

I turned to leave the room again and head down to the bathroom to rub one out in the privacy of a stall. But, I looked back at Daniel and something about his smug, punishing silence caused me to snap. I closed the door and did not leave. I removed my pants and draped them across the back of my desk chair. Then I did something that surprises me even to this day: I marched over to his bed and stood over him.

"I'm sick of your shit," I said.

He sneered at me and turned back to his book. I slapped it from his hands and dropped my boxers. My cock was hard, and it bounced out in the open.

He rose up to his elbows. "What the fuck?"

I pushed him back down and started to jerk off over him, just as he had done to me. I was so worked up, it took only a dozen or so quick strokes for me to unleash a copious load that streaked across his chest and face.

"I hope you are satisfied," he said, looking at me with disgust as he wiped my cum from his face with the back of his hand.

"I hope *you* are," I said. "We've had a good thing – a great thing – going here, and you're fucking it up."

"I'm fucking it up?" he said, standing up as I stuffed my still-hard cock back into my boxers and sat down on my bed.

"You're so fucking full of yourself, you can't get out of your own way. If you don't cut the bullshit, we're going to have a fucking long ass year." The darkness of my eyes matched his, and I crawled under the covers.

"Fuck you," Daniel said, grabbing his towel to head down to the bathroom to clean my cum off of him.

"No, fuck *you*," I said.

He slammed the door behind him.

In spite of our argument and the turmoil that surrounded me, I felt an unexpected peace. Yes, my life was messed up in ways that seemed impossible then to resolve. But, at least I had stood up for myself in a way I never had before. Would this cause a permanent gulf in the friendship I had had with Daniel? I didn't know. Could I ever face Dusty again and be honest about what had happened and how I felt about it? I didn't know that either. What I did know is my life had changed over the past week in ways I never could have imagined. At least with this bold, retaliatory gesture that came from a place I had not known was within me, I demonstrated I had it in me to stand up for myself and not always be so afraid of what might happen. This was just one of the many lessons I had learned and would need to draw upon during the rest of that year and over the course of my life.

9 SNOW BALLS

WHEN I AWOKE the next morning, I lay in bed with morning wood and thought of everything that had happened the previous night. By jerking off on Daniel in the same way he had jerked off on me, I had fought back against the punishing freeze he had imposed on our friendship. In the light of the next day, that felt liberating even if our relationship might now be beyond repair. But, that was out of my control. Now, it was up to him. I also couldn't help but think of what had happened in Shorty's room when we measured his height. As I recalled the glorious sight of Shorty's boner and how it had pointed up to the sky while the rest of us had laughed, my hands traveled beneath the sheets to connect with my own hard cock. It was incredible to think of how Anthony had pressed down on the unexpected surprise of Shorty's boner again and again with unabashed fascination as it snapped back up against his flat belly. Between that spectacle and what happened afterwards with Daniel, it had been quite a night.

I looked over at Daniel as he slept, my throbbing boner imploring me for relief. I squeezed it with my fist, released it, and squeezed it again. I repeated that sequence of gestures, careful not to make a sound as I assessed whether I could get away with rubbing one out without Daniel waking and catching me in the act. Even though having a roommate had caused me to become an expert in the survival skill of stealthy masturbation, I did not want to risk it. It was one thing to pay him back in kind for jerking off on me in anger. It was another to get busted by him the very next morning when the status of our friendship was even more uncertain.

I swung my legs around and set my feet on the floor. I stood up and concealed my boner by binding my towel around my waist. Daniel stirred.

"Morning," he said.

"Morning," I said back. *Great*, I thought. More of the Cold War. More one word conversations. More punishing silence. More calculated remoteness. I was exhausted from living with the sadness as I watched a vibrant friendship wither, and I decided at this moment I was giving up. In love and friendship over the course of my life, I often gave more than I received. I have mentioned I had a weakness of becoming attached to people too easily. I also had a fundamental sense of self-respect, and even I had my limits. It was one thing to love and care without regard to ego. It was another thing to be a chump. I was not going to be a chump.

I turned to leave the room without looking back.

"Wait up, John," he said.

My hand was on the door, but I held it there. Daniel had barely said more than two words to me at a time since the night of *Wonder Breadus Interruptus*. "Wait up, John" was three words.

I turned my head, and he looked at me sheepishly. "Wait up," he said again, swinging his feet to the floor. "I'll come join you in the shower."

I watched as he reached for his towel and folded his morning wood into it in the same way I had concealed mine. I opened the door, and we walked down the hall together toward the bathroom, towels bound around our waists, shaving kits in our hands. And that was that. The Berlin Wall in our room had been torn down. We showered in friendly, naked camaraderie, just as we had before the events of *Wonder Breadus Interruptus*. We stole glances at each other's cock as we stood under the rain of warm water. We talked and shared a laugh as if nothing ever happened, even though something transformative had. We made plans to have breakfast in the dining hall and walk to class together. I felt an upsurge of happiness and relief inside me. I had cared deeply for my friendship with Daniel and thought I had destroyed it. Instead, we were friends again, just like that.

What I didn't know, but would learn later, is that after I had jerked off on him, Daniel had wiped the streaks of my cum off his face with the back of his hand. He had stared at it with curiosity. Then, not knowing what had come over him, he had tasted it. It had been tentative at first, but he licked it off the back of his hand until it was all gone. In the bathroom, he had washed his face and stood for a long while and stared at his reflection in the mirror. He had splashed his face again and then entered a stall where he furiously beat off a load into the bowl at the memory of what happened between us. I didn't know any of that as we stood in the shower and our friendship healed while the warm water flowed down upon us. I told myself I didn't want anything more of Daniel than friendship and tried to convince myself it was true. Even if it wasn't, I was glad he was back.

※

Daniel and I returned to our routines. We ate breakfast together in the dining hall as we had before, just the two of us early risers. We sat next to each other in English and biology. I marked up his Emerging Governments essays and dispensed whispered feedback as we sat knee-to-knee in the hushed silence of the library. We played squash after classes ended. We lingered in the shower as we washed the sweat from our bodies. We lay in our separate beds at night and chatted about everything and nothing after we turned out the lights until we drifted off to sleep. I almost could not have been happier.

I still had what I referred to as "The Dusty Problem," even though Dusty wasn't the problem, I was. With distance between us, I was able to breathe when I thought about the power of that kiss and tried to process what it said about who I am. I had realized I needed to speak with him, even though I had no idea what I wanted to say. If we could just be alone together in private, however, I was convinced the words would flow. But, he had given up on trying to talk to me. He now avoided me in the same way I had been avoiding him. I didn't know for certain what I wanted. But, despite my confusion, I knew I cared deeply for him even if my avoidance of him suggested otherwise. I also knew I needed to man up and fix things. I just needed to figure out how, if it wasn't too late already.

That night, Daniel and I were studying in silence in our dorm room, each of us at our respective desks. But, it was not the strained silence of before. It was a comfortable, familiar silence that was interrupted by the sound of a fist pounding on our door.

"Branson! Wonder Bread! You in there?" It was Anthony, and he kept pounding.

Daniel and I were diligent students in an era when academic diligence was not expected. Not every one of The Magnificent Seven was as serious as Daniel and I were, which was lucky for both of us. Otherwise, we would have missed out on some of the fun that is only possible during a window of your life that is shorter than you imagine at the time it will be. I was too young then to know it, but soon enough the realities of the adult world sweep you away. At least we had Anthony and the other members of The Magnificent Seven to save us from being swept away too quickly.

"It's not locked," Daniel said, more than a trace of exasperation in his voice.

Anthony entered our room and jabbed his finger at the window. "What are you two pussies doing? Can't you see it's snowing?"

Daniel and I both looked outside. It was the first week of November, and it was the start of what would be a long, snowy Vermont winter. Four inches lay on the ground already, which Daniel had brought to my attention earlier. We had both looked out the window with minimal comment and returned to our studying. For Anthony, however, the first snow of the season was an event worthy of celebration.

Daniel shrugged. "It's Vermont. It snows here."

"That's right, Wonder Bread, it does," Anthony said, the deliberateness in his tone indicating he had heard the exasperation in Daniel's voice and was unmoved by it. "That's why we need to go outside and celebrate the natural beauty of the season's first snow."

I have mentioned before that Daniel and Anthony were rivals of sorts. Anthony was a natural leader. He was tall and physically imposing. He was loud, impulsive, deceptively smart, and had an abundance of energy. Daniel was a different type of leader. He was handsome, popular, athletic, and smart. He was polished in a country club sort of way that contrasted with Anthony's brashness. Despite their outward differences, they were more alike than they were not. You would think this would make them closer. Instead, it caused endless friction.

"Sounds good to me," I said and stood up. I liked both of them. I could tell Daniel wanted to resist, not because he didn't want to go. But, because he didn't want to fall in line behind Anthony, which was small-minded and tiresome. I didn't want to get in the middle of anything, and I was eager to take a break from studying and have some fun.

Daniel surprised, me, however, and reached for his jacket and gloves. "I'm always up for a snowball fight. Let's go."

The other members of The Magnificent Seven were already outside having fun when we got there. Howell passed around a flask of whiskey from which we all took hefty swigs. Sasquatch had started drinking before the rest of us and was running around in wide circles with his arms outstretched to the heavens as the snow fell on him. It was thick and wet, which made it perfect for packing snowballs. The other guys were throwing them at trees, the dorm's façade, and at each other. Anthony, Daniel, and I followed Sasquatch's lead and ran through the quad with our arms outstretched upwards like he was. I turned my face up to the night sky and let the cold, wet flakes slap against my skin. It felt like an incredible moment to be alive.

The blitheness vanished when a snowball hit Daniel on the back of the head. He whipped around in surprise, a wild smile erupting from his face. "Who did that? This means war!"

In rapid succession, he packed a half-dozen snowballs that he lobbed at each of us. We all responded in kind, and a frenzied, full blown snowball fight ensued. No one was a match for Anthony's aim and speed, however. Singlehandedly, he sent us scrambling back up to the top steps of the dorm's entrance as he bombarded us with a punishing blitz of cannon fire. As we tried to shield ourselves from the snowballs that exploded on and around us, Sasquatch was struck in the center of his chest by a round with an unexpected force that knocked the wind out of him. Stunned, he wobbled backwards, his eyes widened in surprise.

Anthony called for an immediate ceasefire. "Sasquatch, you okay?" he asked, genuine concern in his voice. "Didn't mean to peg you so hard." Anthony could be rough and forget the power of his own raw strength even if the rest of us never did. But, he never wanted to hurt anyone.

Everyone held their fire and stared at Sasquatch, imploring him to say something. He stared back at us in stunned silence for a long beat. Finally, he blinked a few times, and then he shouted: "Snowballs! I'll show you snowballs!" As we looked on in surprise, he stripped off his clothes. First, he peeled off his sweater, then his shoes, then his pants, and finally his underwear. We all burst out laughing. Fully nude, he thrust his fists thrust upwards into the night air as the wet snow fell upon us.

Sasquatch ran bare-assed naked through the quad in the falling snow. "Snowballs!" he yelled again. "Snowballs!" The snow stuck to the curly dark hair on the top of his head and the tight swirls of black hair that ran down his chest to his feet without interruption and around his legs and up to the crack of his ass, which might have been the hairiest ass I have ever seen. We all were bent over with laughter at his crazy, naked antics.

"Howell, give me a swig," Shorty said, reaching for the flask and downing a few gulps. He handed it back to Howell, and then he tore his clothes off.

"You, too?" Anthony said, as we watched Shorty with his tight, rounded ass bound down the steps. He caught up with Sasquatch, and they ran naked together through the quad.

In almost uniform succession, we each knocked back quick shots of the whiskey in the belief the liquor burning down our throats warmed us up. The rest of us tore our clothes off and raced down the steps after Shorty and Sasquatch. We ran through the quad howling, the snow pelting our bare bodies. The shock of the cold of the air was sharper than I expected, and the snow stung as it struck me. But, I didn't care. None of us did. It was too much fun.

Seeing Anthony's monstrous, wrinkled cock was always a marvel, and tonight was no exception. It was an extraordinary sight to watch it slap from his left thigh to his right and back again as he ran.

Shorty's cock bounced up and down and left and right as he ran, and I couldn't help but notice it hadn't shrunk at all in the cold. If anything, it was longer than it usually was in its natural resting state.

Howell's small cock retracted even further into his body, and all you could see was the roundness of his small dick head buried in his bush.

Daniel's sexy, soda bottle-shaped cock bounced around while he ran, the snow slapping against his taut, muscled body and gravity-defying ass.

When I happened to glance over at Freddy's cock, I was surprised to see it was rock hard. It was big, a solid seven-incher that jutted straight out like mine. It was difficult to see as it bounced in the darkness, but there was no denying he was running around with a boner. I was not the type of guy to call out another guy for having an inopportune boner, and I said nothing. Almost as quickly as it rose, however, it deflated. If anyone else had seen it, no one said anything. That meant neither Anthony nor Howell had seen it, because they definitely would have said something if they had.

By now, we had run to the far side of the quad. Even though I was giddy from the whiskey and my head hurt from the cold, I was acutely conscious of how special this moment was. I was running naked through the campus at night in blinding snow with six of the best friends I would ever want to have. We were yelling and having fun in an expression of naked independence that never would have been possible if we weren't here together. I ~~could not have been happier~~.

The combination of exertion and exposure to the elements caught up with us, and we huddled together under a tree at the far end of the quad. My whole body tingled in pain from the biting cold and the snow.

"My balls are fucking freezing," Anthony said. "They're going to shrivel up and fall off my body."

"Why did we do this again?" Daniel asked, laughing even as the fun was starting to wear off.

Before anyone could answer, the sound of one siren and then another intruded into the night air.

"Campus security!" Howell yelled. From around the corner of the dining hall, a red golf cart bore down on us, the wail and spinning light of its feeble siren slicing through darkness.

"Fuck!" the rest of us yelled in near unison. There was no crime to speak of on campus. But, there was a campus security detail that wrote out parking tickets if anyone parked in the faculty parking lot. They also clamped down on partying when it grew too boisterous and otherwise tried to spoil any type of fun that wasn't orderly.

From the opposite side of the quad, another campus security golf cart bore down on us with a security officer shining a hand-held spotlight in our direction. As much as campus security was an operation we laughed at, running naked through campus was the type of offense that could get us suspended or otherwise mar our permanent records, something all of us were conscious of even in the midst of this drunken escapade.

Instinctively, we fled from the flashing red light of security and ran in the direction of our dorm on the other side of the quad.

"Split up!" Anthony yelled. "There's only two of them. They can't chase all of us."

We scattered and ran in different directions beyond the quad and behind the buildings that surrounded it. The sound of the sirens and the sight of the red flashing lights was a steady reminder this had stopped being fun. I didn't want to get nabbed by campus security and be brought before the campus disciplinary committee for public nudity, nor did any of us. When it appeared the coast was clear, I ran down a footpath in the direction of Canterbury Hall. By now, the sound of the sirens had stopped, but the commotion had caught the attention of residents of nearby dorms. A gauntlet of guys leaned out their windows and doused me with cat calls as I streaked past one of the dorms. But, otherwise it was quiet except for the sound of my feet as they crunched on the fallen snow.

I made my way inside Canterbury Hall, relieved to be back in the warmth of the dorm even though I was far from warm yet. I had almost reached the base of the staircase that would lead me up to the safety of the third floor when I heard hushed, animated voices heading towards me. I glanced at the stairs and then in the direction of the voices, certain it was campus security combing the dorms for us. For cover, I darted into the first floor housemaster's lounge and closed the door behind me. The muffled voices got closer, however. I realized they were coming in here, and I was about to get busted. I scanned the room. The lounge was just a large square room with only a single door, and I was trapped. At the last instant, I scrambled behind the curtains that stretched from floor to the ceiling, the same ones Daniel had snapped shut when he had caught us spying on him on the night of *Wonder Breadus Interruptus*.

I cowered behind the curtains, clasping the two connecting ends together with my hands. It was the height of absurdity, my bare naked ass pressed against the cold window, clearly visible to anyone who happened to be walking by on the outside. I had had enough and wished this could all be over. I was afraid, uncomfortably vulnerable, and I was so cold I thought I might have frostbite. What had started off as fun was ending in misery, and I just wanted to get back to my room.

The door to the lounge opened and then quickly shut. I peered through the gap between the curtains and saw it was Freddy and Shorty. I was relieved it was just them and was about to loosen my grasp on the fabric. But, I halted, stunned at what my eyes caught: not only were they naked, which was not a surprise, but Shorty was pulling Freddy into the room by Freddy's cock, his hand gripped around it. Freddy's cock was rock hard, just as it had been when we were running nude through the quad. They were giggling, and I saw Shorty's cock was hard as well.

 I held my breath as I watched Shorty drop to his knees, open his mouth, and bury his face deep into Freddy's crotch. Freddy gasped with pleasure, and Shorty sucked on the underside of Freddy's balls. Freddy's hard-on throbbed, and he grabbed Shorty's head for balance. This made no sense to me. Freddy and Shorty were friends in the way we all were. But, they were not close in the same way Shorty and Anthony were, for example, or that Daniel and I were. At least that's what I thought until now. Had they done this before? They were so comfortable together, it sure looked like it to me. You would think my cock would have hardened, too. But, I was so shocked at the sight of what they were doing and fearful of how they would react if they caught me spying, my cock stayed as soft and shriveled as it ever gets.

 Freddy's cock was not as thick as mine or Daniel's, but thick enough, and Shorty was enjoying every inch of it. Soon, Shorty shifted his attention from Freddy's balls to the underside of his cock, which he kissed from the base until he reached the crown. Without lingering, he opened his mouth wide and plunged down the length of Freddy's shaft, all the way to the bottom. Freddy gasped and leaned his head back against the wall. Shorty moaned, his head rising and falling as he settled into an even rhythm.

 My eyes followed the slender trail of hair that spread from the crack of Shorty's ass as he knelt before Freddy. I had always admired the compact, muscled frame of his body and perfectly-formed features. With his right hand, he stroked his curved, hefty hard-on as his mouth pumped back and forth on Freddy's cock. It was amazing to see his mouth start at the tip of Freddy's shiny glans and slide with ease down the entire length of his shaft. When he reached the bottom, his face was buried in Freddy's bush, which was neatly trimmed at a time when men generally didn't trim down there. I wouldn't hear the term "deep-throat" until years later. But, Shorty was deep-throating Freddy expertly, his head bobbing with a steady, determined beat.

Freddy's eyes opened, and he gasped louder and deeper than he had before. He grabbed Shorty's head with both hands, and he looked forward for the first time, his breath quickening as he approached the inevitable.

My hand slipped, and the curtain opened.

Fuck!

My heart beat faster in terror. Freddy's eyes locked with mine, and they opened even wider, his face twisted both in ecstasy and surprise. He moaned and increased the tempo with which he pumped his cock into Shorty's mouth. Freddy let out a long, low grown. I could tell by the way Shorty gulped that Freddy was shooting a large load down his eager throat. Freddy's eyes remained glued to mine as his body heaved in pleasure.

I would later learn this was one of the strongest orgasms of Freddy's life, that once the curtains opened and our eyes met at the instant he was starting to cum, his cock surged even harder. The shock of seeing me caused his cock to unleash a load down Shorty's throat with uncommon intensity. As soon as he finished, however, he looked sick with regret. His eyes darkened as they bore into mine, and it seemed as if the coldness in them was meant to threaten me into silence. His load now blown, he dropped his grip on Shorty's head and left without a word. But, the message to me was clear that this never happened, and I better keep my mouth shut.

If Shorty was surprised Freddy would just leave without saying anything, he gave no indication of it. He got up off his knees and stood, providing me with a discreet view of his hard cock, which was flat against his belly. He had been stroking it while he blew Freddy, and he was almost ready to come himself. With just a few strokes, a series of ribbons of cum shot out of his cock and into the air before landing on the rug. It was remarkable to me that anyone could shoot as high into the air as he had, and I filed the image away in my spank bank and would call upon it many times over the years.

I would later tell Shorty that I had seen everything, including how he had rubbed the cum into the carpet with his bare foot before he left the room and darted back up the stairs, naked, to the safety of our floor. He had laughed and not minded at all. That was one of the great things about Shorty: he had thought it hilarious when I described how I had been cowering behind the curtains, my bare ass pressed up against the cold window, as I watched him go to town on Freddy's cock. He cared more about whether his ass looked good than about having been caught on his knees with a dick in his mouth.

After Shorty left the room, I waited a few minutes and then followed, slinking out of there with my shriveled cock between my legs. I ran up the main stairs without being seen. When I reached the third floor, I could hear Anthony's and Howell's elevated voices emanating from the bathroom, and I headed straight there. The guys already were in the shower, trying to warm up their bodies after the punishing cold we had all endured. Luckily, campus security had given up, and no one had been caught.

There are moments when I have felt especially close to The Magnificent Seven, and this was one of them. Anthony and Daniel were laughing about getting chased, and the other guys joined in the laughter. I was so happy to be here with my buddies in the way that I was and to have shared the experiences of the evening we had just shared. I knew Shorty had not seen me in the lounge and had no idea I had watched him blow Freddy. As we showered, Freddy and I made eye contact a few times in a way that felt uncomfortable to me and continued to feel threatening, as if he were trying to bully me into silence. Shorty and Freddy were masters of discretion and gave no indication anything had gone on between them. I didn't want to let Freddy ruin my fun, and I tried to tune him out as best as I could.

When Daniel and I crawled into our separate beds, exhausted, my mind was awhirl at everything that had happened. It had been a night of spirited adventure that had made me feel acutely aware of being alive. At the same time, my mind struggled to process the imagery of Shorty and Freddy together in the way that they had been. I had never seen anything like that in my life. Shorty was a cocksucker and apparently an experienced one. Was I a cocksucker? Watching what I had seen tonight made me want to try it, and I wondered if I ever would. I closed my eyes and thought of Freddy's long, handsome cock and wondered what it tasted like and how it would feel inside my mouth. I thought of Dusty and shook my head with regret at the awkwardness that had arisen between us and wondered if we could ever get past it. I felt uneasy about having had Freddy catch me catch him in the way that he had and the undercurrent of menace that had arisen between us. Whatever this meant, I did not know. But, I knew this was not the end of it. A part of me wanted to tell Daniel about it. A louder part of me told me to keep the information to myself.

10 THE TRUTH

I FELL IN and out of a state of slumber that night, my body twisting with discomfort, my brain searching for solutions to everything that did not make sense and problems I had been unable to solve. My mind replayed on a continuous loop how I had watched Shorty deep-throat Freddy's cock and how Freddy's eyes had locked with mine as he blew his load down Shorty's throat. Oral sex was viewed as dirty and perverted in the 1950s, something decent people didn't do. That made me want to do it even more. I had heard about blowjobs, of course, from friends who had claimed to have received them, and I had imagined in masturbatory fantasies about what it might be like to get one. But, watching one between two guys was something I never thought I would see in my whole life. As my mind raced in circles for solutions it could not find, it was only natural the touchpoints of that blowjob, my perpetual horniness, and my unrest over Dusty would all converge as my active subconscious toiled while I slept.

I was in the shower. It was the night Dusty and I had stood under the warm water as it washed over our bodies that were wracked with unfulfilled sexual desire of a kind of which we could not speak. We had just run together on the track in the late afternoon before we shared the kiss that upended everything

I thought I knew about myself. We had stared at each other with our hard-ons throbbing, each of us reveling in the throes of unexplored sexual desire. Our eyes were heavy with the ache of what each of us wanted most from the other. We stood there with smiling, drunken grins as my cock jutted out towards him, as if it were straining outwards to reach him. He laughed happily as his own banana-shaped cock bobbed in a parallel rhythm.

In my dream, we were not interrupted by the sound of the door opening to the bathroom. The spell remained unbroken. We continued to stand there, our hearts and cocks throbbing with an unfed hunger. Dusty leaned in, and I waited for him to kiss my mouth. But, instead he bypassed it and pressed his lips to the side of my neck. He sucked gently on it as the warm water poured down upon us. I closed my eyes, and I could feel my taint and the starburst of my hole pulse together in synchronicity with my cock. He moved from my neck to my chest and then slowly down toward my stomach. He suspended his downward march as he lingered over my belly button, swirling his tongue around inside it. My cock throbbed and pulsed against his wrist, imploring him to continue on the journey south.

He pressed his cheek against my treasure trail and closed his eyes for a moment to savor the closeness to me. Then he reached up with his hand and started to stroke my cock. It was slippery and smooth from the soap and the falling water. He pressed down on my hard-on and smiled with an innocent wonder as it bounced, just as Shorty's had when Anthony had pressed on his. He cupped my balls and squeezed them with curious fascination. He looked up at me with the cerulean blue eyes that cause my heart to break at the memory of them whenever I lie on my back and stare up at a cloudless sky where the blueness is so deep it extends to infinity. He smiled at me, and while his right hand still cupped my balls, he placed his mouth on the head of my cock. He swirled his tongue in circles on the ridged crown and then sealed his lips around it to form a wet ring of suction.

"Dusty!" I gasped.

I had never had my cock sucked by anyone else before. I had spent countless hours dreaming about it while locked in my bedroom back home, my hands down my pants and my fantasies taking me to the places I most wanted to travel. In this dream, Dusty stepped in and took charge of that fantasy. He looked up at me with his mouth sealed around the smooth helmet of my cock head. His eyes locked with mine, and then they closed as he slid his mouth down the length of my shaft. The seven and one-half inches of my cock that was the width of a cardboard tube in a roll of paper towels was swallowed up deep inside his throat. I leaned back against the slippery wet tile of the shower wall and exhaled. It felt incredible. His lips were pressed against the black tangle of my bush, mashed against my pubic bone. He rose up to the tip of my cock and plummeted back to the base. Then he did it again. And again. And again. His right hand continued to cup my balls as his head bobbed up and down on my cock with increasing urgency.

  He slid the warm wet index finger of his right hand behind my balls and rubbed the narrow pucker of my hole, a sensation I had dreamed of as well, but had not yet experienced in real life outside of my own exploration of it in my bathtub back home. The intensity of the pleasure approached the point beyond which I would not be able to control it. I started to feel that familiar rumbling from deep inside me. If he kept this up, there would be no turning back. And then there wasn't.

  I groaned from the depths of my body as I unloaded a gushing river of hot semen down Dusty's throat. I had never had an orgasm this long or this powerful before. I had only experienced my own hand, never a warm wet mouth except in my fantasies. Yet, here I was with someone I cared about as much as I cared about Dusty. My knees buckled as I leaned against the shower wall. A tsunami of pleasure pulsed through my body from the very ends of my toes up through the top of my skull and my tingling scalp. Dusty gulped and swallowed every drop, sucking the unending streams of cum that pulsed forth from unknown reservoirs inside me. When the pleasure threatened to consume me to the point I felt faint, my eyes shot open and I sat up in bed, gasping.

  Holy shit! My chest convulsed as I caught my breath. That orgasm had felt so real! And it had been. There was a warm, gooey mess in my boxer shorts that was starting to spread across the flatness of my lower stomach. I had had a powerful wet dream, the first one since the first night of school. I struggled to catch my breath and marveled at how incredible it had felt. As the glow of ecstasy ebbed from my body, however, the warm wetness turned cold and liquefied. But, even worse, the memory of pleasure was replaced by regret and the despair of opportunity lost.

I was hit by the realization I did not just want to kiss Dusty again or feel his lips on my cock in the way I had just dreamed about. I wanted much more from him: I loved him. I had tried to convince myself I didn't. But, the truth was there and had been all along. I had just been too afraid to admit it to myself. I loved him. I loved him in the way I had always thought of loving girls. I was almost entirely certain from the way he had been looking at me with such pained desire these past few weeks that he loved me, too. It had to be true – there could be no other explanation. We had been hot for each other from the moment we had met on the first day of school, and it had been building since. I had tried to ignore it, but I couldn't any longer.

Dusty had been willing to open his heart to mine – I was certain of that. But, I had treated that willingness with disregard. Not a disregard born from callousness, but a disregard born from innate fear and my refusal to have an honest conversation with myself about who I was and what I was afraid I might be. I still had strong feelings about girls. Even if it made my head hurt to reconcile those feelings, one thing was certain: I loved Dusty. I wanted more from him, even if I didn't know what "more" meant. It was terrifying to admit that even in my private thoughts. It is terrifying even now to remember what it was like in the darkness of that era to feel what I felt towards Dusty, feelings that were reviled at every corner of society, feelings that were illegal if I acted upon them. Yet, the truth was, I had those feelings. I felt ill at the thought my efforts to trammel on what Dusty felt for me may have been successful.

I looked at the clock: 3:45 a.m. I swung my legs around to the floor and stood up. The cum had liquefied and was running down my leg. I stuffed my still semi-hard cock back into my boxers and grabbed a fresh pair along with a towel. I left the room and headed down to the bathroom to clean up. My mind raced at the recollection of the wet dream I had just had. It had been so vivid. Is that how Dusty would kiss my neck? Is that what it felt like to have your cock sucked? A snug, powerful sheath of warmth and wetness that caresses and sucks the semen from the depths of your body until you can no longer hold back and your cock explodes in spasms of ecstasy? Is that how Dusty would suck my cock if he wanted to suck it? Would he rub his warm wet finger against the outside of my hole? Would I enjoy it in real life as much as I had in my dream? I shook my head. It was all too much to think about.

In the showers, I scrubbed off the mess that had congealed across my groin and streaked down my thigh. I thought of the magic these showers had held in my dream and the night Dusty and I had been in here before we rolled around on the couch back in his room. But, the magic of the dream and that night was missing now. The lights were too bright. The water was not warm enough, and the silence made my soul feel lonelier than I thought possible. I cleaned off quickly and dried myself in front of the mirror.

I felt sick with regret at the prospect my fear and coldness had caused Dusty's feelings about me to wither before they could blossom. Since that evening when we had connected with the potential of such promise, he had looked at me first with desire, then pain, then regret, and then not at all. I had done everything thing I could to shut down and smother those feelings for both of us. From every indication, I had been successful. How long had it been since he had looked at me with the need and the desire he had that night? How long had it been since he had looked at me at all? I didn't even want to think about it any longer. I had an overpowering need to clear things up right now, before it was too late – if it wasn't already.

I left the bathroom. Instead of turning left to head back to my room, I turned right, in the direction of Dusty's. I stopped in front of his door and leaned against it, my heart pounding at the thought he was just on the other side, asleep in his bed.

"Dusty!" I whispered.

"Dusty!" I whispered again. "You awake?"

I closed my eyes, my forehead pressed up against the hard wood of the door.

"Please," I whispered. "I need to speak with you."

I tapped against the door with the knuckles of my right hand. This was crazy. I wanted him to hear me, and at the same time I didn't. He would think I was out of my mind knocking on his door at 4 a.m., and he would have been right.

I tapped again, a little harder this time.

"Dusty!" I whispered, louder than before. Tears formed in the corners of my eyes. I told myself I would count to ten, and if he didn't answer I would leave. I started off slow. When I reached nine, I slowed even further before finally reaching ten.

I stepped back a few feet. As urgently as I needed to speak with him, pounding on his door and waking him at this hour was not the way to go about it. I had resolved to tell him everything – that, I had promised myself. But, now was not the time. I turned away and headed back to my room, the boxers dampened by my wet dream crumpled in a ball in my hand.

Daniel stirred and then rolled over as I entered the room. I climbed back into bed and tried to ignore the top sheet that was damp from my wet dream. As jumbled as my thoughts were regarding the mess I had caused with Dusty, I felt an unexpected sense of calm. Instead of wallowing in regret and attempting to smother the feelings I felt toward him, I had confronted myself in an honest light. That had been the first step. The next would be telling him how I felt about what had happened between us that night. You would think the second step would be more terrifying than the first. But, admitting to myself the truth about what I might be was far more terrifying. I knew even then that in matters of love and passion, you can only do what you can do. The first step was opening your heart, and I had opened mine. The next step was letting your heart be known, and I would make my known in the morning.

I have lived my life by taking chances – not because I am brave, but because I am fearful of regret. I knew if I didn't take a chance with Dusty and tell him my truth, I would be haunted for the rest of my life by tortuous thoughts of what might have been.

MY BARE NAKED HEART

I didn't want that. I wanted to have the certainty of knowing even if things didn't work out with him the way I wanted them to, I had done the best I could. The rest was out of my hands. I drifted off to sleep at peace with the knowledge the next day would bring change even if I did not know what that change would be.

11 MY HEART IN MY HANDS

IN THE MORNING, I was awakened by Daniel's hand shaking my shoulder. "Hey, sleepy head," he said. "Time to get up."
    Startled, I opened my eyes. A habitual early riser, I was not accustomed to sleeping late or being awakened except on my own accord. "What time is it?"
    "7:30. Let's hit the showers and head to the dining hall before class."
    "7:30?" I sat up abruptly. "That late?" I had slept fitfully until my wet dream and then unusually soundly after that. Even with Daniel's welcome hand on my shoulder, my first thoughts went to Dusty and the urgency with which I needed to speak to him while I still had the courage.
    "You okay, sleepy head?"
    "I'm fine," I said, swinging my legs around and standing up. My morning wood strained against the cotton fabric of my boxers. I was aware of it, of course, but was distracted enough to neglect my usual steps to hide it.
    Daniel certainly didn't miss it, however. "Whoa! You almost poked my eye out with that thing!"
    "Sorry about that," I said sheepishly. "I wasn't thinking. I'm still half asleep."

"Don't worry about it," he said. "I've seen it before." We both laughed and looked at it again. I pushed down on it through my boxers and made it bounce like Anthony had done with Shorty's. Daniel laughed again, louder this time. Even though I was on a mission to fix things with Dusty, I couldn't help but appreciate how close Daniel and I had grown and how open we had become with each other.

I laughed, too, and said, "Show's over."

I wrapped a towel around my waist, and we headed down the hall to the bathroom as my boner subsided. He stopped off at the sink to shave and brush his teeth while I headed straight into the shower. It was filled with some of the other guys: Anthony, Howell, Sasquatch, and Shorty. I turned on a faucet, but was too wrapped up in my own thoughts to say anything.

"What's up with you, Mr. Serious?" Anthony asked.

"Nothing. I have a lot of work today."

Anthony gave me a hard look, and I knew he wasn't buying it. The other guys made small talk and were chatting about pro football and how great the Detroit Lions and the Cleveland Browns were doing that year. Normally, I would join in the conversation with my own opinions and predictions. But, not this morning. I kept my thoughts to myself. I wanted to shower and get out of there.

I was all cleaned up and leaving the shower as Daniel was entering. He looked surprised I was already done. "Sleepy and speedy today?"

"A little," I said. "See you back at the room."

Anthony and Daniel exchanged glances. Daniel looked at me a second time, no doubt wondering what was going on. He knew my rhythms well enough to know something was off about me. I could tell by the questioning look in his eye he wanted to ask what was up. But, he didn't, and I wasn't offering any explanations. I left without looking back.

As I headed down the hall to my room, I passed Freddy. His towel was around his waist, and his shaving kit dangled from his right hand.

"Hi, Freddy," I said, nodding at him as we approached each other in the hallway.

He glared at me, but didn't otherwise respond.

"Hi, Freddy," I said again, my tone deliberate.

"Hello, Branson," he said, rolling every syllable off his tongue, his eyes not leaving mine.

It was absurd of him to think he could threaten me with cartoonish scowls laden with menace. The effect was unintentionally theatrical, but it made me uncomfortable nonetheless. Freddy was a good-looking rich kid who had been born with a sense of entitlement. It was driving him crazy knowing I had caught him in the way that I had. I knew even then that people who lived in fear of having secrets exposed were dangerous, especially if they were ashamed of those secrets. In those days, Freddy had every reason to be terrified of what would happen if his secret were to become known. But, I had no plans to divulge anything to anyone. I shook my head and kept walking. If I had turned around, I imagine he would have been shooting dark looks at me until I left his line of sight. I knew I would have to deal with him sooner or later, but I had bigger concerns at the moment.

Back in my room, I dressed quickly. I checked my hair and overall appearance in the mirror before heading down to Dusty's room. My heart was pounding. I hadn't known what would happen that previous night when I had knocked on his door and he had invited me inside as Chet Baker played on the hi-fi and the heaviness of desire hung in the air. I didn't know what would happen this morning. But, I had been lucky once. I hoped there was a chance I could be lucky twice.

I took a deep breath and knocked. I cleared my throat and made sure I was standing up straight and not slouching. I knocked again.

"Come in!" Dusty said. "Door's unlocked."

I opened the door and stepped inside.

I don't think Dusty could have looked more surprised at seeing me, the guy who had ignored him and behaved with such coldness towards him for weeks.

"Hi, there," I said. When I had practiced this conversation in my head, I had imagined myself smiling. In person, I was too nervous to smile. I waited for the words to come spilling out. But, they weren't.

"Can I help you?" The surprise had faded from his face, and his forehead was crinkled in confusion.

"I need to speak to you," I said. I swallowed and cleared my throat. "About that night."

He paused a beat and looked at his watch. "I'm sorry. I can't. I have an exam and was just about to head out."

His manner was formal, as if it weren't me standing there before him and he weren't him. This was not the Dusty who had stared into my eyes and kissed me with everything he had. This was not the Dusty who had wrapped his arms around me and lay on top of me on the leather couch on the other side of the room and ground his boner into mine with hungry, probing intensity. This was an RA speaking to one of his freshman charges.

"Okay," I said, deflating. "I want to talk to you. I need to apologize."

He stuffed his notebook and his textbooks into his bag. "No need to apologize. I really do have to run. See you around, okay?"

I fumbled for something else to say, but I couldn't find the words. I had not expected him to be so distant when I was standing right there in front of him ready to bare my heart. My face was stricken with the regret of unsaid words as my eyes met his. He looked away. It would have been one thing if I had said what I needed to say and he had not responded how I wanted him to. It was another thing altogether to have him not even let me say it. He had his back to me as he continued to pack his bag. I turned to leave.

"Look," he said, his tone softening. "If you want to come back late this afternoon, I should be around after four."

While my heart did not soar in expectation, I allowed myself to recognize he had opened a small window. I wished him well and said I'd be back then. I had not expected the conversation to be easy. But, I had not expected it to have felt as awkward as it had or for it to have been cut short before I said what I needed to say. I had not expected him to look at me with distant consternation, as if nothing had happened between us when something important had. I didn't want to wait until the end of the day to tell him what I needed to tell him. I had been so sure of what needed to be done and how to do it when I had awoken in the middle of the night. I wasn't so sure now.

◊

The minutes passed by with agonizing slowness. After classes ended, Daniel had wanted to play squash, but I demurred. He went off to the courts with Howell instead, but not before turning back to me with a lingering expression of incertitude on his face. I looked back at him and held his gaze until he turned away again and left. I hung out in my room and waited for Dusty to return. I tried to read, but couldn't. I tried to study, but couldn't do that either. I did sit ups until my abs hurt and push-ups until my pecs and shoulders couldn't take anymore. Finally, there was nothing else to do but sit around and wait while I listened to the clock tick.

I was staring out the window at the snow-covered quad when I was startled by a knock on my open door. I looked up and was surprised to see it was Dusty. I had planned on going to his room at four and was caught off guard by his sudden appearance at mine.

"You wanted to talk?" he asked. His manner and tone were business-like, although not unfriendly.

"How was your exam?"

He shrugged. "It went pretty well, I think. But, you never know."

"Good," I said, fumbling for more small talk and not finding any.

Down the hall, someone was throwing a basketball against the wall with monotonous repetition. But, a silence of spoken words hung in the air in my room as Dusty looked at me, his expression guarded while he waited for me to speak. I hadn't thought until now what it would feel like to lay my heart bare in the way I was looking to bare it at the very instant it would be happening. Over the course of my long career, I was in physical danger on numerous harrowing occasions. But, it is not hyperbole to say that I was never as terrified as I was to be an eighteen year old young man in 1957 and tell another man I loved him, particularly the one standing before me.

Here goes, I thought and took a deep breath. "Close the door."

Dusty sat down on Daniel's bed, just opposite from me as I sat on mine. I wondered what he might be feeling at this moment and whether he would forgive me. He had stared at me with such longing in the shower, his hard cock straining to reach me because he hadn't yet dared to touch me. He had kissed me on the couch in his room with everything he had as Chet Baker played in the background. He had smiled at me with unguarded happiness at the realization the connection between us had opened up possibilities for more if only I would have looked back at him in the same way. Instead, I had repaid him by recoiling in fear and withdrawing from him with an unthinking coldness. I shook my head at how callous I had been and hoped it wasn't too late.

"I wanted to talk to you about that night," I said. "I'm really sorry."

He put up his hand. "I'm the one who should be apologizing. It never should have happened."

"I'm not sorry it happened. I'm sorry about how I behaved afterwards. I shouldn't have pulled away like that. I was freaked out."

He nodded his head. "Of course you would be freaked out. That's why it was all a huge mistake –"

"It wasn't a mistake –"

He held his hand up again. "Let me finish. You're only a freshman, and I am a senior. I'm also your RA. What I did was completely inappropriate. I violated your trust and took advantage of you. The fact that you freaked out is all my fault. It's exactly why I never should have done what I did."

"You didn't take advantage," I said. "I wanted it. I wanted it from the first moment I saw you. I was scared and confused the past few weeks. But, I'm not anymore."

He crossed his arms. "You're young, John. You have so much to figure out, and this is confusing stuff. I've had a lot longer to figure things out. That's why this was wrong on so many levels. I'm very sorry."

"Would you quit saying you're sorry? And don't tell me I'm young. I'm old enough to know what I feel."

He reached out to put his hand on my knee, but pulled it back without touching me. "You have a long life ahead of you. What you feel today might not be what you feel tomorrow or next week. I'm not going to be the one to add to the confusion. It never should have happened. I hope you'll forgive me someday."

His words had jagged edges that slashed at my heart. He stood up to go. His demeanor had turned agitated. Even worse, he had been dismissive of my all-consuming feelings towards him, which was soul crushing. In disbelief, my eyes followed the back of his head as he reached the doorway and stepped into the hall. My chest pounded at the realization that all I had hoped for was ebbing away.

I had nothing left to lose, so I blurted out the words I hoped would change everything: "Dusty, I love you."

If my timing and choice of words appear awkward on the printed page, I can assure you it was even worse in delivery. Blurting out "I love you" to someone who hadn't expected to hear it is romantic in the movies. But, I will tell you from experience that the reality didn't match what might have happened on the big screen, at least for me. The words felt desperate and ill-timed as I said them and in my perception of how they were received. Looking back through the lens of an entire lifetime of experiences after that moment, my heart breaks for the young man I was then. I had just laid my heart bare and offered it to the one person I had met in my whole life who I thought would understand who I was and what I might be. I had wanted to feel validation from admitting out loud those words that are among the most very beautiful in any language.

Dusty turned around and stared at me, his face twisted in unbelieving surprise in a way that was not unkind, but felt patronizing in the most painful way after I had just offered him the gift of my bare naked heart. "You don't love me. It was just a kiss. It didn't mean anything."

It felt as if the air was being sucked from the room. "I know what I feel. I love you. I know you love me."

He closed his eyes and shook his head not just to say no, but as if he were trying to shake the words I had just said out of his head, as if they had never been uttered and as if he had never heard them.

"I have to go," he said, and then he was gone.

The remaining air in the room left with him. Time slowed. My legs felt weak. My eyes burned. I felt an overwhelming sense of desolation at the realization I had lost him. I had told him my truth and made myself vulnerable. I had offered him my heart, and he had not taken it. It felt as if something had broken inside me and I would never be the same. He was the only person I had ever known who I was sure shared the secret that went to the foundations of what made me who I am. The fear rose up inside me that love was something meant for other people, not me, and that I would never find it. It took everything I had to remain stoic and keep from falling apart.

I wish I could reach back through time and hug my eighteen year old self as I stood in the emptiness of my dorm room as a light snow fell on the spare landscape. I would hold me tight and kiss my head. I would run my fingers through my hair as I whispered that everything would be okay, that I would get past it even though I could not believe at the time I ever would. I had just laid my soul bare to the person I loved most in the world. I had offered him the gift of me. Instead of feeling the joy of requited affection, I felt the ache and desolation of a broken heart.

I had had enough. I couldn't bear to be in this room any longer. I needed to get out of there and burn off my pent-up energy. I grabbed my running shoes and headed over to the indoor track.

As I ran on the outside lane, my thoughts replayed the pain of my confession. Had I really blurted out "I love you" like that? It had felt like the right thing to say as he turned to flee from me. In hindsight, the dismissiveness with which it had been received made me almost wish I had never said it. Yet, even in my despair and my inexperience in matters of the heart, I found solace in the recognition I had said what I had to say. I had to make myself known to him or else I would always live with the regret of what might have been. As I salved the harsh sting of rejection, I knew I would have regretted not speaking my truth far more than I regretted speaking it. In fact, I did not regret speaking it. I just regretted it had been so awkward and, most of all, too late.

After I hit the two mile mark, I noticed Dusty was running on the track as well. *Damn*, I thought. I had come here to run away from him in literal and figurative ways. Why did he have to come here to run away from me in the same manner?

I kept my pace steady and tried to hold myself together. I tried not to wonder if he would speed up to catch me like he had on the outdoor track on that afternoon when all of this had started. I tried not to wonder if he would pull up alongside me to say what had happened in my room had been a mistake in a different way and that he loved me after all. I couldn't help myself. I also couldn't help but notice he made no effort to catch up with me. In fact, he was making every effort to stay as far from me as possible. That he would now avoid me in the same way I had avoided him felt worse than I could have imagined.

I couldn't take it anymore. I had held myself together with forced stoicism while I tried to stuff the hurt back inside me and pretend it had never happened. But, at this moment, I was on the brink of bursting into tears. I couldn't forget about Dusty if he were right there in front of me. I had run less than half as far as I had intended to, but I finished this lap and left the indoor field house.

The cold air and the snow flurries whipped at my face as I trudged back to my dorm. I wondered if I could maintain a façade for Daniel and the other guys that would be brave enough for them not to know I was dying inside. I wanted nothing more than to crawl into bed, pull the covers over my head, and go to sleep until I could rise up from the devastation I felt. It just hurt so much.

I reached the dorm and the warmth of the lobby that sheltered me from the windy cold and the snap of the flurries but nothing else. As I crossed the lobby, the door from the outside opened again with a bang. I started at the noise and spun around with the expectation the rising wind had grabbed the door and slammed it open. It wasn't the wind, however.

It was Dusty.

He was panting, having run after me all the way from the indoor track. His eyes were dark. His jaw was clenched, and he held his fists tight. My mouth opened in surprise at his unexpected presence and the speed with which he was approaching me. His face was serious and unsmiling. As he raced toward me with such intense determination, I had the unsettling sense he was about to attack me.

He grabbed me by the arms and shoved me against the wall. All in one motion, he leaned in and kissed me so hard I thought he might have broken my nose. He wrapped his arms around me and held me in the tightest most powerful way, squeezing me as if he would never let me go. Our tongues found each other's. Our mouths connected in varying degrees of tenderness and raw, hungry energy. Our cocks jumped to attention and throbbed wildly in our pants as we bore them into each other. The experience of this kiss went beyond just the physical. We connected not just our bodies and our mouths, but I felt his spirit enter my body and connect with mine in a way that made our truths known: I loved him, and he loved me right back.

Looking back over the course of my life and the catalog of first kisses I had shared with every lover I had, I remember every first kiss, but never the second one. Except with Dusty. I have never forgotten the intensity of that first kiss with him in his dorm room as Chet Baker played in the background and my world shifted at the unexpected pleasure of what it meant to kiss and be kissed by a man, especially one as extraordinary as Dusty. I have never forgotten that second kiss with him that came in the lobby of my freshman dorm on a snowy afternoon when I thought all was lost. That kiss had said "I love you back" and enveloped our souls. It also had made our cocks come to life at the unspoken possibilities of what might lie ahead.

Aside from the physical and emotional power of that second kiss, what is so extraordinary is the bravery with which it was exchanged. I have written before of the challenges of that era and how the love we felt was forbidden not just in the romantic literary sense, but also in every legal and social sense. For Dusty to race across the lobby of a college dorm in 1957 and shove me up against the wall and kiss me with such passion, intensity, and open lust was an act of courage that bordered on lunacy. The lobby was empty of people, but Dusty hadn't known that when he raced through it after me.

If anyone had been in the lobby, the exposure of our forbidden secret would have subjected us to certain scorn and banishment. Dusty would have been fired from his RA position and lose the scholarship of room and board that came with it. We would have been brought before the college disciplinary committee and likely be expelled. It would have been impossible for us to work for the Federal Government, including the State Department, which was my biggest professional dream at that time. Our parents would have been notified and mine, for certain, would have sent me to a psychiatrist to cure me of what I knew they thought of as the worst form of mental illness.

For Dusty to have risked everything to race after me and capture me publicly in the way that he did meant he loved me right back. Even a near-lifetime later, my eyes burn with tears as I type these words. Dusty loved me in a way that was beautiful, extraordinary, and human. As he held me, I knew there was nothing dirty or wrong or shameful about what I felt. I had struggled for years with the need to feel normal. With his embrace, he erased all inner doubts that I wasn't. Of the many gifts he bestowed upon me, I have always been so grateful that he validated who I was in these moments without needing to speak a word.

"Let's go," he said finally, and we walked up the north staircase, the same one I had raced up in the nude that night after the frolic in the snow. I was as happy as I had ever been.

Although no one was in the lobby, I would later learn we had not been unobserved. At the top of the south staircase, Anthony and Shorty had frozen in their steps at the sight of what was going on below. They had seen everything from the moment Dusty broke through the door and shoved me against the wall. They had seen us kiss, our bodies grinding together, and our boners throbbing in our pants. Knowing what I knew about Shorty, I would not have been too concerned if had been just he who had seen us. But, I would have been in a state of abject panic if I had known Anthony had watched all of it and said, "Well, well, well. What do you know? Dusty and Branson are a couple of fruit cakes." Anthony had a big mouth, and I would have feared it would be impossible for him to contain the knowledge that there were two fairies on the floor, one of them his close friend and the other the RA of all people.

But, I didn't know any of this yet and didn't feel fear at that moment. I only felt supreme happiness and exhilaration at the possibilities that lay ahead of me now I knew with all certainty that the man to whom I had offered my bare naked heart had taken it after all.

12 THANKSGIVING

THE NEXT WEEK raced by in a blur. Dusty and I reveled in the new found recognition of our mutual truth that we were hot for each other. That it was a secret from everyone else made it even hotter. It was unspoken between us, but I knew Dusty shared my ache for the privacy we needed to explore things further. Privacy of the type we wanted, however, was almost impossible to find in a crowded dorm where everyone was always in and out of everyone's rooms and the behavior we wanted to pursue was forbidden.

Instead, we grabbed stolen moments when we could.

Two days after that second kiss in the lobby of our dorm on that snowy afternoon, we crossed paths in the history department building. "What are you doing in here?" he asked. Without waiting for an answer, he pulled me into the alcove of an empty lecture hall and kissed me for the third time, mashing his mouth against mine and swabbing my tongue with his own. We groped at each other with a passion-filled rush of furious energy until the sound of steps in the hallway caused us to pull apart. We separated and left the safety of the alcove, our chests and cocks pounding with interrupted desire.

The next night, I returned the favor when I found him in the stacks of the library basement. I wrapped my arms around him from behind as he was bending over to reach for a book on a low shelf. He spun around in surprise. My lips met his, and our tongues raced into each other's mouth. Amidst the furtive, fumbling tangle of our tongues and our arms, I reached down the back of his pants and rubbed my middle finger up the cleft of his crack. I was intrigued to find it wet with warm sweat. Our cocks hardened and we ground them into each other until we heard the sound of the door opening from the nearby staircase. When I would later go into the men's room to take a leak, it was no surprise to me to notice my cock was wet with leaking pre-cum. We had other similar clandestine encounters that went no further than passionate kissing and powerful, grappling embraces that caused each of us to ache for much, much more. It was obvious to both of us that we needed to get beyond these hit-and-run encounters or else we were going to burst.

I look back at those first days with Dusty with tender nostalgia. I had risked everything with him to make my heart known, and he had responded in kind. I had said the words, "I love you," and he even though he had not yet said them back to me, I knew by the way his eyes hungered for me that he did. We reveled in the miraculous ether of requited affection. We had not yet complicated the youthful innocence of first love with sex. But, we were tumbling end-over-end in that direction.

I won't tease you and let you wonder whether Dusty and I would eventually make love or not. We would. When we did, it was as hot and gravity-shifting as you would expect from two young men with big cocks, athletic bodies, and the insatiable passion that comes from falling in love for the first time. It was even more intense given how falling in love during that era with another man who loved you back was a secret pleasure you never dared to dream would ever happen to you in this lifetime. Yes, we would make love. But, we would also fuck. Hard. And with abandon. It hadn't happened yet, however. I will let you know all about it in more detail than you would ever want to know. But, if you have been lucky enough to fall in love before, particularly when you are young, you know of what I speak. There is something so affecting about those first steps on the journey down that path you have no choice but to take, when your eyes, your heart, and your whole body are heavy with the ache of unconsummated passion.

The days of that first week of our new truth passed with a flurry of furtive glances and stolen embraces. Even in the throes of our burgeoning relationship, Dusty was measured and focused on all of his responsibilities. He continued to be a steady presence in his role as RA in a way that maintained order on the floor. Inasmuch as he was serious about me, he also was serious about not falling behind in his course load. Final exams hung over our heads like Swords of Damocles that would be dropping in just a few weeks. He also had two big papers and was determined to excel on all of them. I was disciplined in my own right, but Dusty inspired me to try even harder.

I stopped by his room the Monday before Thanksgiving to say I would be leaving the next afternoon. I was hitching a ride home with Daniel and his friend Mike, who had offered to swing by Hartford on their own way home and would be spending the night at my house before heading the rest of the way to Potomac the next morning. Dusty was in his room, reading and taking notes at his desk. I remember even now how sexy it was for me to see him engulfed in his course work. His mind was buried in a text on Ulysses, his expression serious. But, his face brightened at the sight of mine.

"I wanted to say, 'Happy Thanksgiving' in case we don't see each other," I said. "I'm leaving right after class tomorrow and won't be back until Sunday night."

He stood up from his desk and approached me as I stood at the door. He stuck his head out into the hallway and looked left and right to check if the coast was clear. Then, he leaned in close and gave me a soft kiss on my lips. "I'm going to miss you," he whispered into my ear.

My cock hardened.

"What's this?" he said with a sly smile as he stroked my boner through the outside of my khakis.

"You like it?"

"Very much," he murmured.

I closed my eyes. "Feels so good."

"For me, too."

"Happy Thanksgiving," I said.

"You already said that."

"Yeah? I forgot."

He stopped rubbing my cock and stepped back. It was too risky to do that for too long with so many of the guys up and about.

"How are you getting to the airport?" I asked, my cock still pulsating in my pants.

"I'm staying here," he said. "California's too far away for just for five days. I have some studying I want to do anyway." That may have been one of the reasons, though the cost of air travel in the 1950s would have been the biggest factor.

"That's crazy," I said. "Don't stay here. Come home with me and spend Thanksgiving with my family."

Dusty looked surprised, though pleased at the invitation. "I couldn't impose like that. But, thank you."

"No, seriously, my parents would love to have you. I mean it." It was the truth. My parents were the type of people who took great pride in not only having a wide circle of friends and a big social life, but in being perceived by others as having them as well. They were more than happy to have Daniel and Mike stop overnight on their way to Potomac. They would be even happier to have a handsome, young houseguest from California who had nowhere else to go for the holiday.

"You sure?" I could tell Dusty was warming to the idea and had recognized the potential for the same opportunities to be alone of which I had also thought. My mother said yes, of course, when I called her later even though I had never mentioned Dusty to her before. She assured me my friends were always welcome, that she would have Florence, our housekeeper, set an extra place at the table and make sure fresh sheets were on the extra bed in my room. With no further prodding, Dusty said yes.

When Daniel returned to our room later that evening, he paused a beat and stared at me, perplexed as I mentioned to him that Dusty would be driving back with us and celebrating Thanksgiving with me and my family.

"That's very nice of you," he said. "California's a long way to travel for turkey." I knew he wanted to say more, but didn't know what to say or how to say it. I was sure he was wondering why I was bringing Dusty of all people home to spend a major holiday with me and my family. Dusty was the RA, after all. He was the guy who was friendly with us, but not our friend. He was the guy who cracked down on loud noise and excessive alcohol consumption and otherwise enforced the rules of the campus housing authority. Of all the people you would invite to your home for a holiday because their family lived far away, Dusty was an unconventional choice – unless you knew the truth about us, which Daniel surely was beginning to suspect.

The next afternoon, we all piled into Mike's car, a '55 Chevy Bel Air. Mike and Daniel rode in the front with Dusty and me in the back. Was Daniel wondering why I hadn't been myself lately? Was he wondering what he had interrupted that night when he had entered the hallway and caught sight of Dusty grasping my arm? If he was thinking anything further, he wasn't saying it. But, it was obvious to me from the consternation on his face he knew something was up even if he wasn't certain what it was.

As we sat in the car waiting for Mike to load up the trunk, Anthony, Shorty, Sasquatch, and Freddy approached us. I rolled down the back window. Anthony peered inside at us, his eyes widening at the sight of Dusty and me sitting together in the back seat. He leaned in close to me and tugged on my earlobe. "You boys have a good holiday," he said, the corner of his lips curling into a smirk he shared with Shorty. I was so caught up in giddy anticipation at the prospect of being with Dusty for five days, I would not recall the glances exchanged by Anthony and Shorty until much later when I would look back through time and piece the past together through the lens of future events. For the moment, however, I couldn't be happier to be where I was and where I was going. As we pulled away, I waved at everyone and wished them all a Happy Thanksgiving, even Freddy.

☙

My parents' faces lit up when Dusty, Daniel, Mike, and I walked inside my house early that evening after the long car ride to Connecticut. My father slapped me on the back and shook my hand before shaking everyone else's. My mother hugged me first. Then she hugged each of the guys as if she knew them and repeated their names with a vivacious smile and a flirty twinkle in her eye. I had seen that flirtatiousness before when she entertained their own friends, but not mine. I found it mildly embarrassing, but was glad my parents were so welcoming and viewed my new college friends in an adult light they hadn't viewed my old high school friends. Their hospitality didn't surprise me, but their friendly informality did. I have mentioned before how I had hoped for greater closeness with my parents, and I was pleased to be getting some of what I wished for.

There is a special energy in a home when it is filled with young men of the age we were then, our youthful exuberance overflowing as we embarked on the wide open road of the future. I have three sons of my own. Whenever they returned for holidays and summer breaks during the years they were in college, I would relish the life and the spirit they brought home with them. It reminded me of how my friends and I were during the same stage of life as we crossed over the cusp of manhood, and I look back with fondness at that Thanksgiving.

I didn't like Mike much, as I have said. But even with him in the mix, it was great to have everyone at the dinner table in my childhood home, particularly Daniel and Dusty, who were both incredibly important to me. I could tell by my parents' faces how charmed they were by the company of four handsome young men as they asked questions and listened to us talk about the semester and life at Inverness. We were boisterous and overflowing with youthful vitality, and my parents couldn't help but bask in our radiance. My father had served martinis, which made everyone feel grown up. The alcohol fueled the flow of conversation, which grew faster and louder as the evening progressed. Even my younger sister, Kathy, who normally would have fled the table at the earliest opportunity, stayed and called up two friends to come over and join us. It was a great way to kick off the Thanksgiving break.

The evening wound down just after midnight. Daniel and Mike were staying in the upstairs guest room down the hall from my bedroom. Daniel had flashed me a perturbed look as he watched Dusty and me enter my bedroom. We exchanged glances, but I couldn't hold his gaze and looked away. No doubt he was wondering in wild disbelief whether Dusty and I would be fooling around once the door closed behind us. He wasn't the only one wondering. I was wondering myself.

Dusty and I made small talk as he unpacked his bag and we changed into our pajamas. His eyes wandered around my room. He gazed at the Brooklyn Dodgers baseball pennants on my wall, the Pan American airlines poster of Rome, and the Davy Crockett coonskin hat hanging on a hook next to the closet. I was a voracious reader even then, and he browsed through the titles of the books that filled the shelves along the wall next to my desk. He picked up the action figure of Tonto from the Lone Ranger standing on my dresser. He touched the sharp edges of my amethyst geodes, which were left over from an early adolescent phase when I had been an avid rock collector. He was curious about my various trophies from sports victories and the award I had received for the school newspaper essay I had written about the meaning of freedom. It had been picked up and reprinted in *The Reader's Digest*, which would turn out to be my first national writing credit. I had been very proud of that and blushed when Dusty expressed surprise I had never mentioned it to him and told me how impressed he was.

I also couldn't help but notice he had eyed the two twin beds separated by my nightstand. I handed him a towel, and he headed into my bathroom to brush his teeth and wash up. He kept the door open, and we continued chatting. When he was almost finished, he pulled his cock out and took a long leak while I watched and listened to his powerful stream striking the water in the bowl. My cock started to harden.

We grazed against each other as he left the bathroom, and my skin tingled where we had touched. My heart pounded with nervousness and anticipation as I brushed my teeth. When I stood before the toilet to urinate, it took me a few extra beats to get the flow going knowing he was watching and listening to me.

We continued with the pretense of small talk about the knick-knacks of my childhood and the glimpses they gave him into my prior life. But, both of us were thinking of the inevitability of what surely would be happening next. I took a deep breath to calm myself and left the bathroom. I walked over to the door to my bedroom and locked it, the sound of the steel bolt inside the lock mechanism reverberating in my ears.

Dusty was stretched out on top of his bed watching me as I approached him. I turned off the overhead light and sat on my bed. He sat up and faced me. From downstairs and down the hall, I could hear the murmur of low voices and the clamor of closing doors and closets as the rest of the house settled down for the night and as Florence finished cleaning up in the kitchen. Dusty and I didn't say anything. We just sat there and stared at each other, our knees almost touching, our faces illuminated by the reading lamp on my nightstand. It was inconceivable and vaguely terrifying finally to be alone behind the safety of a locked door with him. The sexual tension hung in the air as we teetered on the brink of the unknown that was sure to follow as soon as one of us had the courage to make the first move.

Dusty's eyes met mine, and he held them there. His gaze was serious and steady as he probed my innermost thoughts. His eyes were heavy with desire. His mouth was just the slightest bit open, and I was mesmerized by the fullness of his lips. It was hard to believe this beautiful human being who embodied every fantasy I ever had and ones I could not have dared to conceive was sitting across from me in my very own bedroom staring back at me with open lust.

He placed his right hand on my knee. His mouth wore the warmest smile. "You are so beautiful it almost hurts to look at you. I can't believe how lucky I am to be here with you."

I shook my head in disagreement. I was the one who was lucky, he was the one who was so beautiful. I wanted to say that thought out loud, but I was distracted by the sensation of my pounding heart. I took my right hand and slid it up his thigh. He leaned in to embrace me, and in the next motion, he was on top of me with all of his weight. Our cocks were stone hard and throbbing. We ground them into each other. Our tongues and our mouths mashed together in a wet fury of passion that came from the uncharted territory when love is new and you are embarking on a journey without any thought of direction, only the driving impulse to go. I kissed him with everything I had. I wanted to swallow him up inside me and be swallowed up in return.

Dusty and I had groped each other's body on the outside in our feverish embraces, both tonight and in the stolen moments of privacy back at Inverness. But, we had not yet explored what lay beneath our clothes other than that first night in the shower, when our cocks rose up to meet the other but neither of us dared to let them touch. That was about to change. My rock hard cock had broken through the confines of my pajamas without any manual assistance. No longer encumbered, it jutted straight out through the fly of my pajama bottoms, bobbing brazenly for attention.

He rolled over to his side and stroked the bare skin of my cock for the first time ever. We continued to kiss as his hands explored the exposed parts of my body that no one else had ever touched in a sexual way. He ran his left hand up and down my cock and around the ridge of its crown. He cupped my balls with his right hand and caressed them. He tugged softly on the hair that covered them and probed my taint with his middle finger.

"You have such a beautiful cock," he said, mesmerized by it.

"You have such beautiful hands," I said as I watched him explore the most intimate areas of my body.

He slid off the bed so that he was kneeling at my side and better able to secure a steadier grip on my cock. From just inches away, he inspected it up close in curious fascination. He squeezed it and released it. He inhaled the sexy, musky odor of my groin, a scent I had smelled before on my own hands, but not on anyone else's. As he held my balls with his left hand, he traced his finger up along the major dorsal vein that ran the length of my cock before branching out into the tributaries at the base.

"Your cock's so big, it needs this huge vein to feed it."

I smiled with a combination of amusement and desire. It was impossible not to. He moved his left hand up from my balls and gripped the base of my cock, which surged even harder. The shiny, purple knob glistened. Wet drops of pre-cum dribbled out of my dick hole in quick succession and slid to the curved base of the crown. He touched the tip of his index finger to the top of my cock and smeared the pre-cum in shiny circles.

"Somebody's enjoying this," he said.

"Maybe too much. You better be careful. I don't want things to end just as they're getting started."

"I know what I'm doing," he said. "I have one of these myself, you know." He squeezed my cock at the base and at the crown again. He milked several more drops of pre-cum from my dick hole. The smaller drops converged into one larger drop that he scooped up with a finger he stuck in his mouth and sucked clean.

I leaned back, but was not tempted to close my eyes. I wanted to watch and experience everything. He played with my balls with his left hand. With his right hand, he rubbed my cock up and down in a steady rhythm. By this point, I could only nod. I was too turned on to say anything. I lay there, hyper aware of my labored breath and beating heart that fed the sensations that emanated from my cock and tingled to the far outreaches of my body. I knew I wasn't going to be able to last much longer. My body twisted with pleasure. Our eyes locked, and the rumble in my loins passed the point of no return. I gasped as a large ribbon of semen shot out of me. It spouted into the air before landing with a splatter across my chest. The next burst shot even higher, spraying across me in the same way. The final series followed with diminishing intensity until there was no more left.

As soon as he squeezed the last drop of cum out of my dick hole, he stood up abruptly and dropped his pajama bottoms to his knees. His long, thick, golden banana of a cock bounced out of them and stood at rigid attention, curving up towards the ceiling. He closed his eyes and began stroking it furiously. I was spent, but there was no way I was going to let him finish on his own. I scraped my right hand across my stomach and my chest, scooping up a handful of the still-warm semen that covered me. I pushed his hand away from his cock and wrapped my hand around it, coating it with warm, slippery wetness.

"Fuck, that feels incredible!" he exclaimed.

I swung my legs around on the bed so I was sitting up and my legs were wrapped around his. With his cock slathered in my cum, my hand glided up and down the length of his shaft. I had never touched another cock before. It felt strange to grab someone else's, yet familiar at the same time. I slid my left hand down to the base and placed the bottom of my right on top of the left, end-on-end, encasing his cock inside it. As I alternated the pressure of my grip, he began to fuck the well-lubricated sheath I created with my cum-slathered hands.

"God," he gasped as his hips pumped steadily. "I can't take any more of this." With no other warning than that, he shot a large plume of cum that landed on my cheek and then another that landed on my forehead and streaked through my hair. The remaining fluid spurted onto my bare chest and dribbled down to my treasure trail. He closed his eyes and shuddered before dropping down next to me on my bed. I looked down at my hands to examine the gooey mixture of our cum. I lifted my palm up to my face to examine the smear of white fluid. I brought my hand closer to my face and inhaled as deeply as I could.

He laughed softly. "We made quite a mess."

With his eyes on mine, I brought my hand to my mouth and tasted it with a big, long lick. That it was Dusty's cum and mine converged together made me want to swallow every drop. He smirked as he watched me take another lick. Then, he grabbed my hand and brought it to his face. He took a big, long slurp from the base of my palm up to the tips of my fingers. He paused a moment to contemplate the taste and the sensation on his palate. He looked into my eyes again and then leaned in to kiss me, swirling his cum-covered tongue together with mine. I kissed him back, and we snuggled together until I started to doze off.

By now, the remnants of the cum that streaked my body had turned cold. I was exhausted from the long day that had started in Vermont and had ended here in my childhood bedroom where I had just fooled around with an extraordinarily sexy guy with a beautiful cock, a beautiful body, and a beautiful heart. I wanted him in every possible way and had no question he felt the same about me, the knowledge of which made everything feel even better. Before I fell asleep, I got up and grabbed a towel that I used to wipe the sweat and remaining cum from Dusty's body and from my own. Dusty kissed me goodnight and crawled under the covers of his bed.

"Good night," I said after I turned out the light. I stared into the darkness with sleep already descending upon me.

"I love you," he said.

"I love you, too."

൏

In the morning, I left my room early and went downstairs in my bathrobe to make breakfast for Daniel and Mike before they set out on the remainder of the drive to Potomac. I had taken a long, lingering look at Dusty as he slept and could hardly believe this staggeringly incredible human being I loved more than I could ever imagine was right here in the room of my boyhood and that last night we had shared what we had shared. Kissing him, holding him, jerking him off, and getting jerked off like that may very well have been the highlight of my entire life up until that point. It was amazing to me all of it had happened and how lucky I was that it had. I grinned broadly in the darkness. I had been careful not to wake him even though I had awoken with a hard-on and would have crawled into bed with him if it hadn't been so early and I didn't need to see Daniel and Mike off.

I turned on the coffee percolator and tried to make as little noise as possible as I pulled out a Thermos from the cabinet. I was quiet as I opened the refrigerator and reached for roast beef to make sandwiches for Daniel and Mike to take with them on the rest of their journey. Daniel, however, had smelled the coffee wafting upstairs and soon was downstairs in the kitchen with me. He was fully dressed and his packed bag was at his side.

"Good morning!" I said with more eagerness than was wise if I were going to maintain a level of discretion about my excitement at finally having an opportunity to be with Dusty and be able to do with him what I wanted to do. But, I couldn't help myself. After all of the ups and downs I had had, I was just too damn happy.

Daniel, however, did not share my happiness. I could tell from the quickness with which he had said "Good morning" back to me that he was prickly this morning. He was habitually an early riser, so I knew the early hour was not the cause of his irritation.

I pulled out an iron skillet and turned up the gas on the stove. "How do you want your eggs? Scrambled or fried?"

He looked straight at me, searching for the truth in my eyes. "What's going on here? Is there something I should know about?"

"I don't know what you're talking about. Pour yourself some coffee. Scrambled or fried?"

"Scrambled, and you know damn well what I am talking about," he said, lowering his voice for the last half of that sentence and jabbing his index finger in the direction of the bedrooms upstairs.

I had turned away to reach for a mixing bowl and a whisk, but I turned back to him and returned his stare. "Nothing. Nothing is going on."

"Don't bullshit me, John. It's all very weird how you and Dusty are so tight all of a sudden. He's the RA for God's sake, not one of us."

"He didn't have anywhere to go for Thanksgiving."

"Why did you lock the door? I could hear it lock, you know. I'm not stupid. Mike and I didn't need to lock our door."

"Habit, I guess."

He lowered his voice. "Are you guys fooling around? Were you up there butt fucking or something?"

"No, we weren't. I swear." At least the part about not butt fucking was still true.

There was the sound of steps on the staircase. In a moment, Mike was in the kitchen with us. Daniel's eyes searched mine as I offered Mike coffee and the same breakfast choices I had offered Daniel. I could tell Daniel wasn't buying any of this.

He was not going to let it go until he knew the truth, which I was not prepared to tell him. His tone and manner abruptly turned jovial as soon as Mike joined us, however. We all made small talk about their impending drive home and how all of us were glad to be away from school. Yet, I knew by the sideways glances Daniel shot me when Mike wasn't looking that he was irritated by my evasiveness, and the jollity he was projecting for Mike's benefit was just an act.

While Daniel and Mike finished up their breakfast, I packed them a box of roast beef sandwiches wrapped in waxed paper and several bottles of Coca-Cola. As I poured a large Thermos of coffee for them, Dusty wandered into the kitchen wearing the same pajamas I had pulled off of him last night. I noticed immediately he was not wearing any underwear and his big dick was flopping from side-to-side as he walked.

"Morning, fellas," Dusty said as he reached for the percolator to pour himself a cup of coffee. His curly hair was even more tousled than usual. His eyes were heavy-lidded, and he had a wide, open smile across his face I don't think he could have wiped off if he tried. There was a rosy glow about him, and he had the undeniable demeanor of someone who just woke up after a languid, erotic night. If I had known Daniel was going to choose this moment to cross-examine me about what was going on between Dusty and me, I would have warned Dusty to tone it down. But, there had been no way to warn him Daniel was on to us, and I had not previously confided in Dusty my fears that Daniel had been simmering with suspicion about us for the past couple of weeks.

With his back to the other guys, Daniel nodded his head in Dusty's direction and shot me an arched-eyebrow look of incredulity. "Someone's looking pretty well-oiled, don't you think?" he said in a whisper that was audible only to me.

I glanced over at Dusty and then back at Daniel, but didn't say anything. What could I say? The truth? How could I possibly do that?

Daniel's eyes were dark as he mouthed the words, "When I get back, we are going to talk."

I shrugged in resignation. *Great,* I thought. Daniel was on to me and now knew with every certainty short of an admission on my part that I had not been straight with him in more than one sense of the word. I could tell he was angry about it and that this was not the last of it. This was not going to be a conversation I was looking forward to at all. Daniel had been angry enough at me before to threaten to get a new roommate. Would he be angry enough to end our friendship? Would he make me move out of our room if he had confirmation of the truth about Dusty and me? It was not anything I wanted to think about.

Any regret I may have felt at how my secret was likely to be spilled dissipated as I looked over at Dusty. I slid him a plate of scrambled eggs, bacon, and toast across the counter. Our eyes met, and no words needed to be exchanged between us. I had dreamed before what it would be like to connect with another human being with such love and passion. But, I had never expected it to feel as sublime and spectacular as it felt right now. How could I be so lucky as to share a morning after with someone as extraordinary as Dusty? How was it possible Dusty was sitting here having breakfast - in pajamas with no underwear - in the very kitchen I had eaten breakfast almost every morning of my whole life without anything even close to being this exciting? I would have to deal with Daniel later. As troubled as I was about the prospective ramifications with him, it was hard to think about anything else right now other than how I wanted to run back upstairs to my bedroom with Dusty and lock the door behind us as soon as Daniel and Mike left.

Dusty stayed in the kitchen when I walked outside in the cold wearing only my bathrobe and slippers to say goodbye to Daniel and Mike as the sun of a November dawn rose just below tree level. We returned to the small talk of how long the drive would take and what time on Sunday they would swing by to pick us up for the return trip to Inverness. I handed Daniel the box of food and the Thermos of coffee I had prepared for them. Daniel's handsome face was twisted in a frown, and Mike was oblivious to the dynamic of the triangle between Daniel, Dusty, and me.

I knew Daniel wanted to say things he couldn't say with Mike sitting right there in the driver's seat, and I was glad he could not say them. I still cared very deeply for Daniel, but I had another distraction who was waiting for me inside. It was only when Daniel rolled up the window and stared back at me through the glass without averting his eyes that I realized it had not been anger at all with which he had been looking at me this morning. He had been looking at me with a confused despair and wounded heartbreak he did not fully understand and was struggling to process. His gaze softened, and he did not look away until the car turned and obscured his line of sight.

I watched until the Chevy had driven off before I turned to go back into the house. I wondered about Daniel and whether my realization about him was correct. Could it be? I shook my head. It was too much to think about at this moment. Dusty and all of his charged-up hotness was sitting in my parents' kitchen. I had plans for him today that involved nudity, boners, and multiple ejaculations. My cock was rock hard before I reached the top of the brick steps that led me through the back door and into the kitchen. Dusty looked up at me with the broad, loving grin and the impossibly blue eyes that stared back at me with open desire. He noticed my boner right away and laughed. A circle of pre-cum had escaped from my dick hole and formed a wet blot where my engorged cock head met the comically stretched cotton of my pajama bottoms. He leaned in and kissed me, grabbing my cock as he did.

I smiled as our lips met. "Let's go back up to my room before my parents wake up."

He kissed me again and led me by my hard cock as we raced up the stairs and into my room, closing the door behind us.

13 EXPLORERS

NOW THAT WE were back in the safety of my room, I pulled Dusty's pajama bottoms down as soon as I heard the sound of the door lock. His hefty boner bobbed heavily from side-to-side. I unbuttoned his top, my fingers fumbling in a near-frenzied effort to get him naked.

His cock was a truly glorious example of divine engineering, and I slithered my hand around it thinking it was the best thing I had ever touched in my whole life. While I was exploring its length, contours, and ridges, he pulled my pajama bottoms down. I dropped my robe and lifted my T-shirt over my head. We stood there face-to-face, naked, our cocks hard and throbbing, just as they had that night in the showers when we later shared our first kiss. I have said before how beautiful Dusty's body was: his v-shaped torso, taut muscles, and flawless, golden skin. While I was never the prime specimen he was, my own body was in its heyday then. I was an even six feet tall with a medium build. I was tightly muscled and my stomach was lean and flat with the trace of a six pack, something that is hard to imagine today that I ever had.

We were silent as we stood there, each of us taking in the magnificence of the other's body and the indescribable luxury of having a fantasy-come-true standing before us. Dusty's thick cock curved up to the ceiling in all of its glory. My cock jutted out towards him, the purple knob of my glans as hard and shiny as it ever gets. I admired the breadth of his shoulders, the warm brown of his nipples, and the treasure trail that encircled the indentation of his belly button and lead straight down to the briar of brown pubic hair around his cock. He squeezed his Kegel muscles and caused his cock to throb in a luridly comic way.

I did the same, and we both giggled at the sight of them bobbing at each other.

He reached out and swirled his hands around my pecs and then slid them down across the plains of my stomach on their way to my hard cock. He stroked the length and underside of it, running his thumb in tight circles across the crown. It felt so good, I stopped smiling and looked with the heaviness of arousal straight into his eyes. Still holding my cock in his right hand, he pressed his left hand across my chest and pushed me backwards until I fell onto my bed, bouncing as I hit the mattress.

He knelt down before me. "You have the most beautiful cock," he said. "It's so straight and perfectly proportioned. And so thick." He tightened his grip around the base, which caused the head to engorge with blood and a drop of pre-cum to emerge from the slit of my dick hole. He touched his finger to the drop and then slowly lifted it up. We both watched in curious fascination as the tip of his outstretched finger and the opening of my cock were connected by a thin wet thread of pre-cum that glistened when caught by the light. The thread broke and another drop appeared at the opening, ready to spill over and join the rest. He leaned his head down and nestled the arched tip of his tongue into the slit of wetness and flicked it back and forth. I could feel another drop of pre-cum emerge as his tongue coaxed it out of me.

Without any further warning, his mouth widened and he slid it down over the wet, shiny head of my cock. He held it there as he swirled his tongue in lazy circles before sliding down the rest of the shaft, taking all of it into his mouth at once.

I gasped. I had never had my cock in anyone's mouth except my own, and even that had been only an inch past the crown and only for a contorted moment or two a few times when

I had thrown my legs over my head on this very bed and tried to suck my own cock without any meaningful success. Dusty's mouth was a warm, wet sleeve of pleasure that enveloped my cock with exhilarating sensations. He glided up and down in a steady rhythm that united our bodies in the most magical way. The combination of the heat of his mouth, the pressure of his tongue, and the wetness of skin-to-skin contact thrust me up to a high plateau I had never attained with my own hands. The intensity of the pleasure was greater than I had imagined, and I was alarmed to feel the genesis of that familiar rumbling from within me so soon. I was greedy for the pleasure to last longer – much longer – and was not yet ready for it to end.

"It feels way too good," I said. "Slow down or else I'm going to blow."

He raised himself from his knees and climbed onto the bed and kissed me. His tongue slid into my mouth and swirled around my own. His mouth had the erotic, manly taste of my pre-cum mixed with the warm spit with which he had lubricated my cock. As delicious as that was, I was driven to try something I had always wanted to do: suck a cock other than my own. I sat up and swiveled my torso around so my head was at Dusty's groin, my face just inches from it. I grabbed the base of his cock with my right hand and pointed it in the direction of my mouth. While most of my masturbatory fantasies about cock sucking had me on the receiving end, I was very curious to have one in my mouth nonetheless.

Dusty's cock was a big one, with a large and rounded head that was shiny and smooth in full, aroused engorgement. It surprised me how wide I needed to open my mouth to take all of him in, but I was more than up for the challenge. He moaned as I closed my lips around his dick head and formed a tight, wet seal. His cock surged, and I could feel with my tongue and the insides of my cheeks he was growing even more engorged. It tasted of the smooth and salty pre-cum leaking from him. I inhaled, surprised at how powerful an effect his musky odor had on me. It made me want to swallow him up all of the way, and I opened my mouth wider. I slid it down his shaft until the tip of his cock touched the back of my mouth.

I have always had a quick gag reflex and should not have been as surprised as I was when my throat seized and an angry geyser of bile shot up from my stomach. I coughed and choked. My eyes teared, and I wiped my mouth with the back of my hand. I sat up to pull myself back together.

Dusty laughed. "Take it easy, cowboy. Breathe through your nose."

I laughed - and coughed again - and was relieved I had only gagged and had not vomited all over him. I was determined to get this right, and after I rinsed my mouth with water, I was back at it. I closed my eyes and wrapped my lips around the head of his cock. I swirled my tongue around it. The wetness and salty taste of his pre-cum made my own cock surge. I slid my mouth further down his cock, slower this time, and I remembered to breathe through my nose. It worked. I was able to move my head up and down him with steady consistency. He was too large for me take him all the way in during this first encounter. But, I would later learn to do it like a pro.

I had always thought the ultimate pleasure of cock sucking would be borne by the recipient, but I was finding it incredibly pleasurable to pleasure him in this way. As I settled into an unbroken rhythm, I cupped and coddled his balls with my hand. He hummed with pleasure and ran his fingers through my hair as my head bobbed up and down.

"I want to have you inside my mouth," he said, twisting his head and grabbing my cock, which had been throbbing with the pulse of my heart as I experienced the innumerable pleasures of having him in my mouth. In a single, hungry motion, his mouth found my cock again. In almost perfect synchronicity, our mouths rose and descended on each other. Using my hands, I continued to explore his balls, which were pulled up snug against his body. He gripped my butt cheeks firmly in his hands and pulled me in deeper, all the way to the bottom.

I gasped and pulled my mouth off of him. Having my cock sucked for the first time was a fantasy come true. To be deep-throated like this by him was beyond any dream I had ever had. His grip on my ass cheeks was tight, and I could not have pulled away even if I had wanted too. I brought my mouth back to his

cock and began to suck it again. But, I had barely returned when he began to moan and suck on my cock even harder and faster.
"I'm going to cum!" he said.
I lifted up my head to watch the semen shoot out of him. Just as when I had jerked him off last night, the first spurts shot upwards in impressive arcs over my head and onto the bed. The next several landed on my face and dribbled onto my chest. As he came, his mouth remained wrapped around my cock with diligent dedication to the task at hand. I wanted to hold out for longer in my greediness for the ecstasy never to end. But, I had ceded control to him of my power to ejaculate. He now owned it to a degree I had not thought could be possible by another person. He gripped my ass tighter, and the sensation of my cheeks spreading caused me to pass the point of no return.
"Fuck! I'm cumming!" I said in warning so he could pull his head away.
But, he didn't pull his head away. To the contrary, he sucked even harder and deeper, burying his face against my pubic bone. My cum was suctioned out of my body by him as much as it was shot out of me. He gulped and swallowed every drop as my body writhed and squirmed in the throes of an orgasm more powerful than any I had ever experienced in my whole life, and I had experienced plenty by my own hands in this very bed. My face twisted in ecstatic disbelief, I watched his throat squeeze and contract as he swallowed the load I was pumping down his throat.
My chest heaved, and my body trembled. But, all too soon, the ecstatic sensations of the orgasm I never wanted to end came to an end. He looked up at me, shaking his head with a huge, satisfied smile across his face.
"Fuck, that was hot," he said.
I leaned in and kissed him. "I love you."
"I love you, too."
That was the first of five times we would cum together that day. Now that I had had my cock sucked once, I had an insatiable gluttony for more. But, it was not just the messy confection of cum, sweat, and the inexplicable magic of an orgasm that fed my hunger. It was the experience of sharing it

with Dusty, an exquisite human being I loved more than I ever thought possible to love someone. We would leave the Eden of my boyhood bedroom that day for food and forays into the outside world so my parents wouldn't wonder what the hell was going on up there. But, I knew even then my life had changed in ways that meant there could be no turning back.

☙

The next day was Thanksgiving, and it began in a way like no other Thanksgiving had in my entire life: a jerk-off contest with someone other than just me. It was my idea, though Dusty needed no convincing whatsoever to sign up. The objective was to race from a resting, flaccid state to ejaculation in the shortest amount of time while the other held a stopwatch and monitored how fast it took. I offered to go first and removed my pajamas.

As soon as Dusty said, "Go," I was out of the starting gate. I tugged and twisted my soft cock until it became hard, which was near instantaneous. With him cheering me on, it took me a minute and fifteen seconds until I shot a moderate and not particularly satisfying load that went no further than my belly button.

Then, he dropped his pajamas and handed me the stop watch.

I said, "Go," and he started rubbing his cock. As always, it was a mesmerizing sight to behold as it filled with blood and expanded from limp to full-sized in only seconds. As he stroked it, he reached over to me with his free hand and scooped up a handful of cum that had pooled around my belly button.

"Hey, that's cheating!" I said as he slathered it on his cock.

He laughed and shortly thereafter squirted out a modest load comparable to mine after a total of one minute and three seconds. "It's not cheating," he said, not even out of breath. "There weren't any prohibitions on lubricant."

I looked at him with mock outrage. "You won, but I demand a rematch later," I said as I reached over and smeared his cum in circles across his belly.

He kissed me, and I could not imagine being happier that he - and his hefty cock - was here at my disposal in my boyhood bedroom for the entire holiday weekend. I had a lot to be thankful for.

❧

After we showered and readied ourselves for the day, I called Allison, my high school girlfriend. You may have forgotten about her by now. I had mentioned her at the beginning when I had recounted how I had creamed in my pants as we fooled around right before I left for Inverness and she left for Georgetown. We had kept in touch over the semester through letter writing and phone calls, and we had made plans to attend our high school homecoming football game together.

I am sure you have guessed that if my feelings for Allison were as strong as they were for Daniel or Dusty you would have heard more about her. That is not to suggest she was not important to me - she was - but my life was heading in directions different from the life I had led in West Hartford. As anxious as each of us was to break the bonds of childhood and find our respective ways in the outside world, I welcomed the tie to my prior life and found a steady comfort with her and the connection to home.

Dusty and I drove over to pick her up along with another girl whose name I honestly can't remember after all of these years. I was happy to see Allison and reconnect with my past, without doubt. I was also happy to see old friends from home at the football game even though I had the sense everyone was moving on and things would never be the same. I would stay in touch with a few of them for a year or two longer, and then we would all drift away from each other with no one from my childhood having the draw that could compare to any of The Magnificent Seven.

Allison and her family were spending Thanksgiving at her grandparents' home in Old Saybrook, Connecticut, and she had to leave immediately after the game. I dropped her off back at her house without getting out of the car. Before going inside, she leaned in the window. She gave me a quick kiss on the lips and reminded me of the party she was having for a bunch of our high school friends on Saturday, which Dusty and I were planning to attend. She walked inside, and I was relieved I hadn't had to see her father after what had happened the last time I had seen him.

The rest of the day was a typical Thanksgiving. We watched the Detroit Lions beat the Green Bay Packers eighteen to six in black and white on what was only the second nationally televised Thanksgiving football game ever. My parents hosted twenty-five assorted friends and relatives. Dusty and I escaped upstairs to fool around as we had before. I could not have been happier.

What I remember most about that Thanksgiving is not just the frequency of cock play we were able to accomplish in the haven of my locked bedroom. Sure, that was a big part of it. But, what made it even better was the time we were able to spend together. We slept in the same room. We shared all of our meals together. We had hours just to talk and goof around when we weren't busy with our hands down each other's pants and our cocks down each other's throat. I drove him around town to show him where I had grown up. I introduced him to my friends. He lazed around the house with my family, who had welcomed and adored him from the moment he walked in the door. At a time in my life and in history when people like me and Dusty and what we felt for each other was condemned as abnormal and mentally sick, to be able to do something together as utterly normal and mundane as a visit home for a holiday imbued me with a glow of happiness even if my family had no idea of the true nature of our relationship.

My father was a stockbroker, and he had a standing game of squash on Fridays at the Hartford Athletic & Social Club with a fellow stockbroker named Bud Anderson. Squash habitually was followed by lunch and cocktails. The Friday after Thanksgiving is a trading day, so my father's match with Bud was still on. Before he left for the office that morning, he invited Dusty and me to join them at the club for a match of doubles. I was surprised, but openly pleased at the invitation. Squash was a game I played with my friends, but never with my father. Despite our differences in temperament and interests, I was perpetually hungry for more time with him. He was unswervingly busy with work, his social life, and my mother, which meant there almost never was any time for me. Even though I knew the invitation to the club arose principally out of courtesy to Dusty as our houseguest, I welcomed it just the same.

The squash matches were vigorous and fun. We played four of them over the course of a little more than an hour, with my father and Bud winning the first two and Dusty and I winning the other two. Dusty and I had never played before together, nor had my father and I. It was great to be with both of them and particularly great to integrate Dusty in my life outside of Inverness. I could tell by the eagerness and warm tone with which my father introduced me and Dusty to other members of the club that he was pleased to have us under his charge. It was a pride I would not fully understand until I had sons of my own and would have the pleasure of introducing them to others in the same way. Bud was an easy-going guy with a bawdy sense of humor who poked fun at my father in a jovial, familiar way that was amusing to me given the more formal barriers between fathers and sons in that era, ones I was careful not to create with my own sons.

After squash and before lunch, Bud suggested a swim in the club's pool. Dusty and I, however, decided to have a run on the indoor track while my father and Bud took a swim. I had never been swimming in the club's pool before, but it was no surprise to me the swimmers were all men and all nude. I am sure people today would be surprised to learn that before the 1960s and '70s, indoor swimming pools were usually segregated by gender and males almost always swam nude when women weren't around. It was the same whether you were at the YMCA, school gym class, universities, and private clubs like the Hartford Athletic & Social Club, which did not permit women as members or guests until forced to by law in the 1970s. All of the swimming I had done at the local YMCA, my high school, and Inverness was in the nude. I find it ironic today to look back on that conservative era when there were so many legal and social restrictions on public and private behaviors, particularly of the sort in which people of my ilk were interested. Yet, naked men could glide through water with other naked men with total freedom from all of the other restrictions that life imposed on them. You just didn't think anything of it, that's just how it was.

The hygienic practices of the time required a full, soaped-up shower before jumping in the pool, and that's what Bud and my dad did. Bud was in his forties with a bit of flab around his belly and an average-sized circumcised cock. He had a doughy, good ole boy look and the suggestion he had likely been cute in his college days. He probably still would have been if he hadn't let himself go as much as he had, unlike my father who still had his body and his looks. They stripped down at our lockers and headed to the showers without towels. The shower was a gang shower, of course, a much larger one than the shower back in our dorm at Inverness. It was a big, square tiled room with showerheads that sprouted from outer walls and from an interior bank of walls that rose only half-way up to the ceiling.

Dusty and I headed upstairs to the indoor track, which was on an open mezzanine that hugged the perimeter of the wall and overlooked the pool area. The pool was spectacular, of the type you don't see much of anymore except in old spa towns in Europe that were constructed in previous centuries. It was a large, rectangular aquatic oasis of inlaid tile in a grand open space with a soaring ceiling. The entire building was a beautiful example of early twentieth century architecture that was designed as a monument to civilization, like Grand Central Station and the old Penn Station in New York except on a smaller scale.

Dusty and I ran in tandem along the track and took in the sight of men of various ages and shapes swimming laps in the pool in the unencumbered freedom of being totally naked. It felt so great to be running with him at my side and hear the steadiness of our steps and the rhythmic heaviness of our breathing. As much as I was enjoying the sexual expeditions of the weekend, I was enjoying the intimacy of the non-sexual time I was spending bonding with Dusty just as much. It was unspoken, but I knew from the way I would catch him looking at me he felt the same way.

"Hey, there's your father and Bud," Dusty said, pointing to them below. They each were naked and were strolling casually out to the pool, their cocks and bare asses out in open view.

"You know, your dad is h-o-t hot," Dusty said, looking at me with a devious smirk.

"Stop it! He is not. He's old!"

"He's not old. What is he, forty-one?"

I sighed. "Forty-two." At eighteen, forty-two seemed so old.

"Forty-two is hot," Dusty said. "Your father still has it going on."

"Yeah, if you like older guys."

"Don't knock older guys – ahem!"

"You're only a few years older than me. It's not the same thing."

"Older guys are sexy. They've done it all before. They know what they want and are confident. Plus, your father has a mean ass and a nice, long, thick cock. Like father, like son."

I laughed and squirmed at the same time. "Would you stop?"

"I can't help it. I had to check him out in the locker room. I wanted to see which side of the family you got your size from. Could be his. Actually, his might be a little thicker. Look how it bounces lazily from side-to-side as he walks."

I looked down below while Dusty ribbed me about my father. "Enough about my father's cock! You're making my skin crawl."

"Just admit that it's big."

I jabbed my elbow into his ribs. "Yes, I admit it is big. Enough already!"

"Do you think your dad and Bud ever fooled around?"

"No!"

"No boner contests?"

"No!"

"No sword fights or towel snapping that went too far?"

"No!"

I was happy my father had such a close friend in Bud. But, the thought of anything like Dusty was suggesting made me squeamish, and I didn't want to entertain any such thoughts.

With our eyes still on them, they reached the edge of the pool. Bud knelt down and slipped into the water. He rose up above the surface and then down below it again giving us a clear view of his smooth, but otherwise unremarkable ass. My father stepped up onto one of the racing blocks and bent down to touch his toes in preparation for a racing dive into the water. He had been a strong athlete in his day and still had the body and form that suggested he had been.

"Holy crap!" Dusty said, reaching for my elbow and holding onto it as we ran. "There is a god. Look at your dad's beautiful ass and that sweet hairy crack! You can see his balls dangling between his legs as he's bending over!"

I didn't want to look, but I couldn't help myself. I am embarrassed to admit this even in these pages. But, I had to confess that yes, my dad did have a big, thick cock with a set of hefty, hairy balls. And his ass was a full, rounded, meaty ass that would be considered quite grabbable if forty-two wasn't too old for you. And, yes, from an objective point of view, he was very handsome. He was tall and dark-haired like me. But, he had eyes that were a gun metal gray and a square-jawed New England WASPy look that was befitting of someone with our shared ancestry even if the chisel of those looks somehow had softened when they reached me. I had no sexual interest in my father, of course. But, I will be honest and admit that as I was growing up, his cock held a certain fascination to me as I became aware of the changes going on in my maturing body. I stole glances at it whenever I could and was sometimes hypnotized at how large it seemed to me before I caught up with him in size.

I thought about Dusty's question regarding whether I thought Bud and my father had ever fooled around. It didn't occur to me for a second that they had. I watched my Dad dive into the water and tried to ignore how his bare ass shifted from side-to-side with each stroke of the crawl. I saw how Bud had caught up to him in the adjacent lane and how they swam together in naked unison from one end of the pool to the other and then back again. I had always wanted to know my father better, and you have to understand that in the 1950s, fathers had different familial interactions than they do today. I had always wanted more from him than he had been willing or able to give me.

As I think back in the present how I ran side-by-side on the indoor track with Dusty while down below my father swam nude in the pool with his own pal in parallel lanes, I hoped my father and Bud had the type of friendship where they experienced the close bonds of male camaraderie I experienced with guys in my dorm back at Inverness. Then as now, there is a paucity of friendships in the lives of adult men. Without those friendships, the world can be a lonely place, and it very often is. At least that is how I have felt during extended periods in my adult life and one of the reasons why I so cherish my memories of The Magnificent Seven.

After Dusty and I had finished up a quick two mile run, we decided to relax in the steam room before lunch. We changed and went straight in after rinsing off in the showers. After a few minutes, my father and Bud joined us. We relaxed in the wet heat together for not more than ten or fifteen minutes, each of us sitting naked on our open towels. Bud made some chest-thumping comments about a rematch of the squash game next time Dusty and I were both in town. My father talked about the Lions – Packers game we had watched on television. Until the steam got to be too intense, the four of us relaxed and lingered in the punishing environment bonding in a way you can only do when you have been stripped of every artifice: clothes, pretense, hierarchy, interfamilial order and every other restriction the world imposes on men so that they know and remain in their designated places.

This was still a work day for Bud and my father, and they had to return to the office. We headed for the showers together without reservation or any measure of self-consciousness as we soaped up our bodies, the hair on our heads, and washed our cocks and asses. Bud and my father left the showers first, and we followed behind them. Dusty tortured me by making feigned blow job gestures in my dad's direction while my dad's back was turned and his hairy ass was exposed when he bent over to dry his toes. Luckily, I was spared any more torment once we were dressed and headed up to the dining room for lunch.

MY BARE NAKED HEART

After a meal of pea soup and steak sandwiches, Bud and my father each had a second scotch before they returned to the office. Dusty and I returned to the locker room. We rinsed off in the showers before heading out to the pool naked, of course. The strong smell of chlorine stung my nose. Just three other men were swimming laps. Dusty and I stood before two empty lanes that were adjacent to each other and stepped up on to the starting blocks. Even though there was not supposed to be anything sexy about swimming in the nude here, there was.

As Dusty stood on the starting platform in all of his naked glory, I thought of how utterly beautiful he was. It takes my breath away even now to think about the perfection of his body, the confidence in his gaze, the size and heft of his cock, and the untamed pubes that cushioned it. I had held him up on a pedestal in so many literal and figurative ways, and here he was standing on a real one right next to me. His shaggy blond hair, lean v-shaped torso, solid biceps, and the curves of his high, tight ass were on full display. He smiled and looked back at me in the same adoring way. Without shame, he took a healthy glimpse of my cock with an openness and a knowing sense of ownership.

I smiled back, and I imagine my smile was as big and happy as it ever gets. The time I had spent with Dusty over these past several days had been, without question, the very best days of my entire life. I was experiencing a world I had never dared to dream I would experience, and I never wanted any of it to end.

Dusty dove in first. I waited the extra second or two to watch his lithe, naked body sail through the air, his cock flailing until gravity caused it to point down towards the water. He pierced the surface, and I followed the crack of his ass as he glided underwater. I dove in after him, my body jolting at the shock of the chill. I used the momentum of the dive to fuel my underwater glide, which I followed with the dolphin kick and then the breast stroke, which I maintained without letting my head pierce the surface. I was not the best athlete in every circumstance, but my endurance was one skill I had that let me beat out better athletes. In that regard, I could hold my breath and swim the entire length of the pool underwater. When I reached the shallow end, I touched the side and shot up through the surface, gasping.

"Very impressive, Mr. Branson," Dusty said. "I can't do that."

I shrugged as my lungs heaved, and I tried to catch my breath. "Endurance is my secret weapon."

After a long moment, Dusty and I turned around and swam the crawl back to the other end of the pool. For the next twenty minutes, we swam steady laps. I had never seen Dusty swim before, but it did not surprise me that a child of the California sun who surfed in the Pacific would swim so well and so expertly. I have to confess I can find swimming monotonous if I do it for too long. But, Dusty's strokes were perfect, measured, steady, and strong. He swam with such powerful grace and synchronicity in all of his naked glory, there was nothing monotonous about watching him swim at all.

I tired of the physical activity before he did, my general endurance notwithstanding. I lifted myself out of the pool and rested my bare ass on the wet tile of the pool's perimeter with my legs in the water until he finished his last lap.

"Hit the showers?" I asked.

"Let's," he said, not knowing the showers were only the start of what I had in mind.

By now, in the middle of a Friday afternoon sandwiched between Thanksgiving and the holiday weekend, the vast showers of this downtown club were empty except for us. Still without towels, we strolled bare-assed to the nozzles in the middle of the maze of the massive shower room. We soaped and showered under the water that was far warmer than the colder water of the pool. We lingered under the rain of warm water. Without touching myself, my cock hardened. Dusty noticed almost immediately.

"What do we have here?" he said, stepping closer and cradling it in his hands.

"My big, hard, cock," I said, leaning in to kiss him as the water cascaded down upon us.

"I think your cock is your secret weapon, not your endurance."

Dusty squatted down onto the tiled floor with his knees up and his open crack exposed to the shower floor and the water that swirled down towards the drain. I leaned back against the wetness of the tile as he took my hard cock straight into his mouth, sliding it in a single motion all the way to the back. I moaned from the depths of my body as he deep-throated me. His mouth bobbed back and forth, his tongue swirling over the contours of my cock. With his right hand, he cradled my balls and rubbed his middle finger between my thighs.

"Fuck, you're so good at this!"

I closed my eyes. He massaged my taint, which was slippery from the soap. As the pleasure mounted, I was aware his finger had continued to travel in a new direction. It was sliding back and forth against the wet slit of my asshole, a sensation that was foreign to me. What he did next caught me completely off guard. In a steady, confident motion, he slid his wet finger straight into my hole and buried it all the way up until it met his palm.

I opened my eyes and gasped in disbelief. I had played with my ass a few times before and had even stuck my own finger in once or twice to see what it felt like. But, honestly, it had never done much for me. It hadn't felt bad or unpleasant. It just hadn't felt like much of anything. This was different, however. Some of the shame of the feelings I had about my same sex attractions was the sense the ass was a bad, dirty place. That it could be a source of pleasure somehow seemed very wrong to me. As Dusty slid his finger in and out of my hole and probed my insides to the limits of what a finger could do, it did not feel wrong at all. In fact, it felt way too good. There was no way I could hold out much longer.

He then touched something inside me I had not known was there, but would later realize was the chestnut of my prostate. With my cock buried to the back of his throat and his lips around the very base of my cock where it converged with my pubic hair, he pressed his finger on my prostate with a gentle steadiness. It felt like nothing I had ever felt before. In fact, it felt way too good, and I lost control. I shot a hard, full load of cum that splattered against the back of his throat. He swallowed and sucked every last drop out of me as my knees buckled and my toes curled. In the midst of my own pleasure, I was aware he was fiercely stroking his own cock while he blew me. He moaned, and I felt the warm splats of his cum land on my leg and my foot.

When each of us had finished blowing our loads, he stood up and kissed me, his tongue salty from the cum I shot into his mouth and down his throat.

"You're so amazing," he said, looking me as if he were for the first time. His demeanor confused me in my post orgasmic haze.

"What? No, you're amazing. That felt so good."

He leaned in and kissed me on the lips, without tongue this time. "What I mean is, these have been the best days of my whole life. Spending Thanksgiving here in Connecticut with you and your family has been so special, I will never forget it."

෬

Saturday night was the party at Allison's house. I had been honest with Dusty about my whole history with Allison and had no reservations about the two of them interacting with each other. That dynamic notwithstanding, I had agonized at the embarrassment of seeing Allison's father again after he had caught me with the semen stain the size of a slice of baloney on my pants right before I had left for Inverness. I really hoped I didn't have to interact with him, especially not in his own home. Dusty and I arrived there at the same time as five or six other people, and Allison's mother ushered all of us straight downstairs to their basement rec room. To my relief, her father was nowhere to be seen.

Allison approached me in a manner that was exaggerated and theatrical, which was unlike her. She wrapped her arms around me and gave me a huge hug and a deep kiss of the type you would expect to see on a movie screen, not in a basement rec room where the audience was your old gang from high school. I blushed at such a public display of affection from her, particularly in front of Dusty. I knew what she was doing: she wanted her friends, particularly those without boyfriends, to think she still had one while all of the girls spoke in grand and exaggerated ways about their fabulous new lives in college. As much as I cared for Allison, that type of behavior embarrassed me. She wasn't fooling anyone, and I didn't want to be a part of it. I lingered at her side until I could break away and get myself a drink at the rec room bar, which was fully stocked and open to everyone.

"Sorry about that," I said to Dusty under my breath.

"Don't worry about it, handsome," he said, whispering into my ear. "I know where else your lips have been, and I have a pretty good idea where they'll end up when the party's over."

Elvis played on the record player as I visited old friends and introduced Dusty to everyone. I had a second beer, and Dusty was having a fine enough time. But, an hour and half into the party, I wanted to plot a polite escape. Not even a full three months had passed since we all had dispersed to our respective colleges. But, the conversation was flat and full of reminiscence. It was pleasant enough, but it was clear to all of us in unspoken ways we were all moving in new and different directions. This was the old gang from high school, but everyone had spent the past few months moving on, and no one seemed to be their old normal self. The whole dynamic of the evening was off, and I was ready to leave.

I approached Allison to say good night and thank you. Before I could say anything, she pulled me by my arm into the laundry room. As she closed the door, the last glimpse I had before it shut was of Dusty, his face twisted in a cross of bemusement and confusion. Allison locked the door.

"I've missed you so much," she said.

"I've missed you, too," I said.

"Have you thought about me?"

"Of course. You know I have."

She pressed me against the cold steel of the washing machine and kissed me hard. "It feels so good to kiss you again," she said.

I wondered where this was coming from, and I wanted to pull back. We had fooled around all summer. But, I had always been the instigator and always had the sense I had wanted it more than she did. Our letter exchanges and phone conversations had not been charged with any sexual tension, despite how the Saturday night before I left for college had ended and despite her suggestion we might go all the way at Thanksgiving, something neither of us had mentioned since. Moreover, now I had Dusty, and my heart had moved in a different direction.

She kissed me again with even greater intensity. Her lips felt tender and soft. There was a familiarity with her, and we had a history together. My cock hardened and jutted out prominently at the front of my khakis. Despite the manner in which my cock had betrayed me, this did not feel right, and I wanted to extricate myself without hurting her feelings or causing either of us any embarrassment.

Without warning, however, the door to the laundry room flew open. The blare of *Jailhouse Rock* swooped into the room along with a blaze of bright light – and Allison's father. She jumped back in alarm. Her father's eyes bore into me not just with disgust, but with red-faced fury. He glanced down at the boner jutting out from my pants, the second time he had caught me like this with his daughter.

"You worthless piece of shit," he said to me. In three broad steps, he was at my side and grabbed me by my elbow.

"I'm sorry, sir," I said as he yanked me from the laundry room and across the rec room by my arm. "It's not what you think."

Elvis continued to blare from the hi-fi speakers, and the other party guests burst out laughing at the spectacle before them. Dusty couldn't help but notice the boner that still jutted from my pants. His eyes followed mine in disbelief, and he chased up the stairs after us.

Allison's father marched me to the front door and opened it. "I don't want to see your goddam face in my house again," he said as he pushed me out. "Get out, and keep your hands off my daughter or else I will come after you and make you sorry you did."

I stumbled out onto the front step. The door slammed shut behind me, only to open seconds later to let Dusty out and then slam shut again.

"Geezus!" Dusty said looking at me in disbelief.

My heart pounded in fear and anger. I fumbled for my keys and strutted towards my car with Dusty at my heels. "That was so fucking embarrassing," I said, my eyes hot with tears. "That guy is such an asshole."

Dusty didn't say anything at first. "What the hell happened in there?"

I shook my head. "Nothing happened."

"Nothing happened? You had a boner. I could see it. Everyone could."

"Nothing happened. She started kissing me, and then things started to get out of control."

Dusty nodded in the darkness, but didn't say anything.

I turned to him, his face illuminated by the lights from passing traffic. "Nothing happened, I swear," I said.

He kept his eyes forward, and the remainder of the drive back to my house was in silence.

Back in my room, I had calmed down a bit. I still smarted from the indecorous manner with which I had been expelled from Allison's house in front of everyone I knew from high school. But, I had started to lighten up a bit as the rush of adrenaline faded. "You have to admit, I made a pretty memorable exit."

Dusty laughed wanly. "Yes, you sure did. In fact, I've never seen anything quite like it. How's your elbow? He grabbed you pretty hard."

"A little sore, but it's okay."

Dusty shook his head and looked far away.

We brushed our teeth and washed up with only a little small talk. But, the atmosphere in the room was strained, and I could tell by the way he wasn't looking at me his mind was in motion. He changed into his pajamas, and I could not help but steal an open glance at the cock that had brought me so much pleasure over the past five days. He pulled up his pajama bottoms, and I watched it disappear.

"Good night," I said.

"Good night," he said. "Thanks for a memorable evening."

I rolled over onto my side and reached my hand across the gulf between the two beds. I rested it on Dusty's cock and gave it a squeeze. Polite and firm at the same time, he placed his hand on top of mine. The gulf between the beds was not the only gulf between us.

"Don't," he said.

"I want you," I said. "I'll make it up to you."

He shook his head. "Don't you get it?"

"That stuff with Allison didn't mean anything to me," I said.

"It meant something to me. That ridiculous kiss in front of everyone was one thing. But, no one was forcing you to go into the laundry room. You can't get all hot and bothered with her and think it doesn't matter to me. She got your cock hard, and now you want me to take care of it. I'm not doing it."

I sighed. "It's not what you think."

Dusty rolled over, his back now toward me. "Good night, John."

"Don't go to sleep angry. I'm sorry."

"Good night, John."

I lay there staring at the ceiling in silence, furious with myself for ruining the evening. After several long minutes, I said, "I love you, Dusty. I really love you."

A long beat passed before Dusty said anything. "Let's just get some sleep."

That is not how I ever imagined the evening ending. I was full of regrets and wished I could turn back the clock and change how the events at Allison's house had unfolded. I slept only fitfully that night and still felt shitty the next morning when I woke up. I got out of bed early and went downstairs to the kitchen. While the rest of the house slept, I started up the coffee percolator, fried some bacon, and made myself French toast that I ate in silence in the pre-dawn quiet.

I didn't hear Dusty enter the kitchen until he was there in front of me.

"Morning," he said.

"Morning," I said back.

His hair was tousled, and his eyes were heavy from sleeping poorly. I waited for him to say more, but he didn't.

"Coffee?" I asked.

He nodded. "I'm sorry."

I looked at him, my face twisted in confusion. "You have nothing to be sorry about. I'm the one who should be sorry. Forgive me?"

He shook his head. "Look, this is exactly what we talked about that day in your dorm room. You have to experience everything until you know for sure what you want. I'm okay about last night."

If Dusty was okay about last night, his body language wasn't showing it. He was distant. The vibe was different. Something in him had changed, and I wanted to change it back.

I set down a cup of coffee in front of him. "I'm sorry, I'll make it up to you."

He nodded, and I kissed him tentatively. He kissed me back, but it was not the same as it was before all this. I felt a wave of uncertainty rise up inside me. "Do you want some French toast?"

He nodded again, and I made it for him. We ate in near silence.

Dusty and I, along with the rest of my family, attended church services in town at the Episcopal Church where I had been baptized and attended Sunday school during my childhood. My parents weren't religious, and I never had the sense they believed in God the way I did. It was a part of their social routine, and we went most Sunday mornings as a family. I sat there in the pew with Dusty at my side, our knees close enough to touch.

I knew I was supposed to feel guilty about almost everything about myself and who I was. But, as I sat there with my family and listened to the sermon, I felt no guilt whatsoever. When I prayed, it was not for forgiveness from God for who I was. I prayed I could rectify my relationship with Dusty so we could continue the journey we had begun. I had all sorts of confusing thoughts racing through my head in those years, but I relied on the gift of my faith to bring me strength when I needed it, like now.

Shortly after we returned from church, Daniel and Mike drove up to the front of my house. I had been dreading seeing Daniel and having the conversation he was seeking and I was avoiding. I was agitated about the tension between Dusty and me after the incredible five days we had together. My parents greeted Daniel and Mike as old friends and said farewell to Dusty as if he were a member of the family. My father shook my hand and Dusty's as he warned us of the rematch Bud had promised we would have the next time Dusty returned to West Hartford. My mother hugged him, and they watched us drive off.

Before we reached the end of my street, Mike was snickering. "How was your Thanksgiving holiday, boys?"

"Good," both Dusty and I said in near unison without any enthusiasm.

I could tell by the tone of Mike's voice he wanted us to ask about theirs, so I did.

"We both got laid," Mike said. He let out a holler and pounded his palm on the horn.

I couldn't see Daniel's face head-on from where I was sitting in the rear of the car, and he did not look back. But, I could tell by the way his lips curled into a broad grin it was true.

"Well, well, well," I said. "Spill the details."

Daniel wasn't saying anything, but Mike was eager to talk. "I fucked that girl Delores, and Daniel fucked Carol, the ones from that weekend you ruined for us," he said, referring to me and the weekend of *Wonder Breadus Interruptus*.

"I thought those girls never wanted to see you guys ever again," I said.

"They didn't want to *see* us again, they wanted to *fuck* us again," Mike said, pounding his palm on the horn like he had done before.

The images of the close-up view I had seen through binoculars of Daniel's naked ass pumping up and down on Carol on the couch in the housemasters' lounge passed through my head. I remembered how I had watched his big, low-hanging balls slap against her pussy and how he had pulled out of her when the guys had pelted him with slices of Wonder Bread. We had had a full frontal view of his cock swinging side-to-side like a metronome. It was a pretty sexy and incredible memory I have never forgotten.

"Daniel even went through two rubbers and blew two loads into Carol, one right after the other," Mike said, punching Daniel in the arm.

I could tell by the way Daniel's lips curled into a smug smile again this was also true. He could be tightly wound, as I have said before, and was not the type of guy who would brag about things like that, at least in a carful of people.

"What about you guys?" Mike asked. "Anyone get laid?"

Daniel stopped smiling and still didn't turn around.

"Nope, not us," I said.

The ride back to Inverness was a quiet one. Dusty spent most of the time looking out the side window of the back seat. Daniel spent most of the time looking out the front window and not looking back at me. I wasn't jealous Daniel had gotten laid. But, I hoped we could pick our friendship back up without any strain or awkwardness. I didn't know if that could be possible after the uncomfortableness of the morning before Thanksgiving. A gulf had arisen between us that extended beyond the distance from the front to the backseats of the car. And now a frost had descended upon Dusty and me, which is not how I had ever imagined such a magical holiday break would have ended. At least we were speaking this morning, but damage had been done. I knew I had been callous with Dusty's heart, and I needed to right things that even if righted would not be forgotten.

Whatever happened between Dusty and me and the difficult conversation I was expecting Daniel to revisit once we were alone, I knew my world had changed forever since we all first got in this car earlier in the week and headed on the outbound drive from Inverness back to my childhood home.

14 STALLED

THE DYNAMICS OF my interactions with Daniel and Dusty were thrown askew from every angle during those first few days after our return from Thanksgiving. Daniel's suspicions regarding the true nature of my relationship with Dusty had grown from surprised speculation to near certainty after what he had seen and heard at my parents' house. I would later learn the sound of the lock sealing shut my bedroom door had been reverberating in Daniel's ears with a deafening roar. I held my breath and my body tense, expecting him at any moment to pick up the confrontation I wanted dropped and forgotten even though there was no way for either of us to drop or forget anything. Daniel was tense as well. I knew by the glances I caught from him he had a barrage of questions he wanted to fire at me, but was holding back with his finger on the trigger. He had an inherent self-confidence and did what he wanted without the handwringing I customarily did. If he wasn't asking the questions I was afraid he would ask, it was because he was afraid he would hear answers he didn't want to hear.

At the same time, the rift in my relationship with Dusty persisted. We weren't arguing. In fact, he was exceedingly cordial. But, the cordiality was of tone you would expect from a friend, not a lover. That felt worse than silence or open anger, which I would have been able to address. Anger would have given me reason to confront him about what was really going on in the same way Daniel wanted to confront me. But, Dusty's measured politeness kept me at bay and made it difficult to speak openly of what I wanted to talk about with him. He had too much substance to behave in a manner as petty and obvious as giving someone the silent treatment. But, by speaking to me as a friend instead of a lover, he had erected a barrier that was even more effective in keeping me out as he tried to make sense of us and where we were going.

Adding to my unease, this was the last week of class before the week-long reading period preceding final exams. After a semester that had been full of change as we all adjusted to the new routines and rigors of college life and the freedoms of living away from home, there was an apprehension in the air as the fun died down and the pressure of exams caused everyone to turn dour.

I gave Dusty some distance that Monday and stopped by his room on Tuesday morning to see if he wanted to have breakfast with me. Breakfast was something we had shared at my house, but never at school, where I took all of my meals with my friends and never with him. At least not yet. He looked up at me with a polite, but pre-occupied smile and said he would catch me later, that he had some reading he had to finish up before class. Then he turned his head back to his book. My heart felt heavy in my chest. I could understand being busy if it weren't so obvious nothing had been the same between us since the events of Allison's party. I masked my hurt and wished him a good day.

At least there were plenty of academic distractions from my personal distress. In preparation for final exams, I had notes to review, exam outlines to prepare, and term papers to finish. I received an unexpected surprise in my Emerging Governments class when Professor Johnston passed back the mid-term essay we had submitted a few weeks earlier. I had written a paper on the weakening of the British Empire and how Great Britain could maintain its global influence by fostering economic ties with former commonwealth countries and maintaining the strong military influence promoted by Winston Churchill, one of my great heroes for the leadership he had exhibited during difficult times. My principal thesis was a strong commonwealth of freed colonies meant a stronger Great Britain. I was stunned when I looked at my grade and saw an A+. Professor Johnston called me down to the front of the class and had me read my paper aloud from his lectern while he sat in the first row.

I remember my face had been red hot with embarrassment and pride as I read my words aloud to the class. I was humbled by the unexpected honor. Professor Johnston had never had any students read their papers aloud to the class before to my knowledge. While my face may have been red, I remember my voice had been strong, but without arrogance as I read my words aloud. He then asked me a litany of questions I answered with a poise and an eloquence I had not known I had within me. When I finished, he told the class he had hoped they had paid close attention to me, that my paper had been written in a voice and a level of scholarship worth emulating.

Professor Johnston's praise was empowering for me to hear, and I have never forgotten it. Through the years, whenever I have been in a position to influence the thinking of young people in academic or professional settings, I have remembered how self-inspiring accolades can be, particularly when earned through the levels of passion and effort I had been expending. As a young freshman, I knew I had certain academic talents. But, I was not fully sure of what they were in the same way I was not fully sure of who I was. As I was searching on uncertain footing for my place in the world, my self-confidence was growing, and I was greatly influenced by the professor's encouragement. I had long thought about working for the State Department or having some type of career in foreign relations. That day, however, his praise smoothed over any self-doubts I had in that regard. I would have future stumbles, of course. But, I would navigate them with a confidence born under Professor's Johnston's tutelage.

As inspiring as it was for me to continue to hear his words, I had heard what I needed to hear. I felt self-conscious as I continued to sit there and face the class while Professor Johnston praised me. I didn't know where to look. As my eyes drifted from the ceiling to the clock and down to my shoes while the professor spoke about me, my gaze locked on Daniel for a long moment. There was a sparkle in his eye as he flashed me a warm smile and nodded his head. My heart surged, and I wondered if all might be good with us after all.

When class finished, Daniel punched me in the shoulder as I gathered my books. "Nice work, buddy. What a great honor!"

I smiled, my face still flush. "Thanks. I didn't know he was going to do that."

"I'm so proud of you, buddy. Your paper was brilliant, and you sounded like a professor yourself up there."

I blushed again and thanked him, always happy to hear kind words from him. He asked me if I wanted to play squash after we dropped our books off back at the dorm. I said yes, with some trepidation. Even though we each stood on opposites sides of a valley carved from a river of questions he wanted to ask and I didn't want to answer, I still cared very deeply about my friendship with him. He was smart, funny, sexy, and had a confident aloofness that made him even sexier to me. To have seen him seem so vulnerable before me regarding his uncertainties on where we stood made me want to reach out and hug him tight in a way I knew I never could. Having him as a close friend and the best roommate you would ever want to have had contributed in a huge way to my overall feelings of happiness at Inverness. I didn't want to lose him. I also didn't know how I could continue to lie to him about Dusty when the truth would be so obvious to someone who knew me as well as Daniel did. But, being honest about the truth would take a courage I didn't yet have.

I felt a sense of dread at what might be asked and answered in the confines of the squash court where there could be no escape. Daniel knew what he knew – I was certain of that. He was smart, intuitive, and we understood each other more than we understood most other people in our lives. It made me love him and fear at the same time. Except for Dusty, no one knew me like Daniel did.

I tried hard not to be on edge, which turned out not to be too hard after all. Daniel continued to be full of praise about my paper and the attention it had received in class, particularly after his own efforts to perform well in that course and the help I had given him on his essays over the semester. He was even more impressed when I told him Professor Johnston had invited me to present the same paper at the next political science faculty meeting.

We changed into our shorts and jogged over to the gym in the cold wearing only track shorts on the bottom and sweatshirts on top. When we usually played squash, we would play hard and to win. This time was no different in that regard. Daniel usually beat me, however, and this time he beat me in the first three matches, which was typical. Several times I caught him looking at me, and I was certain he had chosen the confines of the squash court to press me about Dusty and what was really going on between us. With little chance for escape or outside interruption, it was the perfect place for a private confrontation, and I had braced myself for it to happen.

As we were about to start the fourth game, he touched his right foot to the service box on the court and raised his racquet to serve the ball. But, then he lowered it and looked at the far corner of the court floor for a long beat. My mind flashbacked to that afternoon when I bared my heart to Dusty in the cold, awkward silence of my dorm room. It seemed to me Daniel was summoning the courage to bare his heart to me in a similar way. Our eyes locked, and then we each looked away. Then they locked again. Each of us was on the verge of saying something that once said could not be unsaid. But, neither of us did, and he finally he averted his eyes. It was as if he had decided he didn't need to know the answers to difficult questions after all and had swallowed his words deep inside.

After what seemed like forever, but could not have been more than a handful of seconds, he asked, "Ready?"

I nodded. "Go ahead."

I don't know if he let me win the next match or whether I did it on my own. But, I ended up winning it, my only victory of the day, at least on the squash court. Either way, I was happy to finish on a high note when I had expected the worst. Daniel seemed more relaxed as well having made peace however he had needed to about me, even if it were only temporary. On the jog back to the dorm, we were invigorated by the renewed spirit of our friendship and the chill of the outdoors that cooled our sweaty bodies. We laughed and set off into a flat-out running race, which I also won. I knew this was not the end of it. Whatever hadn't been said was not forgotten, but had only been put on layaway. If I had had the wherewithal I have now when it comes to navigating the intricacies of human relationships and if I had had the courage to grant Daniel the honesty he deserved, I would have manned up and confronted the issue head-on and risked the consequences. But, I was just eighteen then and hadn't yet figured out it was better to cast sunlight upon unspoken problems rather than letting them fester under the cloak of darkness. I didn't know where Daniel and I would end up, but I had the sense that everything was going to be okay, at least for now.

After dropping off our squash racquets and sweaty clothes in our room, we stripped down and headed to the shower together with each of us wearing only our towels. Even from the hallway, we could hear the sounds of the other guys in the shower. Anthony's voice overpowered all of them. Once inside the bathroom, we paused for a moment and had a laugh about a sign that had been taped to the stall door in the far corner: "Attention! You must flush your waste and keep appropriate your conduct! Cooperation Please! Thank You from your Custodian!"

Our custodian was named Janusz. At least that was his first name. I don't know if any of us knew his last name, and I don't think any of us gave it a thought. Daniel and I each read the sign out loud, mimicking Janusz's Ukrainian accent and the scramble of his spoken grammar. Janusz had emigrated to the United States right after World War II. To us, he was an old, ill-tempered guy who was in his forties, but looked much older given how his hair was shock-white streaked with grey. How and why he ended up working as a custodian at this preppy college in Vermont so far from wartime Ukraine, I did not know. It seemed to me then and now a pretty lousy job to have to clean up after a bunch of messy, privileged college guys who had no idea how good they had it. I'm sure we drove him crazy.

When Daniel and I entered the showers, Howell, Sasquatch, Freddy, Shorty, and Anthony were already in there after having played a heated game of basketball. They were dissecting Janusz's signs, and Howell was doing a pretty fair imitation of his accent and the intensity of his voice when he was worked up about something. Having to clean up after us was an easy way to set him off, particularly if it were as a messy as a tipped over trash can, spilled beer that had turned sticky, or ashtrays filled to overflowing, all of which were common occurrences in Canterbury Hall. This, however, was even worse.

Howell stepped out from under the shower head and threw his hands in the air as he continued in his mock Ukrainian accent. "This is unacceptable! You must dispose of your waste! Thank you from your custodian!"

As Howell explained, someone in the dorm was getting a kick out of shitting in the far corner stall and not flushing. I knew even then Janusz had a quiet rage about him. There were rumors he had been a partisan who had fought against the Nazis, and I am sure he was apoplectic with rage at having to endure these insults after enduring all he had been through to survive.

"Isn't it his fucking job to scrub toilets and clean shit up around here?" Freddy said. "I mean, c'mon, what are we paying him for? There's no free lunch."

"What are we paying him for? We aren't paying for anything," Daniel said. "Inverness is paying him. And they are not paying him to clean up the shit of some sicko who's not flushing the toilet on purpose. It's fucking insulting, and if you don't think so, you're as fucked up as whoever who is dropping those depth charges in the corner stall."

Freddy shrugged as the luxuriance of warm water of the shower cascaded down upon his shoulders. "I'm just saying if he doesn't want to clean toilets, he should find something else to do. It's his job, and I think he should quit complaining."

Anthony shook his head and shut down the conversation. "That's one of the most fucked up things I've ever heard you say, Freddy. If you think you're being funny, you're not. Maybe because you were born with a fucking silver spoon in your ass. But, guys like Janusz aren't here to clean up after spoiled rich brats who think it's a fucking game to let the janitor flush their shit."

Freddy started to say something else, but Anthony shut him down. "I don't care what the fuck you have to say. If I find out who's doing this, they'll have to answer to me, and I'll give them a fucking pounding."

I have to admit I was both surprised at how Anthony took up Janusz's cause and ashamed at my initial reaction, which had been one of indifference to Janusz's plight and muted bemusement at how fucked up it was someone was soiling the corner stall on purpose, which I found vaguely humorous then even if I do not now. Freddy shrugged, and the rest of us all fell in line. The conversation ended.

When I look back in admiration at Anthony, I often think of how I and others let our prejudices cloud our vision and underestimate him at first. If you didn't know him, you might have thought he was just a handsome meathead with a big personality, a big voice, and a big cock. But, he was also big on character and fundamental decency, particularly when others were low on it, like now. Anthony's family was newer to prosperity than those of us who had grown up on white bread and swimming lessons at country clubs. He had seen the backbreaking work his father, grandfather, and uncles had undertaken as they carved and cut marble that graced public buildings and grand homes in and around New York. He recognized what a gift it was to bathe in the splendor of a warm shower on a December afternoon at an elite private college in Vermont even if the rest of us did not.

After Anthony shut down the sniggering about Janusz, the conversation quickly shifted to our favorite and most frequent topic other than sports, which was sex.

"So, who got laid over Thanksgiving break?" Anthony asked, looking at each of us. "Branson?"

He paused for not more than a short glance at me, and I thought nothing of it. I shook my head in the negative, which was technically true. In retrospect, knowing what I would later learn about what Anthony knew about me, I might have held his gaze for a longer beat or two as he lingered on me in a way that felt more like a courtesy than a genuine inquiry. With no further interest, he turned his attention to Daniel.

"Wonder Bread, my sources tell me your drum stick got some action over Thanksgiving."

Daniel shot me an irritated glare and looked at Anthony even-faced. "I don't know what you're talking about."

Anthony nodded his head in my direction. "Branson didn't tell me. I was just fishing, and you confirmed it with the threatening look you just shot him."

Daniel reached for his soap and lifted his arms up to wash his hairy pits under the stream. He smirked, but wasn't talking. I've mentioned before Daniel could have an edge about him, and he wasn't the type of guy who would brag in a group about getting laid, especially if Anthony were prying about it.

"C'mon, Wonder Bread! Get the pole out of your ass! Tell us about the tail you got!"

Daniel just shook his head. "What about you? I'm guessing you're dying to tell us all about it."

Anthony shook the shampoo from his hair. "As a matter of fact, Wonder Bread, I did get laid."

With a smirk, Sasquatch said, "Was her name Rosy Palm?"

Anthony rolled his eyes. "Her name was Tina. She's from Floral Park."

"Was she hot?" Sasquatch asked.

"Of course she was hot, you dick wad." Anthony soaped up his forearms. As he spoke, he moved his hand down and soaped up the hair on his lower belly. "She went to my high school, and I always knew she wanted my big, fat, Italian sausage." With that mention of his cock, Anthony grabbed it in one hand and slapped it against the wrist of his other hand a few times, each accompanied by the sound of a loud, heavy smack. That gesture along with the sound effect grabbed everyone's attention, and he knew it. I've noticed over the course of my life that it is human nature for a guy to size up another guy's cock if he gets the opportunity to see it. I don't care whether a guy is straight, gay, or somewhere down the spectrum of male human sexuality: a guy can't help looking at another guy's cock, especially if he can get away with it without being seen, no matter how straight he is. I've also noticed if a guy has a big cock and has it out on display for everyone to look at it, all barriers go down, and everyone will look. If the guy also does something as brazen as pick his cock up in one hand and slap it against the other, guys will use that as license to speak about it openly.

"Can you believe that fucking monster?" Howell said. "Sure puts mine to shame."

The rest of us nodded in silent, awestruck admiration. Even Daniel had to acknowledge Anthony's cock was a long, thick, wrinkled monster that had everyone's beat by far. I have mentioned before that on the precipice of ejaculation, Anthony's hard cock was ten inches long and seven inches thick. Those were his self-reported measurements, but given the visual proof we would all get - and, don't worry, I will get into more detail about that later - there was no reason to doubt him.

"Instead of always talking about your admittedly horse-sized cock, why don't you tell us about Tina's pussy?" Daniel said. There was an edge in his voice, and I wished he could lighten up for once and not butt heads with Anthony, particularly now, as Anthony was about to regale us with the tale of how he had slid that monster into poor Tina, something all of us wanted to hear about. Anthony flashed Daniel another look to let him know he had caught the edge in his voice. Then, he turned back to the rest of us, who had mostly finished washing up and were just lingering in the warmth and spray of the steamy showers.

"So, I was saying," Anthony continued, "I knew she had wanted me since high school. Her friend told my friend she was hot for me, which is pretty much as close as you can get to a sure thing. I called her up and asked her out to a movie. I wanted to see *Bridge on the River Kwai*, but I knew a war movie is the worst choice you can make for a date. So, I asked her if she wanted to see *An Affair to Remember*, which was about this couple played by Cary Grant and Deborah Kerr who fall in love and agree to meet at the top of the Empire State Building."

"You wanted to see *An Affair to Remember?*" I asked, surprised Anthony would have wanted to see such a romantic movie.

He laughed and turned his shower nozzle over in my direction, spraying me across the face. "No, you knucklehead. I didn't want to see it at all, but girls like that kind of movie. Going to a movie about romance increases your chances of getting laid about a thousand fold. Taking a girl to a war movie on a first date pretty much guarantees you'll be pounding your pud with your fist by yourself at the end of the night."

I laughed and said, "I'll remember that for next time."

"And even better, *An Affair to Remember* was showing at the Valley Stream drive-in, the town next door. Drive-ins were designed specifically for getting action, and I wanted to do everything I could to make sure I got some. When we get there, Tina slides over next to me, and I put my arm on her shoulder. In the middle of the movie, when Cary Grant and Deborah Kerr are still apart, Tina says, 'I think Cary Grant is so handsome.' I pretend I'm insulted and say, 'You think Cary Grant is handsome? What about me? Don't you think I'm handsome?'"

Daniel laughed out loud. "Only you would have an ego large enough to think you could compete with Cary Grant in the looks department."

Anthony turned to Daniel and looked disparagingly at his cock. "I think I have lots of things that are large enough."

"C'mon guys," Howell said. "Cut it out."

Anthony turned back to us. "Then she said, 'You're like an Italian Cary Grant.'"

"Wow," Howell said. "That's quite a compliment."

"Yep," Anthony said. "I said, 'Thank you.' Then, she burst out laughing and said, 'Cary Grant? You're no Cary Grant. I was just kidding!' I looked at her all surprised and insulted. She was laughing so hard she snorted. 'Cary Grant is a gentleman,' she said, 'and I can tell you're no gentleman.' I was so pissed, I took my arm off her shoulder and placed it back on the steering wheel."

"What a bitch," I said, even though I didn't think there was anything about him that resembled Cary Grant except they both had black hair. Anthony was not suave or debonair, at least not yet. If I had to think of one word to describe him, it would have been "big." Everything about Anthony was big: not just his cock, but his physical size, his personality, his voice, and how his presence could rise up and fill any room he entered if he wanted it to. I thought of Anthony then as more of a handsome, giant puppy that never stopped moving. Years later, however, he and I both lived in Manhattan. I had not seen him for several years during an extended period when I had been stationed overseas, and we had plans to meet up for drinks down near Wall Street. I remember as he turned the corner and walked towards me. The setting sun of an early evening in late June cast a glow about him. He wore a custom-tailored navy blue suit, French cuffs, pewter tie, and shiny black shoes. I thought at that moment how he looked as if he had stepped from the pages of a glossy advertisement for cognac or a European sports car. He was not quite an Italian Cary Grant, but close enough for me to recall this very conversation and compel me to think if Tina could see him now, she would not be laughing.

Anthony said, "There was no way I was going to let her talk to me like that, and I started the car. She said, 'what are you doing?' I said, 'I am not going to sit here and be insulted like this.' She said, 'turn the car off.' I said, 'why?' And she didn't say anything, she just stared at me and gave me 'the look.' I stopped being angry that second, and I leaned in and kissed her."

"What's 'the look'?" Sasquatch asked, his eyes wide.

One of Anthony's many great qualities was he was so much more experienced than the rest of us, and you could ask him a question like that, and he would explain it without making you feel stupid. "It's like this," Anthony said, stepping over to Sasquatch and putting his arms on his hairy shoulders. He stared into his eyes. "You and the girl are looking at each other, right? Your eyes lock, and each of you are thinking 'I want you' and the other person knows what you're thinking, because your eyes are saying what your mind is thinking. Like this," Anthony said, locking his gaze with Sasquatch. Sasquatch nodded his head as he searched for the secret of female desire in Anthony's eyes.

You would think the rest of us might laugh or mock them, but no one did. Anthony's physical presence and unimpeachable masculinity endowed him with the power to place his hands on a naked guy's shoulders in the showers and demonstrate the look a girl would signal when her mind and body wanted you but her mouth was not yet saying it. Out of all of us, only Daniel and Anthony had had sexual intercourse before. The rest of us were virgins, and we would listen to any advice we could get from those fortunate to have crossed over to the other side.

"You got it now?" Anthony asked, stepping back under his shower, his long, heavy cock swaying as he moved.

Sasquatch nodded in awe and gratitude as he etched the lesson into his memory.

"So, we continue kissing, and I immediately pop a rod in my pants. I'm throbbing so hard, and we've barely even gone anywhere. We kiss for a while until I think enough time has passed for me to unbutton her blouse without seeming too rushed. If a girl thinks you're moving too fast and only going after one thing, she'll shut you down, and you'll be choking your chicken by yourself at home instead of heading to tuna town."

Everyone nodded, taking it all in.

"Then, I unbuttoned her blouse, and she had the fullest, lushest, juiciest tits. I played with them a bit, and then I buried my face in between them. She started to moan about how good it felt. I was enjoying it myself, but I had other plans. By now, my cock was so hard, I was afraid it was going to tear my pants. I reached my hand up her skirt, and she didn't stop me. In no time, I had her panties off and my fingers in her wet pussy."

"Holy shit!" Howell said.

"Holy shit was right. She was moaning as my fingers slid in and out of her and around her clit. Finally, I couldn't take it anymore, and neither could she. I opened my pants and pulled out my cock. Her eyes got wide, and she said, 'There's no way that thing is fitting inside me, put it away.' She was fucking scared, so I kissed her on the lips and told her to trust me, that I'd be gentle. She didn't look she trusted me at all. But, I pulled out a rubber and unrolled it down my shaft."

By now, all of us were worked up in various degrees from hearing Anthony's story. Daniel's cock had lengthened considerably, and the broad brown band of his circumcision scar had stretched about three quarters of the way down. Sasquatch's medium-sized cock was showing signs of thickening as well. It was hard to tell what was going on with Howell's cock it was so small, but the round acorn was rosier and plumper. What was truly breathtaking, however, was the sight of Anthony's monster cock, which was waking from its slumber and coming to life. As he spoke of his escapades at the drive-in and his body was buffeted by the warm water of the shower, his cock had relaxed and lengthened to the point his foreskin had retracted part way so that almost half of his glans was exposed. My own cock also had awoken and was now approaching half-mast, much to my embarrassment.

We all listened raptly as Anthony described his entry into a world the rest of us dreamed of. "'Go in easy, I'm scared,' she said. 'I've never had one that big before. If I tell you it's hurting me, you better stop right away or else I'll start screaming bloody murder.' I kissed her softly on the lips and said, 'Don't worry, baby, I'll be gentle,' and then I rubbed my middle finger across the opening of her pussy a few times to make sure she was nice and wet. Then, I climbed on top of her. I rubbed my cock head across the slit of her pussy for a little while to stretch her out and started to work my knob inside her. She loosened up, and I pushed it all the way in to the bottom."

"What did it feel like?" Howell asked.

"It was the best - wet, hot, and tight. I started plunging in and out of her like an oil rig. She was going crazy and telling me how big it was, how I filled her up and she couldn't believe it felt so good."

With those words, I had a clear visual image of Anthony's gigantic cock pumping up and down on Tina, his balls slapping against her. I glanced at Anthony's cock and saw that his large, shiny glans had fully emerged from his foreskin. *Damn*, I thought. This was all too much for me. My semi-erection surged to a full hard-on I could not hide. It was only a matter of time before someone noticed, and there would be nothing I could do about it. I turned my torso toward the shower head and started to think how I might be able to discreetly back my way out of there without anyone seeing my boner.

"I fucked her for a while and finally blew my wad into the rubber."

"Sounds like you really gave it to her," Daniel said. "Did she have an orgasm, too, or just you?"

Anthony leveled his eyes at Daniel and said, "Of course she did. She had five or six of them, one right after another."

"I'll bet," Daniel said, with a snide smirk.

"You're pretty smug for a guy standing in a shower with his cock at half-mast while I tell a story about banging a chick at a drive-in."

Without looking down at his cock, Daniel said, "It's not half-mast."

Everyone looked at it. While it was not quite half-mast, it was close.

And then, I was busted.

"Daniel's not half-mast, but look at Branson!" Freddy said, looking at my cock and then my face. "He's got a full woody!"

I blushed deeply and tried to turn back into the spray of the shower, but Anthony grabbed me with a strong hand and spun me around. My cock was rock hard after hearing his story and was jutting straight out in front of me, purple and fully engorged, as hard as it ever gets. No one had ever seen my boner before except for Dusty and for Daniel. I was embarrassed almost to the point of horror something so private had become public in front of everyone.

Howell gawked unabashedly, his mouth hanging open in surprise. "Holy shit, Branson! You've got a big cock!"

I glared at Freddy, irritated that he of all people was the one calling me out for having a hard-on in the shower, when I had hoped I could have slipped out of there without anyone noticing.

Anthony slapped me on the back. "Pretty impressive, Branson. Didn't know you had it in you. That's a very serious rod you have there."

"Hot damn, Branson!" Sasquatch exclaimed. "After Anthony, you might have the biggest cock on the floor!"

Freddy nodded approvingly at my hard cock. He had a big smirk on his face at having busted me and causing me embarrassment, as if somehow I had received pay back for watching him with Shorty.

Daniel took a quick, but admiring look and said, "I've had enough. I'll let you guys continue your homo boner parade without me. I'm out of here." With that, he stepped out of the shower and was gone.

"What can I say?" I said, my face still red. "It was a hot, sexy story."

Anthony smirked. "Glad I was able to give you a big woody, you little fairy."

I was chagrined enough by now, but I will admit I got a not-so-secret charge from the open-mouthed looks of surprise and admiration I had received. It also occurred to me how close all of us had grown together over the past several months. I thought back to the beginning of the semester, when we were still strangers as we showered together on that first morning. Howell had busted me for checking out Anthony's huge cock, and I had reacted with sheer terror at having been caught, not realizing Anthony's cock already had been the subject of conversation amongst the other guys. When I look back, I should not have been surprised: his cock was so large, it was the elephant in the room someone had to talk about at some point.

Enough was enough, and I didn't want my boner to be the subject of any further discussion amongst the guys, no matter how flattering the conversation had turned. I left the shower and wrapped myself in my towel, tucking my hard cock upwards so it would not be as noticeable as I escaped through the bathroom and back down to the safety of my room. When I reached the door, I was surprised to find it locked. It almost never was.

I knocked on the door. "Daniel? You in there? Open up!"

I knocked again. After a few moments, Daniel opened the door, his face flush. I stole a quick glance down to his crotch and thought I detected a bulge. Had he rushed back in here to rub out a quick load after Anthony's hot story? It sure seemed like it to me.

"Quite a show back there," he said.

I shook my head and laughed. "I'm so embarrassed. I can't believe all of the guys saw me with a woody."

"Everyone gets them, it's no big deal," he said. Then, with a smirk, he added, "Actually, it's a pretty big deal in your case. I thought Howell's and Sasquatch's eyes were going to pop out of their heads in jealousy."

I laughed again. "It was a pretty hot story."

"Actually, it was so hot, I had to come back and jerk off a quick load," he said, and this time he laughed. "Don't tell any of the other guys, especially Anthony!"

I nodded my head. "I thought that's what was going on in here. I hope I didn't interrupt you too soon and you were able to finish."

"Yep, all finished," he said with a smirk. He had a crumpled paper towel in his hand that he tossed into the trashcan where it landed with a heavy thud. "Only took a minute."

ଓ

In the morning, I stopped by Dusty's room again to say good morning. But, he was already gone. We had barely spoken since the incident at Allison's house. He had said there was nothing wrong. But, certainly there was. My heart was heavy as I headed out to the dining hall and the beginning of my day.

At the faculty department meeting, I presented my paper on the British Commonwealth and my analysis of the continuing impact of economic ties between Great Britain and the former colonial territories along with the military strength promoted by Winston Churchill. I was nervous and humbled to have been asked to do this. When I think back to my eighteen year old self, it amazes me I was able to summon poise and presence I did not know I had. I remember how strong and clear my voice was. I remember fielding questions from a dozen professors who challenged me on my thesis. I remember my adamant defense to those challenges. In the end, I held my own. Professor Johnston seemed quite proud to have a star pupil to show off, and I was grateful for the interest he had shown in me.

Later in the afternoon, I was sitting at my desk in my room and was studying my notes from Economics 101, my weakest subject. I was interrupted by a knock on my open door followed by a friendly, "Hey."

I looked up at the sound of the familiar voice I had not been anticipating to hear. My heart leapt.

Dusty was dressed in sweatpants and running shoes. "I'm heading over for a run at the indoor track. Do you want to join me?"

I was busy and had work to do. But, of course I wanted to join him. The irony is, as much as I hadn't wanted to be alone with Daniel so he could confront me about what was going on between Dusty and me, I wanted to be alone with Dusty so I could talk to him about what was going on with us. I changed into my track clothes. It was not hard to notice Dusty's eyes were on my body as I stripped down, and he allowed himself the luxury of a lingering glance as I stepped into my jock strap and pulled my underwear up.

We made small talk about the stress of upcoming exams as we strolled down the hall. We entered the stairwell, and the door closed behind us. Dusty grabbed the back of my sweatpants at the waistband. In the same motion, he pulled me back towards him, and I could feel the knuckle of his middle finger against the bare skin of my crack. He spun me around and pressed me against the wall. He kissed me on the lips once and then again.

"I miss you," he said.

"I miss you, too," I said. It was no secret to me that I missed him, but I kissed him back with a sense of urgency that surprised me. Our cocks grew hard and bulged from our sweatpants as our bodies intertwined in the privacy of the stairwell. He pressed the bulge of his hard-on against mine.

"I'm sorry about what happened with Allison," I said.

He ran his fingers of his hand through the hair above my ear. He leaned in and kissed me again. "You have nothing to be sorry about."

"I don't know what I was thinking. It won't happen again, I promise."

"Look," he said and continued to stroke my hair. "I've said it before. You're younger than I am, and I don't want you ever to think I've stopped you from finding out who you really are and what you really want. My feelings for you aren't going to change, no matter what happens. Let's just be honest and open with each other about everything, and we'll always be alright. Deal?"

I put my hand on his waist. "I love you," I said, my chest tightening with the power of unexpected emotion as I said those words to him. "I really do."

He smiled as if he had never been happier. "I know you do. I love you, too."

We were interrupted by the sound of the door to the stairwell opening two flights up. I will admit that some of the excitement for me of my burgeoning relationship with him was the thrill of secrecy. We each had everything to lose if we got caught, and we did not have the luxury of unlimited privacy to explore what we each ached for and wanted to explore with each other. The moments we had had so far had been stolen moments of intense passion punctuated by the thrill of getting caught. Neither of us wanted that, of course. But, it surely added to the excitement.

With yet another furtive moment interrupted, our boners subsided as we bounded down the stairs and out into the cold of the December afternoon. Dusty and I were going to be fine. As we ran together on the indoor track, I remember thinking how happy I was we were together. Of the countless memories I have of my relationship with him, one of the most enduring is the image of he and I running side-by-side on the indoor and outdoor tracks at Inverness and along the country roads of Vermont. Our bodies were in the prime of young manhood. Our hearts were beating strong, our lungs heaving powerfully, and the sinewy muscles of our bodies taking us as fast as we wanted to go with each other at our sides. To have shared that sensation of truly being alive with another human being as much as I loved Dusty was one of the greatest gifts of my whole life.

CR

The next two and a half weeks were some of the most difficult of my entire academic career up until that time, with the exception only of the College Board entrance examinations. I had worked hard to get accepted at Inverness, and I had hopes for my future that extended beyond college. I mentioned at the beginning of this memoir I knew even before I had arrived here bigger things in life were meant for me outside of central Connecticut. I had had my eye on the State Department for almost as long as I could remember and knew I would need a strong academic record to be accepted into the diplomatic corps. But, I fully believed in myself and what I might be able to accomplish if only I worked hard and had a little luck.

Dusty and I grabbed each other when we could for stolen embraces and limited cock play. But, each of us was distracted by the pain of final exams that eventually ended the last Friday before Christmas. The first semester came to a close, and I was exhausted. As much as I loved my life at Inverness, I was looking forward to going home and doing nothing for the next few weeks.

The last official business that day before people started to leave for Christmas break was an all-hands meeting in the second floor lounge, which Dusty had called in his capacity as RA. It is a testament to the authority he commanded that it took only a little effort on his part to quiet down the room of rowdy freshmen eager to head home for the holidays after the grind of a grueling round of final exams. If anyone wondered what the meeting was about when the notice of mandatory attendance was posted, no one had any doubts when Janusz joined Dusty at the front of the room.

After everyone quieted down, Dusty cut to the chase. The signs Janusz had affixed to the corner stall in the bathroom right after Thanksgiving had not solved the problem. Janusz stood in angry silence as Dusty spoke in plain terms about what we had begun to call "The Mystery of the Secret Shitter" amongst ourselves and what would happen if it didn't stop. "If we find out who you are," he said, "you're heading straight to the disciplinary committee where you'll face possible suspension and expulsion. Am I clear?" He looked around the room.

Freddy raised his hand. "I'm sorry," he said. "I don't understand the problem."

The room, which already had been quiet, went dead silent. Dusty folded his arms. "Excuse me?"

Freddy shrugged. "I don't understand what the problem is."

Dusty's eyes narrowed. "The problem, Freddy, is that it's offensive, anti-social behavior. It has no place at an institution like Inverness. I am not going to tolerate it in a dorm where I am the RA. Period."

Freddy shrugged, and said, "Maybe I'm missing something here, but it's Janusz's job to clean up after us. This seems like much ado about nothing."

I was not a big fan of Freddy's as you may have gathered already. He was a handsome, spoiled rich kid who had been anointed with beauty and family money, and he spent those attributes as if he had earned them. Yes, he had moments of good charm and could be a welcome companion to good fun. But, not now. Sometimes he said stupid, ridiculous things to be provocative or outrageous. This was one of those times.

Anthony thought so too. "Shut up, Freddy. You're being an asshole. We talked about this in the showers, and I said as much then. Cut it out."

"How am I being an asshole?"

Anthony pointed his finger at Freddy. "Don't give me any fucking lip. You shut your fucking mouth right now or else I'll shut it for you."

Freddy crossed his arms. Anthony had shut him down, and there was no further discussion. The whole situation was bizarre, and it was unsettling to think someone in this room was engaging in such anti-social behavior. It was actually even worse than Dusty described. He had omitted the detail known to all of us that someone was also masturbating in the same stall and letting their semen drip down the wall. Freddy's disdainful questions and tone added an ugliness to a meeting that was already starting at a low point and ending up even lower. I didn't think Freddy had anything to do with the shenanigans in the stalls. But, by trying to suggest Janusz did not have the right to object, Freddy had inflamed the situation and added to the tension. I hoped this was the end of it. I could tell by the anger and irritation on Dusty's and Janusz's faces it better be or else there would be more trouble.

Most everyone left for home by the end of the day, including Daniel. He looked drained and exhausted from exams, as all of us were, and he was glad to be on his way home to recover. I was definitely going to miss him over break and hoped our friendship could be reset in a positive way when the new semester started.

Because this was one of the last big trading days of the year, my father was not able to drive up to get me until the next day, which was a Saturday. People like Dusty, who had cross-country flights home, would not be leaving until tomorrow as well. When he and I learned of our mutually belated departure date, a stadium's worth of bright lights lit up in each of our heads at how this presented a unique opportunity to spend the night together in the quiet of a dormitory that was otherwise empty of almost every other student. My cock stirred at the thought of the possibilities. He broke out into an open grin at the prospect of the untold pleasures that would flow from the luxury of an entire night behind a locked door. Our relationship was about to take a few leaps forward, and we both knew it.

15 ANGELS

DUSTY WANTED TO make our big night together special, and he made plans to take me out to dinner at Oriental Garden, a Chinese restaurant in the village of Inverness. Chinese food was far more exotic then than it is now, and a white bread kid from suburban Hartford like me had never had it before. I had also never been on a date with a guy before, which felt pretty exotic as well. I was caught up in the exhilaration of being in love for the first time and the knowledge Dusty loved me right back. It was hard to imagine how I could have been any happier than I was.

There was no blueprint that I was aware of for relationships between two guys during those times. I had never known of men being lovers in a way that men and women were. There were none that I knew of in popular culture, in movies, in any literature I had read or heard of, in school, or in any other facet of public life as I knew it. I had only heard of the furtive aspects of homosexual conduct as perceived by others: the veneer of sleaze, the perversion, the arrests, and the aspersions that were cast upon those who engaged in it. My relationship with Dusty didn't feel like that at all. Yes, it felt forbidden on the outside. But, it felt so natural and beautiful on the inside.

I knew it was illegal for us to have sex back then. I was well aware that people would hate that we loved each other and would be afraid of what that meant. I also knew of the dangers that faced us and the need for discretion if you didn't want trouble, which neither of us did. That's not to say I was ashamed. I wasn't. At all. I was flush with pride and excitement. I knew I had nothing to be ashamed about, and if there was cause for shame, it should be cast upon those looked at us and saw ugliness instead of beauty. I couldn't hold Dusty's hand and walk down the street in public. But, I could go out on a date and have dinner at a restaurant with him, just like the dates I had gone on with Allison. Just like the dates boys took girls on every Friday and Saturday night. It felt like a big step forward, and I could not have been happier to be doing it.

He stopped by my room to get me, and we bundled up for the walk across campus into the village. A steady snow had fallen that afternoon and evening, blanketing the campus in a further quiet that had descended upon it with the departure of most of the students. As we walked to the restaurant, we leaned in towards each other to shield ourselves from the gusts of snow and the cold. Hunched together against the wind, our shoulders would touch every few steps. I felt warm all over inside.

Oriental Garden has a gaudy kitschiness to me in my memories. But, it didn't feel that way to me and my eighteen year old self. As I type these words, I am smiling with bemusement at how sophisticated I felt to be going out with Dusty to a foreign restaurant. The staff was all Chinese and spoke the English of the menu, but little else. The décor was colorful. The high-backed booths were covered with red Naugahyde. Paper lanterns hung from the ceiling. The music of Chinese mandolins and flutes played from an overhead speaker. Wooden chopsticks, which I had never used before, were at every table.

Dusty ordered a variety of dishes for us along with a drink called a scorpion bowl. It was a fruity concoction with a potent amount of alcohol that was served in a large, decorated ceramic bowl that had a volcano rising up from the center. It was meant to be shared, and Dusty and I each drank from it with straws we dipped into the bowl. Our foreheads would touch together as we leaned forward to sip the drink, which felt daring and romantic at the same time. Most of all, it felt so right to share the magic of the evening with someone I had come to love with such intensity it frightened me if I thought about it too much.

"I have something for you," he said, reaching into the pocket of his overcoat. He pulled out a brown paper bag that had a present inside wrapped in Christmas wrapping paper. I immediately felt a sharp pang of regret. We had not discussed exchanging gifts. I had not thought to get him a present, and I was embarrassed he had gotten me one. Despite the love we felt for each other, we had never formally vocalized the nature of our relationship and whether he was my boyfriend and whether I was his. This seemed to say we were, which normally would have made every part of me soar. Now that he had just handed me a present and was sitting there empty-handed, I wanted to kick myself for not matching his thoughtfulness.

"I feel terrible," I said. "I didn't get you anything."

"Don't worry about it! Just open it," he said.

I shook my head in embarrassment and tore open the wrapping paper. When I pulled it back, I am sure my eyes widened and my mouth opened at the unexpected surprise. It was a hardback copy of *The Razor's Edge* protected in a cellophane wrapper.

Dusty's eyes overflowed with pride and excitement. "Take the wrapper off and look inside!"

My heart was pounding with emotion fueled by how exceptionally well thought-out this gift was and who was giving it to me. I opened the cover and flipped to the title page, which was marked with the signature "W. Somerset Maugham" neatly hand-written with the ink of a fountain pen. I wondered if it was what I thought it was, and I looked up at him.

"Yes, it's a first edition signed by Willie himself. Do you like it?"

My eyes burned from the sting of emergent tears that threatened to spill over and down my cheeks but didn't. To say I was moved would be a gross understatement. I sat there in fumbling silence. I could not find words to express the avalanche of emotion I felt. To pull myself together, I turned my gaze to the artificial Christmas tree that stood to the left of the cash register at the front of the restaurant. After a long moment, I turned back to meet Dusty's expectant eyes.

"It's so incredibly thoughtful, I don't know what to say," I said, choking out the words, my voice slow and hoarse. I didn't know what reaction Dusty had been anticipating from me, but I am sure it was not this one, which had to have seemed rather bewildering to him. The truth was, I was stunned and could barely speak. I was so moved Dusty would have made the effort to give me a gift with such meaning. I could not believe anyone could ever have selected a gift with such thought, refinement, and effort – and such expense. What made it even more meaningful to me was that the book was important to him as well. We had spoken at length about the central themes of the story, how the main character, Larry Darrell, searched for meaning and purpose in life, and the idea that love without passion isn't really love. This is all to say nothing of how *The Razor's Edge* had precipitated our first kiss as we each leaned in to grab the book as it slipped from his fingers that night in his room.

The look of bewilderment melted from Dusty's face as I explained all of the above. I could tell by the way he looked at me that if he could have, he would have leaned over and kissed me. Instead, he reached under the table and squeezed my thigh. He held his hand there until our food arrived. His gaze met mine, and he stared at me with those improbably blue eyes that said everything he needed to say without speaking a word. We had spent countless hours so far talking about just about everything in the intense impassioned way that young people speak of ideas and experiences as if they were the ones who had thought or felt them for the first time in the history of mankind. One of the great things about knowing so much about what the other thought is we could have a complete conversation that began with a squeeze of my thigh and be conducted solely by looking the other in the eye and knowing what the other was thinking and where their thoughts would go.

Though we would spend endless hours probing each other's brain with the same curiosity and intensity with which we probed each other's body, tonight was not one of those nights. We were content with small talk, as if we had known each other forever, which it felt we had. It was pretty great just to be out in public with Dusty and do something normal, like a real couple. I basked in the glow of emotion at the impact his gift had upon me. Over the course of my lifetime, I prefer giving gifts to receiving them. That Dusty would think of such a gift and know me so well as to have made the effort to get it for me pulled me into him and his world in a way I never wanted to leave. To this day, that book is on the shelf right next to my desk as I type these very words, and it is one of my most prized physical possessions.

I never imagined as we walked to dinner at Oriental Garden in a small college town in Vermont that my life would change in the way that it did. The irony is that a Chinese restaurant seemed out of place here on a snowy night in Vermont in just the same way Dusty and I seemed out of place in the world. Sure, we had already fooled around in sexual ways and shared the heightened passion of love when it has been found for the first time. But, by going out for a fun meal, sharing a potent drink with paper umbrellas, and sitting in public with Dusty's hand on my thigh underneath the table felt like something regular people did. He had given me a gift selected and received with the greatest love and affection. We weren't deviants in the way that the law and society condemned us. Tonight, we were just a couple of boys out on a date.

The snow continued to fall while we were in the restaurant, and the walk back to campus was more challenging than the walk had been on the way there. But, we didn't care. We were flush from a second scorpion bowl, and we were glowing with the realization that our evening out had served as a stepping stone to a real relationship, even if it was one we had to keep to ourselves. Under the cover of snow and darkness, Dusty interlocked his elbow with mine in a way that was romantic, loving, and brave all in the same simple gesture. My cock was a constant source of pleasure and surprise then, and I remember it was rock hard and throbbing as Dusty's arm connected with mine.

After we passed through the iron gates at the entrance to the campus, we trudged the length of the long mall that was grassy in the summer and a blanket of pure white on this snowy night. It stretched majestically from where we stood at the quad down to the gates of the campus.

As I paused to look back at the distant lights of the village, Dusty dropped to the snowy ground on his back and spread his arms.

"What are you doing?" I asked.

"A snow angel."

"You're crazy."

He laughed. "Give me a break! I never saw snow until my freshman year. I've had to make up for what you East Coasters have been able to do your whole lives."

I dropped down next to him and created my own angel with the outstretched motions of my arms and legs. My face was so cold I could barely feel it anymore, and my clothes were wet from the snow that the heat of my body had melted. I laid there with the snow pelting my face and thought how great this was. I was so happy to be here with Dusty that my heart was soaring as high as it ever does.

As I think back to that night and this image, we really were two angels. We were innocent, happy, and consumed with goodness and the simple joy of being with each other on a beautiful night like this. It was such a hateful, difficult time for people like us who dared to find love with each other. Somehow, we had found it and were able to forget the outside forces that condemned us as we enjoyed the moment. I have seen great beauty over the course of my life and travels. But, it is difficult for me to think of anything more beautiful than the memory of two angel boys in love on a snowy night.

Dusty stopped the arcs of movement from his arms and legs. "Shhh," he said. "What do you hear?"

I listened. "Just the falling snow," I said, which barely made any sound out at all.

"That's right," he said. "It's just us. It's so beautiful - the falling snow, the view, the silence."

My eyes blinked in agreement. I was too taken with the moment to say anything.

"And, most of all, being here with you," he added. He leaned up on his elbow and I leaned up on mine and into him. Our lips met, and we kissed as the snow fell upon us.

※

We were not the only the ones in the dorm, but it was mostly empty. Dusty had a twin bed in his room, as did I. Given the plans we had for each other, however, a twin bed would not do. With Daniel gone, we could pull my mattress and his down onto the floor and push them together so we could spend the night in the same bed, something we had not been able to do before, even at my parents' house, where we had been relegated to sleep in twin beds.

We had made sure no one had seen us enter my room, and I turned out the light as soon as we were safely inside. The luminescence of the outdoor lights reflected off of the snow and bathed the room in a gentle, white light that kept us from total darkness. Knowing we would have the entire night together in the same bed felt unbelievably sublime.

Despite the near emptiness of the dorm, we felt the need to be as quiet as possible, which I must admit felt sexy as well. Some of the most powerful sexual experiences of my life have been when I was having sex when I had to be as quiet as possible because others were about and there was the danger of getting caught. Tonight was one of those nights. We reached for each other in the silence and the semi-darkness. Our lips met first. His tongue slid into my mouth and found mine and began a duel for supremacy that ended in a draw. His arms embraced me, and mine him. He reached with the top half of his hand into the back of my damp khakis and touched his middle finger to the top of my crack, gliding his finger up and down. In unison, our cocks hardened and we pressed them together through our clothes in a mad, hungry, and powerful embrace that each of us knew was just the beginning.

I reached for his belt buckle and fumbled with his pants. They fell to the floor. His hard cock bulged from his underwear, which I yanked halfway down. His cock bounced out in unencumbered freedom. I dropped to my knees and took it in my mouth. It tasted faintly of urine and the saltiness of sweat. The unmistakable musky odor emanating out from his groin made my own cock surge even harder. My cocksucking skills had improved with practice, and I was able to take his long, thick cock into my mouth with relative ease. My tongue slithered around the broad, shiny helmet of his cock head and flicked back and forth across the opening of his dick hole. He moaned my name and a slow, steady stream of pre-cum leaked from his cock into my mouth, coating my tongue with a smooth and salty film.

I moved my head down and created a ring of suction just past the crown where it met the barrel of his cock. I sucked with alternating degrees of tension. He moaned my name again and grabbed my head above each of my ears. I slid my mouth further down and then back up and then back down with several slow strokes. Until meeting Dusty, I had never given much thought to sucking a cock. I had liked to look at them, of course, and fantasized about touching one and jerking off sometime with a buddy, which had never happened. With Dusty, however, I hungered with the ultimate need to have his cock in my mouth. I wanted to smell it, taste it, and wet its smooth skin with my tongue.

He pulled his cock from my mouth and dropped to his knees so we were eye-to-eye. He pulled me towards him and kissed me hard while his right hand flipped the clasp of my belt buckle open. Roughly, he shoved my pants and underwear down and released my cock.

He pushed me back onto the bed I had created and tugged my pants and underwear the rest of the way off of me. He dove onto me as I lay spread-eagle, and he buried his face in my crotch in much the same way I had with him. His tongue swirled around the crown of my penis. In a smooth, singular motion I was not yet skilled enough to mimic, he slid his mouth down to the base of my pubic bone and swallowed my entire cock. I gasped. He had done this before on a number of occasions, but each time it never ceased to amaze me how incredible it felt. It was an ethereal combination of friction, pressure, wetness, and the beauty of skin-to-skin contact. As his head bobbed up and down, he cradled my scrotum between his fingers. He twirled my balls and ran his fingers in marveled curiosity over the tight, wrinkled skin. I gasped for breath.

"Stop!" I withdrew from his mouth just as I was reaching the point of no return.

He flipped over onto his back and laughed. "Your cock tastes so amazing!"

I leaned in and kissed him. He wrapped his arms around me, and we rolled around on the bed entangled in a tight embrace. I remember how strong his arms felt as they enveloped me and how cherished and safe I felt with him. Our lovemaking had a power, a sense of caring, and a sense of insatiable rawness all built into a formidable package of physical and emotional intimacy. We kissed, we explored each other's body, we tested each other's strength, and we searched for new ways to satisfy each other's desires along with our own. I was new to the world of sex with any gender. Yet, I knew even then the difference between sex with just anyone and sex with someone I cared about as much as I loved Dusty.

He reached for my boner, grabbing it with a strong grip and shifting his body so he could rub our cocks together. I looked down and grinned at the sight of our balls snuggled up close in a nest of wrinkled, bulging scrotums and a tangle of black and brown pubic hair. Our cocks were clasped against each other's by his open hand, which stretched to encase them both but could only reach half-way. I brought my hand down to close the circle, my palm against our cocks and my fingers interlinked with his. The sight of a large, hard cock is powerful under any circumstances. The sight and combined sensation of both of our large cocks pressed together between our hands was hypnotic, and we each stared at them. Because my cock juts out straight and Dusty's cock had an upwards arc, the skin of the undersides of our cocks only met until Dusty's curved away. I squeezed my Kegel muscles, and my cock surged. A drop of pre-cum escaped from my dick hole. Dusty did the same and produced a larger drop that spilled over and slid backwards down the underside of his shaft.

I wanted – needed – to taste the drop. I brought my head back down to his groin and ran my tongue up and down the underside of his cock. His pre-cum tasted salty and sweet and made me hunger for more. He spun himself around so he was under me in the 69 position. We bathed each other's cock with our tongues and sucked them. I could only swallow Dusty's cock half-way before I began to gag. But, he could take the full length of mine all the way down to the base.

I grabbed his firm ass with my hands while his cock stuffed my mouth. I spread his cheeks and ran a wet finger over the tight slit of his hole. It relaxed, and I slid my finger inside him. He gasped and sucked my cock even harder. I curved my finger and probed his prostate, which caused him to moan and writhe. He rubbed his finger against my hole, which was tight and not as ready for his finger as his was for mine. With a mixture of pleasure and pain, however, he worked its way inside me. He pressed my prostate, which thrust me over the edge of no return.

I tried to warn him I was starting to cum. But, his cock was down my throat, and I choked on my words. It didn't matter. He knew what was happening. I held back for as long as I could until I exploded with a series of bursts that shot inside him. He squeezed my ass, and at that instant shot his own load in my mouth. Our moans entangled, and our bodies writhed together in simultaneous ecstasy. It was hard to imagine any greater bliss. As the glow ebbed, I rolled onto my side and held Dusty from behind, my moist, spent cock mashed up against the heat of his crack, my chest pressed against his back.

"That was so incredible," he said, his voice woozy with ecstasy.

I could only murmur in agreement. I was spent in every way. Not just sexually, but emotionally as well. My heart swelled at the thought of how lucky I was to be here with Dusty and to have shared with him the extraordinary joy of connecting with him in the way we just had. I remember thinking how beautiful life was and what a miracle I was able to experience it in the way that I was. I was exhausted and felt the pull of sleep.

"I love you," he said.

I clutched him tighter and said, "I love you, too."

The post-dawn sunlight was obscured by the grey, heavy sky and snow that had continued to fall over night. The muted light bathed the room and caused us to stir as the darkness lifted. During the night, Dusty and I had shifted around so I was now curled on my side with him spooning behind me. His chest was pressed up against my shoulder blades, his arms wrapped around me. His cock was snug inside my crack. It was rock hard and twitched against the bare skin of my ass. I had not yet opened my eyes, and I nestled my ass firmly against his pelvis.

We each murmured, not yet fully awake. He reached under the covers and bent his cock downwards and burrowed it between the cheeks of my ass. In slow motion, he slid it back and forth as if he were gently fucking me from behind. Because of his cock's upward curve, its smooth skin slid against my crack and spread the slit of my virgin hole. When it reached the other side, it jabbed my balls and pressed up against the underside of my cock. He gripped my hips and slid his cock back and forth between my thighs.

Now, more awake than we had been, he buried his face in my neck and kissed it. I savored the sensation of his facial stubble against mine. I inhaled his scent, a fragrance borne of sex, sweat, and unbathed skin. He wrapped his arms around me in a tighter embrace and continued to probe his cock between my legs. I reached for the bottle of baby oil I kept under my bed for use sometimes when I masturbated. I opened it and dribbled out a bead of oil, slathering a coat of it on Dusty's cock and on my own. He hummed with pleasure at the increased ease with which it permitted him to fuck the smooth skin between my thighs. His arms tightened around me, and I felt a thrill at the sensation of vulnerability and being dominated by his strength.

He reached down and pushed my hand aside. He grabbed my cock and stroked it while continuing to hump me. The slippery contact of his lubed-up cock against my crack and hole was too much. Without warning for either of us, I sprayed a load of cum across the sheets.

"Oh, baby," he said as he squeezed the last drops of cum out of me. His hips were thrusting powerfully against my ass. "Oh, baby," he said again in combination with a muffled moan of pleasure as he shot his load between my legs. A river of cum splashed across my cock and balls, forming a gooey coating over the outside of my hole. We each shuddered in ecstasy and drifted back into a lazy, shallow slumber.

Dusty stirred first, lifting himself up onto his elbow to check the clock. As incredible as the last twelve hours had been, we each knew without saying it was coming to an end for now. His bus for the airport was leaving in an hour. My father would be up here sometime after that. In the meantime, I needed to pack, return the mattresses to the bed frames, and pull my room back together.

"Hit the showers and grab a quick breakfast?" Dusty asked.

I loaned him a towel so we could head straight to the shower together. I opened the door first to take a peek outside to make sure we were alone. We were. With the coast clear, we headed down the hall and into the bathroom. I was glad no one was there, so I could continue to have him all to myself. I leaned against the sink as I watched him lather up his face with shaving cream and use my razor to shave himself. Then, he lathered up my face and shaved me. He splashed my cheeks with warm water when he finished and patted me dry. So intense were my feelings towards Dusty, even an act as mundane as shaving together felt sublimely erotic to me. I leaned forward and kissed him.

In the vestibule outside the shower, we hung our towels on the hooks. We strolled inside and turned on the faucets and began to luxuriate in the warmth of the cascading water. From out in the main part of the bathroom, we could hear the sound of the door opening. I didn't think anything of it at first, but was surprised when it was Freddy who joined us.

"Good morning, gentlemen," he said, a sly smile on his face.

"I thought you left for home already," I said.

"Nope. Taking the bus up to Burlington and flying home to Cleveland later this morning. You fellas have fun last night?"

Both Dusty and I shrugged, but didn't say anything. Of all people to have joined us in the afterglow of a morning following a night that had been extraordinary on every level, it was disappointing it had to be Freddy. I didn't trust him anymore. After his behavior towards me since I had caught him with Shorty, I had grown increasingly wary of him. Moreover, his comments about Janusz in the all-hands meeting yesterday had caused me to sour further on him. After having had such a magical night, I had been hoping to draw out every moment I could with Dusty before we would be separated over the three week break. I was understandably disappointed at Freddy's presence. Nonetheless, we made small talk about the snow, the upcoming holidays, and the relief that winter break was upon us. But, I didn't linger in the shower and left it before they did.

Before we knew it, it was time for Dusty to start his journey home. The snow had mostly stopped. I walked with him to the college-chartered bus that would take him to the airport. I felt a sense of loss and longing, even if our good-bye would only be temporary. I wanted to hug and kiss him good-bye when we stood by the curb while he waited to board. But, that was impossible, of course. Once he was on the bus, he took a seat next to Freddy on the side where he could see me. Dusty gave me a broad smile through the window and waved. I waved back. Freddy waved as well, probably thinking I was waving at him, too, even though I wasn't. It had been an incredible semester. Dusty was a huge part of my happiness, of who I was, and who I was becoming. These upcoming weeks would be difficult without him. But, I was looking forward to the start of the New Year and what that might bring for us now that I knew with all certainty we were moving ahead together at full force.

16 OUT WITH A BANG

MY FATHER ARRIVED about an hour after the bus had left for the airport, which gave me enough time to get my room back in order. He had arisen before dawn and had been on the road for several hours. He was tired from driving, so I took over the wheel. I was happy to see him, and we talked about finals, the end of the semester, and non-substantive topics until he drifted off to sleep. That gave me a couple of uninterrupted hours to think about Dusty, Daniel, and how lucky I was to have The Magnificent Seven.

I also thought about Allison and how much I had grown away from her since I had started my new life at Inverness. Although we had exchanged brief letters wishing the other well on final exams, we had not spoken since Thanksgiving, which was unusual for us. I wasn't sure what she and I had become, notwithstanding what had happened and not happened in the laundry room at her house over Thanksgiving. But, I knew in my heart where we weren't going. I couldn't move forward fully and cleanly with Dusty if Allison remained on the sidelines, even if the sidelines were on the opposite edges of the playing field. I finally admitted to myself that it was time to discuss with her in person about officially parting ways but remaining friends, and I resolved to do so over the break.

Once I was home, I quickly fell into a routine of not doing much of anything. My mother made sure Florence kept me well-fed. I would eat, sleep, read, and watch TV even though there was not too much to watch in those days. I masturbated when I got into bed each night, in the morning before I got out of bed, and usually at least once more at some point during the day behind the safety of my locked bedroom door. I saw some old friends from high school and was saddened, but not surprised we were continuing to grow apart. I also reached out to Allison to get together for our talk. But, she was on her way with her family to her grandparents' house in Old Saybrook again and wouldn't be back until New Year's Eve. Our parents were social acquaintances and mine had invited them, along with Allison, to the annual New Year's Eve party at our house. I figured that would be as good a time as any to have the talk that would allow both of us to move forward unencumbered.

Another thing I did over break was eat oranges – a lot of them. Dusty's mother had sent an entire crate as a thank you gift to my parents for having hosted her son at Thanksgiving. Oranges were expensive in those days and more of a treat than they are today. The gesture had been well-received by my entire family and particularly me, who was eating most of them. I still have the crate they came in. It is beat-up after all of these years, but I use it to hold old record albums. It sits at the bottom of the bookshelf next to the desk in my study, and you can still read the words that say "McCaffrey Grove" in a faded florid blue script with an orange in place of the "o."

It was not a white Christmas that year, but it was cold enough to light the fireplace while we exchanged gifts as a family. I remember receiving a new squash racquet my father had proudly picked out. I received a few books, including Ayn Rand's *Atlas Shrugged*, and Nevil Shute's *On the Beach*, both of which were best sellers that year. I also received Winston Churchill's *The Age of Revolution: A History of the English Speaking Peoples, Volume 3*, which recounted Britain's rise to world leadership over the course of the eighteenth century. It, too, was a best seller that year, and was of particular interest to me given how Winston Churchill was one of my heroes for his leadership in dark times. Otherwise, Christmas was nowhere near the commercial extravaganza it is today, and the day was mostly quiet.

Later that morning, we went to church. It was crowded with dedicated congregants like my parents along with those who attended only for the major holidays. Despite the ease with which I succumbed to the pleasures of the flesh, I have a strong faith in God. I have never been a big believer in organized religion, however. I enjoy the spirit of community, the music, and the meditative experience of the service. I generally listened to the sermons, but would zone out during the rote recitation of prayers.

This time, however, as I sat with my family and recited the Lord's Prayer with the rest of the congregation, I stumbled over the words "and lead us not into temptation, but deliver us from evil." I mulled those words over in my mind and repeated them to myself. Without doubt, I had plummeted headfirst into temptation with Dusty. I couldn't lead myself away from him even if I had wanted to. The pull was too powerful. I had wrestled for years with my same sex desires and the reconciliation of sin, and I knew I was supposed to believe my conduct with him was the evil about which those words were uttered. But, as I ruminated over them and what they might mean, I knew in my heart they were not meant for us. We were the angels who lay in the snow as our souls radiated with the power of love. We were not abominations, no matter what anyone thought or said. I just had to believe that.

Later that afternoon after church, I was upstairs in my room masturbating. This was the era when masturbation was viewed as self-abuse and a sin with negative health implications. But, that didn't stop me even though there had been times that I had tried. Despite my views on organized religion, however, I used to feel guilty about masturbating on religious holidays in case I had bet wrong and was, in fact, masturbating my way to hell. I would try not to masturbate on Christmas and Easter, but my success rate was checkered. This was one of those years when I wasn't able to keep my hands off myself, and I was upstairs rubbing one out behind the safety of my locked bedroom door. In the middle of my self-depravity, I heard the phone ring and my mother answer it. Her voice raised an octave in delight when she realized who it was. But, otherwise I paid no attention and continued pounding away.

After a few more minutes when I was just about to blow my load, my mother started calling my name.

"Just a minute!" I shouted as I shot my load into the damp towel I had used to shower that morning. It was a rushed, unsatisfying orgasm ruined by my mother's voice and the sound of her approaching footsteps in the hallway.

"John! Telephone's for you."

"Sheesh, Mom! I'll be right there! Give me a sec!"

"It's Dusty!"

"Dusty?" She was almost at my door as I pulled up my pants. I opened it, my face flush in post-orgasmic glow, which I hoped she would not notice.

"He's calling to wish us a Merry Christmas. Isn't that lovely?"

After I shooed her away, I picked up the phone in the privacy of my parents' bedroom.

"Hey, baby," he said. "I miss you."

"I miss you, too."

We spoke in low voices for ten to fifteen minutes. It was incredibly great to talk to him. The five days since we had last seen or spoken to each other had seemed eternal. It's hard to imagine it today when you can call all over the world for practically nothing. But, long distance telephone calls back then, particularly trans-continental calls, were expensive and a far grander gesture than they are today. The connection was marred by static, and he sounded very far away. But, it was terrific to hear his voice, even if it made me miss him more. I whispered, "I love you," into the phone. He whispered it back, and we agreed I would call him at midnight on New Year's Eve.

&cr;

Between Christmas and New Year's Eve, I continued my pattern of eating, sleeping, reading, and jerking off until my cock was raw. As much as I was enjoying loafing about, I was becoming stir crazy and was looking forward to the excitement of a party, even if it was for my parents' friends and not mine. Allison and her parents were some of the first guests to arrive, and I happened to be in the foyer to greet them when they did. Allison's father shook my hand and slapped me on the back after uttering a hearty, "Hey, John! How's college treating you?" without waiting for an answer as he headed down the hall to our living room. Her mother kissed me on the cheek. I smiled at Allison, but we did not kiss or otherwise embrace.

At the time, I couldn't help but think what a phony prick her father was to show up at my house after the way he had wrenched my arm and dragged me up the stairs at his. Subconsciously, I rubbed my elbow where he had pinched it so tight it had been sore for hours. As a father myself, however, I have a greater sympathy for the fathers of daughters who have to fend off horny young guys who wanted to fuck their daughters. I have long since forgiven him for the rough way he treated me, particularly since I realize how terrifying it must have been for him to have seen the boner straining through my pants and my hands on his daughter's hips, even if she had been the initiator of the encounter. That New Year's Eve, however, I remember resenting him with a simmering measure of hatred given the freshness of my Thanksgiving humiliation.

I had been nervous that afternoon at the prospect of officially breaking up with Allison even though I didn't think it would be an unwelcome surprise to her. She had to have realized it would be better if each of us could go forth in our collegiate lives without the tether of a hometown attachment, no matter how tenuous that attachment had become. Our relationship had been intimate and sweet in a high school sort of way. But, I didn't feel the fire with her I now knew was possible since meeting Dusty. I couldn't imagine she felt it either. I knew even at that age, however, that women could be unpredictable and you never knew how they could react, particularly when matters of the heart – or the heartless – were involved.

Now that she was here, however, I was surprised at how happy I was to see her. We had not spoken since the events of

Thanksgiving. All barriers immediately fell now that we were standing here in person. She was dressed up in a pink satin dress with layers of tulle, and I thought she looked really pretty. If you were concerned I would be enough of a clod to break up with a girl on New Year's Eve, you may be relieved to know I knew as soon as she walked in the door this would not be the night for that. I was happier to see her than I had expected to be, and the image of a tear-streaked girl in a pink party dress flashed through my mind. I figured our talk could wait until another day when we could be alone before I returned to school.

Once we escaped from the scrutiny of our parents, we helped ourselves to champagne punch and food from the buffet. We ended up having a giggle about what had happened at Thanksgiving, and it felt surprisingly healthy to laugh at it given how humiliated and angry I had been. Her father had had a long talk with her about the dangers of young men and how they were only after "one thing." He had warned her to stay away from me tonight, which gave both of us a laugh.

Without the presence of people we knew from high school, we fell back into our natural rapport. We caught up and gossiped about our old high school gang. We reminisced. We made discreet fun of our parents' friends, particularly the pompous ones, the overt social climbers, and the phonies. Even though I wished it could always be like this between us, there was a bitter sweetness to the time we were spending together this evening. I had not fully shared all that was going on in my life, and I had the suspicion she had not shared everything going on in hers. That was okay with me. As we sat and shared a cocktail from the same glass, I had the sense tonight was not a mark on a continuum for us. It was a brief reunion from which we would soon split off in divergent directions.

We lost track of each other as the evening wore on. We were each separately corralled by successive chains of inquisitive adults inquiring in sincere terms about how we were faring in college. I had a long, friendly conversation with Bud Anderson. He asked about Dusty and inquired about the status of our rematch. I genuinely liked Bud and could see why my father had enjoyed the company of someone so genuine, without guile, and

MY BARE NAKED HEART

ready for an easy laugh. I could smell the scotch on his breath as he leaned in close and recounted some of the antics in which he had engaged during his own college years. He reminded me in a way of Howell, and it made me like him even more.

The night marched on. By now, it was just a mere half hour until 1958 would begin. It had been a fun evening, but I was tired and had had enough. I was one of the few sober people left and had started to feel out-of-place. Despite the mutually unspoken sentiment about the twilight of our relationship, I had been wondering if Allison might be expecting me to kiss her at midnight anyway. That didn't feel right anymore. If the world were perfect, I would be kissing Dusty when the clock struck twelve. I wanted to avoid any potential awkwardness with Allison if I could and did not want to kiss her.

I left the noise of the party below and went up to my bedroom. I was looking forward to speaking to Dusty at midnight and then going to sleep. I closed the door and lay down on my bed to kill some time before calling him. I thought about how much I wished I were with him. A smile spread across my face at the thought of how lucky I was and how great the year had turned out to be. I thought of The Magnificent Seven and wondered if Anthony was getting laid tonight. I thought of Daniel and how much I cared for our friendship. I thought of Dusty and how much I loved him. I picked up the first edition of *The Razor's Edge* he had given me and flipped through the pages. I was struck again by how much that gift meant to me.

I was startled by the sound of a hand on the doorknob and the sight of it twisting to the right. Allison slipped into my room, closing the door behind her as quickly as she had opened it. My brow crinkled in surprise at the sight of her as she approached my bed and sat down.

"What am I going to do with you?" she asked.

I didn't know what she meant. "It's a fun party, no?"

"I watched you sneak upstairs," she said. "Finally! I've been waiting to be alone with you all night."

I smiled, though her words confused me.

She leaned in and kissed me on the lips. "I couldn't wait until we could sneak off and be alone."

"What?"

"I saw the way you were looking at me. You've been such an incredible flirt all night!"

I know I can be hard to read, but I hadn't been flirting with her at all and didn't see how she could think that. Our interaction over the course of the evening had felt utterly platonic to me. But, she leaned in and kissed me again, sliding her tongue in my mouth as she did. I wanted to pull away. But, I didn't. My cock hardened. My mind was awhirl. This was all so unexpected and was unfolding faster than I was able to process it. Her hand found my boner and started to stroke it through the outside of my pants. The part of me that thought this was wrong and wanted it to stop was overruled by the part of me that wanted it to continue. The draw was too strong, and I just couldn't help myself.

Allison unzipped my pants and my boner popped out of them, bobbing vertically upward. She looked at it with trepidation. She had felt my cock through my pants before, but had never seen it uncovered. To my knowledge, it was the first penis she had ever seen and certainly the first erection. She touched it as if she were testing the bottom side of an iron and snapped her fingers back.

"It's okay," I said. "Touch it."

There was no way I could turn back now. In all honesty, I didn't want to even though I knew I should. I knew why Allison had come in here and what was going to happen next. I had dreamed about it for years, and I was hot with the anticipation it was finally about to happen. As my hard cock throbbed at the thought of the journey upon which it was embarking, I abandoned all rational thinking. I buried any obligations of loyalty and fidelity. I thought solely of prospective pleasure and the desire to cross over into the world I had explored only in my fantasies.

She gripped the bare skin of my cock head and squeezed it as if it were a foreign object with which she had no idea what to do. I slipped my hands under the layers of tulle and pink satin of her dress. I fumbled around in the disarray of fabric for her panties and yanked them down to her knees in my desperation to reach the hot wetness of her vagina. I slid the fingers of my right hand over her opening, which already was moist with arousal. My hand could feel the heat rising from it. I probed my middle finger over and then inside her. She moaned with pleasure. I pulled my hand up from under the fabric and brought it to my face so I could smell her musky scent and taste the wetness. She blushed.

"Do you have something?" she asked.

"Yes," I said, understanding the reference to a condom. I stood up, my pants around my knees, and shuffled over the few steps to my dresser and opened my sock drawer. I had bought three condoms from a vending machine in a gas station restroom a few years before on a family vacation in anticipation of a moment just like this one. I had practiced with one as soon as I got some privacy, unrolling it onto my cock and jerking off into it to see what it felt like. I pulled one of the remaining two out of the drawer and tore open the foil wrapper. Allison watched with a combination of curiosity and fear. I began to remove her dress, but she demurred, saying she did not want me to see her naked. As disappointing as that was to me, there was no way I was going to jeopardize anything, and I didn't protest. With my pants still around my knees, I climbed on top of her and wriggled my way between the confection of pink satin and layers of tulle. The head of my hard cock found the hot opening of her vagina, and I pushed my way in, inserting my glans inside her just past the curved ridge of the crown.

She winced. "Wait, wait! Go slow!"

I stopped. But, I did not pull out for fear she might not let me back in. I wondered if she made me stop now whether just getting the head in meant I had still lost my virginity or whether I had to get my cock all the way inside her for it to count. I remained propped on top of her for what seemed like an eternity, my cock pulsating as I waited for the go-ahead to resume. I said a silent, desperate prayer that I would be allowed to continue.

Her eyes were devoid of desire, and she grimaced in expectation the pain would worsen. It occurred to me at that moment she was seeking experience, not pleasure. She didn't want to be with me. She wanted to get through this and leave her virginity in the wake. The desire in my eyes was more than enough for both of us, however, and I shared her hunger for experience. I could tell by the determination in her gaze and by the way she lifted her hips she wanted me to continue. I slowly worked my hard cock all the way in, inch by inch. I reached some resistance with what I realized was her hymen. I steeled myself and pushed past it. She winced and gasped as I pressed myself inside her until I was all the way at the bottom. Slowly, I pulled almost all the way out. Then, I plunged back in.

Soon, I was pumping steadily up and down on top of her. I remember thinking how surreal this was and how incredible it was that I was finally doing it. Her vagina felt warm and wet on my penis even through the thickness of the condom. I was surprised, however, it did not feel as tight as I expected it would, despite the resistance I received as I broke through her hymen. I was used to the firmness of my dry hand, not the warm, soft canal I had entered for the very first time. I had assumed a vagina would be as tight as my fist, albeit with the added sensations of heat and wetness. The heat and wetness were there, though the active tightness of my well-traveled hands was not. That's not to say it did not feel fantastic, but rather to say the reality was different than I expected.

I could tell by how Allison stared at the ceiling instead of into my eyes she was not enjoying this. I wanted it to go on for longer, but figured enough was enough and it was time to bring matters to a close. I increased my tempo, my pants pulled down to my ankles, my bare ass pumping frenetically up and down on top of her. The pink satin dress and layers of tulle were flipped up on her midsection so that I would feel, but never actually see her vagina. I further increased my tempo and soon ejaculated a load of semen into the condom. It was a long, slow, powerful orgasm, one of the best of my whole life up until that point. I remember thinking how great this felt and how thrilled I was that I was now officially a man.

Spent, I rolled off of her and laid on my back while I caught my breath. Almost without pause, she sat up, pulled up her panties, and straightened out her dress. I wanted to bask in the afterglow of my orgasm and the joy of my newly acquired manhood, but I stood up because she did. I felt a tinge of self-consciousness that she was dressed and my pants were down, my softening cock and pubic hair exposed. Modesty barely mattered, however, because she wasn't looking at me. The condom was still attached to my cock, and it drooped with the weight of the semen-filled reservoir tip. I noticed there was a smear of blood on it.

"Are you okay?" I asked.

"Yes," she said with a distance I might have thought was coldness if I hadn't known her so well. Her mind was awhirl, too.

I pulled the condom off of my cock and wrapped it in a tissue before dropping it in the bathroom wastebasket where it landed with a thud on the empty bottom. She pressed the wrinkles out of her dress and smoothed her hair in the mirror that hung above my dresser. Then she used the bathroom, closing the door behind her. I pulled myself together as well. By the time she exited the bathroom, it would have been difficult to tell anything had gone on between us. I touched my hand to her shoulder and kissed her softly on the lips.

She smiled, turned away from me, and then looked back.

"We should go downstairs before people start wondering where we are," she said. "It's almost midnight."

"You're right," I said, even though no one would have been wondering about us except for her father, and he was pretty well plastered when I had last seen him an hour ago. "Are you sure you're okay?"

She nodded and said she was even though the awkwardness that had arisen between us suggested otherwise. We agreed she would slip out of the room first and I would follow a few minutes later. I wasn't sure what I was supposed to be feeling now. To say I was thrilled to have lost the burden of my virginity would be a wild understatement. I wanted to thump my chest with pride. But, Allison was acting strange and distant. Moreover, all of this had been so unexpected, which made it harder to process. I had planned on breaking up this evening, not consummating our relationship. She leaned up on her toes to kiss me on the lips for a long moment. Then, she was gone.

I looked back at the twin bed where I had spent so many endless hours with my hands on my cock, fantasizing about what it would be like to have sex. My heart sank, and I was seized by a jolt of guilt as my eye caught the first edition copy of *The Razor's Edge*, which had fallen to the floor unnoticed. It was the first thought of Dusty I had had since Allison had slipped into my room and I had ceased thinking about anything other than my own cock and my own sexual pleasure. I felt a torrent of shame at the thought of what I had done to him and what he would think when I confessed to him. He had forgiven me for Thanksgiving. Would he forgive me this time? I shook my head at the thought of it. From downstairs, I could hear the clamor of the party guests counting down the final ten seconds to midnight and the joyous cheers that followed. I didn't feel like cheering. The exhilaration I had felt dissipated as I pictured Dusty's smiling, loving face and the reality of what I may have just done to us.

Allison and her parents left not long after midnight. The gentleman in me returned to make an appearance as I said farewell to all of them while they buttoned their coats in the foyer and prepared to go out in the cold. Allison and I traded shy smiles, but she left without saying anything. I stood in the doorway and watched them walk towards their car. Allison's father had had too much to drink, and both Allison and her mother steadied him as they made their way down the walkway in the dark. I closed the door.

I would not see or speak with Allison for ten years until we met up again at our high school reunion a decade in the future, her husband at her side. In the morning on New Year's Day, she would sit down and write me a letter in girly script that would begin with her telling me I was "so sweet" and end with her saying she "would always remember what we had together." It may amuse you to know that even though I had been looking for a way to break it off with her for the very same reasons she explained why she was breaking up with me, I felt quite stung to be on the receiving end of such a letter, especially given how soon she wrote it after we had embarked on the joint mission to jettison our virginity. I wouldn't know any of this for several days, however. For the moment, I was happy to revel in my newly acquired manhood.

Dusty and I had agreed when he phoned on Christmas Day I would call him tonight just after midnight to wish him well in the New Year. Even though I had been looking forward to this call from the moment we first agreed I would do it, he was suddenly the last person with whom I wanted to speak. I went to my father's study and closed the door to call him. I poured myself some of my father's prized scotch even though it was a taste I had not yet embraced. It didn't matter that night. Scotch was a drink men drank, and I was now officially a man.

Direct dial telephone service was not yet possible between Hartford and rural Orange County, so I picked up the phone and dialed 0 to ask for a long distance operator to place the call. The local operator informed me the holiday telephone traffic had caused a delay of at least an hour before I could secure a long distance operator to place the call. I debated for shorter than I should have about whether I should wait. Just an hour ago, it would not even have been a question. I thanked the operator and actually was relieved to have an excuse to put off the inevitable and figure out what I was going to tell Dusty. My mind was a jumble of emotions, and I was not yet ready to share any of them with him. You probably expected better of me. I expected better of me as well.

Yet, I couldn't just sit on news like this and had to share it with someone. Daniel instantly came to mind, and I reached for the phone. This was a call for which direct dialing was available, and I dialed it myself. A weary-sounding housekeeper answered the phone, no doubt wishing she were back at her own home with her own family and friends rather than helping Daniel's parents entertain theirs. After a few minutes, he was on the line.

"Hey, buddy! Happy New Year!" he said.

"Happy New Year!" I was elated to speak with him, and there was a broad smile across my face. I told him everything that had happened with Allison. He could not have sounded happier as he said, "Welcome, to the club!"

One of the challenges I have found with male friendships over the course of my life is the difficulty men have in forming emotional connections with other men. When close bonds develop in unexpected quarters, complications can arise when it isn't clear where the path is headed and what is possible and what is not. This is particularly true when one or both of them is open even in the hidden depths of their private thoughts to sliding down the spectrum of human sexuality but is afraid of how far they might slide and what it might mean for them. They can be further complicated when those bonds awaken feelings the parties might not have known were there. Daniel was one of the people I cared for most in my whole life, and my relationship with him was riddled with those complications. I didn't know where my friendship with him was going, and I know he didn't know either. At this very moment, however, I could not have been happier to be able to call him in the middle of the night with momentous news of which I was bursting to speak with someone, but not just anyone.

I know you must think my conduct that evening with respect to Dusty was disappointing, and I cannot argue with that. You also might think me guilty of self-serving rationalization knowing I viewed the events of that evening as an unconventional farewell to Allison and my youth and a hello to the adult sexual life I knew even then was likely to be rife with complications. Despite how easily I had capitulated to temptations of the flesh, my sense of right and wrong still had a heartbeat, even if it were a faint one. I planned to come clean and share everything with Dusty after I figured out a way how to do it. I would think all of that through later on. For now, I was happy to think back at all that happened that night and over the big events in my life that had occurred this past year.

After I finished speaking with Daniel and crawled into bed, I jerked off to the still-fresh and incredibly unexpected memory of having lost my virginity. Yes, I was finally, truly a man! At least that's what I thought then, unaware of the challenges that were headed my way. I didn't yet know it, but on the near horizon, I would pass through a shadowed valley that would test me in ways that would alter the direction of my life. After a journey that would be harrowing in ways that make me tremble at the memory even all of these years later, I would rightly be able to call myself a man. But, not yet.

Nonetheless, I had changed this very night and grown up in a definitive way. As the glow of my blown load dissipated, I lay there happy that the year had ended with a bang and wondered what the New Year would bring. I could not yet know it, but it would be a rollercoaster of a year, one of the best and worst of my whole life. I had no inkling of any of that then, however. Gratified for now in more ways than one, I drifted off to a deep and heavy sleep blissfully unaware that unseen forces were setting the course for what would happen in the New Year.

17 SHADOW DANCING

AFTER A FEW lazy weeks, I was looking forward to returning to school with almost as much enthusiasm as I had been looking forward to leaving it for Christmas break. I missed Dusty, Daniel and the rest of The Magnificent Seven. I missed the sex play that had become the new normal between Dusty and me. I was truly in love for the first time in my life, and I just plain missed being with him. I missed how Daniel and I would lie in our separate beds at night and talk in the dark about everything and nothing with the lights out until one of us drifted off to sleep. I missed the drunken fun and the antics of the guys in the dorm. I missed the easy opportunities for innocent mischief that came from living in such close proximity to all of my buddies. I missed the freedom.

My father and I had left before dawn for the drive back to Inverness. I would have rather slept later, but he wanted to be back in Connecticut by lunch time and not spend his whole day in the car. It was hard to argue with that. He dropped me off, shook my hand, and got back into the car. I stood at the curb and wished he would look back at me to wave good-bye instead of driving off, eyes forward, and not thinking of me. I thought of how I had hoped for the same expression of affection back on the first day of school when I had stood in the second floor

MY BARE NAKED HEART

lounge in a pool of loneliness and watched my parents drive off without turning back for one last look at me, their only son.

Yet, it was remarkable to me how different today was than the first day of school when my mind had been a jumble of fear of the unknown and an acute sense of being alone in a sea of strangers. I had felt a sense of panic and turmoil then and had ached for my parents to turn around and offer me even the shortest wave of reassurance as I embarked on my new life where I knew absolutely no one. As this new semester began, however, I felt peace and not panic. I was happy here in a way I had never dared to imagine possible. This was where my life now was. This is where my friends were. This was where my boyfriend was. I rolled that word - boyfriend! - around on my tongue with a broad smile across my face and warmth in my heart. My father may not have thought to turn around for another look at me, but I liked where my life was going nonetheless.

I was one of the first to arrive back, so it was a day mostly spent waiting for everyone to return. One by one, they did. First Anthony, then Howell, then Sasquatch, and so on. The person I had most wanted to see, however, was Dusty, and he had not yet arrived. We had eventually spoken on New Year's Day. The words of what had happened with Allison and how I had dispatched my virginity had been ready to spill out of me. My heart had leapt at how happy he was to speak with me. I could hear the glow in his voice even through the static. How could I tell him? I shook my head at the thought of how hurt he would be. Would he forgive me? I sighed and braced myself to do what I needed to do.

The words I found so easy to share with Daniel were locked inside me. Where was the courage I needed to be honest with Dusty? For the first time since I left my virginity behind in my boyhood bedroom on New Year's Eve, I felt abject remorse. I had tumbled into temptation with someone I did not love and in the process of doing so betrayed someone I did. I chewed my lip and instead told him the lie I had not been able to get through to a long distance operator to place the call until morning. I winced with shame when he mentioned how he had sat by the phone for over an hour waiting for me to call until he had finally given up for the night. It was an image that shamed me. I had thought of Dusty's words after I had been dragged up the stairs from Allison's basement by her father: "'Let's just be honest and open with each other about everything, and we'll always be okay,'" he had said recognizing both his hurt and how he knew college was a time of self-discovery.

In addition to agreeing with those words as a promise, I also had promised what had happened with Allison would never happen again. I knew the bigger promise had been to be honest and open, and I intended to keep that promise. As I opened my mouth to confess the truth into the telephone receiver, however, I hesitated. He sounded so happy to hear my voice. Suddenly, it seemed too big of a confession to make over the phone, particularly when he was on one side of the country and I was on the other with the scratchiness of a long distance connection between us that stretched far beyond the bounds of geography. With every intention of holding myself to that promise, I decided to delay that conversation until I could face him in person. Now that I was back at school and expected to see him in person at any moment, however, it was not as easy as I had hoped it would be to do the right thing.

Daniel arrived back not long after I did. It was great to see him, and I hoped everything would be normal after the awkwardness that had fermented between us since Thanksgiving. Ironically, as much as I feared telling Dusty the truth about Allison would cause a gulf to rise up between us, my midnight call on New Year's Eve to Daniel had the opposite effect. The act of sharing with him what happened with Allison had soothed over some of the wounded feelings between Daniel and me. That's not to say there weren't still unspoken words and questions that hung above us. But, the act of confiding in him my momentous personal news had made us confidants of sorts even if we both knew I wasn't confiding everything.

Anthony, Sasquatch, Freddy, Howell, and Shorty arrived back by early afternoon. With no homework yet assigned, we headed over to the gym to play a game of basketball. I remember thinking how lucky I was to have such an incredible group of buddies and the uncommon closeness we shared. We laughed out loud. We wrestled. We punched each other. We gave each other noogies. Sometimes one of the guys would dry hump someone until the victim on the receiving end could break free. No one said it out loud, but every one of us was glad to be back together after break. We all knew our collective friendship was something special even if it went unspoken.

After building up a sweat during basketball, we returned to the dorm and hit the showers. We stripped out of our jockstraps and shorts in our respective rooms and strolled down the hall to the bathroom. Some of us wore towels wrapped around our waists. Others - like Shorty and Anthony, their dicks flopping from side-to-side - walked with bare naked bravado with their towels over their shoulders.

Once we were in the warm water oasis of the shower, Anthony probed each of us to see whether anyone had gotten laid over the holiday break, just as he had at Thanksgiving. All of the other guys just shook their heads in the negative. Even me. I thought Daniel might shoot me a glance. But, he didn't. He wasn't the type of guy to brag about something so personal, and apparently neither was I. As proud as I was to be looking at my virginity in the rear view mirror, I suddenly didn't feel like sharing the information any further than Daniel. I wanted it to stay that way. I was still smarting from having Allison dump me the very next morning after it happened. That wasn't news I felt like sharing until I could figure a way to spin it in a way that didn't make me look bad in front of the guys. Moreover, I wanted Dusty to hear it from me and not from someone else.

After showering, Daniel and I dressed for dinner and headed out of our room to meet up with the other guys. I glanced at Dusty's door in the obsessive way I had been watching it all day. This time, however, it was open and the light was on. I excused myself and told Daniel I would catch up with him and the other guys in a few minutes. His eyes followed mine, and there was no doubt he knew where I was going. He shrugged and said he'd save me a seat in the dining hall. He gave me a long, hard look as he borrowed from his present thoughts and questions with a discussion that would have to occur at some point, but hadn't yet. If he was thinking anything else, he wasn't saying it.

Without looking back, I hustled down the hallway and swooped into Dusty's room. My heart surged at the sight of him. His back was to me, and he was just setting down his suit cases. He turned around, a bright, enveloping smile on his face. His skin was golden brown, and he radiated with the glow of the California sun in which he had basked these past few weeks. Those brilliant blue eyes that pulled me into his orbit every time he cast them my way sparkled with open pleasure at seeing me.

"Hey, handsome," he said.

"Boy, did I miss you," I said, reaching for his waist to pull him in for a hug, but stopping myself.

"Hold on, close the door," he said.

I pushed the door shut with my foot and locked it. Then, I reached for his waist and pulled him in. He wrapped his arms around me. He hugged me so hard it hurt. Sometimes a hug is just a hug. This was more than that. It was a recognition of the power of the affection we had for each other and how painful it had been for us to have been apart. He hugged me as if he would never let me out of his sight and touch again. I hugged him right back. Our cocks were rock hard and throbbing, as they always were when we kissed and groped each other. Our mouths found each other's and then so did our tongues. We connected with a hunger that was unexpected only in the height of its intensity, which surprised even me. I had never missed anyone in my whole life in the way I had missed Dusty. Now that we were back together, I never wanted to miss him in that way again. I pulled back and buried my face in his neck. I inhaled the scent of his skin, a smell I can remember even all of these years later. It was a clean, but manly scent that smelled vaguely of sweat, sex, and the faintness of Old Spice. I breathed in deeply and held in the essence of his aroma for as long as I could.

Dusty was hungry, too. But, in a different way. He pushed me back, roughly, onto the tattered leather couch and dropped to his knees. He fumbled with my belt buckle and then my zipper with a flurry of fingers and hands. He tugged my pants down past my knees. He yanked my underwear down as well. In an instant, my hard cock was free and bobbing unencumbered. He grasped it with his right hand.

"I've been dreaming of your cock and what I wanted to do with it for the past eighteen hours," he said. "I stared out the airplane window and kept seeing cloud formations that reminded me of it."

I laughed. Before I could say anything, his mouth was on my cock with gusto. He grabbed my balls and twirled them in his fingers. His tongue swirled around the smooth, shiny helmet of my glans. He inhaled the musky scent of my cock in the same way I had inhaled the scent of his skin with my face buried in his neck. During the now uncountable times he had swallowed my cock, he had done so with such skill that if felt as if my cock and his throat had melded into a single, pulsating organ that both received and gave pleasure. This time was no different. He devoured my cock whole, all the way down to the bottom. His lips were jammed against my pubic bone, the hair of my loins mashed against his face.

Because my father and I had left so early, I had not jerked off since last night. I was accustomed to rubbing one out both in the morning when I woke up and then at night before I went to sleep. That meant I was super horny today and would have a big load. Dusty knew my body well enough by now to know what got me off and how to hijack control of my powers of ejaculation. He raised his mouth to the slippery wet crown of my cock and teetered there for a moment before plunging down to the bottom and rising back up again. He repeated this twice more, and I knew I was about to blow. There was no holding back. From the pre-cum that dribbled freely from my cock, I knew he could taste that I was just about to unleash a huge load inside him.

The tell-tale rumble with which I was well-familiar began from deep with inside me. It had been only minutes since I had entered Dusty's room and ascended from a flaccid, resting state to the toe-curling precipice of ejaculation. Since the ascent had been hurried, I expected the release to be hurried as well, and it was. I could feel the ribbon of semen rise up from within me and be drawn into his mouth. With a greediness that matched mine as I fought him in a doomed effort to prolong my ejaculation,

Dusty sucked my sperm from my body. He groaned with primal satisfaction as the first pulse shot against the back of his throat and as he gulped all of it down. I writhed and moaned until I was spent.

"Holy shit," I said, barely able to speak as I savored the ecstasy that still surged within me.

He lifted his head from my cock and leaned back on his knees and looked up at me. His eyes were half-lidded with relief, as if I had just permitted him the greatest favor of letting him welcome my cock and my semen inside him.

"I love you so much, I really fucking do," I said, my voice heavy with miraculous wonder.

His chest heaving with satisfaction, he leaned up on his knees and brought his mouth up to mine to kiss me. He clasped the back of my head with his hand in a way that was both firm and tender. My lips opened to meet his and receive his tongue. He slid it into my mouth along with the wholly unexpected surprise of my own semen, which he delivered off the arched surface of his tongue as if it were a warm, salty oyster. As much as anything Dusty offered me was an offering I wanted, I will confess that having my semen re-gifted to me was not an experience I would have asked for. I had tasted my own cum before, of course, both by scooping it off my naked belly after masturbating or licking my cheeks on the not uncommon occurrence of an errant spurt of semen landing on my face during a particularly athletic ejaculation. It was an acquired taste I had not yet acquired. As sincerely as I would acquire that taste, it was for the semen of others, not mine. But, I loved Dusty, and if he wanted me to try it, I would without hesitation. My eyes locked with his. Through closed lips curled in smile, I swirled my semen around on my tongue. After I swallowed, I opened my lips and so did he. Then we kissed for real.

☙

The next few weeks passed, and January bled into February. Dusty was busy applying to graduate programs in ancient classical history and antiquities at universities in the

Northeast. He had traveled to Boston to interview at Harvard. He also had an upcoming interview at Columbia during the first week of March, and we decided I would make the trip to New York with him. I didn't like to think about his interviews, because they were a reminder he would be graduating in May and moving away, which was an inevitability I wanted to forget. But, I was excited at the prospect of going to New York with him. It would be our first trip together other than the visit home to my parents' house for Thanksgiving. The anticipation of a weekend away with him – and the opportunity to share the same bed – was almost too much for me to think about. Until that could happen, we did the best we could.

We grabbed each other for stolen moments, some longer than others, but none that ever were long enough. Sometimes we would share meals together in the dining hall, which felt daring. If anyone thought anything of it, however, no one said anything. The years between senior and freshman was a wide enough gulf made even wider by Dusty's position as the RA for the floor and the perception that he was stricter than he had to be when it came to decibel levels and excessive alcohol consumption. If Dusty joined me and the rest of the guys in the dining hall, he was welcomed, albeit with some reservations. Even he recognized that salty topics of conversation would make sharp turns to the innocuous as soon as he sat down. I didn't care about any of that. I was just happy to be with him.

I liked my new classes, in particular a European diplomacy course Professor Johnston was teaching. I liked the subject matter and the reading materials. I also very much liked Professor Johnston and his teaching style, which was clearly structured as to form and purpose. He was instructive of his own theories, but wanted his students to develop their own, even if they challenged his. Professor Johnston and I already had discussed how he would be my faculty advisor as soon as I could officially declare international relations as my major at the beginning of sophomore year.

Life in the dorm settled into the same routines as before. The Magnificent Seven did more than our fair share of playing pick-up basketball, drinking, hanging out, farting, and general bullshitting, which was heaven to me. Sure, there were some annoyances. Daniel and Anthony could be testy with each other, particularly when Anthony was spearheading some of the "hijinks" Daniel's father had warned us about. They usually involved alcohol, running around outside in the dark, and making the type of noise that would raise Dusty's ire and which Daniel found childish.

The other annoyance was all of that nonsense with Janusz and the "Mystery of the Secret Shitter." I mentioned previously how someone had been refusing to flush their shit in the stalls in the bathroom on our floor. The same stall often had semen running down the wall. If it had only happened once or twice, I might have thought it funny. But, it had become never-ending and made using the bathroom on our floor hazardous. Semi-miraculously, it had stopped after Dusty and Janusz had the "town meeting" about it right before Christmas break. For the first week and a half after our return, we could shit in the luxury of stalls that glistened with well-scrubbed cleanliness and the antiseptic aroma of Lysol. Then it started up again with a vengeance. Almost every stall was befouled with near constancy, worse than before. Using the bathroom had become treacherous. If I needed to use a stall for its intended purpose, I gave up using ones on our floor and instead would use one somewhere else.

The signs Janusz had posted in the angry scrawl on each of the stall doors returned. He slashed every one of us with jagged glances when he passed us in the halls and common areas of the dorm, as if the guilty party could be exposed with menacing looks. I long had the sense Janusz resented having to clean up after us. But, after Freddy had so publicly tried to put Janusz in his place at the dorm meeting, Janusz saw guilt in all of us. It was unfortunate on every front, particularly because Janusz and I had had always exchanged pleasantries. I thought Freddy had been an asshole, and I didn't want Janusz to think I was one, too. The damage had been done, however. Janusz hated all of us. Aside from that nuisance, everything was great. Really great, as a matter of fact.

During the last week of February, Daniel and I were studying in our room on a Thursday night. I have mentioned previously that for many of the guys in the dorm, weekends started on Thursdays and sometimes on Wednesdays. Daniel and I generally were more disciplined than that. We each had our eyes on the future beyond college and tried to stay focused on our classes during the week, despite the distractions. We weren't perfect, however. I sometimes found myself struggling to resist the night-time shenanigans of my pals, particularly when alcohol was involved. Tonight was going to be one of those nights.

The sound of a fist pounding on our door caused us both to look up.

"Branson! Wonder Bread! Open up!"

It was Anthony. He didn't wait for a response and burst into our room, his exuberance even higher than usual. "What are you two pussies doing?"

"Studying, what does it look like we're doing?" Daniel said, the irritation in his voice unmistakable. I shot him a look, wishing he would just lighten up about Anthony. Daniel was more privileged and polished than Anthony, and it grated on him in the most transparent way Anthony had beat him in the silly competition to have the biggest dick in the room, both figuratively and literally. Daniel was confident, gifted and accomplished in his own right. But, Anthony was taller, louder, stronger, and he had the huge, monstrous cock all of us talked about openly in the way that only close college buddies could talk about, which we actually do sometimes even to this day. No one thought the lesser of Daniel because of Anthony. But, Daniel just couldn't get past his own pique.

"What's going on?" I asked, ready for a study break.

People used to look at Anthony only on the surface and completely miss the intuition and cold smarts that would serve him well and sometimes dangerously later in life. He knew how and why without saying it that Daniel was irked about the rivalry that openly bothered Daniel, but Anthony not at all. He looked coolly at Daniel and said, "What's going on is that Shorty has secured us a few stag films. We're having a special, invite-only cinematic event in the second floor lounge."

211

Daniel dropped the attitude as if he had never had it. "Stag films? Where'd Shorty get stag films?"

Anthony got in Daniel's face and smirked. "We had a camera that night we watched you pump that girl like a jackrabbit in the housemaster's lounge." He gripped Daniel's shoulders and fucked the air in what I must admit was a pretty fair imitation of the frenetic motions of Daniel's ass that night as he pounded his cock into Carol's vagina.

Daniel smiled back coolly without flinching as Anthony moaned and pumped his hips in a way that was comical, accurate, and erotic at the same time.

"Have you had enough?" Daniel finally asked. Knowing what I knew about his pride, I was nervous he might react in way that would blow up the whole evening.

"C'mon, you fruit cakes," I said. "I want to see the stag films, not you guys." That wasn't true of course. I would have given anything to watch Daniel and Anthony go at it naked and see Daniel get punished by Anthony's huge cock. That would never happen, but watching a stag film in the lounge apparently was about to. I had heard about stag films, of course, but had never seen one before. The prospect of watching one was almost too good to be true. I had seen photographs of naked women, but never anything hardcore. I knew from our wide-ranging conversations Daniel never had either. Pornography was illegal and difficult to get back then. Though, as Shorty had demonstrated, it was not impossible. If there was a stag film, I definitely wanted to see it and so did Daniel.

We trailed after Anthony, practically stumbling over ourselves in our eagerness to make it to the special invite-only cinematic event that had been completely unexpected. When we reached the lounge, the door to it was closed and locked. Anthony knocked twice. Sasquatch opened the door and quickly shut it behind us as soon as we were inside. He was careful to lock it as well. No one needed to explain to any of us we had to be as discreet as possible. If we were caught watching porn films, very serious trouble was a given. There was no doubt in my mind it was an offense for which all of us risked expulsion. That didn't stop us, however. The draw was too great.

Shorty was grinning his elfin smile as he stood next to the movie projector he had set up in the middle of the room. He had pulled the screen down from the ceiling, the same screen Dusty had used with his "Getting to Know You" slideshow presentation he had made on the first day of school. The couches had been pulled away from the wall and were set up askew in the center of the room.

"Gentlemen, so glad you could make it," Shorty said. I have commented before that Shorty was a bright spirit amongst our group of friends. He had a smirky smile and an easy laugh. There was no pretense about him whatsoever. He was always up for fun, particular of the raunchy sort. I have never forgotten how I had watched him give Freddy a blowjob in the housemaster's lounge that night after all of us had frolicked naked in the snow. I also had never told anyone about it, either. At the same time, I didn't know yet that Shorty and Anthony had watched Dusty and me that afternoon in the lobby of the dorm, my back against the wall as we kissed for the second time. Incredibly, Shorty and Anthony had kept that information to themselves as well, at least so far.

Anthony, Shorty, Sasquatch, Howell, Daniel, and I were all there – the entire Magnificent Seven, except for Freddy, who hadn't been in his room when Anthony had rounded up the rest of us. Shorty had rented the films from the owner of one of the college bars in the village for twenty dollars, quite a significant sum in those days. Each of us chipped in three dollars – about twenty-five dollars in today's money – for the privilege of watching would turn out to be three short, silent loops. Howell passed around a bottle of whiskey. It was clear to me from the general boisterousness that all of the other guys except for Daniel and me had started drinking earlier. We both chugged from the bottle as Shorty dimmed the lights and started up the projector.

The first loop opened up with a film leader that counted down from eight to two and cut to a title on a placard that read, *Burlesque Review*. It was a compilation of six women in various striptease acts. Judging by how well-worn and scratched the film was, it looked to be about ten or twenty years old. But, no one cared how old it. For many of us, including me, this was the first real pornography we had ever seen. That alone made it titillating.

It was incredible to see the women dance, remove their clothes, touch their breasts, and display their vaginas and asses with absolutely no embarrassment. It was flabbergasting to me, actually, that anyone would ever do that. There was so much shame around sex in those days. Pornography was illegal, which made it forbidden in every sense, not just a moral one. That said, *Burlesque Review* should have been illegal. The women in the reel were not good-looking, and I've never been a fan of big, flabby breasts with saucer-sized areolas, which most of them had. Despite the excitement of watching the women take their clothes off on camera, there was something rather depressing about them, and I did not enjoy this reel as much as what was to come. That's not to say I wasn't turned on – I was rock hard in all of my eighteen year old glory from the moment the very first frames flickered onto the screen.

The next reel was much more riveting. It was called *The French Maid*. Like the first one, this film was older and had been well-viewed. The scene began with a dark-haired man dressed in a suit sitting at a desk, ostensibly working. The woman was dark-haired as well. Unlike the women of the last film, she was attractive and had a good body. She wore a maid's uniform, albeit the maid's uniforms of erotica, not real life: a strapless corset, lace-up back, wrist cuffs, and a satin choker. While the man reviewed papers at his desk, she used a feather duster on the curtains. When she began to use the feather duster on the papers on his desk, he became irritated at the interruption. They had an animated exchange of words, and he wagged an angry finger at her. He returned to his papers and she her dusting. But, not for long. She bent over to dust a low table, and just like that, her skirt flipped up over her ass to reveal she was not wearing underwear.

The man clasped his hands to his face in affected surprise. The camera cut to a close-up of her gyrating ass with a dark tuft of hair tantalizingly visible from below. The man played with her perfectly formed buttocks for a while, and then he spun her around. Her breasts popped out of the corset. They were large and firm, and he buried his face in them, which seemed like a pretty nice place to be. After he sucked on and squeezed them for a spell, she dropped to her knees and unzipped his pants. A long, fat, hairy, uncircumcised cock bounced out of his undergarments, and she grabbed it with both hands.

"Holy shit," Howell said, shaking his head in disbelief. "She has two hands on that cock. It's so much bigger than mine."

"Every cock is bigger than yours, Howl," Anthony said. Everyone laughed, even though it was a jab we all had heard before many times. Through the laughter, I couldn't help but notice from the corner of my eye Anthony had adjusted his cock in his pants. I assumed he had a hard-on. As distracting as his bulge could be, however, it was not enough to keep my eyes away from the hardcore action onscreen.

The "maid" stroked the man's cock, and I had to admit I was fascinated by how his foreskin covered and uncovered the shiny knob of his cock and then covered it again. There was something intriguingly sexy how the head would appear, then disappear, and then appear again. I had seen uncircumcised cocks before, of course, but had never seen a foreskin in action. I was curious about cocks in general, to understate the obvious, and very curious to see how his foreskin worked. The woman was curious as well, though she had other plans for his cock. She slapped it across her face. It must have felt awesome, because she had a laughing, smiling look of beatific joy. I remember thinking I would have had the same look on my face as well if I had been on the receiving end of those slaps. Then he took matters into his hands: he grabbed his cock and slid it into her mouth.

We had been sitting in silent awe until now except for occasional commentary from one of the guys. The movie had no soundtrack, so the only noise in the room was the hum of the movie projector and the flickering of the film. Now, there were audible gasps and catcalling. No one in the room except for Anthony had received a blow job from a woman, not even Daniel, who had fucked two girls, but had never had his cock sucked. I had both given and received blowjobs with Dusty, yet it was still incredibly hot to watch this guy stick his big, hairy cock inside her mouth, particularly since she appeared to be protesting that it was too big and having difficulty fitting it inside her.

At first, the woman pretended to struggle sucking his cock. Soon, however, she was fellating it with hungry skill. In the awkward way porn was edited back then, the film cut abruptly to the man lying on his back on the desk. She was squatting above him, lowering her vagina to his fully erect cock, which stood up prominently in the air. With the lens up close, her vagina slid down the full length of his cock easily enveloping him inside her.

"Holy fucking shit!" Sasquatch exclaimed. There were further hoots and hollers, but for the most part, we sat in awestruck silence. My cock was rock hard and throbbing in my pants. I had to imagine everyone else's was as well.

The camera cut again to a close up. They were still on the desk, but this time she was on her back, and he was plowing her missionary style. The camera was focused in tight on his penis sliding in and out of her vagina, up and down and back again. You could see her untrimmed pubic hair tapering down from her vagina to the insides of her thighs. His ass was dark and hairy, and his balls were covered with thick, black tufts of hair that no doubt had never been trimmed. Majestically, he withdrew the length of his cock and then slid back in repeatedly, his loose balls slapping against her taint. The room was silent except for the hum of the projector.

"That's right, *mon ami*. Give it to her," Anthony said.

The man began drilling her faster. As he did, white streaks of semen spread down the length of his shaft. He continued pumping her, the semen spilling out of her vagina and coating the hairs that fanned out from her vagina onto the insides of her thighs.

"Damn, he just blew his load inside her – without a rubber," Daniel said, his voice low, shaking his head in utter amazement.

The man continued to fuck her without pulling out. His shaft turned a pasty white, streaked with broad strokes of thick, white cum. Clumps of it clung to the prodigious tangle of black hair that burgeoned forth from his large, loose, egg-shaped balls that shifted in his sac and slapped against her taint with punishing repetition.

Abruptly, the film ended. The screen went blank, the bright light of the projector shining on it with the unspooled film flapping against the reel. There was an uproar of boisterous commentary as the guys dove into a dissection of the action we had just seen on screen. Shorty jumped up to tend to the projector and bring the fluttering end of film under control.

"I can't believe she let him shoot his sperm inside her," Daniel said. "Did you see how big that load was? His cock was coated with it. Must feel so amazing to plow a girl with no rubber."

"From a plethora of personal experiences in that area, I have to confess it feels pretty damn amazing to ejaculate into a girl," Sasquatch said. "Amazing, I tell you."

Anthony slapped him on the side of the head. "Fuck you, Sasquatch. You've never seen any pussy, much less 'ejaculate into a girl.' Fuck you!"

Sasquatch was good-natured, as you know by now, and he laughed.

Shorty had brought the flapping reel under control. After he removed it, he entertained us with hand gestures that on screen looked like a dog barking.

Howell passed the bottle of whiskey around, with each of us taking a hefty swig. I felt a healthy, happy buzz already. The other guys had started drinking before Daniel and I joined them, and they had to have been feeling the alcohol a lot more than we did.

"I didn't think nipples on a girls tits could be so big," I said. "Some of those girls had nipples the size of dinner plates."

This got a hearty laugh out of everyone. Howell thrust his fists into the air and shouted: "Saucer nipples! Three cheers for saucer nipples!" Everyone laughed even louder and more raucously. Through the haze of alcohol that had descended upon us like vapors leaking in over a transom, I happened to notice the white screen upon which we had watched the film was now filled with the silhouette of an upward curved, priapic image that reminded me of . . . Shorty's cock!

I turned around in surprise. "Shorty, buddy? What are you doing?!"

The other guys stared at the screen, stunned into incredulity by the image before them.

Shorty had pulled his pants down in front of the light of the projector and was shadow dancing with the singularly beautiful image of his upward curved cock bobbing around, the bright light of the projector shining directly on it. The guys turned their eyes to the screen, then back to Shorty, and then back again. Everyone burst into rowdy, drunken laughter at the sight of the shadowed image of Shorty's boner dancing around on the screen. He stopped for a moment and pressed down on his cock with two fingers, just as Anthony had that night in his dorm room when we held him down to measure his height. He bent it down low and then released it, snapping it against his belly. Everyone laughed again. It was funny and sexy and classic Shorty.

Sasquatch jumped up from the couch upon which he was sitting and approached Shorty and the movie projector. He was always quick to join in fun, so it was not unexpected when he yanked down his pants and his medium-sized boner bounced out. Shorty stepped back from the bright light of the projector so Sasquatch could move into view. The silhouette of his cock bounced from side to side as he shook his hips, the tight curls of the hair on his legs visible on the screen as well.

Anthony roared with laughter. "You guys are such crazy fucks!"

Shorty stepped back into the light of the projector, and it was fascinating to see the difference in their silhouettes. Shorty's muscled, compact frame had a cock that curved up to the sky and was big for his body. Sasquatch's looser, stockier frame had an average-sized cock that was just fine in its own right and jutted straight out from his body. Howell took a swig from the whiskey bottle and jumped up next as Sasquatch pulled up his pants and stuck his boner back in them before sitting down. Howell had a much healthier attitude about the size of his cock than I ever would have. He yanked his pants down, and everyone burst out in laughter at the size of his small, rock hard cock that could not have been more than three and one-half inches. He thrust his hands in the air and yelled, "Yeah!" before tucking it back in. While everyone was cheering and laughing, I grabbed the whiskey bottle and took a big swig. I was not usually the first to join in naked fun, but I had proven by now I was not as reserved as people might think I was.

Daniel looked at me in wide-eyed surprise and burst into laughter as I dropped my pants. My boner flopped out into open view, my pants at my knees. I gyrated my hips from side-to-side at first as my boner bounced around. Then I pumped them as I fucked an imaginary hole. The guys hooted and hollered. I gestured for Daniel to come up and join me. But, he just laughed and shook his head, no. I pressed down on my boner like Shorty had, but instead of bouncing up and slapping my belly, it stopped at the half-way mark and jutted out from my waist.

"Now that's a nice, big cock!" Howell said. "I want one like that."

Anthony clapped his hands loudly. "Very impressive, Branson. I think you have the biggest cock on the floor," he said, as he made his way up to the projector. "Except for me, that is." He shoved me roughly by the shoulder out of the way. Laughing, I stuffed my boner back into my pants.

Then, Anthony unzipped his.

Anthony's huge, monstrous cock was something all of us looked at and talked about openly from time-to-time. It was so big, it was impossible not to. It was one thing to see it loosely elongated in the warmth of a soapy shower, like it was that day he told the story of having sex with the girl at the drive-in over Thanksgiving. But, to see it fully erect was an utterly incredible sight to behold.

When the rest of us had flashed our boners and created sexy silhouettes on the screen, the others had made a lot of raucous noise. When Anthony did it, however, the room sat in stunned silence for a long moment, the only sounds being the hum of the fan in the movie projector and the gasps of awe that came from all of us. Daniel and I looked at each other and exchanged wide-eyed looks of amazement. I have lived a long and adventurous life that took me many times around the globe.

To this day, however, Anthony's cock is by far the largest I have ever seen in person anywhere.

You may recall that everything about Anthony was big – his personality, his voice, and his six foot three height. Soft, his cock was long, thick, and wrinkled, with a foreskin that strained to cover his glans, which was full and wide even in repose. Rock hard, his cock defied all imagination. It was an impossibly long ten inches, with a circumference of seven inches, thick enough that even Anthony could barely get his fingers around it. It jutted straight out from his body with what I can only describe as a sleek upward curve that rose with aerodynamic elegance for the final three inches so that that his glans faced majestically to the sky. It was so hard, it barely bounced in the light of the screen. For full effect, he held it rigid and otherwise unmoving. I would later sometimes see pornography with cocks as big as Anthony's and, rarely, sometimes bigger. Almost always, particularly with white men, those cocks never fully got hard. Not Anthony's, however. It was a firm, rigid masterpiece.

Anthony had brought the bottle of whiskey up to the projector with him and took a swig. "So, fellas," he said. "Now you see it. Pretty fucking, big, right?"

"It's the fucking Empire State Buildings of cocks, I'll give you that," Daniel said, nodding his head with unexpected admiration. "It's bigger than big. It's absolutely gigantic."

Anthony shook it a few times and pulled it down so that it would bounce back up in undoubtedly the most extraordinary silhouette I have ever seen on a movie screen.

"Okay, you fruits, show's over. I know every one of you has wondered how big it gets. Now you know."

The evening would have been extraordinary enough had it been limited to the experience of watching my first ever porno film. Flashing our boners publicly like that was something I never imagined, particularly seeing Anthony's utterly gigantic one. I was truly grateful for the assistance the whiskey had provided in terms of lowering everyone's inhibitions and for the porno flicks in raising everyone's cock.

After Anthony sat back down and we finished the additional commentary on his cock, Shorty started the final film. We settled in and struggled to sit comfortably with the boners in our pants that now everyone knew everyone had with all certainty, except for Daniel, who had not shown his on the screen. I had not expected him to anyway. It was enough of surprise that he had acknowledged the enormity of Anthony's cock, which for Daniel was an act that was the practical equivalent of bowing his head in fealty.

This third film was different than the others in that it was newer and in better condition. The first film with the strip tease dances and the second film, *The French Maid*, actually seemed like they were from France and had been produced before the war. This third one was called *The Peeping Tom*. It also didn't have a soundtrack. But, you could tell right away it was different. The actors and room in which it had been shot looked to be American. It also looked much newer. It began with an attractive blond woman who was sitting at a vanity and applying make-up while wearing only high-waist panties and a classic 1950s style push-up bra. The camera cut to an open window where a young man was spying on her. After she applied her make-up, which frankly was rather boring, she sat on her bed and started reading a magazine, which also was rather boring, except that she had a great body and was wearing only panties and a bra. She must have thought it was pretty boring, too, because she tossed the magazine to the side. Then, she pulled down her panties and started masturbating.

"Now that's more like it," Anthony said.

The woman masturbated in fast circular motions you would assume brought her extreme pleasure judging by her ecstatic facial expressions. The camera cut to the peeping tom who then climbed through the open window. She pretended to be surprised. But, after some limpid back-and-forth as he chased her around the room, they soon were rolling around on the bed and kissing. The man was young, not much older than us. He had a James Dean, neighborhood tough look about him with greased back hair, a tight white T-shirt tucked into khakis, and the sneer of forced machismo.

He began playing with the woman's breasts in a rough manner I realize now with years of experience was delivered with the unschooled belief he was giving women what they wanted. I am embarrassed to admit I followed the cues of that neighborhood tough in my early encounters with women, wholly unaware that despite the actress's head-spinning ecstatic response to having her breasts squeezed and her nipples pinched, that was not what women usually wanted, at least not the ones with whom I would be. Fortunately, I would be retaught by lovers who somehow survived my clumsy, fumbling attempts to pleasure them that I had learned in porno flicks just like this one.

After sucking on her nipples, he unzipped his pants. His cock was soft and circumcised. I remember being surprised he wasn't hard, because I certainly was just from watching. The woman took matters into her own hands, however, and began to blow him.

"Now, that's what I want to see!" Anthony said, not taking his eyes from the screen.

It didn't take long for the guy's cock to get hard. It was a thick, well-proportioned seven-incher with a full, rounded mushroom head. As she sucked on him expertly, the room again fell silent. The camera then cut to a shot of him rubbing the bare head of his cock on her wet pussy and then pushing it in.

"Alright! Give it to her!" Howell said.

"Man, how I ever would love to do that," Sasquatch said, his eyes transfixed on the screen.

I shifted the boner in my pants and noticed right afterwards Daniel had done the same with his. By now, I was so worked up from watching the on-screen action, I actually was eager for it to be over so I could get out of there and rub one out in a bathroom stall. I discreetly pressed on my cock a few times as I watched the young tough's cock slide in and out of the hot girl, his smooth ass grinding against her, his hairy balls slapping her taint. I was starting to get uncomfortable from the building pressure inside me that was clamoring for release.

I was not the only one in such straits, because Anthony abruptly said, "I can't fucking take it anymore." He took a swig of whiskey and then did the most amazing thing: he unzipped his pants and pulled out his big, long, thick, and hard monster cock. He began stroking it furiously. It was already extraordinary enough to have seen Anthony fully erect and shadow dancing his boner on the movie screen. But, to see him pull out his gigantic boner and begin stroking it in front of all of us was a fantastical turn of events.

I don't think any of the rest of us could have gotten away with starting it and convincing the others to follow. But, Anthony's physical and personal presence was so imposing no one would question him about anything. He had pressed down on Shorty's boner out of the curiosity of watching it bounce back and slap against his belly. Everyone had thought it hilarious. No one thought the lesser of Anthony because of it, and no one would have dared question his manhood. In the same way he had seized the mantle and done what he had wanted that night in Shorty's room, he could whip his boner out during a screening of a porn flick and beat off in front of the rest of us. It also meant others were likely to follow him, just as everyone always did.

Sasquatch was the next one to pull down his pants and pull out his cock. As we had just seen before, it was a solid, medium-sized cock. He rubbed it furiously and fast. He seemed to be pretty rough on it and used a grip that was tighter and rougher than I used when I jerked off.

With Anthony and Sasquatch openly and furiously beating off while we watched the young tough plow the hot blond on the movie screen, the rest of the guys followed the leads of Anthony and Sasquatch as they also pulled out their hard cocks and started jerking off. Howell pulled out his tiny cock that was so small it defied credulity in the opposite way that Anthony's did. Shorty pulled out his sexy boner that was big for his stature and curved dramatically upwards. Daniel and I looked at each other. He nodded his head with a smirk across his face. He pulled out the big, hard, sexy cock, which I had seen before, but could never tire of. And then I pulled out my own boner and started to stroke it.

Of the many fun and sexy experiences I would share with The Magnificent Seven over the course of my college years, jerking off in a group with buddies I loved and trusted while we watched the first porno flicks most of us had ever seen was an extraordinary milestone event. If this particular memory were on an actual reel of film rather than in my memory, it would be as frayed as the two pre-war French films. As you might expect, I have jerked off to the memory of that night countless times and still draw upon it today. It also may not surprise you that, by now, the action in the room was more exciting to me than the action on screen. The sight of all of the exposed boners with hands flying and stroking them openly and furiously was one so surreal, I had never thought to imagine anything like it before. I was not the only one to think that way. Even with the action continuing to unfold onscreen, everyone stole open glances at the action around the room. After tonight, there would be no wondering about who had what or how they did it.

It was almost impossible for me to keep my eyes off of Anthony and his cock that was so large it defied all imagination. I had known it would be big, but this was so big, it was difficult to process mentally. How could he fit that thing in his pants? How had it fit inside that girl he had fucked at the Valley Stream drive-in over Thanksgiving? No wonder she had been frightened when he had taken it out. As Anthony rubbed and stroked his gigantic cock, he paused for a moment and pressed his fingers down to the base of it, pressing them into his pubic bone so his cock was on full display in its most erect state.

Daniel shook his head and said, "Damn" under his breath. I shook my head as well with both amazement, and I must admit, desire. I had the strongest urge to reach over and grab Anthony's cock with my own hands and feel its strength and power. I also wanted to see if it really was real, because it was just so damned big, it was hard to believe that it was.

<u>H</u>owell was the first to blow his load. "Fuck! Fuck! Fuck!" he said as half a dozen bursts shot in a straight line of evenly timed and spaced pulses of cum that landed in the same spot in the center of his chest.

Almost simultaneously, Sasquatch was next. "Ohhh," he moaned, low and deep. "Ohhh." Unlike Howell, who had cum in spurts, Sasquatch ejaculated an almost continuous river of cum across his stomach and lower chest. It was white, thick, and matted his prodigious spread of body hair with gooey wetness.

A moment later, the rest of us yanking on our cocks to catch up, there was a rumble in Anthony's voice as he said, "Oh, baby. Oh, baby," over and over again. Everyone turned to look at him. It was impossible not to. Anthony's long, thick, pole was as functionally powerful as it was visually. His cock was in the mightiest state of arousal as he hovered on the cusp of ejaculation. It was at its prime – ten inches he would later brag, and no one who had been in the room that night would doubt him. If you are thinking my account of Anthony and this encounter is yet another apocryphal description of a gigantic cock about which men have been writing and reading since the creation of the written word, I understand your skepticism. A cock of Anthony's size is exceedingly rare, but they are out there. Most people don't have the good fortune to see one like that in the flesh even once during their life time. I just happened to be lucky that Anthony, my good friend, happened to have one and was willing to share it in the way that he was.

In open anticipation, we waited for him to unload what had clearly already begun the journey from deep within his body. What we saw next was something no one in the room could ever forget. Anthony was a strong, muscular guy on the outside, and also apparently on the inside. The first spurt of cum shot to a ridiculous height and arced over his shoulder where it landed with a splat on the back of the couch. He flinched, and the next several spurts shot to eye level and landed on his torso. In the middle of that truly spectacular ejaculation, however, the door to the lounge opened.

The overhead light in the room snapped on. All of us started at the interruption and the realization we had been caught. My head whipped around. As shocked as I was that anyone would have thrown open the door, I was even more startled to who it was.

It was Dusty.

He hovered in the doorway for a moment in stunned silence at the surreal sight of a porn film playing on the movie screen, the young tough fucking the blonde as she rode him on top. He turned to the sight of all of his freshman charges – and me, in particular – sitting there with our cocks out, busted in mid-stroke. His face red with uncharacteristic embarrassment, Anthony squeezed the remaining drops of cum out of his dick hole and exhaled.

"What the hell is going on in here?" Dusty said, the anger thundering in his voice. He stepped over to the electrical outlet and yanked the cord from the movie projector out of the wall. It sputtered to a stop.

"Pull your pants up. Now!" he said sharply to no one in particular and everyone all at once. We fumbled to pull our pants up and stuff our boners back inside them. He slammed the door shut behind him and made sure it was locked. Of course, Dusty could have caught us. It had gotten noisy and raucous in here as everyone had been revved up by the twin fuels of whiskey and porn. He had heard the noise and investigated. The door had been locked. But, he had the key.

"Oh, Dusty, lighten up," Anthony said, having more trouble than the rest of us stuffing his boner back in his pants, a sight Dusty could not help but notice. Even in the midst of his anger, it caused him to pause in astonishment.

"Don't you dare back talk to me, buster," Dusty said, his face red with anger and the tone in his voice matching it. Anthony looked down and nodded in submission. As assertive as Anthony could be with people he thought were weaker than him, there was something about the authoritative and confident way with which Dusty carried himself that caused Anthony almost never to challenge him. He backed down.

Dusty eyed the rest of us. "Do you guys know what kind of trouble you could get into?" He paused a beat. "Do you?"

By now, all of us were chastened, our faces flush with shame. The room was a mess of liquor bottles and couches in disarray. As Dusty continued to rail on us about how we could get expelled for possession of the porn film and for showing it, both of which were illegal and the type of offense for which the school had been known to expel people, I felt regret for the first time. Not just for the conduct, which had started to feel dirty instead of fun as Dusty reminded us of the consequences, which all of us had known but just ignored. But, also because I knew Dusty would be irritated I had joined in. He had caught me with my hard cock out and jerking off with the guys, a part of me I imagine he had thought was reserved for him on an exclusive basis. I was not his only focus in the room, of course. But, he glanced at me more than once, no doubt wondering how the evening had ended up like this, when just a couple of hours before, he and I had been finalizing our plans for our weekend in New York City together.

Getting caught like this felt like another strike, the first having been in Allison's basement at Thanksgiving. I thought of how the loss of my virginity on New Year's Eve would be yet another strike if he knew about it. I wondered how many I had left. I felt sick with remorse and had the sense I was blowing a beautiful thing with him.

As I walked by him on the way out of the lounge, he shook his head and under his breath said, "Geezus, John."

What could I say? I averted my eyes.

The rest of us slinked back to our rooms while Dusty stayed behind to yell at Shorty so he fully understood the potential consequences of what might have happened if someone else had happened upon us. While I know Dusty's concern for us was genuine, he was also concerned for himself. He knew he would be blamed for not keeping order on the floor, and he did not want to jeopardize the free room and board that came along with his RA position. That's to say nothing of his honor society memberships and leadership positions in other campus activities, all of which could be lost. It was an unfortunate end to an evening that had otherwise been electrifying, erotic, and fun.

It was late now, and Daniel and I started to get ready for bed. We both were buzzed from all of the whiskey we had drank. We also were energized about the events that had taken place in the lounge, Dusty's interruption and castigation notwithstanding. We recounted the details of the film with animated excitement. I pulled my shirt over my head and tossed it into the corner. Daniel dropped his pants and tossed them into the corner on the floor. I couldn't help but notice as he pulled his sweatshirt over his head he had a boner that was causing his boxers to tent. I also couldn't help but notice he wasn't doing anything to hide it.

He looked at me as if he wanted to say something. Then, he looked down at his boner. "I'm still pretty horny from those dirty movies," he said.

"Yes, I can tell," I said, not taking my eyes off the tent in his boxers. I was starting to wonder if this might be going where I thought it might be going.

He pressed down on his boner. I could tell how it strained through the cotton boxers that he was rock hard. My cock started to stir as he pressed down on his boner again.

I took a chance. "Do you need to finish what we started back there?" I asked, a suggestive smile widening across my face.

Daniel surprised me by smiling right back. "Yes, buddy, I think I do," he said. "Do you mind?"

"Nah, go right ahead," I said, thinking he was fucking crazy. Of course I wouldn't mind! In fact, I could think of few things I wanted more. I waited a beat before adding, "I might even join you."

Laughing, Daniel pulled his boxers down to his knees. His engorged boner bounced out of them in unencumbered freedom. He grabbed it in his right hand and waved it like a sword in a way that was fun, comical, and undeniably sexy. I couldn't believe this was happening. My own cock continued to harden in my pants.

"Those porno flicks were so sexy," Daniel said, sitting down on his bed, his pants off.

"It was so cool how that one guy shot his load right into that French girl and kept on fucking her until his boner turned pasty white."

Daniel leaned back on his bed and started stroking his cock. "Man, that was the best," he said. "I would give anything to fuck a girl bare without a rubber and shoot a load inside her."

I had already removed my shirt and was standing there with my khakis still on. I couldn't help but notice how he eyed my crotch. I had had so many fantasies about Daniel. I had been drawn to him from the very moment he had walked into our room on the first day of school, my blue blazer folded over my arm. I loved the baritone in his voice and how he called me "buddy." I loved that he was the best friend I ever had. I loved how we would study together in the silence of the library and share our thoughts in private whispers. I loved how we would lay in our beds at night and talk in the darkness. I loved his pale brown eyes flecked with gold. I loved his sandy hair worn in a crew cut. I loved the freckles on his nose. I loved his broad-shouldered wrestler's body and his high, meaty ass. I loved his long, thick soda-bottle shaped cock. The list was never-ending.

I had rubbed my own cock raw at times thinking about the time we had watched him fuck Carol in the lounge that night which could have ended in in disaster, but hadn't. Daniel and I had endured two months of awkwardness as he had wondered what was going on between Dusty and me, secrets he was afraid to know and I was afraid to share. Daniel and I had already seen each other's boner before, both in the lounge tonight and on a few other occasions, including those separate nights we had jerked off on each other in anger. This was different. The realization that we were about to jerk off together with mutual desire caused my mind to spin and my cock to surge to full hardness.

Daniel's eyes were locked on the sight of my cock stretching the cotton fabric, straining for freedom. I turned my back to him for a moment to lock the door to our room. As he continued stroking his cock, I pulled my boxers down past my knees and tossed them onto my bed. I stood before him naked, my boner throbbing in full engorgement. My heart was pounding in my chest. I was nervous and excited all at the same time. It was hard to believe it was happening. But, it was. I started to rub my cock.

Even though we both had boners we were stroking in front of each other, I wasn't sure where this was going and where it wasn't. I sat down on my bed and faced him as he sat on his, each of us masturbating, our eyes on each other's boner. Only a few feet of physical distance separated us. But, my uncertainty about what was really happening made it feel farther. Daniel and I were great friends. We were casual about nudity in the way that roommates are, especially back then. I have said from the beginning that my relationship and my feelings for Daniel were complicated. I had the sense our relationship was getting even more complicated at this very moment in ways neither of us would be able to take back or ever forget.

As we reclined on our respective beds, we had clear views of each other's cock. Daniel leaned back across the width of his bed, and I had an unobstructed view of his strong, muscular legs and thighs. His balls were large, round, and hairy. They jiggled and bounced as he stroked his cock, which this angle fully showcased its length, thickness, and straightness.

As difficult as it was to look away from the extraordinary sight of Daniel's hard cock as he jerked off, I looked down at my own cock. I pulled down on the loose skin and held it tight against my balls so it showed my boner in its most impressive state. I held it there for a long moment and stopped stroking so I could show it off in its full glory. Daniel's mouth opened in amazement. He stopped stroking as well and mimicked my gesture. He pulled down on the stretched skin of his cock and squeezed his cock muscles. His balls were like large, loose eggs suspended in his hairy scrotum. His cock was big, sexy, and powerful. I stared at his, and he stared at mine.

"I never realized your balls were so big," I said.

"I never realized your cock was so big," he said. "I mean, I've seen it before and thought it was big. But, tonight, from this angle, it looks fucking huge."

We looked down at each other's stretched-out cock and then our eyes met. I smiled, and he smiled back. I started stroking my cock again. But, Daniel did not. Instead, he stood up from his bed and moved over to mine, his hard cock swaying from side-to-side. He sat down on my bed and leaned back next to me. Our thighs were pressed together. My cock surged even harder. A smear of pre-cum leaked from the slit of my dick hole.

He started stroking his cock again while he stared at mine. He was mesmerized by my pre-cum. "I've never touched another guy's cock before," he said, looking at my cock and then looking up, his eyes searching mine.

I couldn't say the same, of course. I hadn't been thinking of Dusty. But, I thought of him now and forced myself not to. "Go ahead," I said, removing my hand from my cock. It pulsed with desire that surged through my entire body, including, I must admit, my heart.

Daniel needed no further encouragement. He removed his hand from his own cock and wrapped it around mine. I took a deep breath as I savored the touch of his hand on me. I had had such complicated feelings about Daniel from the first moment I had met him, my blue blazer draped over my arm, my cock betraying my attraction by surging to full engorgement as we shook hands for the first time. I had been drawn to him in ways I couldn't articulate then. But, I needed no words now as he had done the unthinkable and grabbed my cock as we sat here and jerked off together. This moment had been facilitated by the twin fuels of pornography and alcohol. But, the truth was, I needed no excuse. I wanted this and always had.

Daniel's hand explored my cock from top to bottom with tactile fascination. He wrapped his fingers around it and stroked it. He gripped my balls a little too roughly for my comfort, but I didn't complain. He ran his index finger around the ridge of my corona. Then, he touched his finger to the pooled pre-cum and swirled it in a circle until the entire crown was slippery and wet.

"You have a really big dick head," he said, looking up at me.

I returned his gaze. His lips were parted, and they drew me in. I closed my eyes and leaned forward to kiss him.

I felt the firm pressure of his open palm pressed against my bare chest. "Um, John, what are you doing?"

I opened my eyes. "I, I - I was going to kiss you?"

An incredulous smile spread across his face. "Kiss me? You're kidding me, right?"

Considering his other hand was wrapped around my cock and his finger was wet with my pre-cum, I hadn't even thought about how a kiss from me would have been received. I had just leaned in and done it. My eyes searched his to see if he was the one doing the kidding. "What are we doing here?"

The incredulous smile remained on his face. "We're rubbing one out together, like buddies. We're finishing what we all started back in the lounge."

I could smell the whiskey on Daniel's breath, and I am sure he could smell the same on mine. But, this wasn't the whiskey talking, at least not for me. I wasn't just rubbing one out. This was just the start for what I had assumed was more. I wasn't so buzzed, however, not to realize Daniel and I were moving at different speeds. I cleared my throat. I pulled my head back and forced a knowing smile. "Keep rubbing all you want."

Even though kissing was not on the menu, I reached over and grabbed Daniel's cock in the same way he had grabbed mine. His balls were heavy in my hand and the tufts of brown pubic hair that covered them felt unexpectedly soft against my fingers. Pre-cum streamed from his dick hole. I spit on my hand and ran it up and down the length of his shaft. His cock was magnificent. Not quite as big mine, but extraordinary just the same in large part because of to whom it was attached.

My hand was wet and slippery from the spit and his pre-cum. One of the reasons cocks have always been so exciting to me is they are all so different, yet function in the same ways. Daniel's cock was long, smooth, and jutted straight out, like mine. Yet, it was noticeably thicker in the middle than at the base or at the crown, like the sexiest of soda bottles as you have heard me describe him before. With Daniel's cock in my left hand and mine in his right, the joint sensation of jerking off together like this was a special heaven to me, even if Daniel did not want me to kiss him.

The heaviness of our breathing increased. I felt a warm surge within me. His eyes locked with mine. "I'm about to blow," he said.

My chest heaved. "Me too," I said, choking out the words.

The first spurt of my cum shot out and landed across his chest, which was still covered with a T-shirt. The second and third spurts shot straight up and landed across the top of my left shoulder. The fourth landed right on the underside of his cock and dribbled down to his balls. I wiped the cum from the back of my hand onto his cock for additional lubrication that was both warm and wet.

"Oh, fuck," he said. "Fuck!" His cock tightened in my hand, and he moaned. His hand remained around my spent, but still semi-hard cock. As he was coming, he squeezed my cock until it hurt.

My head jolted in surprise as the first shot of his cum splashed against the underside of my chin. The next burst struck me on my neck, with the remaining load striking me on my chest and running down in rivulets to the hair of my treasure trail. I squeezed the last remaining drops of cum from his cock as we both looked down and watched them ooze out the slit of his dick hole. We fell back on my bed to catch our breath.

A whiff of uncertainty wafted into my consciousness as the realization of what we had just done struck me. I couldn't help but think of how I had leaned in to kiss him and how he had pushed me away with a look of incredulity. I cared very much for my friendship with Daniel. Even as the glow of my orgasm ebbed, I felt the fear rise up within me that my friendship with him was altered in ways that were irreparable. Would he feel regret the next day? Would it be awkward between us? Had our friendship come to a fork and we had hurtled in a new direction? As I laid there thinking I wanted to say something, but not knowing what, Daniel burst out laughing.

"Can you believe we just did that?" he asked, shaking his head. He lifted his hand and examined the wet indistinguishable goo of our combined semen. He stood up, and smelled his hand. I smelled mine too. It smelled of bleach and musk and reminded me of the way a salt marsh sometimes smelled at low tide or certain flowering plants smelled in springtime.

"It was fun," I said, allowing myself another whiff.

Daniel grabbed his towel off the hook on the back of our door and wiped the cum off his cock. He tossed me my towel, and I did the same. Other than that, we didn't say anything. I didn't know how to characterize the silence. Was it cool? Was it awkward? Was it filled with regret? My mind was racing. I'm sure his was, too. Even though Daniel had laughed, our relationship had changed. I didn't know if it was for the better or for the worse. My mind was a jumble of thoughts at this moment. I didn't know what to think. I felt self-conscious that I was fully naked and covered in cum. Daniel had pulled on a dirty pair of boxers from his laundry bag. After I wiped the remaining cum off me, I did the same and threw a T-shirt over my head. My mouth was dry from the liquor. I suddenly felt very thirsty and wished I hadn't drunk as much as I had.

An insistent pounding on the door broke the silence.

"Anthony! Enough already!" I said.

I opened the door, but it wasn't Anthony.

It was Dusty.

"What the hell happened tonight?" he asked from the doorway, clearly referring to the events in the second floor lounge.

I shrugged. "We were just having some fun."

"Geezus, John," he said. I sensed by the way his nostrils flared he could smell the whiskey on my breath. I hoped he couldn't smell the unmistakable scent of semen in the room. "I'm really disappointed in you – both of you," he said, the last part of that added as he looked over my shoulder and nodded his head at Daniel. "You guys could have gotten all of us in a whole heap of trouble."

I looked down at my feet. The truth was, I didn't feel bad about the porno flicks and the circle jerk. It had been harmless, drunken fun, at least from my perspective. But, I felt terrible about what had just happened with Daniel, which hadn't been harmless. I also felt terrible from the whiskey, which roiled in my stomach. I shoved past Dusty and ran down to the bathroom at the end of the hall, not sure if I would make it in time. I threw open the door and lunged for the stall without thinking whether it would be one of the stalls that had been tagged by the Secret Shitter. Luckily, it wasn't. I was able to hug a clean bowl and vomit my guts out until there was nothing left.

Dusty had followed me down and waited for me to finish. He helped me clean up and forced me to guzzle a couple of glasses of water. The exceeding care with which he tended to me made me feel even guiltier as I thought of the lack of care I had demonstrated for him, first with Allison and then with Daniel. He didn't mention the events of the evening. I'm sure he thought I had been punished enough. If he only knew.

The lights were out in my room by the time I finally pulled myself together. Daniel had fallen into a drunken slumber and was snoring loudly. Dusty tucked me into bed and kissed me on the forehead. I mumbled a few words of thanks, and he kissed my forehead again. "Don't worry, you're going to be okay," he said. His kiss was unsettling instead of comforting. He thought too much whiskey was my problem that night. He didn't know my real problem was the lengthening list of transgressions I had committed against him, both those that were known to him and the more serious ones that were not.

Through the anxious haze of the alcohol, I had an unexpected moment of clarity as Dusty kissed me on the forehead. I had the realization he was not the temptation that had guided me onto the path of righteousness through all of those years of church attendance when I had spent Sunday after Sunday listening to the sermons that emanated from the pulpit. Dusty was the divine gift who had fallen from the sky, and I had been reckless with what I knew to the core of my being was an extraordinary blessing. Temptation was those other influences that called out to me like the Sirens from Greek mythology. They beckoned me to crash on rocky shores, and I had been heading full speed in that direction. As I drifted off to an uneasy sleep, I hoped it was not too late to set a different course and right myself with him.

18 THE END OF INNOCENCE

THE NEXT MORNING, my mouth tasted like ass, and I don't mean that in a good way. My stomach was sore and growling, even though I didn't feel much like eating. There was a heaviness in my brain, but only mild haze. As far as hangovers went, this one was not bad at all thanks to having puked my guts out before my body had a chance to absorb all of the alcohol I had guzzled. Daniel was in worse shape than I was, and I would not be surprised to learn later the other guys were in worse shape than Daniel was. We shuffled around our room as we prepared for the day, neither of us saying anything. The awkwardness each of us felt was manifest in our silence and averted glances. After a raucous evening, the morning after was off to a disquieting start. If you had thought a circle jerk with your buddies and then rubbing one out with your roommate would have thrown open new doors of freedom, the reality on the third floor of Canterbury Hall was unfolding differently.

The events of last night had gone too far at a number of points that felt right at the time, but didn't feel so right this morning. Jerking off with Daniel and our manhandling of each other's cock and balls had been a dream come true last night. But, in the light of the next day, it felt like a wild leap too far. So did my rebuffed move to kiss him. We showered together with few words, just the two of us in the otherwise empty gang shower. The air between us was unsettled as we headed off to the dining hall in silence. My mind was awhirl as I replayed the events of last night and what they meant and what they didn't. I had to think it was the same for Daniel even if we didn't speak of it.

After we loaded up our trays and left the food service line, he nudged my elbow and nodded in the direction of the table where Anthony, Howell, and Freddy were sitting. We carried our trays over to them and sat down, not even mumbling a greeting as we did. Anthony and Howell oozed the unwashed rankness of not having showered after a night of heavy partying. Both were unshaven. If I could have smelled their breath, I am certain it would have been foul.

I was surprised to see them, though I should not have been. Anthony was a boisterous and prolific initiator of boundary-pressing horseplay that often was fueled by alcohol. But, he also was a stealth academic powerhouse. He had the double distinction among us of being the only first generation American and the only one who was the first in his family to go to college. The rest of us were children of privilege who had never even thought of college as anything but a birthright. Anthony, however, recognized the sacrifices his parents had made for him to be here so that in the New World their son would have opportunities outside of cutting marble and hauling sheets of it to the homes and office buildings of the wealthy in and around New York. It was a trade that had provided a comfortable living but a physically grueling life for generations of men in his family in Italy. Anthony had seen that life close-up and wanted something different. He always showed up for every class, no matter what. In the same way Anthony could lead you to the trough of good times, he could lead you to the lecture hall as well. No doubt, he had dragged Howell here, even though Howell was as privileged as the rest us were in every way except for the poverty of his tiny cock.

"Hey, fellas," Freddy said. "What the hell happened last night while I was at the library?"

"What do you mean?" Daniel asked as he brought a cup of coffee up to his lips.

"The lounge is a wreck. Everyone's hungover. No one's talking. Sasquatch and Shorty haven't even gotten out of bed."

Howell's eyes were red, and I wondered if he might still be a little drunk. "Let's take a vote," he said with a smirk. "Do we tell him?"

"No! Would you fucking shut up?" Anthony said with uncharacteristic sharpness. "Nothing happened, Freddy. So, quit asking."

Anthony didn't embarrass easily, and he had proven with his titanic endowment and the colossal ejaculation that had shot over his shoulder he had nothing to be embarrassed about. But, he made it clear that last night was last night, and he didn't want to talk about it today, especially with Freddy. That was just fine with Daniel and me. We continued to eat without saying anything, each of us in our own silos of quiet detachment.

Freddy let Anthony's sharpness roll off him and, apropos of nothing, started talking about his father's new Cadillac, which, regrettably, I had already heard about.

"My father always buys a new Cadillac, every two years," Freddy said. "He refuses to drive an older car. He always buys the top-of-the line, fully-loaded model...."

I didn't care about Freddy's father's new car. I also didn't care for people who spoke freely about spending money. I tuned him out.

I noticed Dusty sitting by himself a few tables away. He nodded his head in acknowledgment and held my gaze for a long beat until turning back to the notebook he had been studying. I thought of the tenderness with which he had helped me wipe my face last night in the bathroom and how he had tucked me into bed. I thought of how he had kissed me on the forehead and whispered to me I would be okay even though the tears that had welled in my eyes were in regret at the growing tally of my transgressions against him. He had forgiven me for the foolishness in Allison's basement at Thanksgiving. I suspected he would write off last night's special, invite-only cinematic event as juvenile monkey business once he got past his anger at the trouble it might have caused us all. But, if he learned I had had sex with Allison on New Year's Eve and jerked off with Daniel last night in our room and tried to kiss him, I could not imagine he would be so forgiving. He had been generous in his recognition that I was younger than he was and still finding my way. But, the bearing with which he governed his self-regard would allow that generosity only to go so far.

Freddy switched the subject to the weather, which was a frequent and customarily boring topic of conversation in Vermont in the middle of winter. It was either cold or snowy or both, with little deviation. After everything that had happened last night, the weather seemed so inconsequential to me it was hard for me to sit here and listen to him. I looked over at Dusty again and wished I were sitting with him instead of here listening to Freddy.

". . . then my parents are flying to Palm Beach," Freddy said. "First class. They're staying at the Breakers. They always stay at the best hotels – "

I stood abruptly and lifted my tray. The guys looked up, startled by the suddenness of my movement. "I'll catch you later," I said.

I couldn't listen to Freddy prattle on about the weather and his parents' excesses for even another minute, not when Dusty and all of his magnificence was just a few tables away. I walked over and set my tray across from his. I sat down. The guys may have been wondering what I was doing, particularly after the harshness with which Dusty had dressed all of us down last night. But, I didn't care what they thought and did not turn back. Dusty smiled at the sight of me sitting across from him. I had taken a few detours to get here. But, I knew with all certainty I wanted a seat at his table and never to leave it.

"Feeling better?" he asked.

I smiled back. "Much."

The weight of my undisclosed transgressions with Allison and Daniel hung in the forefront of my consciousness. As I absorbed the warmth in Dusty's loving smile, I envisioned how that smile would melt from his face as I unloaded the secret burdens I carried. Heaviness would descend upon his heart. The love he felt for me would be stained with hurt and disappointment as I shared the unwanted burden of my truth.

You may think I chose the coward's way out. But, I knew at that moment I would not confess the behavior that encumbered my conscience, at least not now or any time soon. I was the one who had walked down the path of temptation and engaged in behavior that was unbecoming. Dusty had done nothing but remain steadfast in blissful innocence of how I had betrayed him.

I thought of how the unwanted gift of my truth would set me free and promptly imprison him in a dungeon of hurt. The burden-shifting that would result didn't seem fair to me, particularly since those walks I had taken had led me right back to the table of certainty about the extraordinary love I felt for Dusty. It suddenly seemed selfish to seek relief from my private grief by sharing the pain that caused it with the person it would hurt most. Don't misunderstand: I still felt the pain of that guilt. But, I couldn't see how Dusty would benefit from sharing that pain. Yes, I had strayed onto the well-traveled path of temptation. But, my undisclosed journey had brought me right back to the person I loved even more. For now, at least, I resolved I would carry that baggage on my own.

I knew I couldn't reach across the table and stroke the soft skin of the back of my hand on Dusty's cheek. We couldn't walk to class with the sublime feeling of the weight of his arm slung over my shoulder. We couldn't roll around on the grass in the quad in springtime and embrace in the sunshine. Even with the inexperience of my youth, I knew what Dusty and I had was extraordinary and rare. I didn't know what would happen with us when he graduated and moved away. But, I could well imagine. It was something so unsettling to think about, I just couldn't. But, I knew to the depths of my being I wanted every minute of the next few months with him to count.

Something in me had changed. From that moment forward through the interim weeks until Dusty and I would travel to New York for his interview at Columbia, I was an unlikely fountain of courage. It had taken me my whole life up until then to know with all certainty and without the chaff of third parties or curiosities about outside experiences to know that no one else mattered or could tempt me. I wanted only Dusty, and I wanted him in every way. We weren't brazen in the way we could have been if we hadn't been same sex lovers during those times. But, after the side trips I had taken to get me here, I knew with every part of me I loved him to the exclusion of all others.

We ran together on the indoor track at the fieldhouse and on the country roads around the campus when it wasn't too cold or icy. We played squash together. We sat together in the library, side-by-side in silence at the long tables on the main floor. We took meals together in the dining hall, often just the two of us. We returned to Oriental Garden. We would sit in his room and listen to Chet Baker records on his hi-fi and drink cheap red wine, always with the door open. It was daring to spend time together in the way that we were. That's not to say we weren't careful. We each had way too much to lose. That's also not to say we didn't find time to fool around. We grabbed each other when we could – in empty alcoves of the library in off hours, in unlocked classrooms, in the showers when we were alone, and so on. We each ejaculated with such frequency, our cocks were often sore. But, in one of the many miracles of youth, they never were for long.

At first, none of the guys wanted to talk about what had happened in the second floor lounge. For the rest of that initial day after, we acknowledged each other's presence only with discomfited nods and averted glances. No one spoke of it. We all ate dinner together that night in the dining hall. The conversation was normally free-flowing and loud and it could be hard to get a word in, but not that night. Once again, Freddy did most of the talking. That was fine with me this time and the rest of us. There was an unspoken agreement that what had happened between us would stay only amongst the participants. As impossible as it could be to keep any secrets in the dorm, and particularly amongst The Magnificent Seven, this was one that was still being processed. No one was inclined to share it with anyone else, including Freddy.

We would all get past the initial embarrassment that had set in once Dusty had flipped the lights on and yanked the projector cord out of the wall. As much as there was a collective sense the evening had gone too far for the comfort of most everyone, it broke down the few remaining barriers that had remained between us. At that stage of life, when there is still a veil of shame over the miracles of how your body works and the secrets of who has what and how big it gets, shining a spotlight on your boner and jerking off in front of your friends shatters those barriers. In the immediate aftermath, however, we each retreated back into our own cauldrons of private thoughts. But, there was no doubt we all had become even closer because of it.

Daniel and I worked into our own groove as well. After a few days of awkwardness, we settled back into our friendship with a familiarity that is difficult to characterize. We had become closer without question. We had for many months been casual about nudity to almost every degree. Since that night, there was no modesty between us at all. We used towels to dry ourselves, but not to cover up. When we woke with morning wood, neither of us took any efforts to hide it. It was just a normal extension of who we were and how our bodies functioned. I would not avert my eyes to avoid a glimpse of Daniel's healthy rod nor would he would do the same with me. But, the interest with which both of us peeked was more natural curiosity than any blatant sexual desire. After everything, we each knew what the other had and how it worked.

I sensed there was a part of Daniel that wanted to forget anything had happened between us. It had happened, however. Both of us had wanted it, and there would be no forgetting. But, the tension that had existed between us had evaporated on that night. We were undeniably close. We trusted each other. There was an unspoken affection between us that transcended ordinary friendship but did not breach the intimacy that lovers otherwise would have shared. That's not to say it wasn't magical in its own right. But, what I had with Dusty was so much more.

☙

When I think back to the excitement I felt on that first date Dusty and I had at Oriental Garden, it was nothing compared to what I felt as we headed off to New York together. Normally, I can think of few things I would rather do less than spend seven hours on a bus. But, setting off on an adventure with Dusty made it thrilling. We each had a bag stowed below in the luggage compartment of the Trailways coach that belched exhaust and groaned in low gears as it climbed the mountain roadways and traversed the countryside of rural Vermont on the journey to New York.

New York both excited and terrified me back then. I had been fascinated by it enough to have applied to NYU and frightened by it enough to have passed it up in lieu of Inverness. I had only been a few times with my parents. Dusty had never been. That added even more to the sense of adventure. The plan was we would arrive late Thursday. Dusty would interview at Columbia on Friday, and we would have the rest of the weekend to ourselves. I was keen to visit New York, of course. But, even more tantalizing was the prospect of spending the night in the same bed with Dusty, something we had not been able to arrange since the night before Christmas break.

We were staying at the apartment of an Inverness graduate named Will Brewster who was a friend of Dusty's. Will attended Columbia Medical School and lived in a married students' apartment building with his wife, Claire, whom he had married right after graduation. They would be there Thursday evening, but were leaving for the weekend on Friday after class, which meant Dusty and I would have the apartment to ourselves. Knowing we had the whole weekend together and two full nights alone was almost too exciting to think about.

Our anticipation grew as the countryside and then the suburbs of metropolitan New York gave way to the congestion, the tall buildings, and the swarming masses of people. As much as I enjoyed sitting knee-to-knee with Dusty, we both were eager finally to get there and get off the bus. It dropped us off at the Port Authority Bus Station on West 41st Street, which was a shithole we both wanted to escape as soon as possible. By the time we made it up to Morningside Heights, we were exhausted from our travels. At the same time, however, we had the energy of youth and wanted to explore the immediate area even if the neighborhood was sketchy.

Will and Claire were easy-going and hospitable. We all went out for dinner at a local diner and then for beers at the campus pub. Will and his wife were both twenty-four, which seemed old to me. They were so mature in a way that underscored how young I was. It also underscored the age difference between Dusty and me. Will introduced us to some of his friends from med school, and we had a good time even though I felt like a kid amongst grown-ups who knew where their lives were going. As much fun as we had that evening, however, it was easy for me to picture Dusty here, which was a painful thought. I didn't want him to leave Inverness. I didn't want him to leave me. I didn't have my head in the sand, and I knew it would happen in the not-too-distant future. I just didn't want to think about it.

By the time we returned to Will and Claire's apartment, it was after midnight. We had had a long day that had begun in Vermont and ended in what might be Dusty's new home depending on how everything worked out. The apartment was a small one-bedroom with a pull-out couch in the living room. There was a brief conversation about whether one of us would toss a coin to get to sleep on the couch with the other one taking the floor. But, then Will said, "Don't be silly. It's not as if you guys are a couple of fruitcakes. Share the bed, and one of you can sleep in our room over the weekend after we leave."

Dusty and I looked at each other and shrugged our acceptance. When Will turned his back, we exchanged wry smirks as we changed into our pajamas. When it came time to crawl into bed and turn out the lights, Will and Claire said goodnight and closed their bedroom door. We lay there in silence for a handful of minutes, not sure what would happen, but knowing something would. It would have to. I never tired of the magic of Dusty's cock or the pleasure it gave me to have him share the gifts that mine could give. Finally, he reached over and slid his hand underneath the elastic of my pajama bottoms. My cock was soft, but not for long. I reached over and felt his, which was hard and had poked through fly of his pajamas. I stroked it gently while he stroked mine, each of us careful to minimize the noise.

From behind the closed door, I could hear the soft, rhythmic sound of the bed creaking as Will and Claire coupled quietly. Dusty heard it, too, and we exchanged amused, knowing glances. It gave us each a charge to know our hosts were going at it and taking failed pains for us not to hear. As the creaking continued with metrical steadiness, Dusty lowered his head under the sheets. His mouth found my cock and in an instant, he swallowed me all the way to the very base of my cock – and then some – as his face mashed against my pubic bone. He rose up and bathed the head of my cock with his lips and tongue before plunging back down. I struggled to contain the moans and gasps that fought to escape from within me, the effort of which only served to intensify my pleasure. I knew I couldn't hold out for too long.

As Will's tempo reached a quiet crescendo that signaled he was on the verge of finishing, I reached my own point of no return. I choked back the noises of my orgasm and came in virtual silence with only a single, quiet gasp as my fingers squeezed the curls of Dusty's hair. When he had sucked me dry, my head collapsed back onto the pillow. I closed my eyes as I savored the waning tendrils of ecstasy for as long as I could. Dusty rose up from under the covers and knelt above me. He slapped his engorged glans, slippery with pre-cum, against my mouth. My lips parted, and he squirted his own load in my mouth before the ecstatic glow ebbed from my body. He collapsed onto the bed and pulled the sheets above us. Exhausted after a long day that had begun in Vermont and ended in the exalted pleasure of a shared pull-out couch with Dusty, we each fell into a deep slumber.

☙

In the morning, Will made an obligatory joke about whether Dusty and I had stayed on our respective sides of the pull-out couch. Dusty and I exchanged smirks as we made up the bed and prepared for our day. We thanked Will and Claire for their hospitality as they left the apartment and gave us a key. As happy as Dusty was to see an old friend, I knew without hearing it he was happier for us to be able to spend the weekend alone in their apartment without them.

Dusty had dressed for his interview in a form-fitting two piece black suit with a crisp white shirt and skinny black tie. In addition to looking stylishly handsome, he also looked like a grown-up. I felt like a kid in my khaki pants and blue button-down shirt as we walked across campus to Hamilton Hall, the imposing Gothic Revival building that housed the Classics department. Dusty walked briskly and confidently. The efforts I undertook just to keep up with his pace made me feel I was behind in more ways than just chronological age. I couldn't help but think how this ivy-covered campus could become his new home.

On paper, his record was impressive in its own right. He was a leader of most every honor society at Inverness and had a transcript that all but guaranteed he would be graduating *magna cum laude*. Student Body Honor Society President, Antiquities and Classical Studies Honor Society Chairman, Student Liaison to the College Housing Administration, and so on, were among his other accomplishments. I was biased, of course, because I loved him so damn much. But, I couldn't imagine how Columbia wouldn't want to have Dusty in their daily midst once they met him and saw he was even more remarkable in person than he was on paper.

I had a couple of hours to myself while Dusty was busy with his interview and the meetings he had requested with students already in the program. As I have mentioned, I genuinely wished him the best and wanted everything to go well for him today. But, being alone while he was off discussing a future that went beyond Inverness and the life I had hoped to have with him there in my quixotic fantasies only left me feeling unsettled about us and what might happen. It was a disconcerting couple of hours for me in the noise of this urban campus that seemed bigger and foreign in ways that dwarfed Inverness. As excited as I had been to join him on this trip to New York, my mind went to dark places as I thought of what life would be like for me after he left. I tried not to think about it, but it was impossible not to.

After browsing around the campus bookstore, I sat on the steps of Hamilton Hall and waited for him. It was a few minutes past noon, and Dusty was half an hour later than he had said he would be. My mind continued to spin. What was going to happen to us? How could I have been so excited to visit here before, but so close to tumbling into despondence at this moment? Would he get swallowed up and enchanted by New York and this ivy-covered campus and lose interest in me?

I felt the firm squeeze of a hand on my shoulder and looked up. It was Dusty.

"Sorry," he said. "I didn't mean to keep you waiting so long."

"How did everything go?" I asked. But, I knew from his broad smile, the breathless way with which he spoke, and the light in his eyes his interviews had gone well. He filled me in on his morning. He was openly exhilarated about the prospect of doing his graduate work here, and Columbia was now his first choice.

"We're going to be okay," he said, placing a hand on each of my shoulders and searching into my eyes. "Don't worry. I'm not letting you go anywhere. Do you understand?"

I nodded my head and tried to swallow my fears. I hadn't said anything about my private thoughts. I didn't need to.

"I mean it!" he said. "You have to believe me on this."

I wanted to believe him with every part of me. But, I couldn't think about it anymore. Dusty's assurances we would be okay notwithstanding that we both knew he would be leaving in a few months felt off balance and unsubstantiated. We both knew whatever happened, the "we" that had become "us" would be different, no matter what we said or wished.

"Let's get out of here," he said. He took a long, sweeping gaze of the exterior of Hamilton Hall and the quadrangle upon which it sat. I kept my eyes forward.

We returned briefly to Will and Claire's apartment. They had two suitcases packed for the weekend and waiting in their living room for them to pick up when they returned from class. As hospitable as they had been, the sight of the suitcases portended in the most favorable way that my weekend alone with Dusty would officially begin with their departure. He changed out of his suit into more casual clothes, and we left armed with our guidebook to the city.

Our first stop was the United Nations, which Dusty had suggested, because of my interests in diplomacy. We spent the afternoon there and toured the UN General Assembly, the visitors' galleries, and walked through the gardens that surrounded the complex. As a surprise, he had reached out to Professor Johnston to help arrange for us to visit the office of the US delegation to the UN. While we were there, Henry Cabot Lodge, Jr., the US Ambassador to the UN, passed through the lobby of the office with his entourage. Our guide, who was an Inverness alum and former student of Professor Johnston, introduced us to him. I could not have been more thrilled. Henry Cabot Lodge, Jr. had been appointed by President Eisenhower, had a career I had followed in the press, and I could not believe I had met someone in that universe. I would go on to meet many famous people over the course of my career, but he was the first one I would ever meet. Meeting him and seeing the UN like this made the professional future I dreamed of seemed real.

After spending the afternoon at the UN, which was more enthralling and inspiring for me than it was for Dusty, we headed down to the Empire State Building, which was then the tallest and most famous building in the world. Neither Dusty nor I had ever been in a building taller than ten or fifteen stories, so ascending to the 102nd floor observation deck was a unique and extraordinary experience made all the more fun because we were sharing it together. We arrived in the very late afternoon as the sun had started to set and cast the city with a warm glow.

Dusty had flown in an airplane, but I hadn't yet, so the view from so high up was like nothing I had ever seen before. We could literally see for miles, which was amazing to me in a child-like way. The cars, buildings, and bridges spread out below us were all so small they barely seemed real. At the same time, the view through scattered clouds was so beautiful, majestic, and powerful. We were mesmerized and lingered on the observation deck as the sun set and the lights of the city turned on below us like a carpet of sparkling light. Clouds began to roll in from the distance, and the air turned colder. As we stood at the railing looking out at the world, Dusty locked his elbow with mine.

When no one was looking, he brought his face in to the crook of my neck and inhaled the scent of my skin. Then he kissed me on my cheek and whispered, "I love you."

I had many extraordinary moments with Dusty. But, the intimacy of this gesture in this iconic romantic location is one that has stayed with me as one of the most spectacular of my whole life. Yes, the setting of the top of the Empire State Building at sunset is one that has been seen before in film, television, and popular culture to the point of becoming a clichéd destination for lovers to kiss and proclaim their passion. But, that's why the memory is so special to me. It may have been common for straight lovers to share the moment Dusty and I had shared. But, it was a forbidden impossibility for lovers of the sort we were. For a man to whisper, "I love you" to a man and kiss him in a near public display of affection in a quiet corner of the top of the Empire State Building in 1958 is something I had never seen before or ever thought to imagine. My heart aches to think of it even to this day.

I took his hand and squeezed it, which felt frighteningly daring. Our eyes met, and I hungered to kiss and embrace him in feverish recognition of the beauty of everything I felt at that moment in the magic of the sparkling world below us. He squeezed my hand back, which was an act of courage in its own right and would have to do in place of the passionate embrace we each desired with all of the various parts of our bodies and souls. We forced ourselves in unspoken unity to swallow the moment and stifle the outward manifestation of affection that was anything but unnatural, no matter what anyone said.

As happy as we were then, it saddens me to write how we suppressed any further demonstrative expression of the sweet, simple love we felt for each other. It pains me to remember how I felt a whiff of danger from even those chaste, innocent gestures. How I wish we could have enjoyed those moments in a different and transparent way. But, it was not to be. Eventually, we descended from the observation deck to street level. Our time spent up there had been such an exquisite experience, there was a part of us that would never come down from it.

We began walking in no direction in particular, since the UN and the Empire State Building had been our primary tourist destinations of the afternoon and we had nowhere else to go. We ended up near Times Square, which was a hub of seediness in those days. It had started to drizzle. Underneath the glow of billboard lights, the sidewalks were slick with wetness. People milled under theater marquees. Bums begged for money. Prostitutes lingered on street corners and everyone seemed to be living a life on the extremes of open desperation, indifference, or hurried purpose.

We eventually bought dinner at a Horn & Hardhart automat and watched the masses of people, which was part freak show and part theater crowd and part just about anyone else you could think of who was out in a sketchy neighborhood as the evening grew late. Eventually, we tired of walking and looking and made our way back to Will and Claire's apartment after midnight. We both were exhausted, but we were looking forward to the secret pleasure of sleeping in the same bed and what that might facilitate.

The suitcases that had sat in the living room at midday were gone, which heralded Will and Claire's departure and denoted that it was officially just Dusty and me. I could not wait to crawl into bed with him. I was perpetually horny back then and looking forward to fooling around despite my fatigue. He washed up first and crawled into Will and Claire's queen-sized bed. He leaned back and smiled, his eyes heavy with a combination of desire and exhaustion. I kissed him and went into the bathroom to brush my teeth, wash up, and get ready for some cock play and whatever else might happen.

When I finished in the bathroom, Dusty was still lying on his back, his arm folded behind his head. But, his eyes were closed. I stood there for a moment and thought how beautiful he looked and how lucky I was that I was about to slide into bed with him for the night, even if he had fallen asleep before anything could happen between us. I kissed his forehead and thought of the care and tenderness with which he had kissed mine the night of the special, invite only cinematic event when I had the gift of clarity about everything I thought or might have felt about us. I turned out the light and removed my boxer shorts.

Naked, I slid into the bed and sidled up to him. I could feel the smoothness of his skin against mine. I could hear the sound of his breathing. I could smell the scent of his skin. I leaned my head against his chest and could hear the sound of his beating heart, which was one of the most fantastical sounds I would ever want to hear. Even to this day, I can savor the memory of that sound in my head if I only close my eyes and listen for it. It had been an exhausting, but phenomenal day, and I quickly drifted off to sleep in the arms of the man I loved more than everything.

☙

In the morning, I woke before Dusty did. We had shifted positions during the night so that he had nestled up to the cleft of my bare buttocks. He still wore his white briefs, but his cock had escaped at some point during the night. It was rock hard and buried between my legs. I could feel the smooth skin of his shaft against my hole. His pronounced upwards curve caused the engorged head of his cock to press against my balls and the inside of my groin. I squeezed my glutes and tightened my anus against his cock both for my own pleasure and to check if he was awake. He wasn't. At least not yet. As much as lying there naked in bed, my bare ass pressed against Dusty's divine organ was a heaven I never wanted to leave, my bladder telegraphed urgent messages to my brain that it needed draining. I loosened the grip of my buttocks on Dusty's cock and pulled myself away as gently as I could so as not to disturb his slumber.

I did my business in the bathroom and decided afterwards to brush my teeth and shower. While I was in the shower, Dusty entered the bathroom.

"Good morning, sweetheart," he said.

"Good morning, sleepy head." I peeked around the shower curtain and smiled at him. His cock was rock hard, curved and pointed at the sky. He was perched above the toilet and attempting to relax his morning wood enough so he could urinate. I closed the curtain and a moment later heard him emit a quiet gasp of relief followed by the powerful sound of his urine splattering into the bowl.

"Keep the water running," he said while he urinated. "I'll join you."

I heard him gargling mouthwash. Then, he pulled back the shower curtain and joined me inside. One of the many things I loved about Dusty was how his face always brightened and his smile widened whenever he saw me. I could never tire of either. His intense ardor for me could have gone unspoken, because his outward expressions made it perfectly clear he loved me with every part of him. One part that was never bashful in demonstrating his affection for me was his cock. It had been half hard when he joined me in the shower. But, now that he was in here and naked with me, it took only moments before he was rock hard again.

"Happy to see me?" I said, reaching to grab his cock.

"Very," he said, pulling me in and kissing me. His mouth tasted minty fresh. His tongue was strong and forceful as it probed my mouth. My cock hardened and jutted against his thigh. He grabbed it as he kissed me. It was still slippery from the soap, and his hand traveled over it with increased ease. It felt so good that I closed my eyes as he kissed me. My lips vibrated against his with a stifled moan. It almost felt too good. "Careful," I whispered, not wanting to blow my load too soon.

He pulled his lips back from mine and spun me around so my ass was facing him as the warm water continued to splash down upon us. He ran his soaped hands over the smoothness of my buttocks.

"Your ass is so beautiful," he said.

"You think so?"

"I love it," he said, sliding his hand down past my taint to the slit of my hole. "Small and tight." He tapped the tip of his middle finger against the opening of this most private of places. I had held a hand mirror down there a few times to get a better glimpse of what I could feel but not see. It was a place foreign even to me, one I did not fully understand even though it was part of my own body.

He wrapped his elbow around my neck and leaned in to kiss me. Our mouths met and our tongues clashed as the water cascaded upon us. Our cocks throbbed, our knobs brushing against each other's thighs. It was always electrifying to be in Dusty's embrace, particularly when we were naked and our bodies knew that embracing was only the beginning. He kept his hand mashed between my legs, his hand and fingers slippery and probing. The tip of his middle finger repeatedly found its way back to the outside of my hole with both persistence and a steady insistence that made me wonder – and fear – what else he might have in mind for me. His eyes locked with mine. That nettlesome finger slid in with a pop, past the tightness of my sphincter and into the warmth and hot wetness of my ass.

Despite the natural resistance from my virgin hole, Dusty continued to slide his wet, slippery finger inside me. The muscles in my ass gripped it involuntarily. But, as he kissed my mouth, the resistance inside me dissipated. He spun me around and pressed his left hand between my shoulder blades while he reinserted his middle finger inside me. I leaned forward against the wall of the shower, my buttocks arched upwards to facilitate the entry and motion of his finger. While he fucked me gently with it, I closed my eyes and relaxed as the warm water sprayed down upon my back. He probed me, pressed against my prostate, and I tingled from the sensation of having him inside me even if it was just a single finger.

Dusty knew my body better than I did and was aware by the way my hips moved in a slow but steady grind that I was about to cum. Abruptly, he withdrew his finger. My hole quivered. The sensation of his finger lingered, and my body hungered for it to be reinserted. He spun me around and hugged me tight, his boner crossing with mine as he pressed his body against me. He turned off the water and stepped out of the shower. He reached for a towel he used to dry me off first before drying himself off. Then I grabbed his hand and led him into Will and Claire's bedroom where we tumbled onto the unmade bed in which we had slept.

Dusty's cock had fallen to half-mast, a deficiency of which I set out to fix. I wrapped my mouth around it and sucked it in mere seconds to full hardness. I lifted my head and admired his cock from up close: it was rock hard in its full glory, slick with spit, engorged with blood, a long, thick, curved golden banana. It was a cock that would be extraordinarily beautiful under any circumstances. Having it attached to someone who entranced me as much as Dusty did made it desirable beyond all reason. I lowered my head to continue sucking it, but he shifted his weight and placed his hand on my shoulder, pressing me to lay on my back, my head against the pillow.

I stroked the hair behind his ears as he sucked my cock. He slid his mouth down to the base in a single, fluid motion. I gasped, always amazed he could deep-throat the entire length of my shaft without gagging. His mouth glided up and down my whole cock and back again. His hand gripped my balls and twirled them in his fingers. His brilliant blue eyes were open the entire time and locked with mine. As he gauged my reaction to the pleasure with which he bestowed upon me, he adjusted his tempo and the pressure of his mouth and tongue.

My cock leaked pre-cum, and he could tell by the way my breathing increased and my eyes became heavy-lidded I was close to coming. He stopped, lifting his mouth from my cock to allow me to pull myself back from the brink. I took several deep breaths and exhaled. He kissed the base of my cock and then kissed the inside of my legs on each side of my balls. He pressed his nose against my scrotum and inhaled deeply over and over again. Then he moved his mouth and kissed the smooth skin beneath my balls, a sensation that was exciting in its newness to me.

"That feels so good," I murmured, my fingers running through his curly locks of hair.

He took my legs and bent them back towards my chest, which startled me with the strength and suddenness of the motion. Then he did the most shocking thing: he kissed my hole. It was fully exposed in this position in a way that made me feel vulnerable and self-conscious. This most private part of my body was on full and open view in a way I had never even seen myself. With tenderness, he kissed it again and slid his tongue in broad, insistent circles across it. In the same way that kissing the smooth skin beneath my balls was something new to me, the knowing touch of his soft, wet tongue on my hole was a new sensation I had never experienced or ever even imagined. As with other aspects of the natural mysteries of sex between men, it had never entered my mind that anyone would do such a thing. To say it felt great would be a wild understatement. But, it also felt very wrong. I squirmed and tried to free myself of the grasp he had on my thighs.

"What are you doing?" I asked, my mind and body swirling in the most confusing vortex of ecstasy and mortification. This was insane. Dusty had his mouth on my ass? He was licking it? Bathing it with his tongue? The thought was revolting. Yet, it felt so good. I had never heard of or imagined such a thing ever. I had never seen any photographs or descriptions of it. I had never heard anyone speak of it.

"What does it look like I'm doing?" He flicked his tongue against my hole, his eyes locked with mine, his mouth curved into a devilish smirk.

"You're licking my asshole!"

He continued to flick his tongue against my hole. I continued to squirm. He continued to hold my thighs in place against my chest and not let me move.

"Do you like it?"

"No! It's embarrassing!" I didn't like having my hole on such open display.

Dusty leaned up and kissed me on the lips. "Trust me," he said. "Relax."

Of the myriad feelings I had towards Dusty, trust was one of the strongest. I trusted him implicitly about everything, including my life. If I could trust him with that, I figured I could trust him about this. I leaned my head back on the pillow in resignation and let him resume. If I was honest with myself and forgot the bewilderment I felt at what was happening, I had to admit it was one of the most incredible physical sensations I had ever felt in my whole life. He blew gently on my hole and then licked around the stretched-out pucker of my skin. He flicked his tongue, teasing me. It left me twitching, aching impatiently for more.

He placed his mouth full-on over my hole and sucked it hungrily. I gasped for breath and moaned involuntarily. Using his hands, he stretched my anus open wider and pressed his tongue inside me as far as he could get it in. His tongue was rigid and moist, and he used it to fuck my hole with a warmth and a slippery wetness that felt so incredible, I almost felt as if I were levitating above the bed with pleasure. How could something like this feel so good? How come I had never heard of such a thing before? I laid there, moaning, my head rolling side-to-side on the pillow as his mouth and tongue worked unspoken magic on this most hidden of places on my body.

He adjusted himself and knelt above me, still pressing my legs to my chest.

"No, don't stop," I said.

"See? I told you to trust me. Now trust me about this." He spit into his hand and rubbed it on the length of his cock and around the crown that already was wet with pre-cum. When it was fully lubed and wet, he tapped the head of his cock on my splayed hole. I had a good idea what he had in mind, and this scared me in a different way. Was this really happening? It was one thing to have a finger, whether mine or Dusty's, in my ass. But a cock? And one as big and thick as Dusty's? I had heard of butt fucking, of course, and could well imagine it in a way that I had never imagined getting my ass eaten out with such gusto. But, imagining getting fucked and wanting it were two different things, and I didn't know if I wanted it. He teased me, continuing to rub his hard, slippery dick head against my ass. My hole was wet and surprisingly relaxed. I was afraid. At the same time, I ached with curiosity. I loved Dusty, and at this moment, I wanted – needed – his cock inside me. I pressed my hips and my hole against his cock.

He smiled. "You want it, don't you?"

I nodded. "Don't tease me. Give it to me."

His smile faded, and his expression turned serious. He pressed his wet, engorged cockhead inside me and then stopped once the crown was fully in. Our eyes locked. My eyes searched his and his searched mine right back.

I was afraid this would hurt, and it did.

"Don't worry," he whispered. "I'll go slowly. Trust me."

Those words again. I nodded, indicating for him to continue. He pressed his cock further into me, but the pain was too much. My face crinkled in pain. I arched my back, and my hands gripped the sheets of the bed. As much as I loved Dusty and wanted him inside me, I didn't think this was for me.

"Push out, like you're going to the bathroom," he said, his gaze not leaving mine.

I nodded again, not saying anything, but trusting him not to hurt me. I pushed my ass muscle against him as he pressed his cock inside me. He slid in further and deeper. My hole felt like it was on fire. I was not enjoying this.

"Stop," I said. "It's too big. It's never going to fit."

This time he smiled and looked down at where his cock was buried inside me, all the way down to the base with his pubic hair mashed against my taint. "I told you to trust me. I'm all the way in."

I took a series of short, shallow breaths. "Don't move. Let me get used to it."

I felt surprisingly emotional at this moment. Dusty was inside me all the way. He was holding me. My hole hurt, and he knew it intuitively. His eyes were staring into my own, scanning my mind, gauging the threshold of where pain crossed over into pleasure, which he desired both to give and receive. In the most loving, careful, and attentive way, he had coached me through something I had feared and wanted at the same time. My anal canal twitched in rebellion as it fought the battle over whether to expel or welcome Dusty's long, thick cock.

"Shhh," he whispered and leaned in to kiss me. "I love you."

With his arms wrapped around me and his cock buried in the depths of my body, we kissed. His mouth and tongue connected with mine with knowing tenderness. My cock and my heart surged. I loved this beautiful, incredible human being inside and out, and he loved me right back. My breathing slowed. I relaxed.

Dusty began to withdraw his cock, slowly rising until only his purple knob was in me. My hole squeezed it involuntarily, and he smiled at the recognition of what I was doing. Slowly, he descended back into me, all the way to the base of his cock. He rested there without moving as my ass loosened and became more accustomed to having him in it. Then he repeated the sequence again. By the time he had slid back into me all the way to the bottom, the pain had morphed into supreme pleasure. He leaned forward and kissed me again. I ran my hands over his firm ass, which was clenched tight. He squeezed his cock muscles, which made it even harder. He thrust into me, more forcefully this time. I had one hand on each of his cheeks, my fingers meeting in his crack, and I pulled him deeper into me.

He pulled his chest up from mine and braced himself with one arm on either side of me. My legs were spread, my cock hard and throbbing. His biceps were extended and his pecs were stretched tight. The tenderness was a memory now that my ass had opened up and hungered for him. He began to pump me vigorously with the force I had feared before but now craved.

"Fuck me," I begged. "Give it to me."

His breathing was heavy, his facial expression serious as his eyes bore into mine and his cock drilled my ass. As much as I loved Dusty and his beautiful body, getting fucked was not something I had ever dreamed about. I had always associated it with dirtiness and shame. Butt fucking was thought of as louche then, one of the most sordid of sexual acts, even among male lovers. "Brownie queen" was the phrase I had heard whispered about it, an act committed by lower class gays, not lovers like us.

Now that it was happening to me, however, I hungered for it in a way I never wanted to stop. Dusty's cock was long and thick and his body powerful. The upward curve of his cock caused the hard, shiny smoothness of his glans to slide along the top of the inside of my ass, gliding along and expertly pressing against my prostate, a powerful, extraordinary center of pleasure I never even knew I had until I met Dusty. I had never felt more aroused, more alive, or more in love than I did at this moment.

My cock was rock hard and jutted straight out, as erect and aroused as it ever gets. As Dusty continued to fuck me, he slowed and arched his head down. Because both of our cocks were long and Dusty had the flexibility of athletic youth, he was able to bend down and suck the top half of my cock while his cock was still inside me. The twin sensations of pleasure – his mouth on my cock and his cock in my ass – defied the expectations of every fantasy I had ever had. How could two bodies converge in such an incredible way to create such extraordinary bliss? How was it possible to feel such astonishing passion to a degree that made me feel is if I were soaring and had escaped the bonds of gravity?

Dusty lifted his head, and the reduction of pleasure was actually a relief. It meant I could concentrate on the multitude of pleasures of his cock was creating by sliding in and out of my hole. A singular strip of semen dribbled out of my dick hole, forced out by the pressure of his cock against my prostate. He leaned forward and licked it off of me before rising again. The act and the taste excited him even more. He pumped me hard and furiously, his cock sliding in and out of me. His balls slapped against my ass, the crush of his pubic hair tickling the underside of my balls.

His eyes were heavy and darkened, his breathing intensifying. "I love you, baby," he said, before closing his eyes and throwing his head back. "Oh, baby!" He moaned, and his body twisted as he unloaded his semen inside me. My face was transfixed on his. His eyes were closed, and his features were contorted in what looked like pain, but I knew was the pinnacle of pleasure. He squirted a river of semen inside me, his younger lover I knew with every part of me was the one soul on the entire planet he loved more than anyone or anything. I could feel his cock pulse as he injected his semen into me, and I swear I could feel the sensation of the first two bursts striking me on the inside.

He opened his eyes and continued to fuck me, even though he had shot his load. I could feel the hot wetness of his semen-coated cock slide in and out of me. The knowledge he had inseminated me and the unexpectedly heightened and extended sensation caught me by surprise. My cock was rock hard, as hard as it ever gets, and my hole pulsed as it gripped his cock. I felt that familiar rumbling from inside me as his cock head pressed against my prostate. But, this was different. It was deeper.

As I lay on my back, my legs wrapped around his waist, my cock jutted straight up into the air. I gripped the sheets with my hands as if the waves of pleasure that convulsed through my body would sweep me away. The pre-cum that had been leaking from my dick hole switched to a thick string of semen that streamed down the side of my cock in a slow steady orgasm that surprised me both with its intensity and because neither my hands nor Dusty's were touching my cock. The root of the orgasm came from within me and the primary sensation of Dusty's hot, hard, slippery cock that had just pumped me full of his semen.

As I groaned, however, Dusty took his hand and wrapped it around my oozing cock and rapidly stroked it. The combined sensations of both internal and external friction caused the cum to stop oozing and start to shoot out of my cock in rapid bursts that splashed onto my chest. I moaned, groaned, and gasped in near delirium as my body was rocked in a way it never had been. As the orgasm began to fade, I opened my eyes, and they met Dusty's. He had been watching my face the whole time. He smiled and leaned forward to kiss me. The waves of pleasure that had convulsed through me morphed into waves of emotion. I loved Dusty more than I ever thought I could love another human being. I knew by the way he looked at me and held me that he felt the same way. I wallowed in the sublime physical and emotional manifestations of love and passion. We kissed and held each other, our bodies glistening with post-coital sweat and stickiness.

Dusty's cock was still thick, even though it was only half hard by now. It slithered out of me as he shifted his body to lay next to me. He smiled at me in the sweetest way. His eyes glistened. "I love you, baby. I really do."

I leaned in and kissed him. I closed my eyes and let the post orgasmic sleep wash over me as I recovered from an explosive journey into a beautiful, secret world Dusty and I had traveled to together.

☙

We never made it to Central Park. After we woke from a brief snooze, Dusty's cock was hard again. My ass was sore, but I was eager to have him inside me again. He opened the nightstand on Claire's side of the bed and pulled out an unmarked bottle he assumed was a personal lubricant. He opened it up and poured a drop on his hand. He was right. He lubed up his cock and the outside of my hole. As Dusty lay on his back, I slid over and positioned myself on top of him. I spread my cheeks as I lowered my buttocks down on his erect cock. With less effort than before, I was able to accommodate him inside me. I raised and lowered my ass, my hard cock bouncing in front of me as I did.

Now that my ass virginity was already an hour in my past, I was curious to move beyond tenderness and Dusty was eager to satisfy that curiosity. When my hole had relaxed and I was able to take him with greater ease, he flipped me over on my back with my legs in the air. He held them against his chest, my feet resting on his shoulders. He was attentive to how much I could take and when. Soon he was pounding me hard with a degree of force I had not thought possible I could take. Yes, it hurt. But, there can be a blurry line between pain and pleasure. I was skirting the outer limits of both. That's not to say he was rough. He wasn't. But, there was no mistaking he was fully in control and that my hole was his.

He contorted me into several different positions, and we ended up with me on all fours as he fucked me until I shot my load into the sheets. As he sensed my hole tighten and grip his cock, he moaned, "Oh, fuck! Oh, fuck! Oh, fuck" as he shot his load deep inside me, the front of his thighs slapping against the back of mine, his hands gripped tightly on my hips as he pounded me. Panting, he fell off of me and collapsed onto his back on the bed as the ecstasy ebbed from his body. Even though he had just fucked me with abandon, this second coupling ended with a tender cuddle and a series of gentle kisses just as before.

We eventually found our way out of the bedroom and journeyed down to the Statue of Liberty, which I had never visited on my previous trips to New York. We had both seen pictures of it, of course. I had even written about it in that high school newspaper essay I had written about the meaning of freedom, the one for which I won an award and had been published in *The Reader's Digest*. The majesty of the statue as we arrived at Liberty Island by ferry from lower Manhattan on that brisk March afternoon was a spectacular sight made even more memorable by my acute awareness of how exhilarating it was to be there with Dusty. Ever since that first visit to the Statue of Liberty, it no longer had a primary association for me as a symbol of freedom. Instead, my primary association of it is with Dusty and our weekend in New York. I also associate it with how sore my ass was after getting fucked all morning and how three loads of his semen leaked out of me all afternoon. Climbing the 377 steps from the main lobby to the crown exacerbated the pain and cemented the memories in my mind.

Dusty's birthday had been the first weekend of March, just a week before. As a present for him, I had purchased tickets for us to see *West Side Story* on Broadway. Neither of us had seen a Broadway play before. *West Side Story* had just premiered in the fall and was one of the most sought after shows of the year. The soundtrack to the show was also one of the most popular albums of the year, and Dusty owned it. We had played it many times on the hi-fi in his room as we drank cheap red wine from the water glasses he had lifted from the dining hall. We dressed up for the show, of course – it would have been unthinkable to do otherwise back then. It makes my heart ache to think of how young, handsome, and happy we were that night as we sat in our balcony seats dressed in suits, starched shirts, and shiny ties.

We didn't speak of it, but I couldn't help but think of how Dusty and I were similar to the lovers in the drama that played out on stage. Like us, they were consumed by a deep, forbidden, and passionate love, the kind that defies those who condemned it. In the darkness of the theater, Dusty reached for my hand. He squeezed it and held it on my thigh until the show was over and the lights came up.

When we returned to Will and Claire's apartment late that night, we both were horny again, which was not a surprise. After a long day and night, we both showered and climbed into bed.

My ass still hurt from the punishment it took that morning, and there was no way Dusty was going to be able to fuck me. But, that didn't mean there weren't other things we could do. I was curious about so much of what Dusty and I had done that morning in bed, and there were things I wanted to try.

The first item on my list was eating his ass. I flipped him over and admired the curves of his firm, muscular ass and the smooth, creamy whiteness of his skin. I started off slowly at the top of his crack and made my way down. Even though I had never imagined doing such a thing until Dusty did it to me, I wasn't revolted by Dusty's ass or the thought of sucking on his hole. To the contrary, I loved every part of him and wanted to try it. I spread his cheeks and dove in.

It is hard to explain how truly delicious and intimate it is to kiss a lover there, in this most private, forbidden place. It tasted uniquely of him. Its incomparable, musky smell made me ravenous, and I burrowed my face deeper between the warm, wetness of his cheeks in an insatiable quest for more. He moaned a high-pitched whimper as he writhed in ecstasy and begged me not to stop. After indulging in this act, there are few sexual barriers between lovers. I couldn't do it just to anyone. But, to Dusty, I could do it all night. In the same way having my ass eaten caused the resistance within it to melt, Dusty's did the same. I knew by the way he moaned and ground his hips into the bed he wanted me inside him in the same way I had wanted him. I spit on my hand and lubed up my cock. Then, I tapped my wet, hard, slippery knob against his hole and pressed it in.

"Careful," he whispered. "Go slow."

I kissed his neck and lowered myself on top of him. My cock slid into him far more easily than his had slid into me. Once I was all the way inside, I rested the weight of my body on top of his, my chest pressed against his back.

"You doing okay?" I asked.

He smiled and murmured affirmatively.

I took that as license to increase my tempo. I gradually began to pump his ass harder. It felt different than when I had had intercourse with Allison. I had had to wear a rubber with her. But, with Dusty, I was able to experience the magic of the bare skin of my slick cock against the bare skin of the inside of his ass. The magic was not just the skin-to-skin contact or the intensity of having my hard penis stimulated in this primal way. It was the knowledge I was deep inside the man I loved so much.

There was no way I was going to last long, and I didn't even bother trying. My chest still pressed against his back, I buried my face into his neck and wrapped my arms around him. I humped his tight, meaty ass. A powerful surge rose up from within me. As I thrust my hips against his buttocks, I began to groan.

"Fuck! Fuck! Fuck!" I exclaimed as I delivered a load of semen deep inside his ass, my long cock jammed inside him as far as I could get it in.

"Don't pull out of me yet," he said. We shifted into the spoon position, each of us on our sides, my cock still inside him. He jerked himself off, shooting his load into the sheets. I could feel his anus pulse and clench my cock as he came. When he was finished, he pulled himself off my cock, which slid out of his ass and flopped onto the bed. My cock was still semi-hard, even after cumming. I reached down and rubbed the head of it in my semen that leaked out of him. My cock was numb, but nonetheless began to harden, and I eased it back in. Exhausted after a long, spectacular day of firsts, we fell asleep, our bodies still entangled, my cock still inside him.

☙

In the morning, we conducted a repeat performance of the night before, with me on top again. My hole was still way too sore from yesterday to let him back inside me. Despite the supreme pleasure it had given me to bottom for Dusty and feel his thick, curved cock probe my insides and welcome his semen into my body, I wondered if I might like being on top even better. Dusty was an inch or two taller than I was, and his body a little thicker and more muscular than mine. He was also older than me, so it had originally seemed more intuitive to me that he would take the insertive role. But, I seemed to like being on top better than bottoming, and he seemed amenable to being receptive as well. I didn't worry about it too much and figured we would have plenty of time to figure things out.

We left Will and Claire's apartment as clean as it was when they had departed on Friday. Then we headed down to the Port Authority Bus Terminal. We felt a waterfall of sadness when we closed the door on the private Eden that had allowed us to explore the passion that consumed us in directions we otherwise would not have been able to explore back at Inverness. Our balls were sore from ejaculating with great frequency over the past several days. Our asses were sore in a different way, mine more so than Dusty's, after taking that further leap forward on the extraordinary journey upon which we had embarked together. We had changed forever in profound ways, and neither of us needed to say that we would never forget this weekend.

As New York receded behind us on the long bus ride back to Inverness, we each were lulled to sleep by the rumble of the engine and the monotony of the drive. Even with the incumbent exhaustion from an Earth-moving weekend, we didn't sleep the whole way, of course. But, we did for large parts of it. Just when I didn't think the ride could go on for any longer, we finally turned off the main road and onto the local road that lead to Inverness. The turn and the slowing rumble of the engine had caused me to awaken. I looked out the window as we passed along the roads that lead through the village.

Dusty was still asleep, the blond curls on his head pressed against the window. His mouth was open, and a drop of drool had collected on his lower lip. He looked so beautiful and peaceful to me. He had wrapped his jacket around himself for comfort and warmth. It may sound trite, but I never tired of looking at him even after a long day of travel. As much as I would have been happy just to continue staring at him, we were almost there. To wake him, I reached my hand underneath the jacket he had spread across his chest and lap. My fingers found his crotch. I squeezed it. When I did not get a reaction, I did it again. Gently, but firmly, I manipulated his crotch until finally, his eyes still shut, he closed his mouth and his lips curled into a smile.

"Are we there?" he asked, still smiling, eyes still shut, his cock starting to stiffen.

"Yes," I said, smiling back.

As we pulled up to the bus depot, I was surprised, but pleased, to see Anthony, Daniel, Sasquatch, and Howell standing there in a line along the curb to welcome us, their arms crossed as they waited. Daniel cupped his hand to his forehead, scanning the faces of the passengers inside the bus. I saw him and waved, thinking how lucky I was and how incredibly great my life had turned out. I had arrived at Inverness last September, nervous and uncertain about who I was and what my year would be like. I had made the most extraordinary friends I had always dreamed of having. I had the most extraordinary boyfriend – that word again! – I had never dared to dream of having. I was thrilled to see my buddies and drunkenly happy to have Dusty at my side. I don't think I had ever been at such a truly contented stage of my life as I was then, particularly after a weekend like that, and particularly at the sight of the friends I cared for so much.

Daniel waved back. He tapped Anthony on the shoulder and pointed in my direction. If I had been paying attention, I would have noticed despite Daniel's wave, he was not smiling. I would have wondered why Daniel and Anthony were together in concert when generally they didn't hang together unless they had to. Anthony's face was dark. He did not wave at us, but instead nudged Sasquatch and Howell with his elbow. They raced to the bay the bus had turned into. But, I didn't see any of that. I was too caught up in my own damn happiness.

If I had known what I would soon learn, I never would have woken Dusty, and I never would have gotten off that bus. I would have kept on going to the end of the line, wherever it was. Anthony, Daniel, Sasquatch, and Howell hadn't come to the depot to greet us. They had come to us in frightened desperation to warn us of impending peril. As I type these words, my hands tremble with anger, and my chest rumbles with fear at the memory of what was about to happen. My heart weeps at the thought of how young and radiant Dusty and I were. I was just eighteen and he was newly twenty-two. We each were in the throes of first love, a love we had thought was reserved for others, not for people who loved like we did. We disembarked with such innocent happiness, not knowing we were stepping into a dry desert gulch just in time to be swept away by a raging river of shit.

19 INQUISITION

I HAD NEVER set foot in the campus administration building before, yet here I was in an august chamber aptly named the "Trustees Room," because it generally was reserved for meetings of the college's board of trustees. Oak paneling covered the walls and matched the lacquered wood of the furniture. Olive-colored leather covered the stuffed chairs. The room had the faint, acrid smell of stale cigarette smoke. The windows rose from floor to ceiling and let in the bright sunlight that belied the darkness of the proceedings happening inside. Today, there were no trustees within miles. Rather, this sunny room was the setting for a special meeting of the college disciplinary committee that most unfortunately was seeking to discipline me.

Dean Hoffman, the platinum-haired sexagenarian who had held the position of Dean of Students since before I was born, glared at me over the top of his reading glasses. His icy dark eyes bore into me. "Mr. Branson," he said, "I will remind you that you are under oath, and I will ask you again: Are you or are you not a homosexual?"

I blinked under the bright lights, my young, unhardened heart pounding in my chest with a speed as frenetic as that of a baby robin knocked from its nest. I felt wretched in every physical and emotional way as I sat, alone, at a long wooden table and looked up at the dais where the five people facing me waited impatiently for my answer: Dean Hoffman; the head of campus security; Dr. Oswald, the college physician; Professor Johnston, who was there in his role as the faculty advisor to the disciplinary committee; and a student representative who was a senior I had seen around campus but did not know.

I struggled to reconcile the horror of what was happening to me. How had I ended up here, in the worst sort of trouble you could ever expect to be in? I was the quintessential "good boy," the type of kid grown-ups trusted with the car keys, the type of kid who ate his vegetables and brushed his teeth without being told, the type of kid who writes a naïve and foolishly optimistic essay on freedom that gets picked up by *The Reader's Digest*. I never got in trouble, yet here I was on trial by the Inverness disciplinary committee on charges of homosexuality and sexual perversion, the worst sorts of things you could ever say about a person back then. Even though I had been naïve enough to write that essay on the meaning of freedom, I was not so naïve to think the committee's case against me wasn't a slam-dunk or that this wasn't a show trial which was the antithesis of the freedom about which I had written.

I knew without being told the official punishment would be expulsion, with public humiliation and banishment from the known circles of my life as unofficial collateral punishment. My academic and professional aspirations would be over before they started, snuffed out by the pink "H" that would be stamped across my permanent record in both figurative and literal ways. No other college would want me once they knew sexual perversion was the reason for my expulsion. The US State Department wouldn't want me either, and the career in diplomacy that had been my dream for as long as I could remember would be an impossibility.

It was painful to think about how my family would react and the probability my deviant shame would be reason enough to be banished even by them. How could they show up for tennis and cocktails at the country club with a son who was a proven fairy? How could they entertain on weekends with Florence serving canapés baked in the kitchen while the guests sipped gin martinis and averted their eyes as they gossiped in hushed voices about the tragedy of the sex pervert lurking about? How could my father ever bring me back for squash, a swim, and lunch at the Hartford Athletic & Social Club when friends like Bud Anderson would come to learn of the shame that had befallen the Branson family? I could hear the whispered words said with a cold, sharp smile: *Poor Charlie. His son's a cocksucker, you know. He and Helen are devastated, of course. A pity. At least if they ever need a florist or a hairdresser, they'll know where to find one.*

Was I a homosexual? That was the fear that had terrified me to my core for so long. The truth was, I didn't know the answer. I loved Dusty. The perceived evil of loving another man was the reason I was here on trial. But, I had ached to distraction for pussy in the same way I had ached to distraction for cock. I had had sex with Dusty, of course. But, I also had had sex with Allison and enjoyed the magic of how it was different and fundamentally similar all at the same time. How could that mean I was a homosexual? How could my feelings for Dusty mean I was not?

I knew I had to be mortally careful how I answered. There was no way I could admit to it. Even suggesting uncertainty would put the life I knew to an end faster than it appeared to be ending on its own. The evidence against me was as damning as you would expect. Even though I had begun to brace myself for my fate, I stuck to my strategy: admit to the small things that don't matter, but categorically deny the things that do.

Dean Hoffman cleared his throat in angry exasperation. "Mr. Branson, we don't have all day. I will ask you for a third time: Are you or are you not a homosexual?"

"No," I said, my voice weak.

"No, what?"

"No, I am not a homosexual."

The room was silent except for the sound of the scribbling of penciled notes recorded by all of the committee members except for Dean Hoffman and Professor Johnston. It was obvious to me Dean Hoffman was predisposed to find me guilty. I hoped Professor Johnston, my great mentor, was predisposed to find me innocent and help assure the other members that I was a good kid, the best sort of student any college would want to have. But, I couldn't tell by the lack of expression on his face what he was thinking. The virtual silence belied the roar of terror inside my head.

"Let's start at the beginning," Dean Hoffman said. He licked his index finger and flipped through the pages of his notes on a yellow legal pad. "Have you ever had any homosexual experiences?"

"No."

"Never?"

"No."

Dr. Oswald cleared his throat and asked, "Have you ever had any homosexual thoughts or desires?"

I shook my head. Dr. Oswald had already asked me that when he had evaluated me privately in his office. He had asked me a whole litany of questions regarding my interior thoughts, my masturbation habits, and my sexual experiences with girls. He had asked what my interests were, whether I liked sports and whether I was musical, artistic, and creative. He asked about my parents and how they interacted with me, whether my mother was over-bearing and if my father was a dominant figure or a weak one in our household. I knew these questions were laden with peril for me, and I answered each one with regard to my welfare rather than the truth. I then had submitted to a medical examination in his office. He had me strip naked. He examined my eyes and my facial features. He took measurements of my skull. He instructed me to bend over and inserted a gloved finger into my anus and conducted a digital examination of my rectum that lasted far longer and included more movement than any other such examination I have had since. He examined my penis and my testicles. He tested me for venereal diseases. I submitted to all of it without resistance.

"You will have to state your answer out loud," Dean Hoffman said.

"No, I have never had any homosexual thoughts or desires."

Dr. Oswald continued, "Have you ever had any homosexual dreams?"

I shook my head. "No, I have never had any homosexual dreams."

After Dr. Oswald was finished, Dean Hoffman continued: "I am going to ask you a number of questions regarding your conduct since you arrived at Inverness. Have you ever danced naked in the showers in front of other students in a lewd, indecorous, or lascivious manner?"

"No," I said.

Dean Hoffman fell silent and flipped through his legal pad. After a long moment, he said, "I have a description here of an incident in which you were in the showers in Canterbury Hall. You gyrated your hips in a lewd manner. Your genitals were spinning, an act you referred to as 'helicoptering.' You incited the other boys to do the same. During this display, Edward Olsen referred to you as 'the boy next door with the dirty parlor tricks,' and you replied, 'it's the boy next door you should be worried about.' Did that incident happen? Yes or no."

I paused to collect my thoughts. I was stunned by the specificity of the description Freddy had given them and wondered what else he had said to save himself. I had never trusted Freddy very much, and I despised him with every part of me at this moment. While Dusty and I were away for our long weekend in New York, our world back at Inverness was being pulled apart, with Freddy doing some of the pulling. Janusz had caught Freddy and Shorty butt fucking in the first floor housemasters' lounge, the same room where we had all watched Daniel fuck Carol on the couch and where I had watched Shorty give Freddy a blow job, my bare ass pressed against the glass after The Magnificent Seven had cavorted naked in the quad as the snow fell upon us.

As Shorty had explained to me, Freddy was fucking him as they were standing up, with Shorty bending over as Freddy took him from behind. Freddy's bare ass was facing the door in the darkened room. Janusz had unlocked the door to clean the room, thinking it was empty. Startled, Freddy had turned, a movement that uncoupled him from Shorty and given Janusz a clear view of Freddy's hard cock as the light from the hallway streamed into the room.

While Janusz fumbled for the lights, Shorty managed to pull his pants up during the commotion and jump out the window before Janusz could see who it was. Freddy was not so lucky. As he tried to flee and pull up his pants at the same time, he tripped and fell to the floor. Janusz grabbed Freddy by his feet and dragged him out into the hallway with such force, he received a rug burn across his buttocks.

Janusz had seethed with a quiet rage he had felt towards all of us as a result of the affront caused by the Mystery of the Secret Shitter. He had fumed with a palpable animosity towards Freddy after the humiliating town hall meeting Dusty had called where Freddy had posited that it was Janusz's job to clean toilets and if he didn't like it, he should find another job. Catching Freddy with his dick up another guy's ass and reporting it to campus security was no doubt the sweetest act of revenge for which Janusz ever could have hoped.

While Dusty and I toured Columbia and visited the Empire State Building, Freddy was interrogated by campus security and Dean Hoffman. Dean Hoffman viewed himself as the steward of the college's moral reputation, which would be in tatters if it were thought to be a fairy playground. Freddy was understandably frightened at the trouble he found himself in, and he figured the surest way out of it would be to drag the rest of us into it. He quickly named Shorty as the receiving party in the act Janusz had interrupted.

Mindful of depravity and the school's reputation, Dean Hoffman was eager to stamp out any scourge of deviant behavior. He was hell-bent on finding out whether there was a ring of homosexuals in the dorm, since everyone knew the homosexual was on a never-ending mission to recruit new members to their sleazy world of sin. That was the conventional thinking back then and partly why it was so feared. Incandescent with rage, he demanded Freddy furnish the names of other guilty parties. At a loss to name anyone he knew for certain, he took a short leap and named Dusty and me. It worked. Naming the three of us was enough to save him from this inquisition and mitigate a punishment that was still undetermined. Dean Hoffman and campus security dragged Shorty in to be questioned. When they tried to find Dusty and me, however, they learned we were off for the weekend in New York. Our current fate was sealed.

"Mr. Branson," Dean Hoffman said, the disdain in his voice unmistakable as he unrolled the syllables of my name. "Do I need to repeat myself? Did this 'helicopters' business happen in the shower?"

"No, I don't recall any of that."

"None of it?"

"No."

More sounds of scribbled notes by the committee.

"Mr. Branson," Dean Hoffman continued, "I have a description of another incident in which you again were in the showers of Canterbury Hall. You openly admired in a lustful way and commented on the size of Anthony Toscano's penis as he showered. Your penis was erect as you stared at him, a sight seen by everyone else in the shower. You then flaunted your erect penis in front of the other students in a sexually provocative manner."

"I don't recall that," I said.

"I see," Dean Hoffman said. He stared at me over the top of his glasses with a disdain that conveyed his disbelief. Professor Johnston looked at me with disillusion, no doubt disappointed a prodigal student like me could be suspected of such illicit behavior. Dr. Oswald eyed me with an air of clinical detachment as he searched for confirmation of his diagnosis of the mental disorder of homosexuality. The head of campus security, a former police officer, looked at me as the perpetrator of criminal behavior. The student representative looked at me with supercilious disregard, no doubt grateful I was not in his social circles.

"Your roommate is Daniel Wright," Dean Hoffman said. "Or should I presume you don't recall that either?" This comment elicited wry smirks from Dr. Oswald, the student representative, and a thin-lipped smile from himself.

"Yes, Daniel is my roommate."

"In October, Daniel Wright met with the housing office and requested he be assigned a new roommate."

That statement jolted me. Daniel had said he was going to do that after he blamed me for the events of *Wonder Breadus Interruptus*. But, he never moved out, and we repaired our friendship. I hadn't known until this moment he had followed through with his threat to obtain a new roommate. I really had almost lost him.

"We had an argument," I said.

"Did Daniel Wright request a new roommate, because he thought you were a homosexual?"

"No," I said.

"What was the argument about?"

How could I explain we had watched him fuck a girl on the couch in the same first floor lounge that had been the scene of Freddy and Shorty's crime? Fucking a girl in the dorms may not have been cause for expulsion as it would have had it been with a boy. But, it was grounds for suspension, and I could never sell Daniel out like that. How could I explain he had been furious for catching me masturbating at the memory of it, and that he had jerked off on me in anger? I just couldn't and didn't even think to. "I don't recall."

"I see."

I cleared my throat. Even though I hadn't lost Daniel last fall, I was rattled by the thought I almost had. It drove home how much I cared for him and how much I cared for my life at Inverness. I had found great happiness here in ways I could never replicate somewhere else. I had so much to lose, and I could see no way out of this mess.

"Dustin Robert McCaffrey is the resident advisor on your floor. Correct?"

I nodded my head. "Yes."

"Are you engaged in a homosexual relationship with Dustin Robert McCaffrey?"

"No," I said, my voice weaker than I had hoped.

"No? I remind you again you have undertaken an oath to tell the truth."

"No, I am not engaged in a homosexual relationship with Dusty."

"Has Dustin Robert McCaffrey ever performed an act of sodomy on you?"

I gulped. "No."

"Have you ever performed an act of sodomy on Dustin Robert McCaffrey?"

"No."

"Do you understand that homosexual sodomy is illegal in the State of Vermont and throughout the entire United States of America?"

"Yes," I said, swallowing the word. I felt like I was dying inside.

Dean Hoffman paused again. He moistened his index finger with his tongue and flipped through the sheets of his legal pad. He whispered something to Professor Johnston and then looked back at me.

"On the night of December 20, the eve of winter break, did you cavort in the snow in a lewd and indecorous matter with Dustin Robert McCaffrey? In the quadrangle, underneath the oak tree at the entrance outside of Canterbury Hall?"

I thought my pounding heart would jump out of my chest. Freddy had seen that? "No," I said, barely able to choke out the word.

Dean Hoffman stared at me for a long moment, perhaps as long as a minute. The room fell silent. It felt like forever. "I remind you again, Mr. Branson, you are under oath. I have a sworn witness statement that describes in specific detail how you and Dustin Robert McCaffrey were rolling around in a lewd and obscene manner in the snow outside of Canterbury Hall on the night of December 20."

My eyes blinked under the bright lights. Freddy had spied on us from the window and witnessed a beautiful moment I had assumed had been private. The dorm had been mostly empty that night. But, he had been there, and so had we. That was the night Dusty had given me the first edition autographed copy of *The Razor's Edge*, a gift that had made me tear up with emotion. No wonder Freddy had shot us a sly smile as we joined him in the shower the next morning. I thought of how Dusty and I had lain on our backs in the snow and created angels with our outstretched arms and legs. It had been one of the most beautiful, powerful moments I had ever experienced: two angel boys in love on an enchanted snowy night. The thought that anyone could characterize it as lewd or obscene and that I had to sit here and defend it tore me up. The little resolve I had left started to crack.

I shook my head, but did not look up.

"A sworn statement, Mr. Branson. A witness swears under God that you did. Either this witness is lying or you are. Which is it?"

Over the course of my adult life, I found myself in significant physical danger on far more than one occasion while on assignment. I was robbed at knifepoint in Phnom Penh, Nairobi, and São Paulo. I was robbed at gun point in Los Angeles (twice) and Washington, D.C. I was held in a cell in customs and denied exit for days in the USSR, Iran, Burma, and the Sudan when no one knew where I was. I also had found myself in troublesome personal and professional situations that did not quite rise to the same level, but were challenging in their own difficult ways. Despite the pain and fear I felt in those other situations, I never felt more violated in the entirety of my long life than I did sitting in this sunny room as this committee of monsters forced its way into my most personal intimate thoughts, thoughts I had struggled to admit to myself much less out loud to other people. It felt as if I had been stripped bare and tied down by hostile enemies as they clawed at the most personal aspects of my mind, my body, and the most private, sexual thoughts and explicit details of the loving relationship between Dusty and me.

I loved Dusty more than I ever thought it possible to love another human being. It was the purest and most beautiful connection two human beings could ever have. Yet, I was forced to deny it even existed. I was forced to admit that if it did, the feelings and private behavior that went to the core of who I was were criminal and I was a mentally ill sex pervert.

It was obvious to me by the tone and the questions this was all for show. Once they were done with us, we would be banished and tossed out the gates of this prestigious college for which I had spent years of hard work to gain admittance. My sterling academic record would be worthless. Even Professor Johnston, the mentor who had coddled me with promises of my promise, viewed me now as if I had none. The head of campus security had suggested the possibility this would be turned over to the local police. It was utterly terrifying to think of my shattered future and the great shame that would be cast upon me and on my family.

    I wish I could tell you I summoned a hidden reserve of courage and stood up before my inquisitors and launched into impassioned oratory in my own defense. Or that I demonstrated inner bravery by sitting up straight in my chair with proud stoicism. But, I didn't. The hours I had spent under the bright lights of this crucible had ground me down. I was humiliated. I was profoundly sad. I was broken. I thought of the beauty of Dusty and me as snow angels and how a loving act so innocent had been characterized as so perverted. Something inside me snapped. As Dean Hoffman repeated his question again, the tone in his voice turned harsher as he zeroed in on the weakness that bellowed from my crumpled demeanor. I held my head down, and I started to cry. If there had been any doubt of my guilt, it was extinguished completely by the tears that streaked across my down-turned face and the quiet sobs I tried to stifle, but couldn't.

20 DARKNESS AND LIGHT

IN THE EVENING, I lay on the bed in the small white room in the infirmary and stared at the ceiling. I didn't want to think about what was going to happen to me, but it was impossible to think of anything else. My mind replayed on a continuous loop the horror of the disciplinary committee hearing and how disastrous my performance had been. I had comported myself with precisely the weak, pathetic, and untrustworthy behavior they would expect from a fairy. Dean Hoffman had continued to question me after I stopped sobbing. But, I had reached the end of what I could say. I did not answer, not even saying "no" or "I do not recall." Periodically, I would wipe the tears from my cheeks with the back of my hand. But, I said nothing further. I no longer looked at my interrogators. I no longer listened to them. I turned my gaze away to the bright, improbably sunlit world on the other side of the glass and wondered what awaited me on the outside.

There was a knock at the door. "Come in," I said.

The door opened. It was Shorty, as I presumed it would be. The housing office had moved us both to the infirmary a week and a half earlier to protect the other students from the perceived danger we presented. Until campus security and the disciplinary committee completed its investigation, Shorty and I were required to stay here alone, just the two of us in the entire building. We were permitted to attend our classes, but we were not allowed back in the dorms or to eat with the other students in the dining hall. They had moved Freddy across campus to an empty room in a dorm for upperclassmen. I had heard Dusty had been moved to an apartment in off campus housing. But, I had not seen or spoken to him since that first night back.

After Anthony, Daniel, Sasquatch, and Howell warned us upon our arrival of the trouble that was fermenting, an officer from campus security was waiting for us back at the dorm and summarily ordered us to collect our books and pack a bag of clothes. Dusty and I were separated and required to stay away from each other until the investigation was complete. Our torment began. It was as if the dreamland of our weekend in New York had never happened.

"I ordered us a pizza and a six pack," Shorty said. "It just arrived."

I shook my head. "I'm not hungry."

He flipped on the light switch. "You think I am? You can't just lie there on the bed and stare at the ceiling in the dark. C'mon. At least sit with me. I was able to get a signal on that old TV down the hall. *The Phil Silvers Show* is about to start, and then there's a new episode of *Wyatt Earp*."

I didn't think Phil Silvers was very funny, and I didn't feel like watching a western right now. But, I cared very much for Shorty. As bad as my situation looked, his was even worse. He had been caught by a live witness bending over with Freddy's dick up his ass. The elfin grin and the sparkle in Shorty's eye was mostly a memory now. I knew he was suffering as much as I was throughout this whole ordeal, if not more. Shorty had wanted to become a lawyer and join the white shoe Wall Street firm with his grandfather's name over the door. There wouldn't be much chance of that happening once all this was done. He also had the same kind of family background I did. I had met his parents when he had introduced them to us at parents' weekend in the fall. I remembered his mother's thin-lipped smile of disapproval of Anthony's ethnicity and the outer borough she thought she smelled in his accent, clothes, and his manners. If Italians

weren't welcome in her life, it wasn't difficult to imagine a gay son wouldn't be either.
 I hadn't lost every sense of friendship. Even though humiliation, sadness, and terror had burrowed into my bones, I knew Shorty needed me at this moment in the same way I needed him. I relented without him having to ask again. "You're right," I said. "I haven't eaten all day."
 The warm pizza and cold beer were unexpectedly refreshing, the first food and drink I had found remotely pleasurable since we had moved into the infirmary. I was cheered up in this small way, and I always enjoyed Shorty's company. I raised my beer up in the air and found it in me to smile. "Great call."
 He raised his beer to touch mine. "*Santé.*"
 "*Santé.*"
 We each took long swigs of our beer. Shorty let out a loud belch that rumbled from deep within him. I did the same, and we both laughed. Shorty was always great fun, even in misery.
 "Dusty really loves you," he said. It was a statement, not a question. Either way, I didn't want to comment. I had been sitting opposite him as we ate and drank. At these words, however, I stood and walked over to the TV. With my back to him, I fiddled with the antenna and pretended to try improving the reception, which I already knew was as good as it was going to get. The fear returned, and I didn't respond. What could I say? What did he know? I had never said anything to Shorty or to anyone about Dusty, not even this week as we had been holed up together in the solitude of the infirmary.
 I had learned that one of the worst, most destructive side effects of being ensnared in a witch hunt is you question friendships you never would have questioned, particularly when the accused are relentlessly pressured and threatened to name the names of others to save themselves in the way that we were. I had not thought of Freddy as much of a friend lately. But, I hadn't thought of him as an enemy, either. Yet, he had been quick to sell me out solely on the basis of his suspicions about my admittedly suspicious secret conduct with Dusty. The irony is I had watched Freddy shoot a load into Shorty's mouth, and it

never occurred to me to rat on either of them, not even now. Freddy was cut from different cloth, however. I realized he had sold out me and Dusty before I had a chance to sell him out, something I never would have done.

Could I trust Shorty? Yes, we were friends. Great friends, as matter of fact. But, as bad as things looked for me, they looked worse for him, and they looked awful for Dusty. Dusty had become the primary focus of the investigation. Shorty had heard Dusty's questioning had been unduly blistering, and there had been shouting coming from the room. Dean Hoffman was openly enraged in his accusations that Dusty had abrogated his duties as an RA and violated the trust of the college and his freshman charges by allowing a perverted den of iniquity to fester on the third floor of Canterbury Hall. He had been accused of corrupting me and recruiting me to his filthy world. Presumably, if Shorty could implicate Dusty and me, he would save himself by naming others in the same way Freddy had. All it would take would be a simple, whispered, "Yes."

I changed the subject. It was just too dangerous. "Sergeant Bilko is hilarious, don't you think?"

"I'm serious. Dusty really does love you," Shorty said, undeterred. "I saw you that day. There was a light snow. You had just entered the lobby of the dorm. He ran through the doors at full speed, chasing after you. You turned around. He rammed you up against the wall and kissed you with everything he had. You kissed him back, and he held you so fucking tight, it was as if he never wanted to let you go."

I looked back at him and sat down, stunned. I dropped my guard. "How could you know that?"

Shorty smiled at the memory. "I was at the top of the stairs. Anthony was with me. We saw everything."

I felt vaguely sick. "You did? You never said anything."

He shrugged. "It was none of my business. The truth is, I was so fucking jealous. It was the hottest, most passionate kiss I've ever seen. Better than anything in the movies. Only someone who loves you with every bone in their body kisses someone like he kissed you and you kissed him back. Do you know how lucky you are to have been kissed like that? Most people never get kissed like that in their whole lives, not even once."

My face was flush. "Anthony never said anything either?"

"He said something like, 'Well, well, well - what do you know? Dusty and Branson are a couple of fruitcakes.'"

My mouth went dry. "No, I mean, did he tell anyone else?"

Shorty's face twisted into a grimace of insulted surprise that I would even ask. "No, of course not. Friendship means everything to him. It's in his blood. He's Italian, remember? They're like that. They don't rat out their friends."

We both smiled. My entire body surged with emotion at the realization Shorty could have sold me and Dusty out to save himself, but hadn't. It had never even occurred to him, even though he had everything at stake. It was a hugely powerful lesson in honor for me, and I have never forgotten it. Shorty will have a special place in my heart for the rest of my life because of it. I had been crippled with fear since all of this began. I didn't know who to trust. I wondered if there was any decency left and had started even to question my own. In these quiet moments in the exile of the infirmary, Shorty restored those beliefs inside me. Over the course of my life, I would always search for them in people. I had learned from this experience that even in the darkest times, the strongest maintain their honor and decency when the weakest don't. "Thank you," I said. I wanted to say so much more, but couldn't find the words to articulate what I felt. "Thank you."

He raised his hand and slapped the air. "Stop. Please. I would never."

I took another long sip of beer with a renewed gratitude for Shorty's friendship.

"Freddy never kisses me like I saw Dusty kiss you," Shorty said. "He never kisses me at all."

"Do you love him?"

"Very much. It's totally fucked up. I love him, and he . . . he loves how I suck his cock and take it up the ass whenever he wants to get off. I can't believe he sold me out like this, you know? I never would have done that to him." He shook his head, and a wave of despair and disappointment washed across his face.

"I know. It's totally fucked up."

"You know the sad thing? I forgive him. How sick is that?"

I didn't know what to say. I was furious with Freddy and didn't feel like saying anything remotely good about him, even if it might make Shorty feel better at this moment. Freddy had fucked all of us to save himself, which was bad enough. But, what Freddy had done to Shorty was worse. Shorty had let Freddy into his heart and into the most private parts of his body. Shorty had allowed the essence of Freddy's handsome but unworthy spirit into him by swallowing Freddy's semen and welcoming it into his ass, the significance of which I well understood from personal experience. In return, Freddy had betrayed him. Freddy had sold out a lover, and that was unforgivable to me.

"I saw you guys, too," I said, wanting Shorty to know he could trust me as well. "It was more than a kiss, though."

"What! That's impossible! Don't bullshit me, "Shorty said. He opened another beer for himself and handed me one, too.

My smile broadened. "It was that night after we ran around naked in the snow storm. I was hiding in the housemaster's lounge behind the curtains. You two walked into the room. You were pulling Freddy by his boner."

Shorty laughed. "You were there! Freddy's got a sweet one, doesn't he?"

Even though I hated Freddy, I could admit to Shorty that Freddy had a nice, long boner that actually looked pretty much like mine. "Yeah, it was pretty good. You were squatting down in front of him. I couldn't believe how expertly you blew him. You don't even have a gag reflex."

Shorty's grin grew broader, and it was nice to see him smile again after all we had gone through. "What can I say? I'm a pro. Did my ass look good?"

I broke out into a grin. "It looked great. When you jerked off and shot so high in the air, that was pretty great, too."

"Man, you saw everything!"

We each laughed heartily. But, behind the laughter was the renewed sense of trust we felt in each other. It had been such a rough time for both of us. As much as we hoped it wouldn't, we each sensed without saying it we knew things would get even rougher. At least for now, I knew I wasn't alone. Shorty was someone I could trust with anything, whether it was the most intimate secret or unswerving support in the darkest of times.

Shorty stepped over to the television to turn up the volume just as *The Phil Silvers Show* started. The reception was snowy and unstable to a degree that would be considered unwatchable on the high definition televisions of today. But, we each got lost in the program, and it was a mercifully welcome distraction after all we had been through. At one point, I looked over at him. My eyes burned with tears both at the pain of our predicament and the beauty of our friendship in such a perilous time. I thought of how we were alone in this big building on a dark night as we feared for our futures and the inevitable ensuing wreckage. It felt as if our lives were in shambles when they were only just beginning. It was terrifying, and we were terrified. Yet, watching an unfunny TV show with one of the great pals of my entire life as a world of hate condemned us outside the isolation of the infirmary was the first moment of solace for me during this whole awful predicament.

When I crawled into bed, I fell into a deep sleep, the deepest since all of this had begun. My mind took me to places far from the infirmary. I found myself in a dream that felt familiar and different at the same time.

I was in a room bathed in white light that streamed through Venetian blinds across a gigantic bed. I had been in this room before. Or had I? I was confused. I looked down at my cock. It was hard and throbbing. It was longer than I knew it and thicker. Not as big as Anthony's, but almost. A thread of pre-cum hung to my knees and blew in a breeze without detaching. There was a nude body on the bed lying face down, waiting for me. I remembered where I was. I had been in this room with Allison. It had been the setting for the wet dream I had had about losing my virginity to her back on the first night of school. I had blown my load inside her with three short strokes of a cock that felt like mine, only bigger. When I had awoken, I had been embarrassed Daniel had seen my sheets and boxer shorts stained from my wet dream, which I hadn't thought he had seen until I later learned he had. But, this wasn't a dream. Or was it?

The nude body that awaited me was not Allison's this time, but Dusty's. He turned his head sideways on the pillow, and I could see he was smiling. "Hey, baby," he said. "I've missed you."

"I've missed you, too," I said. "You have no idea how much." I climbed onto the bed and lay on top of him. I instantly felt a comfortable familiarity with how our naked forms fit together like pieces of a puzzle. Instinctively, I reached down and burrowed my hard cock into the crevice between his buttocks.

As my cock pulsed in the warmth between his thighs, I buried my face in his neck and inhaled the scent that was only his. It was a scent I could recognize today if you were to hand me a T-shirt he had worn and I were to hold it to my face. I kissed him and wrapped my arms around his waist, squeezing him tight. We lay there like that, the full weight of my body stacked on his. I had missed him so much, my body had ached and felt incomplete without his for so long. I forgot the pain of our separation and savored how laying there with him beneath me completed us almost, but not quite. I hungered for a full reconnection and set out to complete it.

I lifted myself up off his back and the heaven of his ass. Then I kissed him from the fine hairs of his neck and commenced a slow journey down the ridges of his spine. When I reached the top of his bottom, he arched his athletic, meaty butt upwards, and I buried my face deep in his crack, nestling it firmly between his cheeks. I inhaled the sexy, musky smell of his ass and wet the tip of my nose with the bead of sweat that stretched from his tailbone, down over the slit of his hole, and to the smooth skin of his taint. My cock surged even harder.

I loved Dusty with every part of me and wanted to savor every inch of his body with every sense of mine. My tongue found his hole and flicked it lightly. He twisted with pleasure and moaned my name. I held back until he squirmed, teasing him, and then flicked his hole again and again. I spread his cheeks with my hands so I could nuzzle my face and my tongue in deeper. But it wasn't enough. I flipped him over and knelt down next to the bed. I lifted his legs and rested them on my shoulders to enhance my access to his open ass. I ran my tongue in broad, wet swirls around the outer limits of his hole and then up and down the slit, forcing it inside. The taste, the smell, the texture of the smooth, damp skin of this region that had been unknown to me before him were each tantalizingly erotic in their own way. I wanted – needed – more of everything his body was offering and my senses were craving. I ached for him in every way. I hungered for his ass, which was an opening to the world I most wanted to go. I placed my mouth over his hole and sucked on it more insistently than before. I moaned myself from the pleasure it gave me to pleasure him. He writhed, and I knew this would not be enough for either of us.

I stood and pressed his legs against his chest, his hole at optimum exposure. I reached down and slapped the big, juicy, purple knob of my cock against his primed slit. He gasped, and I knew even before he begged me for it that he needed my cock inside him. I eased the rounded head and the first two inches inside. His ass was warm, wet, and deliciously tight. But, more than that, I belonged here. I belonged inside him. I eased my cock the rest of the way, all the way in until my balls slapped against the smooth skin of his taint. I leaned down to kiss his lips, slowly grinding my hips against him as I waited for him to fully loosen up. He was relaxed from my having devoured his hole, and I knew from the way he nodded his head he was ready for me. I had an overpowering urge to pound his ass – not to hurt him, but to take him. By the sly look in his eye, I could tell he was eager to be taken.

"You're in so deep," he said, his improbably blue eyes probing mine.

"I wish I could be deeper." I looked down at the sight of my pubic hair mashed against the opening of his hole, my cock buried inside him as deep as it possibly gets. My cock pulsed with pleasure at the sight of it.

He smiled, his eyes heavy with desire and what I knew was unconditional love for me. "I love you," he said.

"I know." I kissed him again as I pumped my cock in and out of him with no resistance on his end, despite the length and thickness of my shaft. "I love you so damn much, you know that?" The tempo with which I had been fucking him increased with a steady drum beat towards the climax that had been building within me. My eyes were locked with his. I wanted to hold out longer, but I couldn't. He surprised me without warning by shooting a long spurt of cum out of his dick hole as his hands clenched my ass and as my hands held his legs in the air.

"Whoa!" we both exclaimed, laughing as the uncommonly copious load shot out of him and strangely didn't seem to be diminishing as the sprayed cum doused each of us.

That triggered my own load, a long slow orgasm that churned up from within me. I closed my eyes as a river of semen shot out of my dick deep inside his ass and continued to fill him up with pulse after pulse of toe-curling ecstasy I never wanted to end.

I wanted to savor the bliss that reverberated through my body for as long as I could. But as ethereal as it was, the pleasure ebbed, and I opened my eyes. When I did, however, it was not Dusty with his smiling, loving face beneath me. It was just the twin bed in the infirmary, my face buried in the pillow, my hands gripping the sides of the mattress. An expansive spread of sticky wetness had pooled around my entire mid-section. It was still warm, but rapidly turning cold.

I rolled to my side and propped myself up on my elbow. The recognition of where I was and why returned with an instant heaviness. I reached my hand down to the gooey mess that clung to my groin. *Damn*, I thought. It had been a wet dream of biblical proportions. Ever since the nightmare of the investigation had begun ten days earlier, I hadn't felt any sexual desire at all. It was as if my cock and balls had shriveled up and retracted into my body cavity. I had been separated from Dusty, so I hadn't had sex. And for the first time since I had discovered the miracle of masturbation five years before, I had had no inclination whatsoever to jerk off. My cock had gotten me into this trouble in the first place. The last thing I had felt like doing was indulging it any further.

The truth that I hadn't beat off in ten days gives you an idea just how bad off I was. It also gives you an idea how large my load was. It was a big, wet, sticky mess that was a mixture of white and yellow cum, the thick kind mixed with the runny. It would have been fun for me to watch it shoot into the air in a series of geysers. It would have been better to blow that ten day load inside of Dusty and let him savor it inside him all day. I would have been happy with either. I wished I could return to the heaven of that dream and be with Dusty anywhere but here.

I hauled the wet sheets down the hall to a linen closet and pulled out a set of clean ones. On the way, I had stopped to listen at Shorty's door and was happy to hear him snoring softly. We each had bemoaned to the other the sleepless nights we had endured during the agony of the previous ten days. I was glad that at least on this night, we had shared a few laughs and he was able to get some rest. Shorty was such an extraordinary human being, the most decent pal you would ever want to have. He didn't deserve any of this trouble and heart break. Neither did I.

As I carried the clean sheets back down the hall, I stopped at a window. I stared out at the moon that lit up the night sky. I marveled how the light reflected off the layer of icy snow that blanketed the ground. I wondered where Dusty was at this moment and whether he had been thinking of me as much as I had been thinking about him. What would happen to him? What would happen to me? What would happen to us? What would happen to Shorty? I wanted all of these troubles to end and wondered how they possibly could without it being utterly disastrous for all of us. I leaned my forehead against the cold glass and prayed silently in the moonlight that we would all be okay even though there was no reason to hope that we ever would be.

21 JUDGMENT

THE REMAINDER OF the week passed with agonizing slowness. Shorty and I were called in for additional questioning as the committee neared the end of its investigation. We both were just as terrified as we had been during the initial round, if not more so. We each knew how detailed and invasive the questions could get. We each sensed a determination of guilt was all but a formality at this point. How could the result be any different? They knew too much of what they knew they knew. They believed too much of what they thought they knew. If an essential strategy of a witch hunt is breaking its targets, I was broken. Shorty was, too. But, this time I maintained my dignity as I lied my way through the questions. My voice was even, my demeanor calm as it masked the resignation inside me.

This round of questioning was scheduled in back-to-back sessions for each of us. Shorty and I sat together in the quiet outside the Trustees Room while we waited for our turns. We saw our friends come and go from behind closed doors as they were barraged with another round of intimate and incriminating questions about us. We saw Daniel enter and leave, his face somber as he nodded at us. We saw Anthony as well. We had had heard the muffle of raised voices when he was in the room and wondered why Dean Hoffman was shouting and why

Anthony was shouting back. He was somber, too, his face uncharacteristically flush as he left. I thought of how he knew what he knew about me and was grateful he had kept it to himself.

We also saw Dusty enter and leave the room, the first time I had seen him since all of this began. My heart surged at the sight of him. I wanted to stand and go to him, but I didn't. At least not at first. He looked at me and held my gaze as he walked past. It was hard to believe what I saw. He was not the same Dusty I had known. Everything was different about him. The color from his face had drained. There was a heaviness in his step and a dip in his posture. The light had left his eyes. The natural aura that once emanated from him and drew people into his world so they never wanted to leave had deadened. It was as if his heart and spirit had been ravaged by unseen forces. The fear rose up inside me that this was a good-bye, that I might not ever see him again. That fear pulled me from my torpor. This time, I stood and stepped towards him to make contact.

"Dusty!" I exclaimed. "Dusty!"

He just shook his head to himself and kept on walking down the hallway, not looking back as he did. The door slammed shut behind him.

Shorty and I exchanged glances. The sound of the door slamming shut reverberated in my head. I felt the worst sort of emptiness. Dusty had looked right through me, as if he weren't really here and I were only a distant memory. The thought of it wrenched my insides. I had the horrific sense if there had been any remaining hope everything could be okay, it vanished when the door slammed shut.

◌

That Thursday night, Shorty and I ordered pizza and beer again. We each had received notes during the afternoon to report to the committee the next morning for what we presumed would be the pronouncement of our fate. I joked that this was the collegiate version of The Last Supper. It elicited wry smiles from each of us, but only underscored our collective sense of resignation. We watched *You Bet Your Life*, a comedy quiz show hosted by Groucho Marx, which was really funny and helped us to forget ourselves and our situation at least for a little while. I can't remember what else we watched. But, we stayed up until the station signed off at midnight, the signal turning to static after playing the national anthem with the American flag rippling majestically in a fierce wind.

When I crawled into bed, I jerked off for the first time since all of my troubles began. I didn't feel horny in the slightest. But, I did it in the hope it would help me drift off to sleep so I wouldn't spend the entire night tossing fitfully. It worked, and I slept straight through until the morning light streamed into the room.

When I think back to those two horrible weeks, one aspect I recall was my memory of the sunshine. It was two of the sunniest weeks of blue sky on the cusp of springtime in Vermont. I don't remember any cloudiness, haze, or inclement weather of any kind during that time. I only mention this, because it contrasted so sharply to the darkness that engulfed me. I feared everything I knew and hoped for in my life was on the precipice of destruction. An expulsion for the synonymous offenses of homosexuality, sexual perversion, and dishonorable conduct would thrust me on a journey far different from the one I had chosen for myself. That life in the rest of the world could go on with sunny brightness while I suffered in the worst sort of hell was difficult for me to reconcile and added to my sense of disbelief.

Shorty and I walked together across campus back to the administration building. I felt a calm sense of terror as I headed to face the fate I feared. I could feel and hear the breathing of my lungs. But, my heart no longer reacted to the terror by pounding in my chest as it once had. The terror felt more like an alien presence in my body that dominated my thoughts and tingled through to the tips of my extremities. I had the sense my life was about to change in the most profound way, and I would leave the administration building a different person than the one I had been when I had entered it. I wished the walk would take forever and never end.

All of the other interviews had been conducted separately, so Shorty and I were surprised this final meeting was one in which we appeared together. Just before we entered the room, he looked at me and whispered, "*Ne laisse pas les bâtards te descendre.*" Don't let the bastards get you down. He winked, and I saw the sparkle in him that had been dimmed, but not extinguished. I don't know that I ever cared as much for him than I did at that moment. I had learned so much about friendship and about myself from him during this horrific ordeal. I had learned about honor. He could have sold me out to save himself, and I could have done the same to him. But, we hadn't. It hadn't even occurred to us. Despite the collapse of my composure during that first session when I shut down and cried before my tormentors, I hadn't sold anyone out. Perhaps I had shown courage and dignity after all, even if it had all been rather messy. I squeezed his shoulder and felt an unexpected sense of peace descend upon me as we entered the room to face our fate.

The five members of the committee watched as we entered and sat down. Dean Hoffman recited the points of inquiry the committee had been investigating, a pointless formality since it had been all Shorty and I could think about since our ordeal began. There was no way either of us could have forgotten anything. Dean Hoffman paused and flipped through the pages of his legal pad before closing it. He stared at both of us over the top of his glasses, his eyes as icy and dark as they had been on that first morning. My breathing stopped, and I listened with every part of me as the words fell from his mouth.

"After a long and thorough investigation, the committee has reached its decision. We have concluded there was chronic disorder and poor supervision on the third floor of Canterbury Hall. That notwithstanding, we have found no credible evidence to support the allegations that were made against John Branson and Edward Olsen. Unless the committee learns of new information that would convince us otherwise, we are terminating the proceedings and will take no further action."

Shorty and I exchanged stunned glances, shocked that such a result was possible given the specificity of the allegations and the venom with which they were pursued. How was this possible? It made no sense.

Dean Hoffman continued. "You are free to leave. But, let me warn you: my office takes allegations of the dishonorable conduct that has been the subject of this inquiry extremely seriously. The homosexual is a dangerous element that undermines our society and honorable institutions like this one. If you are truly innocent, guard your person, because you don't always know when they are about. On the other hand, if you are truly guilty and have made a farce of these proceedings, we will re-open them if there are any further accusations of homosexual conduct of any kind."

Shorty and I sat there, waiting for more, not realizing we had just been dismissed.

"You are free to go."

We stood, each of us dazed at what had just happened. Could it really be? We had entered this room just minutes ago with every expectation our lives were about to be catapulted in a different direction. Instead, we were free to return to Canterbury Hall. Despite the daze of the unexpected outcome, Shorty and I each felt a palpable sense of euphoric relief that immediately rose up within us.

Professor Johnston left the room shortly after we did, and my eyes caught his. Despite my elation, I was embarrassed he had heard everything that had been said about me. He had stayed mostly silent during the proceedings. He almost certainly had come to doubt a student in whom he had once seen uncommon promise. I recognize today, of course, that I had been a victim of outrageous hatred and discrimination. The disciplinary committee should have been embarrassed for its behavior, not me. But, I didn't feel that way then. I felt profound shame to have been accused of sexual perversion and dishonorable conduct, particularly before a professor who had influenced me so much and whom I admired greatly. It stung to think of how I surely was now diminished in his opinion of me.

"John," Professor Johnston said before pausing, searching in the air in an affected manner for the words he was forming in his mind. "You have considerable promise and academic talent.

I hope you have learned something from these proceedings and that you will get past this, this – moral failing."

The words "moral failing" reverberated through my head. I had been found not guilty. But, as I would later learn in life, no one is innocent until proven guilty. The reality is, people are presumed guilty until proven innocent, no matter what anyone says. There is also a difference between being found not guilty and being proven innocent. I didn't know that then. But, I knew at that moment that the stigma of these proceedings would linger and follow me. I was lost to a great mentor who had helped steer me in the direction I most wanted to go. I was the quintessential good boy to the end, however. Always respectful of order and authority, I said two words I truly am embarrassed to repeat in these pages: "Thank you."

Professor Johnston nodded with a self-satisfied smile as he accepted my thanks, no doubt pleased with himself that I had accepted the generosity of his gift of encouragement to get past my flawed personal conduct.

Daniel was sitting at his desk studying when I walked into the room without notice and set down the bags of clothes and books I had carried from the infirmary. He stood up with such alacrity, his chair tipped over. "Are you back?"

I nodded, nearly overcome with emotion at the sight of him, who I cared about so much. He had assumed he had lost me for good. A wave of relief washed across his face as he rushed over and hugged me so hard it hurt. "I'm so happy you're back, buddy," he said, his voice cracking. "I didn't think you were going to make it."

"I didn't either."

"What about Shorty?"

"He's okay, too."

Daniel sighed. "I am so happy, you don't even know. Now, everything can get back to normal. It's not easy hanging out with Anthony all the time, you know."

I laughed at the thought that Daniel's desperation for companionship had lead him down the hall to Anthony, his long-time antagonist. Daniel laughed, too.

"Is Dusty back yet?" I asked.

Daniel shrugged. "I haven't seen him."

I peered out into the hallway and saw the door to Dusty's room was partly open. He was back! My heart swelled. During the darkness of the quiet nights in the infirmary when I had twisted and turned in my bed without sleeping, I had been wracked by a persistent fear we would be pulled apart, and that I would never see him again. I had been afraid I had loved him too much and the heavens would punish me for it. All of that was behind us now. I don't know if I had ever ached for another human being as much as I had ached for him at that moment. I sped down the hallway, my heart racing along with every part of my body at the prospect of seeing him again after the awful pain of our separation.

When I reached his door, I threw it the rest of the way open in my excitement. What I saw, however, shattered me. His room was empty. Broom clean. All of his belongings were gone, and so was he. Fear and desolation swelled up inside me. A silent scream shouted from the depths of my soul, but stopped at my lips. I felt the crush of despair, fear, and the most barren form of sadness you could ever imagine. Nothing of him remained. He was gone. But, he was not just gone. It was as if he had never been here.

22 COMMENCEMENT

DUSTY NEVER DID come back. He had been banished to an off campus apartment and permitted to go to class and to the library. But, that was it. He had been ordered to stay away from the dorms, the dining halls, his former freshman charges – and me, in particular. He had been branded a pariah, all but excluded from every aspect of campus life.

Dean Hoffman had leaned in close to Dusty's beautiful face to hiss that failure to comply with the committee's directives would result in expulsion and withholding of the degree for which he had been striving for the previous four years. He would have nothing to show for all of his hard work and his family's sacrifices. He would have no meaningful future. Dean Hoffman knew something had happened on the third floor of Canterbury Hall, even if he did not have the tidy confessions and testimony he had hoped to have. He believed Freddy's accusation that Dusty was a confirmed homosexual who had recruited me to his deviant world even if he could not prove it. He believed the more ambiguous claim that Dusty had been derelict in his RA duties and fostered an environment where the possibility of perverted behavior could have existed even if he had no evidence it had. He was disgusted at the thought of it and enraged that a student as prominent as Dusty – an entrusted RA and president of the Honor Society, among all of his other honors – could be accused of such dishonorable conduct.

The committee held its decision on Dusty in abeyance, leaving him in the vice of a purgatory where he was the subject of an investigation that remained neither open nor closed. It left open the possibility of criminal prosecution for sodomy and sexual perversion. It left open the possibility of disclosure to his family and future employers. It left open the possibility of disclosure to the PhD programs to which he had applied, all of which would likely reject him if they were to learn of the allegations that had been made against him. Despite a lack of evidence, the committee was determined to take action, and Dusty took the hit for the rest of us by languishing in an Escher-like limbo from which the only way to survive was capitulation.

To avoid further trouble and to try to salvage his future, Dusty had complied completely and without question. He had looked right through me when we would pass each other on campus. He would not speak to me even though I tried. I am not ashamed to tell you I begged and pleaded with him with the desperation of someone who had lost everything dear to him and had nothing further to lose. It was not pretty, but I am not ashamed I made every effort. It was to no avail, however. He treated me as if we never were.

To say I was destroyed would be a gross understatement of the absolute and utter devastation I felt. It was as if every part of my body, my mind, and my heart had been gutted. I felt abject despair. I felt violated to my core. I felt profound sadness. I felt that the rarest and dearest gift I had ever received in my whole life – my requited love for Dusty – had not just been stolen from me, it had been forcibly wrenched from me, defiled, and stomped on with the intention it be obliterated from the face of the Earth. To have endured the horrific ordeal of the disciplinary committee investigation and come out on the other side of hell without Dusty at my side simply wrecked me.

Aside from what had had happened to Dusty and as much as Shorty and I had been informed our ordeal was over, it clearly was not. Daniel had been offered the opportunity to replace me as his roommate if the thought of having me return caused him any discomfort. He just needed to give the word, and it would happen. The housing office would move me out, and I would disappear from his world, as if I also had never been in it. Sasquatch was offered the same option with Shorty. No questions asked and no explanations needed.

Neither of them accepted, which were choices not entirely without risk for them and ones neither Shorty nor I would ever forget for the rest of our lives. We each had had the most private parts of our minds and, by association, our bodies, laid out naked for display and dissection by those who sought to hurt us. It had been an inquisition of the worst, most intimate, violative sort. So much had been broken inside us, there was no way any of it could ever fully be forgotten. To know, however, that extraordinarily loyal and courageous friends like Daniel and Howell chose to stand by us in times of terror meant more than either Shorty or I could ever express in mere words.

Freddy stayed in the single in the upperclassmen dorm on the other side of campus. That was more than fine with me and the rest of us. He had sold all of us out to save himself. In the end, however, it hadn't exactly worked out that way. We were still here, and he wasn't. He had lost The Magnificent Seven forever, and that was an awful lot to lose if you ask me.

If you're wondering how Shorty and I escaped from the bear trap in which the disciplinary committee had ensnared us, I had wondered, too. The case against us had been overwhelming. Some of the allegations had been true, and the ones that weren't admittedly were plausible. The hysteria of the times mandated that people accused of what we had been accused of to be expunged from conventional society and elite institutions like Inverness College. Even the whisper against a man or a boy of an allegation of the type that had been shouted against us would brand him a danger to others and to society.

There was no salvation in the truth. In the end, it was the courageous untruths of our friends that saved us. To a person, Daniel, Anthony, Sasquatch and Howell were united in their denials that there was anything suspect or untoward about those of us who had been accused. Acting in concert, all of them called into question Freddy's character and Janusz's mental state as a counterbalance to the questioning of mine, Shorty's and Dusty's. As a joke, Howell had originally saved a dozen or so of Janusz's paper signs handwritten with the angry and suspiciously foreign scrawl and taped them to the walls of his room, the ones that read: "Attention! You must flush your waste and keep appropriate your conduct! Cooperation Please! Thank You from your Custodian!" During his testimony, he had laid them out one after the other on the table as evidence of Janusz's anger and had raised the suggestion that he was mentally imbalanced. Sasquatch was also equally unflappable and adamant in his defense of our character.

Daniel and Anthony each took matters further. As I think about their uncommon courage and dedication to friends in trouble, I have had to remove my glasses and wipe the tears from my eyes while I type this recollection of the efforts they undertook to save us. For Daniel, it was not just enough to issue a series of denials regarding his observation of any suspicious conduct on my part. After he had been dismissed following the initial round of testimony, he had returned to the committee, unsolicited, to express further outrage that the allegations had ever been brought.

I have mentioned before that Daniel had a steady consistency about him even then. He had a quiet conceit that came from not truly caring what others thought of him and the arrogant self-confidence that would later serve him well in the medical profession. He knew what he knew about me and had his own future at risk. Yet, he had marched back to the committee to express the measured outrage that an Inverness man like me had been accused of sexual perversion and dishonorable conduct. Daniel reminded them he was an upstanding member of this collegiate community. He stated flat out that if he and the other members of our floor were doubted, it called into question the integrity and honor of the entire school. *

Anthony wasn't satisfied with just denying the allegations. He wanted to control the outcome in the same way he would try when he later would be accused of fraud during the junk bond scandals a few decades in the future. I will never know how much his height, his bravado, and the self-confidence that came from the sausage that swung between his legs came into play. But, Anthony had marched into the disciplinary committee on a mission and with a swagger. He had sworn under God that Shorty had been playing pool with him the night he had been accused of being with Freddy, and that it would have been impossible for Shorty to have been caught in any compromising position whatsoever. He stated flat out that Janusz had to have been lying, and, moreover, had the motive to do so because Freddy had called out Janusz in a public way during Dusty's town hall meeting regarding the Mystery of the Secret Shitter.

With every confidence, Anthony vouched for my character, Shorty's and Dusty's. Not intimidated in the slightest by the disciplinary committee, Anthony had testified before them with all certainty that they had had it wrong, that there was no one more honorable, or wholesome, or All-American than us. In the same way he questioned Janusz's intentions, he argued that Freddy had no credibility, because he had the motive to fabricate the allegations against others in exchange for a lesser punishment. When Dean Hoffman shouted at Anthony for arguing instead of just answering questions, Anthony stood up and shouted right back.

In the end, I have no doubt Dean Hoffman knew Anthony was full of it. But, with the entire case against us children of privilege hinging upon the testimony of Janusz – a foreigner and a powerless custodian – and Freddy's coerced confession, there was no way such a verdict would survive the scrutiny that most certainly would ensue. The chances would be even less if Shorty's family law firm were brought in, which is what Anthony had insinuated would happen. That's not to say they believed him or us. In fact, the follow-up treatment of Dusty clearly indicated they did not. But, it was enough to save Shorty and me without condition and to save Dusty from expulsion when he was just a couple of months from graduation. It was also enough for Janusz to be fired, and he disappeared completely from our lives.

Despite that outcome, I never did make it to the State Department. Even though I would dedicate the entirety of my college years in pursuit of my long-time dream of serving in the diplomatic corps, my application would be rejected on three separate occasions. For years, that confounded me. I knew with all certainty I had done everything right, and it was hard for me to imagine a candidate more qualified than I was. I would eventually earn a degree in international relations, *magna cum laude* with departmental honors and be elected to Phi Beta Kappa. I spoke three languages. I had impeccable references and Washington internships. Even a graduate degree from the Fletcher School of Diplomacy couldn't help get me in. Eventually, I gave up. I ended up falling into a lucky and successful career as a foreign correspondent for *Newsweek* magazine and wrote a dozen books that won me a few Pulitzers and other notable awards along the way. As well-suited as I was for that career, however, it was not the one I had dreamed of. It was the fall back from the one I had earned, but had been denied to me because of who and how I loved.

Many years later, I would confirm the nagging suspicion that my run-in with the disciplinary committee had derailed my dreams and set my life on a different course. I had an inside source pull my State Department file. By then, I was not completely surprised to receive confirmation that I had failed the background check process of my candidacy. But, I was hugely disappointed to learn it had been Professor Johnston, the mentor who had once seen such promise in me, freely disclose to the CIA officers conducting my security clearance his opinion that I was a homosexual and, therefore, a security risk of the type that did not belong at the State Department or in any other form of government service. Those simple words were all they needed to hear. The career of my dreams was over before it even began.

ଔ

Dusty's room didn't stay empty. He was replaced by a new RA named Ralph Henderson who moved in a few days after we had been allowed back. Ralph was a senior and a theology major who had agreed to serve as the RA for the remaining eight weeks of the semester as a personal favor to Dean Hoffman. Dean Hoffman was his faculty advisor and personal mentor in the same way Professor Johnston had once been mine. Ralph was chubby and wore his pants a little too high, even for the times, which is a fault that always caused me to doubt a person's awareness of the world. He was not a bad guy. But, he was not a good one, either. He had plans to become a minister, which he eventually fulfilled.

Somewhere along the road that lead Ralph to us, however, he had chosen to ignore the Bible's admonitions on not judging others, even in the silence of one's heart. The judgment of others is a manifestation of the deadly sin of Pride, and is one from which I have always tried to refrain. If there had been any doubt we had been found not guilty but not innocent, it was in the meeting Ralph had called to introduce himself and lay out his rules for order and conduct on the floor. He took great pains, his voice taking on a stentorian manner as he did, to admonish us that this was an opportunity to redeem ourselves from the collective sins of our behavior that had been called into question by the disciplinary committee. I remember wishing the chair in which I had been sitting would swallow me up so I didn't have to hear any more of what he had to say.

In the same way I wish I could tell you I had exhibited noble stoicism while I had been interrogated by the disciplinary committee and had not cried in front of them, I wish I could tell you I recovered from my ordeal and bounced back with at least a modicum of resilience. But, I didn't. For the first few days, I felt relief that I had not been expelled, that my parents had not been informed, that neither Dusty nor Shorty had been expelled, and that I had been free to resume my normal life, whatever that was anymore. Then the realization I had lost Dusty in all of this set in. I simply collapsed. I fell apart. I had followed him after class to learn the address of the off campus apartment to which he had been banished. I had knocked and pounded on the door, knowing with every certainty he was on the other side.

"Please, Dusty. I know you're in there," I had begged. "I'm dying inside. Please, just talk to me, even for a minute."

After a long silence, without opening the door, he said simply, "Leave me alone. Just go away."

His cold dismissal caused me to plunge into an abyss. I could not believe he would abandon me after the trauma of our ordeal. I had held him up on a marble pedestal for as long as I had known him. In the figurative shrine I had created for him, he was perfect and would be there for me always. Now, when I needed him most, he would have nothing to do with me. Yes, I understood his fear more than anyone. But, I thought we were bigger than that, that no matter what, there would always be an us. His rejection of me after all we had been through just gutted me. I became a shell of my former self. I felt damaged in ways that could never fully be repaired. I went to class and buried myself in my studies, rarely leaving the library or my dorm room. I undertook anything I could to keep my mind away from the swirl of everything I had lost. I tried to accept Dusty was gone, but I just couldn't.

I lost an alarming amount of weight in a short amount of time. I couldn't eat. I ran for miles on the track and on the country roads around campus in an effort to flee the agony of my heartache. Anthony was the first to take note of it, his mouth dropping in shock at the sight of my skinny, naked body one morning when all of the guys were in the shower. He always had a lot to say, but he kept the thought to himself and stopped by my room later to give me a pep talk in private. He hugged me as he left, and I thought I might cry at his kindness. Shorty kept checking in on me as well. We had been good friends since the beginning of the year. But, we had been great friends since our shared ordeal and the time we spent together in the isolation of the infirmary. He had bounced back better than I had and implored me to pull myself together. If I didn't, he said, I was letting the bastards win. I tried, but I just couldn't.

At the end of April, my birthday arrived. I wasn't feeling celebratory, but that didn't stop Howell from buying me a cake and gathering the guys in my room to sing "Happy Birthday." Sasquatch had bought nineteen trick candles he had stuck in the frosting. My unsuccessful efforts to blow them out got a laugh out of everyone, including me, even though I felt hollow on the inside.

I am normally not such a sad sack, but I just couldn't pull myself out of the hole I was in. I realize now I was suffering from a form of post-traumatic stress disorder, a condition for which there were no words in those days. The ordeal of the investigation had been humiliating and terrifying. The forced intrusion into the most private of my inner thoughts had felt violent to me. My biggest fear, that I would lose Dusty, had happened. I wasn't coping well at all. I just wanted the hurt to stop, but it didn't. I wanted to forget everything, but wasn't able to. I sure could have used professional counseling, but there wasn't any such thing, at least not where I was and the kind I needed.

After I crawled into bed that night of my birthday, I crashed to the bottom of my existence. I had held out hope until the moment Daniel turned off the lights that Dusty would reach out to me with birthday wishes. I couldn't believe how much had changed in the six weeks since we had celebrated his birthday in New York with tickets to see *West Side Story* on Broadway. Throughout all of this, I had held out the belief he would come back to me once he realized how much he missed me, the prohibition on contact with me notwithstanding. To have my birthday come and go with no word from him, however, crushed me. At that moment, I just knew I wasn't going to hear from him again. I cracked in the darkness and started to cry, the first time I had cried since I had broken down under Dean Hoffman's interrogation. I didn't want Daniel to hear me, and I tried to stifle myself. But, I couldn't. It just hurt so damn much.

"You okay over there, buddy?" Daniel asked in the darkness.

I was crying too hard to say anything.

"It'll get better," he said. "I promise. Just give it time."

As much as I wanted to believe him, I couldn't and continued crying.

What Daniel did next was an act of extraordinary tenderness when I most needed one. He left his bed and crawled into mine to hold me while I cried. He soothed me with mellow whispers in the baritone in his voice which I always loved to hear. He spooned me from behind and gently stroked my head and my arms and warmed me with the heat of his body. His cock hardened, and there was no ignoring it as it pulsed through the thin fabric of his cotton boxers and pressed against the crack of my ass.

"Sorry about that," he said, pulling away from me. "I don't mean anything by it, I swear. It just has a mind of its own."

I was still crying and didn't want Daniel to go anywhere. I pulled him back toward me and was embraced by the warmth of his body and the sensation of his cock. It swelled and softened throughout the night as he held me close. In the morning, he left my bed, and we never spoke of it again. I still felt profound sadness through every part of me. But, I had started to heal.

☙

In 1986, I returned to Inverness for the first time in the twenty-five years since I had graduated. I had been invited to give a lecture on the future of communism and Soviet influence around the world. Ostensibly, the invitation had been issued by the political science department, but the reality was the college president's office was behind it. I had just won my first Pulitzer, and my latest book had just hit the *New York Times*' Bestseller List. I was entering the prime of my renown, and the college hoped I might inspire impressionable students to aspire to a career like mine. That was totally fine with me. I had mixed feelings about Inverness by then. But, I always enjoy speaking with young people as they form their futures and pursue their dreams before others try to quash them. I also figured it would be therapeutic to return to the place where so much had happened to me during the formative years of years of my life as I set out in one direction and ended up going in another.

To accommodate everyone who wanted to hear me speak, the lecture was held in the gothic chapel on the campus that was still as idyllic as it was in my memories. I approached the podium to thundering applause. I opened the manila folder containing the neatly typed words of my speech with the portentous title, "The Future of Communism and the Downfall of Global Soviet Influence." I ran my eyes over the first page as the applause died off. It was a well-worn speech, one I had given many times before. I looked out at the sea of bright, curious faces of the young men and, since the arrival of co-education in the 1970s, the young women who had joined the student body after my time here.

I looked off to my left at Professor Johnston who had taken a seat on stage after introducing me with the pride that he had recognized my promise way back in his freshman Emerging Governments course more than twenty-five years ago, long before everyone else had. He described how he had had me present that paper on the British Commonwealth and post-war Winston Churchill to the class and to the department faculty, an honor he had not conveyed on anyone prior to me or since. He described his lack of surprise when he learned of my early successes and my first *Newsweek* cover story back in the 1960s. I twitched with irritation at his flattery, because I had never discussed the possibility of a career in journalism with him. I had had other plans he had known about. He didn't talk about those, even though I knew by now his role in what had happened to them.

I looked down at my oldest son, Chris, who was sitting in the first row. He had ridden the bus up from Hanover, New Hampshire earlier in the day. He was a freshman at Dartmouth, the college that had been my first choice and had rejected me. It had been a sore spot Allison's father had sprayed with salt the Saturday night before I left for school when he had said, "Good luck at Dartmouth" knowing full well where I was going and why. That Dartmouth had accepted my son early decision had thrilled me even though the sting of rejecting me had long been forgotten. At least mostly forgotten, that is.

Chris had dressed up in a blue blazer and was wearing a navy and burgundy-striped repp tie that had once been mine. He looked mostly like his mother on the outside. He had her sandy blond hair, her prominent cheek bones, and her gazelle-like sleekness. He looked mostly like me on the inside. We were the ones who cared most about feelings. We were the ones who shared. We were the ones who worried about the problems of the world with a heavy dose of compassion and could be prone to bouts of melancholy. He also had my shy smile and the brown eyes that open up to my soul if you look at me in the right light. I had a sense he might be like me in other more private ways, ones I had wanted to talk about with him but never had.

The applause had died down, and my silence had drawn on for long enough it had started to seem awkward. Chris held my gaze, and I thought how handsome he looked and what an extraordinary, loving, decent human being he was. It was hard to believe he was the same age I was when I had arrived at Inverness, my lean body still young, my heart still unbroken, and my naïve outlook on the world and the hopes I had for my place in it still intact. Chris and I were extremely close, and I was a more attentive father than mine had been. But, there were parts of my life I had never told him. I carried secrets and wondered if he did, too. He nodded his head, a direct hint that I should begin. I smiled broadly at him. I held his gaze, and he held mine. I knew then I couldn't give the speech I had planned to and that I might make a more meaningful impact if I spoke on a different topic.

I closed the manila folder and cleared my throat. "I am going to talk to you this afternoon about 'Moral Failing.'"

For the next hour, I spoke about my life on the third floor of Canterbury Hall and The Magnificent Seven. I spoke of the lessons of friendship and the power of human connection. I spoke of falling in love with Dusty and the confused feelings I had had for Daniel. I spoke of the kiss I had shared with Dusty in the lobby of the dorm after he had run after me across campus and kissed me so hard as he shoved me up against the wall that I thought he might have broken my nose. I spoke of the terror I had felt as a young man in 1957 to tell another young man I loved him. I spoke of the courage I had felt when I had picked up my tray in the dining hall and marched over to sit where I really wanted to, which was with Dusty. I spoke of the magical weekend Dusty and I had had in New York City, and how he had kissed me at the top of the Empire State Building, a gesture that would have been unremarkable if our love had not been so forbidden.

I spoke of the horror of the disciplinary committee proceedings and how they nearly wrecked our lives. I spoke of my destroyed dreams of being a diplomat and serving my country in the State Department. I spoke of the accident of my journalism career and Professor Johnston's role in how it came about. I spoke of the persecution of homosexuals in the US and how President Eisenhower had issued Executive Order 10450 in 1953, which branded homosexuals as sex perverts and mandated that every one of them be fired from all government jobs and from every company that held government contracts. I spoke of how thousands of gay men and lesbians subsequently lost their jobs and had their lives and dreams derailed. I spoke of how UN Ambassador Henry Cabot Lodge, Jr., whose hand I had shaken during my tour of the UN with Dusty, had threatened UN Secretary General Trygve Lie that the United States would withhold its funding of the UN if the remaining homosexuals in the Secretary General's office were not fired. And so on.

I held myself together as I spoke, mostly measured, sometimes laughing, and sometimes angry. But, then I recounted how the previous summer Shorty died a terrible death he had not deserved, an early victim of AIDS. I started to crack at the tragedy of his life cut short and the beauty of how he had been cared for by Anthony and his family when Shorty's own family had abandoned him. I wept openly, and I am sure I was quite a spectacle. But, I didn't care. I had said what I needed to say and where I needed to say it. I had spoken from the depths of my heart and with passion, and I was not ashamed. At all.

If this had been a movie instead of real life, I might have received a standing ovation. Maybe I would have received one today. But, at an elite, preppy New England college during the Reagan years, that would have been too much to ask for. I received confused, tepid applause that was polite, but scattered. Most sat in silence, but at least no one booed. Professor Johnston left the stage without speaking to me. I looked down at Chris, who sat with a wide, proud smile across his face as he applauded heartily and louder than anyone. When I stepped off the stage, he rushed over to hug me.

Chris and I walked around campus for an hour as I pulled myself back together. I showed him where I had lived and where these events had happened. No father ever wants his son to see him in the type of shape I was in. But, Chris had been predictably sanguine upon learning this new news about me. It further opened up a dialogue between us that continues to this day. I kissed him and hugged him tight as I put him on the bus back to Dartmouth. He had waved from the window and watched me until the bus had rounded the bend and I left his line of sight.

That night, I blew off the faculty cocktail party and the dinner that was held in my honor. I went back to the village inn and drank an entire bottle of wine by myself and was not surprised or disappointed that no one came to look for me. When I climbed into bed, I jerked off to the memory of making sweet love to Dusty. Afterwards, I passed out from the tandem effects of the alcohol and the load of spunk that had landed with a splat on the headboard behind me.

ଊ

I made it through the remaining few weeks of school, although it was not easy. After scraping the bottom of the abyss on my birthday when Daniel held me as I cried myself to sleep, I began to recover from the loss of Dusty and the rape of the beautiful, intimate, and most private parts of me that had occurred during the invasive days of the disciplinary committee's investigation. I had mentioned previously I now recognize I was suffering from a form of post-traumatic shock. I could have benefited from speaking with a professional if there had been someone who could have helped instead of causing further damage. Even though loving a man the way I loved Dusty was viewed as a mental health disorder by the medical community back then, I never doubted my love for Dusty had been perfectly beautiful. Whatever cure they could have offered me was not a cure I wanted, even if it could have worked. What I needed was a cure for heart break, and I don't believe there is any such cure.

That didn't stop the guys from trying. Over the course of my professional life and travels, I have seen the extremes of people at their best and at their worst. One of the lessons I have learned is the extraordinary power of love, friendship, and human connection. Daniel, Anthony, Sasquatch, Howell, and Shorty saved my life by helping me onto the path to recovery. They knew I was crushed in the worst way. I know it was alarming to them that a reliably steady force like me had unraveled so quickly and so fully from the ravages of a heart that had been mangled in the way mine had. The uncommon care, attentiveness, and love they had shown me was the most potent medicine any human being could ever hope to be offered.

It would have been so easy to give up on me, particularly when what I mourned was little understood in any positive way and easily condemned in every negative way. They didn't. They checked on me daily. They never let me forget there was a great, wide, beautiful Earth out there waiting for me to rejoin it when I was ready. They tried to cure me with humor. They tried to cure me with fun. They tried to cure me with anything they could. The enduring image of Daniel, Anthony, Sasquatch, and Howell standing at the curb with crossed arms as they awaited the arrival of the bus from New York so they could warn me of impending peril is seared into my memory. I will never forget it. I will love them all forever for their extraordinary gifts of friendship.

I wrote early on here that my relationship with Daniel was complicated and that I was responsible for many of those complications. It may amuse you to know that many of those complications continue even until this day, despite our respective ages and a near lifetime of knowing each other. Daniel made sure I ate during the darkest days of that semester when I didn't feel like it. He made me sleep when I couldn't. He made me play squash and basketball when I didn't want to and only wished to lay in bed and stare at the ceiling. He refused to let me wallow. He held my hand in every figurative way as I returned to the world of the living. My soul weeps in love and gratitude to him.

My parents had left on a last minute trip to Bermuda right as my final exams ended. That meant I needed to pack up my belongings and find my own way home for the summer, which I hadn't planned on having to do. Luckily, Daniel and his father helped me bring my things to a storage facility outside of the village. Otherwise, I don't know what I would have done. They also offered to drive me home to West Hartford, which they professed not to mind even though it was several hours out of their way.

Daniel's dad was waiting down in his car while Daniel and I did one last sweep of our room to make sure we hadn't forgotten anything. As much as I was looking forward to the freedom of the summer, I was going to miss my friends and the life I had created with them. I was going to miss Daniel in particular. When the door to our room shut behind us, we both felt a slap of sadness at what we were leaving behind. Ralph waved from the room that had once been Dusty's. Daniel and I looked at each other without waving back to him, and we left without saying a word.

Dusty and I never reconnected during the remainder of the semester. We had seen each other on campus, of course. But, we never spoke, not even once, after I pounded on the door to his apartment. He would avert his eyes when he saw me, even though I would never drop his gaze. We had never had any closure, never any good-bye. It had been brutal. It had felt violent. I felt a crushing sense of loss. I felt broken on the inside in ways that would never fully heal. Please forgive me for the pathos, but I don't know how else to describe it. As I drove off with Daniel and his father, I said farewell to Dusty in the silence of my thoughts and wondered how I could ever get over him.

The drive back to West Hartford was surprisingly chatty. Daniel's dad was laid-back for a dad and very easy to talk to, which I found rather amusing given how Daniel could be so uptight. He had gone to Inverness as well and peppered us with questions about our courses, campus life, and details on any "hijinks" that may have taken place. Daniel was not biting, and neither was I, even though I was envious Daniel's dad was so accessible. "My son can be a bit of a stick-in-the mud sometimes, in case you haven't noticed," he said, winking at me in the rear view mirror as Daniel stared ahead, unmoving. "I apologize for that and assure you I had nothing to do with it." I liked that about his dad and wished I could have such an easy rapport with my own.

After we pulled up to my house a few hours later, Daniel got out of the car to say good-bye. I missed him already, and he hadn't even left yet. We spoke again of how he had invited all of us down for 4th of July weekend at his family's summer house on the Chesapeake Bay. Anthony was going to have all of us down to his family's house in New York at some point during the summer as well. I didn't want Daniel to leave. I had cared for him so much and had come to count on him for everything. Intuitively, he knew that and hugged me even though his father could see us.

"You should go back up to graduation next week," Daniel said. "It's not far for you."

I looked at him, surprised. He wasn't saying why, but I knew he meant because of Dusty. Daniel and I still had unresolved business between us, and I was moved by how generous that was of him.

"At least you know for sure he'll be there," he said. "You owe it to yourself."

I was still fragile from my ordeal, and I tended to be easily overcome with emotion when people showed me even the most basic kindness. I didn't know what to say. I hugged him tight and said, "Have a safe trip back. I'll see you for the 4th of July."

I stood in the driveway and waved as they drove off into the afternoon sun.

My younger sister, Kathy, was on a week-long class trip to Washington, D.C., the fortuitous excuse for my parents to sail off to Bermuda at the last minute. It was also fortuitous for me, because it meant I had the house to myself. I didn't feel like calling up any of my old friends from high school, though I thought it rather telling no one called me up either. I went to the movies by myself. I watched too much TV. I ordered in pizza and drank cold beers in the back yard. I ran through the house naked. I masturbated like a fiend and made a game of jerking off in every room in the freedom of the empty house. I was the happiest I had been in a while, even if I had rubbed my cock raw.

The following Saturday, the day before my parents were to return, was Inverness's graduation. I had awoken at 3 a.m. in a panic, my subconscious mind awhirl about Dusty even though I had tried to convince myself I was moving past him. The thought resounded in me that this might be the last time I would ever know with probable certainty where he was. After he graduated and left Inverness, he could be anywhere. It was one thing knowing where he was even if he wasn't speaking with me. It was another thing to let him go out into the broader world to live the rest of his life without me and not know where he was at all.

By 4 a.m., I was in my father's Cadillac driving to Vermont. By 7:30 a.m., I was having breakfast in the diner in town, the one right next to Oriental Garden. I was wearing pressed khakis that had been wrinkled from the drive, a starched white shirt, a blue blazer, and the blue and burgundy striped repp tie I would later give to Chris. I didn't fully know what I was doing here. But, I knew I had to see Dusty one last time, even if from a distance.

I sat in the stands during the commencement ceremony. I watched as Dusty received his diploma and received only light applause from the audience, a level of recognition that surprised me with its indifference given his prominence on campus. He had been popular amongst his classmates and had been head of the Honor Society until Dean Hoffman had revoked that honor along with all of the others. None of that mattered to me, of course. I stood up and gave Dusty the hearty applause he deserved. I even whistled. I wished him the best, no matter what had happened with us.

After the ceremonies ended, the graduates clustered with their families and friends. I watched from a distance as Dusty posed for photographs with his parents. He looked very distinguished in his cap and gown. His parents beamed with pride, and his mother clutched his diploma in her hand. I had noticed in the commencement ceremony's printed program that Dusty had been listed in the column of *magna cum laude* recipients, but had not been included on the list of Phi Beta Kappa inductees. He was the only *magna* graduate not on the list. I could only assume Inverness had not submitted him for the honor, which required the nominating institution to vouch for the nominee's moral character.

I moved closer for a last look at him before I left, not wanting to intrude on the private moments with his family. He saw me and then looked away. I didn't think I had any hurt left in my body, but the coldness I perceived in that gesture reawakened the caustic pain of loneliness I had tried to convince myself had been dissipating even though it really hadn't. I turned to leave and did not look back.

"John! John!"

I had not heard that voice in so long. I turned around and saw Dusty and his parents looking at me. His mother smiled and waved. Dusty gestured for me to join them. I thought my heart would pound its way out of my chest as I jogged over to them.

"I'd like to introduce you to my parents," Dusty said, as if the past two months of silence had not gone by.

His father shook my hand, and his mother did as well. "I'm Virginia McCaffrey," she said, shaking my hand longer than she had to. "Dusty's told me so much about you."

"It's nice to meet you," I said. "I'm really going to miss him."

"You'll have to come visit us in California," she said. "We would love to have you."

"Thank you," I said, knowing that would never happen. Commencement is a tricky word that signifies both an end and a beginning. This felt like an end. I glanced over at Dusty. He smiled an uncharacteristically shy smile and looked down at his feet. He didn't say anything.

Dusty's mother said to his father, "Hand me the camera. I want to take a picture of the boys."

Dusty moved next to me and slid his arm over my shoulder, which felt like heaven. I wrapped my arm around his waist. It was the first time in two months we had touched each other. I ached with sadness at the sense it would be the last.

Dusty's mother was not what I had imagined. I had expected Doris Day, but Virginia McCaffrey was prematurely gray, and she had the sinewy limbs and sun-damaged skin that were the byproducts of years of running the family orange grove in Southern California. She had a kind manner about her, and I had heard from Dusty of her sharp intelligence and desire that he have a different, more lettered life than she had. She had poured so much of herself into her son so he could live the dreams that had been hers, and I could tell by the way her eyes followed him how much she loved him. She smiled at me, and I knew at that instant she knew who her son was and what he meant to me. I smiled back and nodded in tacit acknowledgement. She raised the camera to her face and focused it on us.

"Move in closer," she said, and Dusty tightened his grip on my shoulder.

"I'm so sorry for everything," he said in a whisper only I could hear, his voice choked with emotion.

My eyes were wet with unspilled tears at the agony of this farewell. At the end of the day, he would leave with his parents and fly home to California. I would drive back to Connecticut. Our lives would spin off in different directions, and we would be separated by geography in addition to the other forces that had separated us. I thought of how the world had laid waste to our relationship and smothered what had meant everything to me. I had lost faith in so much which had mattered to me over the last half of the semester. I had been damaged in ways I knew could never be fixed, and I felt a bitterness rise up alongside the sadness inside me. Dusty squeezed my shoulder, and I thought of how this was the end of us. What I had forgotten at that moment was the enduring power of love and human connection. If I had understood that power in the way I do now, I would have known when Dusty squeezed my shoulder that this was not the end of us, but only the end of the beginning.

ABOUT THE AUTHOR

David Avery was born in Los Angeles in 1970. He attended college in New England and lives in Manhattan. He is currently writing his next novel.

Made in the USA
Middletown, DE
10 March 2018